D0201196

slaves
of
new york

slaves of new york

STORIES BY

tama janowitz

CROWN PUBLISHERS INC NEW YORK

acknowledgments

"Modern Saint #271" appeared in *NYB*; "The Slaves in New York," "Engagements," "Physics," "Spells," and "Patterns" appeared in *The New Yorker*; "Sun Poisoning," "Matches," and "Kurt and Natasha, a Relationship" appeared in *Interview*; "You and the Boss" appeared in *Spin*; "Ode to Heroine of the Future" appeared in *Mississippi Review*; "Lunch Involuntary" appeared in *Lo Spazio Umano*; "On and Off the African Veldt" was published in *Snowy Egret*; "Case History #4: Fred" appeared in *Harper's Magazine* and "Case History #15: Melinda" appeared in *New York Talk*.

"Modern Saint #271" appeared in *Top Stories* in a totally different version.

"The Slaves in New York" was reprinted in *Brutus*, Japan.

with thanks to:

The National Endowment for the Arts; The Fine Arts Work Center in Provincetown; CAPS Foundation; The Ludwig Vogelstein Foundation; and CCLM/General Electric Foundation for Younger Writers.

"Ode to Heroine of the Future" was a winner of the 1984 CCLM/General Electric Foundation Awards for Younger Writers.

Published by Crown Publishers, Inc., 225 Park Avenue South, New York, New York 10003 and represented in Canada by the Canadian MANDA group

CROWN is a trademark of Crown Publishers, Inc.
Manufactured in the United States of America
Library of Congress Cataloging-in-Publication Data
Janowitz, Tama.
  Slaves of New York.

  I. Title.
PS3560.A535S56   1986   813'.54   86-8812

ISBN 0-517-56107-7
Book design by Dana Sloan
10 9 8 7 6 5 4 3 2 1
First Edition

THIS BOOK IS FOR
Phyllis, Lillian, Gwyneth, Anne, Julian, Joellen, Mary, Paige, Andy, Gael, Wendy, Caroline, Sam, Peter, Lizzie, Betty, Laura, David G., Ronnie, David J., Cynthia, Steve, Patrick, Agustin, Michael, Lulu and Beep-beep.

contents

But it wasn't a dream, it was a place. And you—and you—and you—and you were there. But you couldn't have been, could you? This was a real, truly live place. And I remember that some of it wasn't very nice—but most of it was beautiful.

DOROTHY, IN *The Wizard of Oz,*
MGM PICTURES

modern saint #271

After I became a prostitute, I had to deal with penises of every imaginable shape and size. Some large, others quite shriveled and pendulous of testicle. Some blue-veined and reeking of Stilton, some miserly. Some crabbed, enchanted, dusted with pearls like the great minarets of the Taj Mahal, jesting penises, ringed as the tail of a raccoon, fervent, crested, impossible to live with, marigold-scented. More and more I became grateful I didn't have to own one of these appendages.

Of course I had a pimp; he wasn't an ordinary sort of person but had been a double Ph.D. candidate in philosophy and American literature at the University of Massachusetts. When we first became friends he was driving a taxicab, but soon found this left him little time for his own work, which was to write.

When my job as script girl for a German-produced movie to be filmed in Venezuela fell through, it became obvious we were going to have to figure out a different way to make money fast. For a pimp and a prostitute, Bob and I had a very unusual relationship. As far as his role went, he could have cared less. But I didn't mind; I paid the bills, bought his ribbons, and then if I felt like handing over any extra money to him, it was up to me. At night I would come in for a rest and find him lying on the bed reading Kant, or Heidegger's "What Is a Thing?"

Often our discussions would be so lengthy and intense I would have to gently interrupt him to say that if I didn't get back out to work the evening would be over and I wouldn't have filled my self-imposed nightly quota.

I was like a social worker for lepers. My clients had a chunk of their body they wanted to give away; for a price I was there to receive it. Crimes, sins, nightmares, hunks of hair: it was surprising how many of them had something to dispose of. The more I charged, the easier it was for them to breathe freely once more.

As a child my favorite books had been about women who entered the convent. They were giving themselves up to a higher cause. But there are no convents for Jewish girls.

For myself, I had to choose the most difficult profession available to me; at night I often couldn't sleep, feeling myself adrift in a sea of seminal fluid. It was on these evenings that Bob and I took drugs. He would softly tie up my arm and inject me with a little heroin, or, if none was available, a little something else. For himself there was nothing he liked better, though he was careful not to shoot up too frequently.

Neither of us was a very good housekeeper. Months would go by, during which time the floor of our Avenue A walk-up would become littered with empty syringes, cartons of fried rice, douche bags, black lace brassieres, whips, garrotes, harnesses, bootlaces, busted snaps, Cracker Jacks, torn Kleenexes, and packages of half-eaten Ring Dings and nacho corn chips. The elements of our respective trades.

I was always surprised to realize how intelligent the cockroaches in our neighborhood were. Bob was reluctant to poison them or step on them. He would turn the light off and whip it back on again to demonstrate his point.

It's obvious they're running for their lives, he said. To kill something that wants to live so desperately is in direct contradiction to any kind of philosophy, religion, belief system that I hold. Long after the bomb falls and you and your good deeds are gone, cockroaches will still be here, prowling the streets like armored cars.

Sometimes I wished Bob was more aggressive as a pimp. There were moments on the street when I felt frightened; there were a lot of terminal cases out there, and often I was in situations that could have become dangerous. Bob felt it was important that I accept anyone who wanted me.

From each according to his ability, to each according to his need.

Still, I could have used more help from him than I got.

But then Bob would arrive at the hospital, bringing me flowers and pastrami on rye and I realized that for me to change pimps and choose a more aggressive one, one who would be out there hustling for me and carrying a knife, would be to embrace a lifestyle that was genuinely alien to me, despite my middle-class upbringing.

When I was near Bob, with his long graceful hands, his silky mustache, his interesting theories of life and death, I felt that for the first time in my life I had arrived at a place where I was growing intellectually as well as emotionally. Bob was both sadist and masochist to me; for him I was madonna and whore. Life with him was never dull.

In any case, I liked having the things that money could buy. Originally I hailed from a wealthy suburb of Chattanooga, Tennessee, from one of the few Jewish families in the area. My great-grandfather had come from Lithuania at the turn of the century, peddling needles, threads, elixirs, yarmulkes, violin strings, and small condiments able to cure the incurable. All carried on a pack on his back; his burden was a heavy one, eight children raised in the Jewish persuasion. Two generations later my father owned the only Cadillac car dealership in town. I suppose part of my genetic makeup has given me this love of material objects. Or maybe it's just a phase I will outgrow as soon as I get everything I want. Even saints have human flaws; it is overcoming their own frailties that makes them greater than the sum of their parts.

I went to college at an exclusive women's seminary in Virginia. Until my big falling-out with Daddy, when I sent home F's for two successive semesters, and got expelled after being suspended twice, I had my own BMW and a Morgan mare, Chatty Cathy, boarded in the stables at school.

But I could never accept the role life had assigned to me; I fell in love with Jimmy Dee Williams, the fat boy who pumped gas at the 7-Eleven, and though the marriage only lasted six months, Daddy never felt the same about me. Well, he said, there are treatment programs for people like you. I didn't mind the time I spent in the institution. Fond recollections can be found in all walks of life. Yet if I had been allowed to go to a co-ed school I know things would have turned out differently for me.

Back in college the other girls would spend long evenings drinking beer and sitting on the rocking chairs that ringed the great plantation hall—the school had taken over many of the original buildings on a tobacco estate, and the new buildings were built in a Georgian style in a great semicircle facing the old mansion—gossiping about boys and worrying if they would pass French. But meanwhile I had to show them that I was wild and daring; I would pick Jimmy Dee up when he got off work and the two of us would smoke grass and drive around, bored and restless in the heat. One evening I drove right up onto the lawn and Jimmy Dee pulled down his pants to press his great buttocks, gleaming white, against the cool air-conditioned glass window of the car. That was the second time I was suspended from school; the first was when I had an affair with one of the black cafeteria workers in my dorm room, a man with only one arm who tasted of bacon and hair oil. . . . The only reason I was allowed to stay after that was that Daddy donated money to the school to build a new swimming pool. He never understood that no matter what he did, they were always going to think of him only as a rich Jew. . . .

I was finally asked to leave for good when Jimmy Dee and I were caught sneaking into the school pond, which was closed for swimming after dark. Both stark naked, dripping with mud and algae. . . . I tried to explain to Miss Ferguson, the dean, that I always got wild when there was a full moon, but, prim and proper in her mahogany office, smelling of verbena and more faintly of shit, she said she could see no future for a girl like me, that never in the course of all her years . . . I had to laugh.

Before Daddy could find out about my marriage and divorce and take the car back from me (and have me locked up again? But there are no convents for Jewish girls), I had driven north to New York, sold the car for $2,000, found an apartment, and bought some new clothes. I landed a job in an internship program at a major advertising agency, even though I didn't have a college degree. . . . Once more Daddy spoke to me on the telephone; Mother and Mopsy even came up for a visit. . . .

I might never have found my vocation if I hadn't been evicted from my apartment, and after finding a new place in the East Village, met Bruno (ah, Bruno, that Aryan German, pinched, brittle in his leather trenchcoat, rigid as a crustacean —even a saint has her failures), who offered me the job of script girl on the film he was making in Venezuela, which in the end didn't work out at all.

But one thing leads to the next (doesn't it always?) and it was through Bruno I met Bob, and now at night, cruising the great long avenues of the city, dust and grit tossed feverishly in the massive canyons between the skyscrapers, it often occurs to me that I am no more and no less, a thought that I hadn't realized until my days as a prostitute began. (True, I have my bad days, when I cannot rise from bed, but who can claim he does not? Who?) I could have written a book about my experiences out on the street, but all my thoughts are handed over to Bob, who lies on the bed dreamily eating whatever I bring him—a hamburger from McDonald's, crab soufflé from a French restaurant in the theater district, a platter of rumaki with hot peanut sauce in an easy carry-out container from an Indonesian restaurant open until 1:00 A.M., plates of macaroni tender and creamy as the sauce that oozes out from between the legs of my clientele.

As in the convent, life is not easy . . . crouched in dark alleys, giggling in hotel rooms or the back seat of limousines, I have to be a constant actress, on my guard and yet fitting into every situation. Always the wedge of moon above, reminding me of my destiny and holy water.

the slaves in
new york

There was a joke that my cousin told my brother Roland when he was five years old. The joke went, "Fat and Fat Fat and Pinch Me were in a boat. Fat and Fat Fat fell out. Who was left?" And my brother said, "Pinch Me," and my cousin pinched him. So when my brother got home he told my mother he was going to tell her a joke, and he said, "Fat and Fat Fat were in a boat. Fat and Fat Fat fell out. Who was left?" My mother said, "Nobody." My brother repeated the joke, and when my mother said "Nobody" a second time, my brother kicked her.

Twenty years went by . . . I was always older than my brother, and my mother still talks about my brother's fury at her incorrect response. All he wanted was to do to her what had been done to him. So now I'm living in New York, the city, and what it is, it's the apartment situation. I had a little apartment in an old brownstone on the Upper West Side, but it was too expensive, and there were absolutely no inexpensive apartments to be found. Besides, things weren't going all that smoothly for me. I mean, I wasn't exactly earning any money. I thought I'd just move to New York and sell my jewelry—I worked in rubber, shellacked sea horses, plastic James Bond–doll earrings—but it turned out a lot of other girls had already beaten me to it. So it was during this period that I gave up and told Stashua I was going home to live with my mother. Stash and I had been dating for six months. That was when Stash said we could try living together.

We've been living together in his place in the Village about a year now. One room, it's big, but he has a lot of stuff here—boxes, closets full of papers. Well, he's been here for ten years, and after his divorce he hadn't lived with anyone in six years or so.

I'm getting used to it. In the morning I clean up some, I walk his Dalmatian, Andrew, then I come back and cook Stash two poached eggs, raisin tea biscuits, coffee with three spoons sugar. Usually around this time of day, the doorman buzzes on the intercom and I have to go down to pick up a package, or run to the store for some more cigarettes, whatever. Then Stash goes off to work. He's an artist, he works for himself, so he doesn't have to go in until late, except recently he's been out of the house by ten, since he's nervous about getting ready for his show coming up soon at his gallery on Fifty-seventh Street.

I watch a few soap operas and have a second cup. Then usually I start to plan the evening dinner. I'll make, let's say, Cornish game hen with orange glaze, curried rice, asparagus, or it could be fettuccine Alfredo with garlic bread and arugula salad. Nothing too fancy. I take Andrew to the Key Food and tie him up outside, return the empty bottles. Stash likes Coca-Cola, Cracker Jacks, eats marshmallows out of the bag.

Well, I'm getting used to it. He still complains a lot if I leave makeup on the back of the toilet. He kept saying, "Eleanor, look at this sin," until I pointed out to him he was regressing to his Catholic childhood. I forget what else bugs him. If I do the dishes and there's, let's say, a little spot of grease on the floor from where I carried the roasting pan over to the garbage pail—this just drives him crazy. Clothes—if I leave any clothes out, or if after I wash them I put them away where he can't find them. If I buy the wrong kind of deodorant—why, he has to take fifteen minutes to explain to me why he only uses deodorant and not antiperspirant. Antiperspirant clogs up the pores and prevents you from perspiring, it's unhealthy,

whereas deodorant just masks the odor. Well, it's his apartment, and if we have a fight or something I sometimes get this
panicky feeling: Where the hell am I going to go?

I have a couple of girlfriends in the city. One is renting out
her second bedroom for $650 a month. The other has a three-
year-old baby, and I'm sure she'd be glad if I slept on her
couch in the living room in return for day-care services or
whatever, but would I be better off? Anyway, I'm trying to
learn how to get along with a man.

So what happens is, I went out to this party without Stash.
He wasn't feeling too well, and once in a while I really make
an attempt to go out without him. It's one of the most difficult
things in the world for me to do. I'd much rather go out with
him, and when he's saying hello to all his friends I can kind of
lurk behind him and smile every once in a while, but I don't
actually have to come up with anything to *say*. For instance, at
a nightclub some guy comes over—well, he isn't talking to me,
he's talking to Stash, about business or the softball team they
both play on. What do I have to say? I don't have anything to say.

Anyway, this party was a housewarming for this couple,
Mona and Phil. I didn't know them too well. They had just
found a new apartment on Fourteenth Street, $1,500 a month
—Mona had some money from her parents—a real find, a
sixth-floor walk-up. Phil was a carpenter, and so he could in-
stall the toilet and fixtures himself. Most of their boxes and
stuff hadn't yet been unpacked. For a while I sat on the couch
drinking a margarita that had been mixed up in a blender and
listening to Mona's mother and father talk about their trip to
China. They had deluxe accommodations at some hotel in Pe-
king, and there was a lottery among the members of their tour
group, and Mona's mother and father won and got to stay in
the Grand Suite, which had a fully stocked liquor bar.

When I finished listening to them, I turned around and there
was a totally stunning man sitting on a chair next to me eating
some Kentucky Fried Chicken. Mona and her husband, Phil,
had made their own dipping sauce, but since they were in the

middle of moving they went out and got the chicken at Kentucky and arranged it in a linen-covered basket. I wasn't eating anything. I had already made dinner for myself and Stash, and because he wasn't feeling well I kept the meal simple and just served homemade black-bean soup with macaroni and cheese and a small salad. I felt sort of annoyed at first when I saw this guy eating fried chicken and staring at me, because it occurred to me that (a) he was far too gorgeous, with his green eyes and curly black hair, and (b) he was probably an actor, because he seemed to be reenacting the dinner scene from *Tom Jones,* that old movie with Albert Finney. Stash always tells me I have "buggy-whip" arms, and it made me uncomfortable the way this guy was eating a scrawny chicken wing and looking at me. You know, I just wanted to tell him to knock it off and be a person.

He introduced himself and we started talking. It was the first time in ages I had talked to a man, other than Stash. Stash is half-Polish and half-Italian, so conversation between the sexes doesn't go over so good with him.

This guy's name was Mikell and he was from South Africa and wrote novels, political-type novels, so he had been thrown out of the country some time back. They didn't actually throw him out, they just confiscated a work-in-progress. I asked him if he knew Jimmy Gwynne, who is from Cape Town, and naturally Mikell knew Jimmy—in fact, he had shared a flat with him in London about six years ago. He had come to the party with Millie, who I had always wanted to meet—Millie was one of the few successful woman painters in New York. So I said hello to Millie, and it turned out we had gone to the same college but at different times and she had graduated some eight years before me. I never thought Mikell and Millie were actually together, I thought they just came to the party at the same time. Whatever. Millie excused herself, and Mikell went back to talk to me.

As it happened, I gave Mikell my address and phone number without bothering to mention that I lived with someone. Let me tell you, at this point there was nothing devious going on in my head. Stash was always encouraging me to develop a life of my own. This Mikell had eyes that were truly sickening— green pools like you never see and never want to see: when he looked at you, it made you weak in the knees, which in actual fact made me mad. So I didn't respond—I mean, come on already, I didn't let my knees get weak, I just talked to Mikell like he was one of my girlfriends. Come to think of it, that was the only way I knew how to talk to anyone anymore.

A few days later, after Stash had gone off to work, Mikell called, and I agreed to meet him for a cup of coffee. It turned out he lived only a few blocks away. I sat in the back corner of the White Horse Tavern, hoping no one would be able to see me if they walked past the window and report me to Stash or anything.

Mikell showed up. Such white teeth, like you wouldn't be- lieve (they must have something in the water over there in South Africa), and those eyes—brilliant green (maybe he wore contact lenses). I couldn't even believe it. He had a copy of his novel for me. It had been published in England and he was looking for an American publisher. It was called *Registered Alien*. After a while, I had to explain that I lived with a person, and Mikell asked me how it was going. I said okay, but that my dream was that someday I would get some bucks and then maybe I could move out. I said I got along all right with Stash, but that he never wanted to have anyone over, we had no couch, just a bed, all his stuff was all over the place, it hadn't been painted in ten years, and my dream was to have a real apartment, maybe with a little terrace, geraniums, and then I'd have dinner parties for eight or ten every once in a while.

Well, it turned out that Mikell lived with Millie. They had met in L.A. Millie went out there for a show and Mikell was living there reading screenplays for a production company. So Mikell invited Millie to South Africa, she met his mother, and they got along really well. Mikell took Millie to meet some Zulus and she danced with them; they stayed up all night drinking some local concoction, and Millie had a great time. When Millie went back to New York, she invited Mikell to move in with her—New York was where the publishing was. Mikell said yes, they got along great, there was only one problem, which was that they fought all the time.

What the situation was, Millie owned her own co-op, and her former boyfriend, during the time they were engaged to be married, had purchased the co-op next to hers, and they had torn down the walls between the two apartments. So now Millie's former boyfriend rented out his half of the space to Mikell at a very, very tiny rent, a rent so small that even though Mikell was absolutely broke he was able to afford living in New York, which was where he wanted to be. The reason the former boyfriend rented out his half of the co-op to Mikell at such a reduced rate was that it would have cost a fortune to rebuild the walls between the two apartments, and Millie absolutely refused to live with a complete stranger. But it was lucky for Mikell that Millie didn't consider him a complete stranger, otherwise he would have had to go back to Los Angeles and his job, when that was something he had nothing for but contempt.

We both just sat there. Mikell put his hand over mine. It wasn't a sexual thing, not really, it was just the two of us sitting there at a wooden table in the White Horse Tavern, looking at each other and sitting there. We were both in the same position. Things might have been different if one of us had our own apartment. It wasn't that Mikell wasn't very fond of Millie— he was. But they had a lot of fights, and he wasn't allowed to go out by himself at night, and Millie didn't feel like going out all that often, and Mikell would have liked to be able to see some of the New York scene now that he was finally here.

When we got up to leave, I let Mikell pay for my coffee. He said he would call me in a couple of days. I asked him to call only between the hours of eleven and one, when I could be certain that Stash would be out. I asked him to sign his novel. He wrote, "To Eleanor by the River, with love from Mikell." So I said, "Listen, why don't you write down your number, in case I have to give you a call?"

It was all totally out in the open. I just wanted to keep him like a girlfriend, and that was why I told Stash about meeting Mikell. I figured that things would never work out between me and Mikell because we were both in the same position, but maybe as a foursome I could be friends with Millie and Stash could go shoot some pool with Mikell. It was important to bring new people into a relationship, to make new friends, and if you're part of a couple, well, then it's easier to have new friends who are also a couple.

Stash almost had a nervous breakdown. For two days he wouldn't speak to me, then he started screaming. He told me to go move out so I could start sleeping with this guy, and said how dare I bring home little love notes from some cretin.

I said, "Well, Stash, I wouldn't have told you about it if there was anything going on. All I did was tell Mikell about you and how great you are, and he talked about Millie."

Stash said, "Don't give me that, that's how it begins—you go out and talk to each other about your relationships and then jump into bed with each other. Maybe we should just end this," he said. "You're beginning to bore me."

This went on all day. I started crying. I said, "If you want me to leave, then I won't stay here any longer. You know how much I love you, and I can't understand your reaction." I said, "I thought you'd really like this guy—he's interested in seeing your paintings, and I thought I could be friends with her."

"Who?" Stash said.

"The girlfriend," I said.

Stash said, "You want me to call her up and go out with her? Is that what you want? Fine. You're doing this out of insecurity. What is it about you I hate the most?"

"My messiness?" I said.

"No."

"My personality?"

"No," he said. "Your insecurity. That's what I hate about you the most. You are so damn insecure. Why don't you stop?"

I couldn't figure it out. I mean, I'm insecure, but I couldn't see how this related. My having coffee with a man didn't seem to illustrate this character defect. I cried all day Sunday, and Stash went out with his friends and played softball.

Mikell called at twelve-thirty. I tried to sound happy and bright. He really was intelligent, and it was beyond me how Millie could ever think of anything to argue with him about. I wanted to see him for coffee, except my eyes were all swollen up. I just broke down and told him how things had been hell around here for three days, how Stash went insane because I told him I had gone out for coffee with a man.

Mikell said, "Actually, that's what's been going on around here. She's gone totally out of her mind."

There was a silence. I said, "Well, let's meet for coffee tomorrow."

He said, "I can't. How about Wednesday?"

I said, "Let me call you in the morning, since I'm not sure if I can make it."

There was a silence. He said it would be better if I didn't call him.

We did get to meet one other time. It was really sad. After that, I bumped into him once at the bank. He was with Millie, and she gave me a strange smile. I had no makeup on, and I was wearing my glasses, which were pointy and had little rhinestones at the corners, and maybe she only half recognized me. I mean, at the party, the one other time she had seen me, I had been wearing my contact lenses and had on a lot of my original jewelry, things like my James Bond/Oddjob necklace and earring set. When Millie went to use the cash machine, Mikell came over to me and asked if I was going home after the bank.

Luckily, when I got home Stash wasn't there, and Mikell called a few minutes later. We spoke briefly. Mikell said things would be best if we didn't speak for a while. He was talking in a whisper. I said, "But, Mikell, I must meet you to continue our mad, passionate affair."

There was a moment of silence.

"Just kidding," I said.

After that, whenever Stash was home in the afternoons I just prayed the phone wouldn't ring.

I tried to keep the apartment clean. My mother lived upstate in a one-bedroom apartment. I couldn't escape to her. I got up at seven-thirty to walk Andrew. Things went okay. Stash bought me a coat, Day-Glo orange wool with a green velvet collar. It wasn't the one I would have chosen—I guess I would have selected something a little more conservative. But it was nice to have a new winter coat.

My friend Abby called me up from Boston. She was all hysterical. It's like this. She's been living with this guy for a few years. He was an art director for an advertising agency, and she has a good job teaching at Simmons, tenure. But it's Roger's house, an old Back Bay brownstone that he's fixed up, and now he's lost his job and he wants her to start making some financial contribution, but he still doesn't want to marry her. Just at this time Abby's old flame reappears. He wants her to move to New York and live with him.

"What are you going to do?" I said.

Abby said that even though this old flame, Bruce, was a jerk, she was bored with Boston and Roger. "I could live in New York with Bruce," she said, "and fly up to Boston to teach one day a week, and maybe I'll meet someone I like better than Bruce in New York."

I said, "Abby, don't do it. In the old days, marriages were arranged by the parents, and maybe you ended up with a jerk but at least you had the security of marriage, no one could dump you out on the street. In today's world, it's the slave system. If you live with this guy in New York, you'll be the slave."

"Well," she said, "I'm used to Roger cooking for me. Would I have to cook for Bruce?"

She already knew all about my dinner menus, the frantic daily preparations. "Yes," I said. "You'd have to cook for Bruce. What are you going to do if you two have a fight and he tells you to leave? With your salary, you'll never be able to find an apartment."

"I know Bruce is a creep," she said. "But I thought I'd be with him while I looked for someone else."

I said, "Abby, forget it. You think you'll be making an improvement, but that's not the case." I didn't want to tell her this before, because I didn't know the situation with Roger, but quite frankly it didn't sound so bad. I said, "If you live with Bruce, you'll be the slave. It's not the same in other cities, the rents aren't so high. Roger doesn't have the same power over you, because you could always threaten to move out and get your own place in Boston."

"I didn't know," she said. "I'm going to reconsider. Are you sure there're no available men in New York?"

"There're women," I said. "There're hundreds of women. They are out on the prowl. And all the men are gay or are in the slave class themselves. Your only solution is to get rich, so you can get an apartment and then you can have your own slave. He would be poor but amenable."

"Are these women, the ones that are prowling—are they attractive?" Abby said.

I could tell she hadn't been listening. "Abby," I said. "It's New York. They have hundred-and-seventy-dollar haircuts and wear black leather belts with sterling silver buckles."

"Oh," she said. "How are things otherwise?"

"Stash and I are getting along very well," I said. "He just bought me a new winter coat. I should probably go. Andrew needs his walkies."

After I hung up, I thought about what I should have told Abby: See, Fat and Fat Fat fell out, and in New York all that's left is Pinch Me. But I'm not sure she would have understood. I remembered when my brother Roland was five he wore these little boots with metal toe caps, and after my cousin told him the joke and pinched him my brother kicked him. My cousin was really enraged at Roland's behavior and called up my mother to complain. He had a black-and-blue mark. My mother was ashamed: obviously she was doing something all wrong in her child-rearing practices. Now Roland is a first-year resident in obstetrics/gynecology down in Texas.

engagements

It was easy to find an apartment in New Haven, although my classes in feminist criticism were starting in a few days and most of the other grad students had arrived at Yale the week before. I rented a two-room flat, sunny but dingy, across the street from a punk-rock bar, and overlooking the edge of the ghetto. The manager of the building—I nicknamed him Père Goriot—sold me two twin beds for $10 each, and a battered fan. It was late August, the city felt airless. At the Salvation Army I discovered a shabby Victorian sofa in worn blue velvet for $60, a major investment, but I bought it anyway.

At a mixer at the Art and Architecture School, I met Ray Connors. He had small, worried eyes and fine, babyish hair, already receding. His back was hurting him; two years ago, at a New Year's Eve party, he had fallen down an elevator shaft. He was graduating from the Architecture School in January. He went off to get me a glass of wine; by the time he came back, I had practically forgotten his existence.

A few days later Ray showed up at my apartment. I offered him some Minute Maid lemonade, but Ray preferred Perrier, which I didn't have. "Listen, Cora, I was wondering," he said. "I'm going home this weekend and I wondered if you'd want to come into the city on Friday or Saturday night—you could meet my parents and see our apartment, and we could have dinner."

I don't know exactly why I agreed; it was difficult to think up a fast excuse, and I really had nothing else to do. I neither liked Ray nor disliked him—he just wasn't there.

He met me at Grand Central Terminal on Friday afternoon. I was wearing a black-and-white flowered dress with rhinestone buttons from the Salvation Army and an old forties straw hat the woman who lived next door had given me, white lace gloves, and ankle-strap sandals. I caught sight of myself as we went in the front door of Ray's parents' apartment: there were wall-to-ceiling mirrors opposite the front door. Though I wasn't wearing makeup, my face was shiny; to my surprise my outfit, which I had thought quite razzle-dazzle in New Haven, now resembled something worn by a person just off the train from Mississippi. In the mirror, with my moony, freckled face, I looked as gullible as a horse. This was not at all the image I had hoped to project.

The apartment was huge, with wall-to-wall carpeting, steel-colored, and a great view of the city. Eight or ten people were sitting on pigskin sofas around the living room, wearing frosty, pale cottons and linens, and gave off a certain New York type of elegance, as if they were in a photo session for a Bloomingdale's catalog. The room was stuffy with perfume and conditioned air. I shook hands with the various middle-aged men and women. Though the room was crowded, I felt like shouting out, "Hello, is anybody home?" These people seemed so smooth, correct, as if they were leading their lives according to standards set by *Better Homes and Gardens*.

Ray's mother insisted I go with her into the bedroom. She was frisky and plump, with hair the shade of cedar chips, and told me right away that she ran an independent film company —she ran the New York office for her brother, anyway—and Ray's father designed mattresses, one of which was now in the Museum of Modern Art.

In her bedroom, clothing was piled several feet deep on the floor. That morning, she told me, she had had a woman come over and go through her wardrobe to show her how to wear her stuff: what skirts she should throw out, which old sweaters went with newer things, what she should buy. The woman charged $150 for two hours, but her assistance was worth it. I thought for a minute Mrs. Connors was going to offer to give me her old dresses—which I would have happily accepted—but all she wanted was to show me some slacks which she still thought were nice but which the woman insisted she get rid of.

It made me nervous to think I wasn't envious of this sort of lifestyle. What could be wrong with me? Had I no cravings for a milky-white fur coat, an ice cream maker to spin gelato from invisible threads—or whatever it was those machines did—or a baby with hot, sweaty palms to cling to me like a marsupial? Aside from somebody's old clothes, I couldn't think of anything to want: I even lacked the desire to go on a macrobiotic diet and have my cards read by an Indian master. Once I had read about a person who had had a lobotomy—I could empathize with this, at least when I was in the presence of others.

We went into the terra-cotta-tiled kitchen, whose ceiling was covered with hanging stainless-steel pots and pans. Ray's father came in and kissed my hand. Mr. Connors had iron-gray hair and was really good-looking: he was taller than Ray, and very sexy. I imagined him as my father-in-law, chasing me around the sofa late at night. He made me a Tom Collins and told me how he could converse with their cat—a Maine coon cat weighing at least twenty-five pounds. I thought he might mention something about Ray, but Mr. Connors seemed almost to have forgotten him. I liked Ray's parents much better than Ray. Despite their ostentation, they seemed younger than Ray, and livelier.

When Ray came back into the kitchen, his father gave him a slap on the back.

"Jesus, Dad," Ray said. "My back! I'm already in agony, and you're trying to kill me."

Ray's parents wanted us to stay and have dinner with them after the guests left, but Ray said he was taking me out to a Japanese restaurant nearby. I had never had Japanese food before, so Ray decided to order portions of everything: chunks of raw tuna, abalone, mackerel, some stuffed into rice and wrapped in seaweed, more lying pinkly on little wooden tablets with legs. Pieces of fish flopped from my chopsticks. To cover up I gulped the plum wine. I felt like I was being forced into re-creating a bout of seasickness I had once experienced on a boat trip. "You didn't try the California-make," Ray said. He dabbed a piece of sashimi into a dish of green mustard and wiggled it in front of my nose. I realized my palms were sweating. I wondered how much this whole business was going to cost. My mother and I had been broke our whole lives; I had a loan from Yale that barely covered my expenses. Ray would probably expect some form of compensation for this meal, this much I knew from past dinners with men. I tried to put it out of my mind.

We had nothing to talk about, though Ray told me more about Max, the cat, and his younger brother. Then he fell silent and stared down at his hands. I thought of a few topics: my courses at Yale, my feminist professor. Ray didn't seem very interested. I mentioned my father, whom I hadn't seen in twenty years. My parents had been divorced when I was four. My father, whom my mother called "Captain Ahab," had re-married and moved to New Zealand in order to avoid nuclear fallout. There was a thirty-three-percent chance that New Zealand wouldn't be affected. But Ray apparently wasn't listening; his eyes wandered to his reflection in the mirror behind me and he reached across the table and jabbed my elbow with a chopstick.

I pretended this hadn't happened and Ray asked for the check. Before he paid with his charge card, I got a look at how much the dinner had cost: two weeks' worth of groceries. The food was barely touched. I wasn't used to eating so well. At night, alone in my apartment, I ate a takeout sandwich from a vegetarian place up the block, of lima beans with melted mozzarella cheese. By eleven-thirty I had said good night to Ray and was back on the train to New Haven, a takeout paper bag in my hand.

A few nights later Ray called to ask if he could drop by. I was surprised to hear from him; though I hadn't felt any elementary particles hopping between us, I decided to go to bed with him. The prospect seemed somewhat boring, but I thought I might as well get it over with. Perhaps I'd be fonder of him if something physical happened between us.

When Ray showed up, he had a carload of furniture from his apartment to give me: two chests of teak, with many tiny drawers and compartments, three chairs, an expensive floor lamp, very modern. "When will you need this back?" I said. I assumed he was just lending it to me, or storing it with me for the moment.

"No, it's for you," Ray said.

"For keeps?" I said.

"Yeah, yeah," Ray said. "My father has a whole warehouse of furniture." He looked pleased.

After carrying the furniture upstairs we went out to an espresso place a block away. Cappuccino coffee was two dollars, so I had never gone there. I had one of the coffees with whipped cream, and a big piece of carrot cake. I ate the cake eagerly, cramming it into my mouth as if it were a drug, somehow feeling this would give me strength for whatever was to happen with Ray. "I like to watch you eat," Ray said, looking at me dreamy-eyed. I wiped off my chin with a napkin; the cake had abruptly become quite tasteless.

Ray stopped at his car to get a bottle of wine out of the trunk. He put his arm around my shoulder as we walked back to my apartment. It was after midnight. I sat on one of the twin beds; it had no frame, just a mattress and box spring on the floor. Ray sat on a chair, uncorking the wine. I figured either he'd make a move and I'd go to bed with him, or he should go home. I was tired. Once again, I felt we had nothing to say to each other, but Ray told me the plot of a movie he had just seen. This is a symptom. I've noticed how any time a man tells me the plot of a movie, it is a kind of declaration of love.

After about fifteen minutes, just as I was ready to suggest

he leave, Ray went over to the closet. He took off his shoes
and socks and put on my favorite pair of high heels, red leather
pumps. "How do I look?" he said.

A wave of rage rose within me. He walked all around the
apartment in my shoes. I didn't dare say, "Listen, Ray, you're
going to stretch out my favorite shoes," because he had just
given me all that furniture, and I didn't want to embarrass
him. My mother always said, "Lend people your clothes, but
don't wear other people's shoes or lend yours, because your
shoes conform to your feet and other people's feet are different
shapes and will stretch them out." Ray didn't have very large
feet, but I just didn't see how he could fit them into my shoes,
which were definitely small. I didn't have the money to replace
them, anyway.

Then Ray tried on my straw hat. Maybe he was trying to be
playful. But it was almost one in the morning, and he was
walking around in my straw hat and shoes. I couldn't laugh. I
finally said, "Well, I'm tired and I have class in the morning."

At the door Ray kissed me good night and looked at me
pleadingly. It was too late. I felt a rush of incipient hyperten-
sion, but I tried to calm myself. When Ray had finally gone, I
examined the shoes. They weren't ruined after all, but I
pushed them to the back of the closet.

I was the youngest in my family, but now I'm an only child.
When I was eight, Ellen, my sister, then twelve, died of leukemia. When Ellen got sick she asked for a dog and got a
Chihuahua named Midnight. It lived until four years ago. Now
it's just my mother and I. I rarely think about Ellen. My mother
doesn't like to talk about her, and for me she's become
bleached to an image on a flickering movie screen. Photographs show me standing next to my sister: she had wispy
blond hair, horn-rimmed glasses, and a pointy chin. Once,
during a squabble, I ran into the kitchen and came back at
Ellen with a handful of pepper which I threw in her face. Just
after that, she got leukemia. I also have three half-brothers,
whom I've never met. After Ellen's death my father offered to

pay for a ticket to New Zealand for me, but I didn't want to go
—or perhaps my mother didn't want me to—and the offer was
never repeated. The boys are now fifteen, thirteen, and six. In
September my father sent me a miniature jade baseball bat,
highly polished, and a note congratulating me on my accep-
tance to the Women's Studies Program at Yale. With the jade
bat was a card saying this was a replica of a Maori war club. I
brooded about what my father had meant by it, but I was too
busy with my courses and schoolwork to think about it for long.

At the beginning of the semester my courses seemed quite
interesting; but a few days after Ray tried on my shoes I was
sitting in class, taking notes as usual, when it became apparent
that not one word that was being said made the slightest bit of
sense. The teacher, Anna Castleton, a well-padded, grayish
woman with clipped, poodle hair, was discussing a conference
she had attended the week before—a Poetics of Gender collo-
quium—where she was severely attacked for her presentation.
I carefully wrote down everything Anna said but when I got
home that night I reread the notes and found they still sounded
as if they had been written in a foreign language.

Status of empirical discourse.
Post-structuralist account of dissolving subject precludes
  formation of female identity.
The notion of the subject in progress.
It was assumed she was calling for a return to fixed iden-
  tity.
Post-gendered subjectivities.
If gender is constructed—a gendered identity 99% of the
  time is built onto a person who has a sex.

Here I had made a little sketch in the margin: a picture of a
beaver, paddling frantically, with a tree stump clutched in its
large buck teeth.

The only text of rupture is right wing.
To speak of identity is to speak of racism.
Anyone who throws out the word "essentialist" believes

that there is such a thing as real women who are trans-historical.

ANYONE WHO THROWS THIS OUT AS AN OPENING
  REMARK IS PROVING THEIR MIDDLE-CLASS
  PARANOIA.

*The most important thing about Marxism is positing a
  historical subject. Now, you can say as a Marxist you
  want to dissolve "woman."*

*Without using the word "class," she argued for a more
  complicated view of women as historical subject.*

Yet she was attacked for this—brutally attacked.

Then I had written down the words of one of the other students: "Angela Davis said that Elizabeth Cady Stanton's decision to separate a middle-class reformist movement in the
name of feminism was implicitly racist—there is such a thing
as nonessentialism."

To this the teacher responded, at least according to my
notes:

*It isn't complicated, it's simple: the unreworked biological
category, where you locate yourself to take action. The
language becomes the primary basis for working things out
—in other words, can you top this? The privileging of the
complicated.*

I wondered whether the teacher had burst into tears following the attack on her. The two hours of class were devoted to
a retelling of the attack, couched in this language which so
gracefully circled a subject without ever landing to make a
point.

At the end of the semester I gave an oral report for the
Castleton class in which I discussed mysticism and Eastern
philosophy and some of the similar themes that emerge in the
writings of Virginia Woolf. I had hoped to please the teacher;
throughout my lecture she wrote furiously in a notebook. When
I finished, she looked up and said, "You're wrong." The other
women in the class all turned to catch my reaction. I felt as if
I had been electrocuted on a television game show. Anna went

on to say that I had fallen prey to a traditional male put-down: placing women in the category of weak, dreamy mystics and thus denying them power. I knew that the most successful reports in class were those which merely repeated what the teacher herself had said; but how could I repeat what made no sense? I found myself arguing, trying to defend my position. I left the class feeling as if my leptons were no longer in orbit.

That evening I sat in my apartment, on one of Ray's chairs, trying to figure out what had happened. It was strange to find something that had once absorbed me so quickly transformed into musty, foul-smelling words. I thought of Dostoyevsky, chattering away in his icy locker room, seized with the flu or perhaps remembering his near-execution. Charlotte Brontë, trimming her cuticles by the open fire. Florence Nightingale, sanctimonious in her bandage-strapping. These people had lust, infectious greed to live, a passion in life. If smallpox and polio vaccines hadn't been developed, I figured I would have been one of the ones to keel over by now. Maybe I was just tired; it would be good to have a break at Christmas.

But I didn't feel any different during vacation; by New Year's Day I decided not to go back to Yale.

Half the reason I had decided to go to Yale was that I didn't get an apartment I fell in love with in New York. The summer before I had landed a job as editorial assistant on a magazine —I would be taking over for a woman who was going on maternity leave in September. I had a whole month to find a place to live, but after several weeks of looking I still couldn't find anything, not even a share. Nell, my mother, came into the city to help me look. She wore her tattered cardigan with holes in the sleeves and her Red Cross shoes, practical for walking. She said that the way to find an apartment was simply to wander up and down the streets until we saw a sign in a window saying APARTMENT FOR RENT.

"Ma," I said, "maybe that was how you could one time find an apartment, but not anymore." But she insisted, and on the afternoon of the second day we did see a sign on the first floor of an old brownstone on Third Avenue in the twenties. Nobody answered the bell, but we went next door to an antique store and the woman gave us the key to the place and said that she was handling the rental for the landlady.

The place was fantastic. It held the sediment of many lives: gilt ceilings, molding in a pattern of vines and leaves, covered with many layers of paint, an intricate puzzle-parquet floor, like a Parcheesi board, cracked and dented in places, the wood still beautiful. The apartment was two stories high, with a spiral staircase in the dining room that led upstairs to a small balcony with a sleeping area. There was a second bedroom in front, off the living room, which had an ornate marble fireplace. The bathroom was elaborate, with a claw-footed tub and a pedestal sink. The place came with its own backyard, fenced in, though bare of plant life. How calm and happy I felt here! It was a place to sit morosely by the open fire in a velvet dress, entertaining an assortment of people I would surely meet. I would plant a willow and peach tree in the backyard, get a cat. "I'd never be able to afford this," I said. "I bet it's twenty-five hundred a month."

"You could get a roommate," my mother said. "Maybe it's not so much." My mother, on her stiff stilts of legs, never allowed her face to express much emotion, but I could tell she liked it.

We spoke to the woman in the antique store. She said the rent was $600 a month, and had scarcely finished the sentence before my mother wrote out a check as a deposit. The woman said she would call the landlady—she didn't see that there would be any problem. I took the train home with my mother; the whole trip we discussed the apartment. She said that maybe the landlady would reduce the first month's rent so that I could get metal security gates installed over the back windows. At $600 a month, however, it was hard to complain.

When we got home the landlady called: she hadn't spoken to the woman in the antique store when I saw the apartment, but it had been rented only a few minutes before we looked at the place.

"Goddammit," I said to my mother. "That was my apartment. It *felt* like my apartment." The flavor of lemons and chalk filled my mouth, the taste of disappointment. This loss was an indication that my whole life was out of sync. Nell was also disappointed. There was nothing she could say or do, but she did show me an article in *Fate* magazine which suggested that possibly I had lived in the apartment in another incarnation but was not meant to now.

Luckily I had something to fall back on; Yale had accepted me the previous spring, and though I had told them I wasn't going to come, now that I changed my mind they said I could still attend, but without the scholarship.

Though I had enjoyed living in my own apartment in New Haven, I didn't mind being back at home with my mother. She lived in Southampton, on a back suburban street, far from the large mansions that lined the waterfront. The tiny house had been built in the 1930s, before the Hamptons became so popular and expensive. Some summers, my mother went away on a trip and rented out the house for $5,000 a month; this summer she had a job as librarian at the Southampton library.

In her house we were constantly tripping over each other, but we didn't get on each other's nerves: we called each other, as a joke, "Letitia" and "Hermione." Though we had never seen the movie *Grey Gardens*—about a mother and daughter, related to Jackie Onassis, who never went out of the house and grew old and eccentric together—this was what we imagined we were like. We lived on quick-cooking Ramen noodles, spinach, and snow peas; tuna fish, direct from the can, frozen corn fritters heated in the oven; or baked potatoes topped with Cheddar cheese.

In the afternoons I rode my bike to the beach and walked up the mile stretch and back, scuffing my feet through the foam at the edge of the sand and waves. I spent a lot of time thinking: What makes me the way I am? Okay, I figured, I was a combination of genetic and environmental accidents. On the other hand, surely my personality wasn't *entirely* beyond my control. It disturbed me that I seemed to be totally uninterested in men: when I went out with them, it was only in order to be able to study them as if they were natural history museum exhibits. Captain Ahab couldn't be blamed completely for this. That I *wasn't* worried about finding someone—this wasn't normal, according to the magazines. Even Anna Castleton had turned away from men only because they had proved to be so rotten.

The way I felt now, I wasn't really interested in any aspect of life. Not in the least bit. Perhaps I really would live at home, my mother and I growing older, more set in our ways, graduating to higher degrees of oddness. Yet what would become of me when my mother grew too old to support us both? Abnormal. I tried to imagine myself decked in a purple fez, smoking a cigarette in a long ivory holder, sipping absinthe or crème de menthe and actually speaking to people—having what is known in books as "conversation." Murmured voices, the sound of brittle chatter across a ruby-lit nightclub. Yet my imagination couldn't pick up the words.

There were so many ways to fill up a day, let alone a life. I didn't see how I could possibly cram anything—anyone—else into my hours. For example, one afternoon I spent three hours reviewing the contents of a sweepstakes brochure that came in the mail. It took hours to figure out the rules of the sweepstakes; apparently one had to purchase an item of jewelry for $4.99 before the entry form could be considered valid. Though I knew I'd never enter, I felt obliged to read about each item of jewelry: elegant "love" ring with genuine diamond; Pegasus pendant with genuine ruby and swirl of faux diamonds; Princess Di's famous sapphire-and-diamond engagement ring; the Diamond Wedding Cross, Symbol of Eternal Unity. The descriptions were written in a style as interesting to me as my feminist crit. courses had once been.

In May I received a letter from Ray. He had been looking for me all semester, and had asked Yale for my address but they refused to give it out. As a last resort he decided to write to me in care of my old address, and the letter was forwarded.

All spring I had been gardening with a frenzy: the small fenced-in backyard hadn't been touched in years. On her days off my mother sat in the yard in a screened-in tent house from Sears—insects bit her even when no one else was bothered—and watched me at work. I spent hours in the sun, stooped over the splotchy faces of pansies, puffy foxgloves, inebriated day lilies, glossy as honey, quivering with palsy. The flowers trembled in the salt air. My fingers were raw, I refused to wear gloves and my hands were permanently veined with dirt.

"Go ahead," my mother said. "Call him. You haven't spoken to anyone besides me in months."

"I don't like him," I said. "He makes me feel like he's going to throw me into a coffin and walk around on top of it." But I called him up and asked him to dinner; he was ready to come out that night, but I told him to wait until the weekend.

For his visit I made chili and corn bread and a salad; I supposed I really had been cut off for quite a while. I found myself going out of my way to dress up, make the dinner elegant. When my mother came home from work we went out to the yard to sit in the tent house. This was our ritual almost every night. I had a beer and she had a concoction made from soda, piña colada mix, and sometimes ice cream. So far she hadn't questioned me about what I wanted or planned to do. I knew she was glad to have me here. We sat in the light of the citronella candle—even inside the screen house insects somehow managed to bite her—and listened to the crickets and barking of dogs down the road. The aroma of the raspberry bushes in the yard and the sour potato smell from the potato fields a half-mile away filled the night air.

At eight o'clock we ate our salad; Ray was supposed to have come at seven. My mother decided to eat her chili. "You and Ray can eat alone," she said.

"Ma, I don't even like this human," I said.

"Well, what did you ask him to come for?"

"*You* told me to invite him."

So we bickered, gently. Still, it was a way to pass the evening. Maybe I had been too harsh in my previous judgment of Ray. Maybe she would find Ray genuinely charming.

At nine o'clock he called from a gas station; he had gotten a late start and there was a traffic jam.

"He's not even close," my mother said. "Why don't you just tell him to go home? By the time he gets here it'll be ten o'clock."

Ray arrived at ten-fifteen. He brought two bottles of expensive wine: the price stickers were still on them—$29 and $18. I didn't even like wine. I wondered how my mother, a tall, thin woman, nearly five feet ten, with the presence of a dyspeptic duchess, garbed in a frowsy old sweater, must have appeared to Ray. He was freshly shaved, smelled of aftershave, and wore raiment that might have been ripped from the pages of some men's magazine. He barely came up to her shoulder.

Ray wasn't hungry, but we ate a little chili and salad and then went out for a walk. At the end of the street was an empty lot someone had turned into a vegetable garden, with neat rows of asparagus, tomatoes, eggplants, and peppers. None of the plants were very big yet. The evening was cool, murky, with a shimmery liquid quality to it. Ray cleared his throat. "How's your brother doing?" I said.

"Fine," Ray said. "He has a beautiful Swedish girlfriend. He just got home for the summer."

"How's that crazy cat?" I said.

"Max?" Ray said. "He's fine." We turned around and walked the other way.

"Listen," he said. "I really want to get married."

"Oh?" I said.

"I mean, maybe you think this is coming out of left field."

"Not if that's what you want to do," I said. "When are you getting married?"

"No, seriously," Ray said. "I was thinking we could go steady."

"I don't even know you, Ray," I said.

"Well, that's okay," he said. "You'd get to know me."

I turned to look at him, but he wasn't smiling. I thought I

had never met a person who had less to say; nor did I feel any doglike waves of love coming from him. There was simply no connection.

"Do you want to go someplace?" he said. "To a roadhouse?"

"No, I'm pretty tired," I said. I walked with him back to his car.

"Will you call me if you change your mind?" he said. "Think about it, anyway?"

"Don't you want to take your wine back?" I said. "We didn't even open it."

"No," he said. "It's for you. Listen, I don't mean to keep bugging you—"

"That's okay," I said. I rubbed my forehead for a second.

"I have to go into the hospital next week," he said. "They're operating on my back. I'll be in the hospital for a while. Could you come and visit me?"

"I guess," I said. "Sure, sure. How did it happen that you fell down an elevator shaft, anyway?" It was strange that I'd never bothered to ask him before.

"My fiancée," Ray said. "It was a New Year's Eve party, and we were engaged—in fact we were going to be married in a week—and I bumped into her in the bathroom with some guy. I just started running, and it was in an old loft building, and the elevator door opened, and the elevator wasn't there."

My mother was still awake when I went to her room. "Did you have fun?" she said. "I can't believe he brought such expensive bottles of wine. Who drinks that stuff?"

"He wants to get married," I said.

"Go ahead," she said. She turned back to her book. "He has small, eloquent feet and hands," she said to the page.

"He likes to try on my shoes," I said.

"As part of sex?"

"We never slept together," I said. "His feet might be small, but I still don't like him wearing my shoes."

My mother shrugged. "If you like him, maybe you could find him a pair in his size at the thrift store."

The hospital room, on the twenty-second floor, was crammed with masses of expensive floral arrangements: scarlet blossoms sprang out of moss, and there were heathery clouds of purple and violet. I knew just one of the bouquets probably cost enough to feed and keep me for a week. The room had one large window with a panoramic view of stubby, toylike buildings and a soiled ribbon of East River. Ray was lying on his back, tubes emerging from his arms. He looked white and shrunken, but the operation had been a success. "Sit down, sit down," he said. "Do you want some candy or something?" I shook my head. "There's some lemonade—Minute Maid—if you want."

"So, how are you feeling?" I said.

"Okay."

I sat in a chair by the window. "Nice flowers," I said.

His mother swept into the room. She was wearing an expensive-looking outfit in baby pink: trousers, a linen jacket, slingback pink high heels with rosettes, strands of pink and gray pearls. I studied my feet, realizing too late I should have stood up. Mrs. Connors came over to my chair, bent to embrace me, and pecked me on both cheeks. "Just look at you two," she said. "What a couple of deadbeats. Cora, where have you been? Ray was frantic when you left New Haven. Now, I don't want to interfere; you just tell me to shut up. I don't know what's been going on with you two. But why do you have to live together? Why don't you just get married?"

"Ma," Ray said from his bed.

I smiled. "Those earrings are wonderful," I said. Mrs. Connors was wearing large mulberry-colored cubes, spiked with gold branches like tendrils. They resembled some living entities found in a coral reef.

"Look how she tries to change the subject, Ray," Mrs. Connors said. She put her hand up to her ears. "These old things," she said. "They're not real." She unclipped them and handed them to me.

"Nice," I said, studying them.

"They're for you."

"Oh, no, I couldn't."

"No, no, they're for you. I insist, don't make a fuss, or I'll be very angry."

"Well, thank you," I said. I stood up, with the earrings in my hand. "I guess I'd better go now," I said. "I have to catch my train."

"Where are you going?" Mrs. Connors said. "Back to South-ampton? Don't go. You'll stay uptown with us—you can have Ray's room."

"I didn't bring anything with me," I said.

"Oh, we have everything," Mrs. Connors said. "We'll go out right now and buy a toothbrush. Ray talks nonstop about you, and I've hardly gotten a chance to see you."

"I really can't stay," I said. I went over to the side of Ray's bed and bent to kiss him goodbye.

"You'll call me later?" Ray said.

He pulled me down by the arm. I thought he was going to whisper something to me, but when he didn't I said, "I'm glad the operation was a success."

I made my mother answer the phone, but Ray didn't call. In the fall I found a job working for a publishing company in Manhattan and began the rounds of looking for a place to live. On Monday morning there was an ad for a studio apartment on a block near Central Park West. I had already checked out that block—mostly brownstones—and the blocks nearby; it was a nice area. The apartment was dark, but the building was quaint and I could almost afford it. I left a small deposit with the landlady. The woman was going to call my references and I was to leave my security deposit and first month's rent with her that afternoon.

I had the rest of the morning to fill. For some reason I de-cided to go back downtown to the area where I saw the apart-ment with my mother the previous summer. I still felt as if that were really my apartment. Maybe by chance the previous ten-ants had moved out and there would once again be a FOR RENT sign in the window. For less money than I would be paying on the uptown place, I could have had a whole floor in a building, sunny, with a yard. As I got near the address I felt the strong feeling—the sense of place, whatever—coming back even more intensely than on the previous visit.

Standing in the front entrance of the building was Ray.

"Hi," he said.

"Ray," I said. "What are you doing here?"

"My father bought the first floor," he said.

"I don't believe this," I said. "I tried to rent this place last year. I came back to look."

"The building went co-op a little while ago," Ray said. "We're in the middle of renovating." He seemed pleased with himself; I wondered if he thought I came looking for him. "Do you want to come in?" he said.

The first floor had been completely stripped. Now the rococo molding was gone, there was wall-to-wall carpeting over the floor and track lighting. The bathroom was replaced with modern equipment. It was probably neater and cleaner, but the crazy charm of the place was gone. Now that it had new windows and different doors, it was just like a million other apartments.

I looked out the windows to the backyard; it had been paved over with bricks, and small trees were stuck into redwood planters. It was too cold to go outside, but Ray said I should sit down for a minute. He pointed to a gray sofa. "I'm in the middle of working on a project," he said. "For my parents. They bought a house upstate and hired me to renovate."

I said I was about to go and give a deposit on an apartment uptown.

"We're just subletting a place right now," Ray said. "As soon as this place is finished, in a couple of weeks, then we can move in."

"Who's we?" I said.

"I got married last month," Ray said. He looked at me with a wry expression. I thought he was waiting for me to burst into tears. "My father got us this place as a wedding present."

"Oh, how great," I said. "Congratulations! Who is she?"

My voice sounded artificial, not because I was upset over this news but because I just didn't care. "Someone I know?" I said.

"No, no," Ray said. "She's a secretary at my firm; she just started work there a few months ago."

"You didn't know her before?"

"No," Ray said. "It was just one of those things that happen fast."

"Great," I said. His small, worried eyes looked at me with a combination of rage and love.

"I have to get back to work now," Ray said. "I'm glad you stopped by. I had hoped we wouldn't lose touch. Listen, would you like to have dinner with me? Just the two of us?"

"When?" I said.

"I don't know," Ray said. "Tonight."

"Um," I said. "Well, I have a bunch of things to do. Why don't I call you later this afternoon?"

"Okay," Ray said. "And if you can't make it tonight, maybe we could have lunch next week. Do you still have all the furniture I gave you?"

"Oh, yes."

"I'll also give you my number at work."

I took his phone number, written on the back of a card. Out on the street I went to a nearby phone booth and called my mother, who was having lunch with friends in the city. We met on Thirty-fourth Street to go shopping for shoes. My mother bought me two pairs: gray pumps, with a medium heel, and a pair of purple sandals, which resembled, at least as far as I was concerned, those worn by French prostitutes. They weren't practical, but I liked them.

A while later I saw Ray's father on television—a morning talk show—kicking a mattress to demonstrate construction. He was a vigorous man, and he chuckled to the host as he ripped open the ticking and pulled out the stuffing.

you and
the boss

First, you must dispose of his wife. You disguise yourself as a chambermaid and get a job at a hotel where Bruce is staying with his wife on the tour. You know you are doing the right thing. Bruce will be happier with you. Does Bruce really need a wife with chipmunk cheeks, who probably talks baby talk in bed? You are educated, you have studied anthropology. You can help Bruce with his music, give him ideas about American culture. You are a real woman.

You go into Bruce's room. His wife is lying on the bed, wearing a T-shirt that says "Number 1 Groupie" and staring straight up at the ceiling. You tell Bruce's wife that Bruce has arranged for you to give her a facial and a massage: it's a surprise. "Isn't he sweet?" she says with a giggle.

You whip out an ice pick, hidden under your clothes, and quickly give her a lobotomy: you've watched this technique in the Frances Farmer story on TV. Bruce's wife doesn't even flinch.

After the operation, you present her with a bottle of Valium and an airplane ticket to Hollywood; the taxi's waiting outside. To your amazement, she does exactly as you tell her.

You're a bit worried about how Bruce will adjust to her absence, and your presence, but when he returns to the room, at three in the morning, he doesn't even seem to notice the difference. You're dressed in her nightie, lying in bed, looking up at the ceiling. Bruce strips down to his Jockey shorts and gets into bed with you. "Good night, honeybunch," he says.

In the morning he still doesn't seem to realize there's been a change in personnel. In real life, Bruce is larger than life. Though he appears small on television and on record covers, when you stand next to him for the first time you understand that Bruce is the size of a monster. His hands are as large as your head, his body might take up an entire billboard. This is why, you now know, he must have guitars made specially for him.

At breakfast Bruce puts away a dozen eggs, meatballs, spaghetti, and pizza. He sings while he eats, American songs about food. He has plans, projects, he discusses it all with his business manager: the Bruce Springsteen Amusement Park, the Bruce Springsteen Las Vegas Casino, a chain of Bruce Springsteen bowling alleys.

Bruce decides that today you will buy a new home.

You are very excited about this prospect: you imagine something along the lines of Graceland, or an elegant Victorian mansion. "I'm surprised at you," Bruce says. "We agreed not to let my success go to your head."

He selects a small ranchhouse on a suburban street of an industrial New Jersey town. "You go rehearse, darling," you say. "I'll pick out the furnishings."

But Bruce wants to help with the decoration. He insists on ordering everything from Sears: a plaid couch, brown and white, trimmed with wood; a vinyl La-Z-Boy recliner; orange wall-to-wall carpeting. The bedroom, Bruce decides, will have mirrors on the ceiling, a water bed with purple satin sheets, white shag carpeting, and two pinball machines. Everything he has chosen, he tells you, was made in the U.S.A.

In the afternoon, Bruce has a barbecue in the backyard. "Everybody's got to have a hobby, babe," he tells you. He wears a chef's hat and has his own special barbecue sauce— bottled Kraft's, which he doctors with ketchup and mustard. Though he only knows how to make one thing—dried-out chicken—everyone tells him it is the best they've ever had.

You think it's a little strange that no one seems to notice his wife is gone and you are there instead; but perhaps it's just that everyone is so busy telling Bruce how talented he is that they don't have time.

Soon you have made the adjustment to life with Bruce.

The only time Bruce ever feels like making love is when the four of you—you, Bruce, and his two bodyguards—are driving in his Mustang. He likes to park at various garbage dump sites outside of Newark and, while the bodyguards wait outside, Bruce insists that you get in the back seat. He finds the atmosphere—rats, broken refrigerators, old mattresses, soup cans —very stimulating. He prefers that you don't remove your clothes; he likes you to pretend to fight him off. The sun, descending through the heavy pollution, sinks slowly, a brilliant red ball changing slowly into violet and then night.

When Bruce isn't on tour, rehearsing with his band, recording a record or writing new songs, his favorite pastime is visiting old age homes and hospitals, where he sings to senior citizens until they beg him to stop. His explanation for why he likes this is that he finds it refreshing to be with real Americans, those who do not worship him, those who do not try to touch the edges of his clothing. But even the sick old people discover, after a short time, that when Bruce plays to them they are cured.

The terminally ill recover after licking up just one drop of Bruce's sweat. Soon Bruce is in such demand at the nursing homes that he is forced to give it up. There is nothing Bruce can do that doesn't turn to gold.

One day Bruce has a surprise for you. "I'm going to take you on a vacation, babe," he says. "You know, we were born to run." You are thrilled. At last you will get that trip to Europe; you will be pampered, you will visit the couture houses and select a fabulous wardrobe, you will go to Bulgari and select a handful of jewels, you will go to Fendi and pick out a sable coat. You will be deferred to, everyone will want to be your friend in the hope of somehow getting close to Bruce.

"Oh, Bruce, this is wonderful," you say. "Where will we go?"

"I bought a camper," Bruce says. "I thought we'd drive around, maybe even leave New Jersey."

You have always hated camping, but Bruce has yet another surprise—he's stocked the camper with food. Dehydrated scrambled eggs, pancake mix, beef jerky. "No more fast food for us," he says.

You travel all day; Bruce has decided he wants to visit the Baseball Hall of Fame. While Bruce drives he plays tapes of his music and sings along. You tell him you're impressed with the fact he's memorized all the words. "So what do you think?" he says. "You like the music?"

Though your feet hurt—Bruce has bought you a pair of hiking boots, a size too small—you tell him you think the music is wonderful. Never has a greater genius walked the face of the earth.

Unfortunately, Bruce is irritated by this. The two of you have your first fight. "You're just saying that," Bruce says. "You're just the same as all the rest. I thought you were different, but you're just trying to get on my good side by telling me I'm brilliant."

"What do you want from me?" you say.

Bruce starts to cry. "I'm not really any good," he says.

"That's not true, Bruce," you say. "You mustn't feel discouraged. Your fans love you. You cured a small boy of cancer just because he saw you on TV. You're up there with the greats: the Beatles, Christ, Gandhi, Lee Iacocca. You've totally restored New Jersey to its former glory: once again it's a proud state."

"It's not enough," Bruce says. "I was happier in the old days, when I was just Bruce, playing in my garage."

You're beginning to find that you're unhappy in your life with Bruce. Since Bruce spends so much time rehearsing, there is little for you to do but shop. Armed with credit cards and six bodyguards (to protect you from Bruce's angry women fans), you search the stores for some gift for Bruce that might please him. You buy foam coolers to hold beer, Smurf dolls, candy-flavored underwear, a television set he can wear on his wrist, a pure-bred Arabian colt. You hire three women to wrestle on his bed covered in mud.

Bruce thanks you politely but tells you, "There's only one thing I'm interested in."

"Me?" you say.

Bruce looks startled. "My music," he says.

To your surprise you learn you are pregnant, though you can't figure out how this could have happened. You think about what to name the baby. "How about Benjamin Springsteen?" you say.

"Too Jewish immigrant," Bruce says. "This kid is going to be an American, not some leftist from Paterson."

"How about Sunny Von?" you say.

"Sunny von Springsteen?" Bruce says. "I don't get it. No, there's only one name for a kid of mine."

"What?" you say, trying to consider the possibilities. Bruce is sitting on the couch, stroking his guitar. The three phones are ringing nonstop, the press is banging on the door. You haven't been out of the house in three days. The floor is littered with boxes from Roy Rogers, cartons of White Castle burgers, empty cans of Coke. You wonder how you're going to fill up the rest of the day; you've already filed your nails, studied the Sears, Roebuck catalog, made a long-distance call to your mother.

At last Bruce speaks. "I'm going to call the kid Elvis," he says.

"What if it's a girl?" you say.

"Elvis," Bruce says. "Elvis, either way."

You fly to Hollywood to try to find his real wife. Finally you track her down. She's working as a tour guide at the wax museum. "Admission to the museum is five dollars," she says at the door. "The museum will be closing in fifteen minutes."

"Don't you remember me?" you say. "I'm the person who gave you a lobotomy, who shipped you off to Hollywood."

"If you say so," Bruce's wife says. "Thank you."

"I made a mistake," you say. "I did wrong. I have your ticket here; you'll go back to Bruce."

His wife is willing, though she claims not to know what you're talking about. "But what about my job here?" she says. "I can't just leave."

You tell her you'll take over for her. Quickly you rush her to the airport, push her onto the plane. You tell her to look after Bruce. "He can't live without you, you know," you say.

You wait to make sure her plane takes off on time. A sense of relief comes over you. You have nowhere to go, nothing to do; you decide to return to the wax museum and make sure it's properly locked up for the night.

You have the keys to the door; the place is empty, the lights are off. Now you wander through the main hall. Here are Michael Jackson, Jack the Ripper, President Reagan, Sylvester Stallone, Muhammad Ali, Adolf Hitler. You are alone with all these men, waxy-faced, unmoving, each one a superstar.

Something violent starts to kick, then turns, in your stomach.

life in the pre-cambrian era

I forgot that my mother planned to pay me a visit that day. Or I would have cleaned up. Maybe. Now I, Marley Mantello, hesitate to speak too highly of myself. But even as a toddler, reenacting imaginary scenes of death on the roof of my mother's run-down house, garbed in a matador's tweedley-dee, it was obvious—to myself, to my mother—that I was a boy genius.

Example: my Hollywood-inspired paintings of the Crusaders fighting the Moslems, and in the sky, emblazoned in black letters, the word "GOD." And beneath this word a black cross. Not bad for a kid of eight. But what good does any of this genius do me? There are times when I think that to leave my mark upon the world is simply to curse it with another smear. . . .

After art school I became a starving artist. I starved with a vengeance. My mother approved. All this was for my art. Still, in another sense, it didn't matter one way or the other: I knew I wasn't going to live very long, I expected to keel over at any minute. Every day I had to think carefully: Was I well enough to get up today? Did my stomach hurt? Was an unhealed cut on my finger a sign of cancer? What should I eat for breakfast? And none of these things would have been enough to get me out of bed except for the fact that I had to go paint a picture.

But as much as I wanted to paint, often it took me most of the day to prepare myself for it. First of all, I had to go to the

bank to take out another dollar or two. I am a fast walker, but
my bank is very far away. It was one of those big banks on
Wall Street, an unusually gloomy place, built in a neofascist-
religious style. It should have had one of those big organs at
the back, or at least a baptismal font. If my bank had had any
sense, it would have commissioned me to turn the interior into
a chapel. It would have been a real investment for them. It
gave me great pleasure to walk down there, even though it
generally took me about an hour. I liked the fact that my bank
was far away, this way I wasn't tempted to spend money as
quickly.

On the streets crowds of people were staggering this way
and that, newly released from their office tombs. Grim faces,
worn down like cobblestones, never to make anything of their
lives. These were the worker bees and drones, who had been
imprisoned in American thought-patterns since birth, with no
hope for escape but the weekly million-dollar lottery. Walking
at a slow speed, which drove me crazy. But what would have
motivated them to move more quickly?

I stood out. With my long, lanky stride, my scuffed Italian
loafers, and my beat-up, faggoty Italian jacket. It had deep
pockets on both sides, ripped because I kept a lot of variables
and disregards in the pockets—and the shoulders had a little
padding in them, by now somewhat lopsided.

It didn't bother me, the looks and stares I got. People were
angry with me, and why? Because I was some sort of freak, an
artist. They were trapped, and I wasn't. So I felt smug, even
though I was starving.

But when I got to my big mausoleum, I found I only had $10
in my savings account: I took out nine. Ginger, my dealer,
owed me money. I had at least two grand coming to me, which
was going to have to go for the rent. I hadn't paid the rent in
months, in protest. The crummy landlord, Vardig, hadn't
turned on the heat. So even if Ginger paid up, I would still be
broke after Vardig got what he was owed.

Meanwhile, as I was waiting for the cash machine to excrete
my receipt, I could hear snickers coming from behind me on

line. This made me mad. I walked out of the bank in a fury. Who needed this kind of attention? I strolled up the streets like a panther, grimacing and ready for food.

So I stopped off at the restaurant nearby I liked to frequent. This place had been around since the days of J. P. Morgan. Wood-paneled walls redolent with coffee smells, the ceiling blackened by ancient grease and cigar smoke.

I bought the *Times* and sat at the counter, a fudge brownie before me. The counter woman, Marion, was very frisky today. Our acquaintance went back over a few years. But we weren't intimate, normally she spent our conversations racking up complaints against the customers. What a skinny little salamander she was, with a pitted face and eyes the color of lime juice. "How's the painting going?" she said, scouring the counter with a rag held in one clawed hand. "You paint pictures, right?"

"Great," I said. "I've got this idea for a painting—"

"I could tell you a thing or two about artists," she muttered. "You see that man sitting over there?"

On the other side of the counter was a small creature wearing a hearing aid and a binocularlike pair of glasses: a poor denizen crawled up perhaps from the subway. "I see him," I said.

"He's not supposed to drink coffee because of his ulcer," Marion hissed at me. "But does so anyway. Some people have no more sense than a can of peas. He's been married four times, and left every one of them for various complaints. Where does he get off thinking of himself as so desirable that any woman would come running for him?"

She left me to bring the man a plate of cinnamon toast, though I hadn't noticed him ask for it. He gave her the royal nod, and she came back to me, the salamander relegated to the scullery.

Well, that was poor old Marion for you. I could tell she was depressed, each of us has been gifted from birth with our own problems. In her case it was her appearance. But she cheered up when I told her my idea for a painting: I wanted to use her as a model. Already in my head I could see those salamander thighs topped with a pink pot of geraniums and a cluster of frog's eggs. "Me? Me, a model? That's a joke," she said. Still, she was pleased. She straightened herself up and began smashing the coffee cups with a little Mae West twist of her tail. With a certain neat flick: I half expected she lived at night in some sort of hole beneath the counter, so much a part of the room were her movements.

After this we were best buddies—she slapped an extra goo-brownie on my plate at no charge. I got out my notebook, and would have sketched her, too, right then and there, with her two slabs of breasts like day-old cupcakes on what was other-wise an amphibian physique. Only I remembered. My mother was scheduled to visit me that day. I was late, it was already early afternoon.

When I got back to my building, my mother was waiting in the lobby. More overweight than ever, if such a thing was possible. From the top of head to ankles, one piece of flesh, indisposable. Without joints—nor did I believe there were bones underneath that skin. Then beneath, the tiny feet, little figgys. "I told you yesterday I was coming to visit," she said. "Do you know how long I've been waiting? Where've you been?"

"Aw, Ma," I said. I gave her a smack on the cheek to placate.

So we went upstairs. To distract her from the mess I took her around and showed her the latest frescoes on the wall and ceilings, which I started when I ran out of canvas: goddess and nymph and semitropical vegetation. The God of Baseball, play-ing a game of billiards with Bacchus. I was proud of the God of Baseball, in his Yankees cap, chipmunk cheek filled with a plump throb of chewing tobacco. One hand fiddling with his crotch. But my mother barely seemed to notice. "How can you live in this pigsty?" she said. "You're twenty-nine years old, Marley. A person can't go on this way. I was hoping you'd be able to support me in my old age."

Listen, with remarks like this I was titled to my irritation. Old Vinnie van Gogh never sold a painting in his life, but at least his brother was there with support. My mother, of all people, should have worshiped the ground I walked on. "A pigsty?" I said. "You call this a pigsty? Who did I learn my housekeeping habits from if not you?"

"Not like this, though," she said.

"Oh, yes," I said. "Like this. Listen, Ma, all your life you've lived in a dream. You haven't had it easy, I'm willing to admit that. This perpetual fog that surrounds you can't be much fun to be in."

"I had a hard life," my mother said.

"That's true," I said, without feeling sorry for her, "Grandfather disowning you when you got knocked up with me. That so-called husband of yours, Marco, running around the world to play the violin, then all of a sudden dying. It wasn't much of a marriage, I guess. But for all these years you've basically ignored me. Now you show up, a stranger—I'm nearly thirty years old—and tell me I live in a pigsty!"

My mother didn't even look surprised. "Yes, yes . . ." she muttered. "It's true." She sat heavily on the couch. I noticed she wasn't making any effort to clean the place up, either. Well, at her great weight it took a lot out of her just to rest.

"You were brought up to expect one thing," I told her. "You were a rich little girl, no one told you life wasn't going to be chipped beef on toast forever. If you had married someone from your own background, Grandfather wouldn't have disowned you and things would be different for me today. But you've always done exactly as you pleased. Well, why don't you sell those stocks in Marvel Comics"—for I had discovered this secret wealth she had managed to squirrel away the last time I went home and was looking through some of her papers —"and use the money to help me out?"

"Oh, I don't know, Marley," my mother said. "At one time I thought you'd make these paintings, which seems to be all you're capable of, and make some money, and in this way things would work out for you. A boy like you, from an un-

known background, without connections—what choice did I
have but to encourage you? But let's face it, other, younger
artists have come along who are by now a big success. Your
shows don't even get reviewed. I wish you'd get out of this
business, which is making you neither rich nor happy. It's not
too late, you could still change. There are schools to learn the
computer—"

"I have my own goals, Mother. If you don't want to help me,
then say so. But let's not pretend you couldn't do it if you
wanted to."

My mother, however, wasn't listening. Yet even though I
was mad, I still adored her. I happen to think my mother is a
brilliant woman who has not let modern civilization or the
twentieth century disturb her in any way. That mass of Valkyr-
ien hair, mostly gray. Those washed-out blue eyes, always
looking at a person who wasn't in the room. The thin lines just
beginning to form around her mouth.

It gave me an idea for painting Athena after she reached
middle age. No longer interested in getting her own way as
much as being left alone. Standing in the middle of a nightclub,
filled with baubles. Tired out, overweight.

But because I adored her, my fury was greater. "Hello!" I
said, waving my hand in front of her face. "Anybody home?"
But my mother was still in her trance. "Listen, Ma, you've got
to understand what I'm trying to do! After all, you did marry
my father, who, from what I can gather, was an artist."

"An artist," my mother said, blinking. "Oh, well . . . if you
want to look at it that way. I married him because he could
play the violin and I was fed up with Vassar. At the time he
was playing with Django Reinhardt . . . I met him during
Christmas vacation in Paris."

"I don't care to hear this story again," I said.

"I was supposed to be studying French. All the girls fell for
him, though physically he wasn't a paragon of beauty, with his
large nose and shock of dirty blond hair, a Northern Italian
who smelled of garlic. Actually, you take after him."

"Mother, what are you talking about," I said. I was insulted.

"Lay off trying to tease me at this time. You know I don't have much of a sense of humor when it comes to myself. Ten years ago I could have been a male model. What a different life I would have been leading now. But you always encouraged me in my artistic ambition."

"I think I'm pregnant," my mother said, looking at the ceiling. "I don't know what to do. I've always had a healthy appetite, but this is different. . . ."

"Once again you're changing the subject on me!" I said. "Well, Mother, I've told you for years to go on a diet."

"This is a different kind of fatness," my mother said. "This is the kind of weight gain due to something being alive inside my stomach."

"Did you see a doctor?"

"At my age I'm embarrassed to go to a doctor."

That's the kind of logic my mother always thought was acceptable. "Ma, what makes you think you're pregnant?" I said.

"A few months ago, visiting Andrea at her summer place in Maine, I had an affair with a young man. He was an instructor at Berkeley in the politics of television, and we had sexual intercourse twice, without using birth control. Neither time was very much fun."

"I thought, Ma, that you said you had been through the menopause."

"I never paid much attention to that sort of thing."

For a few minutes neither of us said anything, each occupied with our own thoughts. I supposed, if she went ahead and actually had this baby, that I would offer to take care of it and raise it as my own child. Would she have done the same for me? This was doubtful; besides, I would never let any child of mine fall into her hands. It wouldn't be so bad. My brother, my son. I would name the kid Achilles, it could talk to me while I painted.

And I might have opened my mouth to make my offer had not my mother opened her mouth to insult me once again.

"I can't go on worrying about you forever, Marley," she said.

"You're twenty-nine years old and haven't gotten any more mature since you were ten. I wonder if I should have given you more vitamins."

"Crazy old bat!" I said. "Old cow! Who asked you to worry about me? You're the one who screwed up your life and mine!"

My mother was like a little kid with a lot of toys, and I was just a toy she had forgotten about a long time ago. Once in a while she saw me up on the back of the shelf. When I was a kid, I waited for the times when she would dust me off. Then it was great, it made up for all the rest.

But I thought I had worked through all this. I hadn't meant to snarl at her; I really didn't want her bucks, nor did I need them. I didn't mind not eating, it was part of what I had chosen for myself. "Oh, that's not to say, Ma," I added guiltily, "that you didn't always make me feel capable of doing anything. I have to hand it to you for that. You had confidence in me— and look how I turned out, a genius of the first degree!"

This was a compliment of the highest order. But all my mother said, looking at the floor and not at my paintings, was, "You've always sounded so pompous to me, Marley. I wonder if other people feel the same way about you that I do? Or is it just because I'm your mother that you come across as pretentious. . . ."

Let's face it, my mother was in outer space. She made me mad. There was no use in my trying to talk to her. I got up and walked out, leaving my mother alone in the loft.

Well, I really just went up the street to buy some beer. I only wanted to get away from her for a couple of minutes. But when I got back with the Rheingold, she was gone. This made me feel even worse. Because the neighborhood was not exactly safe, and it was already past dark. All the Cuban fritter joints had closed up for the evening and there was nobody out on the street but a bunch of men standing around drinking. Which was okay for me, because though I'm a skinny guy, I've always been tough. But for my mother, wandering around pregnant with my brother . . .

I cracked open the quart of beer and there on the table my

mother had scribbled a little note. It was lucky I found it, the table was so covered with old paint rags, napkins, telephone numbers, and unopened bills. The note was short: "As long as you have confidence in yourself, Marley, I suppose that's what's important. I'm leaving you five dollars, buy yourself something to eat."

My mother had never outgrown a certain girlish style of writing, at least in her personal correspondence. And yet her monthly pet column, appearing in various women's magazines, which she churned out with regularity, was highly professional, though the subject matter was generally quite deranged. Articles on homosexuality in the household pet; hookworm; rabies, and other lurid topics.

I was so mad at myself I went over to the sink and smashed the three plates I hadn't yet broken. I'm a very volatile type of guy. Why had I spoken to my mother that way, calling her an old bat? Maybe it was the cold, my apartment was without heat. I have never done well in the cold, nor in the heat either, for that matter. The cold hadn't seemed to affect the cockroaches, however, they were more active than ever. I figured the least I could do would be to poison the roaches, a task I thoroughly enjoyed. In this way I supposed I would be pleasing my mother. I would use the money she had left me to go buy roach poison and some ice cream. If my mother thought I was looking skinny, she who had never before paid the slightest attention to my appearance, then I really must be looking frail. So I threw my coat on and went back out.

On the street I realized I felt extremely giddy. Here I was, Marley Mantello, a genius of an artist, and shortly about to have a new brother. Already I thought of the kid more as my own son. The discussions we would be able to have! All that I knew about art would be his by osmosis. It was as if I was in a cyclotron, whirling about. I could feel the various amoebas and molecules inside me hopping like Mexican jumping beans. Oh, it was amazing how lucky I was, though it was no more than I deserved.

I couldn't control myself; once inside the grocery store I

leapt up, accidentally knocking over a package of Japanese rice cookies. Oh, I was an elegant chap, and though my Italian almond-colored loafers were scuffed, what a team my son and I would make once he arrived! It would be him and me against the world.

Then I spotted an artist friend of mine, standing next to the piles of dried apricots and nutmeats. "Larry!" I said.

"Hello, Marley," he said, in the voice of a zombie. Humped over alongside the apricots that way, he gave me quite a jolt. It was screwy, the way he was standing, one shoulder lower than the other as if he had got the plague. Maybe he was trying to steal the fruit, though I could have told him that this wasn't the place to try. "How have you been, Marley?" he said.

The last time I saw Larry, he looked like a human being. Now he had slithered into some preliminary reptile. On his head were a few sprouts of hair with a lot of skull in between. Dull lizard eyes. He was dressed in some sort of shabby camouflage. A terrible odor, reminiscent of cauliflower and old cheese . . .

"I'm great!" I said. "My work is going fantastically, I'm designing a giant altarpiece, ten by twenty feet long—see, I've applied to build a chapel in Rome, right near the Vatican. And I have a feeling I'm going to get the grant. But the real reason I'm excited is that I'm going to have a kid. Would you believe it? Me. Marley Mantello—" Meanwhile my voice trailed off. The guy obviously wasn't doing too well. I felt embarrassed to run into him like this, in my black Italian sweater with neon-blue stripes like an early Frank Stella, my elegant rumpled old jacket, my gold, angelic hair. There was a pause. I thought at least the guy would congratulate me.

"Didn't you hear, Marley?" he said.

"Hear what?" I said.

"You must have heard."

"No."

"I'm not doing so well, Marley," he said. "I have cancer."

"Cancer!" The word leapt out of my mouth before I had a chance to close it up.

"Yes, Marley," he said listlessly. "Kaposi's sarcoma. You really didn't know?" I shook my head, taking a step backward toward the Campbell's soup. He took a step closer to me. His thick tongue crept out of his mouth and gave his lips a lick. "Well, Marley, I haven't been feeling well for about a year. Two months ago I went to a specialist in Boston. I had these giant purple welts all over my body. It's the first, contagious stage of AIDS, Marley." He stepped forward and clasped the edge of my coat.

"Wow!" I said. I shot backward about a foot.

"Don't worry," he said. "It takes intimate contact to spread it. But you know, Marley, at least now I know I'm not a hypochondriac. Of course, this isn't exactly helping to increase the value of my paintings. Who wants to buy something by an unknown artist who's got AIDS?"

"God, Larry, what can I say? Are they . . . doing anything for you?"

"Oh, I'm on chemotherapy. I had a course of radiation treatment. That's why I lost my hair. Does it look very bad?" I tried to shake my head. "You know what, Marley? Since I've gotten it, I can't have sex with anyone . . . and I'm horny as hell!" He leaned forward like a leering, toothless old lion in the zoo, sighting a toddler with a pop.

"Well, Larry, best of luck—" I edged away.

"Ah, don't worry, Marley. I know which side my butt is breaded on. I'm going to use this to get one hell of a lot of publicity. Don't catch anything now, you hear?" For I was backing off rapidly. Unable to find the insect repellent, I purchased my eggplant-chocolate-chip ice cream and staggered out of the store.

He had cancer, and the first stages of AIDS! All I could think was that this probably meant I would get it next: he had said it was contagious. Thank God soon my son would be born. Someone to visit me in the hospital. Poor Achilles, he would be fatherless, as I had been. Tears came into my eyes, thinking about the kind of life he was going to have ahead of him. Before

I knew it I was walking alongside the Hudson, preoccupied with my thoughts.

An offering to the gods! I threw my ice cream into the water. The river was gray and choppy. I buried my hands in my pockets and wrapped my scarf around my nose, looking out. I could see all kinds of gooey things swimming around in the water, all sorts of primordial, primeval sludge. It was the land of the dinosaurs, out there in the water, with giant amoebas and lobster tails sashaying back and forth. Everything was alive, even though the water was so cold there were chunks of ice in it.

There were globules eating oil—these were the hungry enzymes from millennia ago that had survived through this day —and invisible lizards slithering through the waves. And volatile guy that I was, a great feeling of joy and happiness swept over me. I was not some primitive sponge or barnacle or anchorite. I was not Larry, walking around with a condition similar to leprosy. I was not my mother, in a dream world without clouds. But I was myself, Marley Mantello.

Oh, Marley, I thought, my boy, there is nothing you can't do. It was unfair, I was so much more alive and talented than any human being had a right to be; and if I had the financing I could have shown this to my son and to the world, by writing books, making movies, forming a rock-and-roll band and various other plans I had in mind for myself once I got rich enough to hire slaves.

I felt quite weighted down with the voluptuousness of my thoughts. Then it occurred to me that quite possibly I was weighted physically as well: an overabundance of hair. I always cut my hair myself. I was so good at it I didn't even need to look in the mirror.

So I sat down on the bank of the Hudson and got my scissors out of my key chain. It was true, it had been a long time since I had last cut my hair, which always grew quickly. No wonder my thoughts were crazed and tangled, with so much hair like violent worms feeding on the juice within my brain. My strength was slowly being sapped. I crossed myself: though I wasn't Catholic, it couldn't hurt.

Besides, this was penance of a sort. Like the monks of yore, I would remove my worldly vanity, my golden curls. Or at least give myself a trim, in the name of poor Larry who had AIDS. It wasn't fair to give him this illness on top of the fact that he wasn't a very good painter, while I was in the prime of life and a genius to boot. And now to be graced with this offspring, little Achilles. The gods no doubt needed placating, a sacrifice to keep them on my good side.

It was only with difficulty, sitting there on the bank, that I was able to trim off the bottom hair and then lie back in the cold dirt, tired out. The hell with the top: though I had not a mirror to hand, I had probably done a good job and would be pleased with my appearance. I certainly felt dizzy. Well, what had I eaten today? Practically nothing.

It would have been nice to go now to the bistro on the corner and sit quietly at a table, eating a lovely, juicy hamburger with a mound of French fries alongside. And how very quietly I would sit, eating my hamburger and asking for an extra plate of raw onions and consuming an entire bottle of ketchup.

But my pocket, as always, was empty. Meanwhile, thinking these thoughts, I rose, leaving my piles of curling blond hair to blow along the shore. Whosoever discovered these hairs would no doubt have good fortune shine upon his life; such was the nature of all that had been touched by me, Marley Mantello. And before the last hair had blown away, I snatched it up and stuffed it into my back pocket—this I would present to my son, whether I was alive or dead, so that he could turn out like me.

case history #4: fred

Fred had a problem: he liked to approach strange girls on the street and offer to take them shopping at Tiffany's. As he was an out-of-work musician who lived in a cold-water walk-up near the Williamsburg Bridge, this often got him into trouble.

The first time it happened he was leaving a midtown record company (he had gone there to drop off yet another of his tapes) and across the block he saw a tall girl with short cropped hair and a certain elegant hard way of walking. He crossed the street against the light and came up alongside the girl. To his surprise, he found himself saying, "Listen, I like your linear definition. I was wondering—just for the hell of it—would you let me take you shopping at Tiffany's? It would give me a great deal of pleasure, and naturally I wouldn't expect payment of any kind."

The girl looked at him and said, "Buzz off."

If anything, Fred was energized by the experience. A few weeks later, while shopping for artichoke-chocolate-chip ice cream at Di Roma's in SoHo, he saw another girl with skinny elbows and a wry, pixieish face. He looked over her shoulder; she was purchasing a can of cream-of-asparagus soup. "Good choice," he said. "Listen, I know this might offend you, but I'm a millionaire and I get a kick out of taking young women shopping at Tiffany's. Would you like to go? You can pick out something nice—a bracelet, whatever."

"Okay," the girl said.

They got in a taxi. On the way uptown the girl explained that she was from Ohio and was visiting her sister. Fred said that he didn't do this sort of thing all that often, just when the mood struck. "It must be nice to have all that money," the girl said.

"Oh, it's not bad," Fred said.

In Tiffany's the girl grew very excited. "I can't believe this," she said. "Wait till my sister hears about this. She'll just die. This is like something out of the movies."

For almost an hour Fred and the girl perused the trays of emerald rings, chunky lapis bracelets, silver and pearl neck-laces. Watching the girl, with her gingery freckles, her mut-tered cooing, and her skinny, twitching elbows, Fred was nearly overcome with love. At last the girl selected a $3,000 belt of alligator and silver. "Very tasteful," Fred said. "A good choice. But don't you think you'd rather have a pin?"

The girl looked worried. "Well it's up to you," she said. "You're paying. I mean, you can decide."

Fred knew the girl really wanted the belt, but he selected a tiny choker of pink coral and small diamonds.

Just as the salesperson was about to write up the purchase, Fred searched his pockets and his wallet. "Damn," he said. "I've forgotten my credit card. How stupid!"

The girl looked wistful but said she understood absolutely.

That night Fred replayed the event over in his head. He felt he had never been more aroused, more attuned to life, than he had been in that hour and a half spent in Tiffany's. Yet ob-viously this was not normal. He remembered reading about how when Nietzsche, the famous German philosopher, was fifteen years old and in boarding school, a sadomasochistic nymphomaniac countess snuck into his dorm room late one night dressed as a man and beat him until she was sexually aroused enough to make love.

Though Fred didn't quite remember all the details of this incident, he did know that in future years, when Nietzsche was grown up, he developed his superman philosophy, in which the virile, powerful individual would dominate in life and society.

In Nietzsche's case it was obvious how the primary, or key event—that of his rape by the blond nymphomaniac countess —led to the creation of a new philosophy.

But Fred could not understand why he himself had this penchant, this need, this lust to approach strange women on the street and offer to take them shopping at Tiffany's. He'd never had a key event. Maybe he'd never had any events.

For a few more times he was able to get away with his harmless ruse; but eventually the salespeople began to recognize him, and at last one of them, upon seeing him enter Tiffany's with yet another woman, called the police. He was detained and questioned for several hours; the woman also. She wept bitterly as she explained she had never seen Fred before. Tiffany's decided not to press charges provided Fred never entered the store again.

He thought about asking women to shop with him at Harry Winston's, but his original enthusiasm had worn thin, his pleasure in women had dimmed, even his new musical compositions seemed to lack the old zip and snap.

sun poisoning

You never wanted to take a vacation. Just to stay home requires all of your energy, and when you go away you not only have to do all the normal, exhausting things, you also have to run around getting tickets, contact-lens solution, do the laundry, et cetera. You'd much rather just lie in bed and think about how much fun everyone else is having. But your boyfriend has a show of his paintings and decides you should both get away for a few days.

It takes days of preparation to get ready for your Haitian vacation. You take the big plunge and have your legs waxed. This is one of the most horrifying episodes you will ever undertake. By the time your appointment actually comes, you are prepared for an operation more painful than an abortion. You wonder who thought up leg waxing. It involves a tiny woman screaming at you in Spanish while she pours boiling hot wax over your legs and rips out the hairs.

You wish women's styles would change and that hairy legs on women would become a new trend. Somebody made a big mistake when they assigned you to a female sex role; you'll never get over feeling like a female impersonator.

You spend all of Monday searching for the right kind of expensive sun tan oils and lotions; the Bronx Zoo has come out with a line made from cobra and turtle grease. You don't know why you spend half your life trying to scrub your body free from essential oils and the other half smearing stuff onto it.

You can't wait for the day when humankind is so far evolved that bodies are completely unnecessary and people are nothing but large, flabby gray brains in Plexiglas boxes. Then maybe you'll be appreciated for yourself. As it is, your body has evolved far past the mainstream of society already. You've never been interested in physical exercise. Your highly developed mind inhabits a braincase balanced on top of a large, larval body with feeble, antennalike arms and legs.

The food on the plane trip is not to be believed. Exquisite! Those chefs must have worked hard in the back of the plane: you are served a whitish material resembling chicken, delicately seasoned in a saliva-colored sauce; some unusual pressed vegetable matter shaped like green tubes; and a salad with real lettuce and actual pieces of tomato. This is to be the last fresh food you'll taste for five days.

In order to help your boyfriend calm down—he finds airplane travel extremely erotically stimulating—you feed him your piece of cake, topped with voluptuous sandy frosting. With the coffee comes tiny packets of a white substance, which, when mixed with the coffee, reconstitutes itself into something quite similar to cream. That such food can be served miles above the ground is an amazing feat of modern man: it must be difficult to raise the chickens, lettuce, and so forth so far off the ground.

You are staying on an island about an hour from Port-au-Prince. It's curious how, at the travel agent's, the brochures of Haiti showed an island filled with palm trees and natives with excellent dentures; they must have rented palm trees just to shoot the commercials, because there is no vegetation to be seen on the entire place.

The only thing on the island is the hotel. You are told at once by the hotel clerk not to drink the water or eat any fresh fruits or vegetables. A surly, superior lackey leads you to your cottage, carrying a thermos of drinkable water. The cottages are A-frame, Swiss chalet type residences; whoever built this hotel saw *Heidi* and *The Sound of Music* one too many times. All the buildings are Swiss chalet type. It is as if Walt Disney had a nervous breakdown and got the plans for Bali H'ai and the Swiss Village at Disney World mixed up.

You go in for a dip and when you come out the surly lackey tells you that dinner this evening will be a barbecue by the swimming pool. You can't take a shower because the water isn't working in your cabin, but you are told this condition is only temporary.

You dress and go to look at the view. A large pink man, whom you've seen earlier, comes and stands directly in front of your picnic table, blocking the way. "You're right, Linda," he says, "I can't see any fire, just smoke."

"What's burning?" your boyfriend says. "Is that a fire in Port-au-Prince?" Across the bay, near the lights of the city, black, crackly-looking clouds of smoke rise into the white, moonlit sky.

"It's not in Port-au-Prince," the man says. "It's much closer, a brush fire."

Your boyfriend strikes up a conversation with the overweight man. His girlfriend, sitting at the other table, is named Linda; she's also somewhat overweight, but it looks as if she has gained weight just to keep her boyfriend company. "We're professional travelers," the man says. He gestures for Linda to come over to your table, where he is standing with his stomach resting along one edge.

"No, we're not, Michael," Linda says.

"Well, what would you call us?"

"We travel," Linda says.

"What do you know about buying paintings in Port-au-Prince?" your boyfriend says.

"They're all alike," Michael says. "Someone manufactures them. What do you want them for?"

"I'm an artist—" your boyfriend begins.

"Me, too," Michael says.

"No, you're not," Linda says. "You're a computer graphics designer."

"And I like to buy these paintings," your boyfriend says. "I put them together and I paint over them."

"Why?" Michael says.

"I don't know."

"Do you show?" Michael says. "In New York?"

"I just had a show," your boyfriend says. "I took a vacation to get away afterward. I'm wiped out."

"Oh, yeah," Michael says. "We've experienced something similar—Linda's father was nominated for an Academy Award last year—"

Here you manage to interrupt the conversation by saying it's time for the barbecue dinner and time to get on line. By dragging your boyfriend over to a table, you escape further conversation with the professional travelers.

After a sleepless night slapping mosquitoes, you get up early and spend the day roasting on the beach. The maître d' comes over to your lounge chairs and asks if you want one of the two offerings that night for dinner: boeuf bourguignon or churkey. "Jerky?" you say, thinking this is some sort of Haitian dried meat specialty.

It turns out the maître d' doesn't speak any English. You try to ask him, in French, if it would be possible to get a couple of lobsters for dinner. When you finish talking, the maître d' gives you a puzzled look. "You choose. Boeuf bourguignon or churkey."

You realize what you have in fact said to him was something along the lines of "We are wishing for a need for the lobsters to be prepared for the luncheon event." You are furious with yourself. You have studied French for years—elementary school, high school, college. But apparently none of the lessons have sunk in.

At every meal a three-piece band plays. The band only knows two songs. You call this band "The Royal Haitian Zombie Trio." You are sitting on the porch of your alpine hut, while your boyfriend sits under a tree on the beach listening to his Sony Walkman, when the three-piece combo band comes along. They are going from tree to tree, playing the two songs they know—"Yellow Bird" and "Que Sera, Sera"—to each group of sunbathers, for tips. When they arrive at your boyfriend's seat, one starts playing the bongo drums right next to his ear. Your boyfriend can't hear them, he doesn't even turn around. After a minute or so, your boyfriend feels the vibrations from the drum and he turns to look. He points to his ears, covered with headphones.

You start to laugh. One by one the band stops playing. By now they can hear you laughing, and they slink off. This is the only time during your stay that the band doesn't finish a tune.

The second night your boyfriend tries to figure out some sort of rigging to keep the mosquitoes from biting his ears. Finally he comes up with the idea of wearing your bikini bottom over his head. Just his face sticks out. "They're not going to get me tonight," he says.

It's strange to see a man wearing the bottom half of a bathing suit around his head, but you don't say anything. For a while before you fall asleep you watch the little Watchman TV. Both of you can't imagine traveling anywhere without it. There is only one channel, playing the Jim Jones/Guyana movie massacre dubbed into French. Then an elderly, pudgy singer, who resembles Liberace, sings rock-and-roll songs in French while three girls wearing duck masks dance behind him.

"It's funny," your boyfriend says, "I was just thinking, for kids who grow up not speaking any English, American rock-and-roll music must seem really strange. I mean, it can't make any sense to them."

You are pleased that, away from the pressures of New York, you and your boyfriend are actually communicating on an inti-

mate level. Now you are glad you have refrained from telling
your boyfriend not to wear your bathing suit bottom around his
head, even though he is probably stretching it out.

The next day your boyfriend can't get out of bed. You tell
him he got too much sun the day before, but he says he has a
tropical fever and goes back to sleep. He doesn't wake up all
day.

You have always been a shy person; by the evening you are
feeling lonesome. You go across the beach to the bar and have
a hideous drink made in a blender, wishing you had the nerve
to talk to someone. You decide you are mad at your boyfriend.
He has a lot of nerve, bringing you here to the middle of nowhere and then falling prey to some jungle ailment.

Next to you are two glossy American boys, tanned, blond
hair. They are very sure of themselves. They are hard at work
sizing up a pretty French girl who is with her family. "How old
do you think she is?" one says.

"Old enough!" the other says.

These guys might be anywhere in the world, it doesn't matter. They travel with their own permanent frat house over their
heads. You would give anything to be so sure of yourself, so
American. You decide the reason they're not speaking to you
is that your nose is now bright red from the sun.

By the next day your boyfriend wakes. You spend another
day on the beach. The food served at the restaurant has gotten
worse and worse. For dinner that evening you are served bean
and cabbage soup, piping hot; cubes of beef swimming in
brown sauce and masses of potatoes. This would be a perfect
meal at a ski resort. The temperature this evening has dropped
to 85 degrees. Everyone eats with resignation. All the diners
appear to have spent too much time in the sun. They look
hectic, stricken—as if this were some peculiar sanatorium
where one arrives in good health but shortly deteriorates.
Where are all the delicious curries with coconut, the gumbos

and lobsters? The chef must really be deranged. The food seems to have been shipped from some terrible high school cafeteria.

All of a sudden you realize that the chairs in the restaurant are the most uncomfortable you have ever sat on. You figure you'll go and sit down on the couch in front of the reception desk. You have to get away from these restaurant chairs, even just for a minute. "I have to sit down over there," you say to your boyfriend. You are totally nauseated.

Your boyfriend looks surprised. You go and sit down on the couch, but after a minute you realize you can't sit there, either. You go back to your table. "What happened?" your boyfriend says. "You're all white."

"I can't stay here," you say. "I'm going to our room."

Your boyfriend helps you to your alpine hut. On the way things start to get a little black around the edges. "Aren't you going to have dinner?" your boyfriend says.

"I have to lie down," you say.

In the room you look in the mirror. Your tan is totally gone. It's just disappeared. Your skin hurts so much—especially on the back of your legs—that you can hardly stand up straight. You lie down on the bed and pass out.

A while later your boyfriend comes back with a roll and butter but you are too sick to eat.

The next day you sleep until early afternoon. Finally your boyfriend lets you go to the beach, wearing a T-shirt, long pants, his baseball cap, and sunglasses. You feel extremely fragile and feeble. Your skin is burned so badly you can only hobble a few steps at a time, but your boyfriend arranges a chaise longue for you in the shade under a tree.

You had so wanted to look glamorous, garbed in resort wear and with a dusky tan. You are not that kind of person. You now have skin like fried chicken, extra crispy.

"You know what?" you say to your boyfriend. He is fondling a chunk of coral, a large, smooth white object shaped like a pipe. The beach is covered with such pieces. "I've decided I'm tired of being female."

"How come?" your boyfriend says.

"Oh, I feel like a female impersonator. All these hormones crashing around have nothing to do with me. It's like a facade. I'd much rather be a man. Would you still go out with me then?"

"You're hallucinating," your boyfriend says. "Sun poisoning."

You think, as the sun sets, there are plenty of good opportunities for tropical description. Purple sky, orange moon, yellow stars, dry silver leaves. It really is like a trashy postcard, complete with balmy winds and sea air. Once again the band plays "Yellow Bird."

snowball

Victor sat on the toilet; his nerves made him constipated. His body had abandoned him, at forty-two his hair was white and falling out daily. His fingernails were split and soft. He had to face the day as if it were a hallucination; at night he couldn't sleep. Around five each morning he would drift off, and by the time he managed to stagger into the gallery it would already be after noon. He missed important interviews, meetings with collectors; curators from San Francisco stopped by and left after forty-five minutes when he hadn't shown.

Nothing was going Victor's way. He should have spent more on real ceramic tiles. The linoleum in the gallery was already cracking near the bathroom on the upstairs floor. Gray squares creased with pink, this should have been elegant, but in comparison to Betsy Brown's black and white Italian tiles there was no comparison.

He had spent hours talking to Mark-Paul, going over his paintings, telling him how to improve them. A show was arranged for January. Then one afternoon it was let slip that Mark-Paul had gone over to Betsy.

Prosperity! Prosperity was always just around the corner at Betsy Brown's gallery. She had managed to steal Mark-Paul Lachine right from under Victor Okrent's nose. How many days had he spent with Mark-Paul, taking him out to eat at the most important restaurants, lecturing him, filling him in on all the art history Mark-Paul had been too stoned to bother with.

Meanwhile, his backers were at his throat: though he was asking for more money, they were asking when the gallery would start to make a return. He should never have taken money from the diamond dealer, though Schmuel—Sam—was one of his oldest friends. Now Sam claimed to be twenty million in debt and couldn't keep shoving money into Victor's gallery. Then there was the mistake with the group show last summer: he had bought everything himself, as an investment, and had held onto the work even when the collectors would have taken it off his hands.

He had to do everything, all by himself. He had to go through slides, make sure the paintings went out on time to the art fair in Madrid, insurance, every single thing his staff should have taken care of had to be checked and double-checked by him. And Sistina, the Italian-American princess! How had he ended up with her? The sides of the bathtub were lined with hundreds of bottles of shampoo, it was impossible that any human being should use so many varieties. She had already gone off to work, leaving a coffee cup behind the toilet, a confectioners' sugar of talcum powder sprinkled over the floor, and the cat box uncleaned. One furious paw waved under the bathroom door. The cat was insane, he was allergic to its dandruff, he had told her a hundred times to get rid of that animal.

But what Sistina didn't want to hear, she didn't. This morning he had woken to find the animal asleep on top of his face, trying to suffocate him. What a way to wake up, with a mouth of fur and a fecund odor and the sensation of drowning. *She* was out of the house by eight, a showroom model for Bill Blass —with a great intelligence she insisted on covering up with platitudes and inanities.

Pushing the cat away from the bathroom door, he went into the kitchen. He was running water in the kitchen sink for the espresso machine, which he had to wash first—Sistina drank her coffee and left the hot wet grounds in the machine—when the cat, a moldy, white animal named Snowball, jumped up onto the kitchen counter, ran across its length, and dove into the sink, splashing him with soapy water.

He would have thrown the animal off the terrace—twenty-seven floors up—if not for Sistina. In any event he would have been consumed with guilt. And his head. He suspected Sistina hit him over the head while he slept, he had the feeling of having been bludgeoned.

He lit up a Player cigarette while the coffee perked. The cat sat preening itself with a reptilian tongue. While he was waiting, in his shirtsleeves, for the operator at the Palace Hotel in Madrid to put him through to Gabriele, the cat came out of nowhere, leapt up, and bit him in the elbow, leaving a jagged tear in the sleeve of his shirt.

The animal was insane, it would have to be put to sleep. The shirt had cost $150. He had never seen anything like this, luckily his skin wasn't pierced, but the shirt was ruined. He lunged out to give the cat a whack but it had already sprung halfway across the room and run off to one of its secret lairs. Therapy! He was going to insist that Sistina go back to her shrink.

He lit another cigarette. Gabriele wasn't in his room, now he had no way of knowing if any of the paintings had made it through customs. Ten-thirty, a splitting headache. Just as artists could be divided into those who were great and those who were merely second or third rate, so the world at large could be broken up: A people, B people, and C. Now, while he hesitated to place himself in the A category, on the other hand surely he was not a C person. At least, eight years before, he had had the sense to realize he was never going to be a great artist, but as a dealer he might easily be among the top-notch. He had a skill, he might instruct artists in how to improve their work. Yet his artists refused to listen to him. Betsy Brown had two top-notch artists. About his own he could not be certain, except perhaps for George Lodge, who painted the same picture over and over again: dull faces like African masks, primitive and heavy-lidded.

He dialed Madrid again, this time a different operator at the Palace: either Gabriele hadn't yet checked in or was already out. He took his cup of coffee through the sliding doors in the living room and out onto the terrace. Christopher Chin, the well-known fashion photographer, waved at him from the far end. The terrace extended across the length of the two apartments.

He carried his coffee over to Christopher's metal table. "We should get someone up here to paint the terrace," he said. They had both put in money to have a raised wooden platform built out there two years before, lifting the floor up by five feet. Now they could look out over the pillared cement railing.

"What happened to your sleeve?" Christopher said. A plucked-looking man, he wasn't holding up too well. He had just come back from Haiti; the sun had beaten his face into a thick surface of cow hide.

"What can I do?" Victor said. "Do you know anyone who wants a cat? You talk to her, I can't get through to her. Before she moved in, I got the apartment painted once a month, I had people over to dinner almost every night—" He had used his apartment as a gallery for two years before he got the backing for the SoHo space. Now, with Sistina's terrible taste—she had brought with her a giant overstuffed couch, grandmotherly, chintz floral, as well as boxes, chatchkas, a collection of salt shakers in the shapes of cacti, kittens, windmills—his apartment was a mess, there was no educating her.

Christopher was writing the introduction for a book of photographs. His eyes glazed over at Victor's litany. "I can't get any sleep, hemorrhoids, none of my staff are able to follow any of my orders and I end up doing everything myself."

"Relax, you've been this way for too long. Why don't you take Sistina and go away on a vacation? Haiti was fabulous," Christopher said. Christopher Chin. Not Oriental, but the name had apparently affected him: little slits for eyes, puffed up from too much drink. A tuber of a nose, stiff hair, glasses easing themselves halfway down his face, held up only by the budding growth of nostrils.

"Yes? I can't go away. I have too much work to do, there's no one I trust enough to leave the gallery with."

"I thought you were going to get your brother in there as an accountant. You trust him."

"An accountant isn't the same thing. All he knows is numbers, he doesn't know about running a gallery." His brother, Leo, was coming that afternoon. He looked out across Twenty-ninth Street. The roofs of the buildings, tetrahedrons, gristly bricks, dull copper pyramids in shades of lichen green. Meanwhile a taste like salad oil welled up in his throat. Flowers for Mother's Day. He had told his secretary the week before, but it was unlikely Sasha had remembered. His parents had settled, finally, in Arizona. German-Jewish refugees, they had gotten out—to England—just in time, not through any intelligence on his father's part (his father would never have left at all had it not been for his brother, who had emigrated to London back in the twenties). The two brothers were not alike. His father, a dapper hypochondriac, had been a doctor in Cologne. Somehow he had never managed to fill out the required paperwork, take the proper tests, to practice in England. Eventually he went into business with his brother, import-export. The brother, a vigorous man who gambled, smoked cigars. Though married, in middle age he dated Playboy bunnies. Victor had been born three years after the move; they lived in Golders Green, a grim house filled with Oriental junk furniture. Both parents spoke English with heavy German accents. Leo was nearly four years younger than he. His mother's life had been devoted to his father's health. They had never made friends, though they had joined the synagogue. Both he and his brother had been bar mitzvahed; only Leo continued to practice. He never felt himself to be Jewish, or English; he had ended up dropping out of Cambridge. Though he knew everyone in the London art scene, he never really felt at home.

The juice of New York was something he could understand. American rage, freedom from European classicism and the deathly Common Market. Still, he had problems with his stomach. It was fifteen or sixteen years since he had moved to New York. Now his artists were famous for painting cartoon char-

acters, primitive computerlike drawings, rip-offs of Navaho
and African art. He was riding the crest of the future, it was
better that he hadn't stuck with painting. He had been involved with a revolutionary group, in the 1960s: one of the
members had gone up to the offices of a famous art publication
and chopped off his finger on the desk of the senior editor.
This was a statement. He and two others had bombed the
information desk at the Museum of Modern Art. It was a small
bomb; none of them expected that a few paintings would receive smoke damage, shrapnel. Only a Miró was beyond res-
toration. A year's suspended sentence: ten years later, people
still tried to fight with him in bars. But his old self no longer
seemed to have any relationship to his present one.

He had told George Lodge he would go up to his Forty-
second Street studio to look at his new paintings that afternoon; by now it was too late to go to the gallery first. He took a
cab uptown. The streets, even this early in the summer, were
unbelievably filthy; the pavement seemed to be oozing its own
sediment, the reek of grilling meat, hot dogs, shashlik, burnt
and greasy, was like the smell of some garbage incinerator. He
had to fight his way around the hustlers, past the electronic
junk stores, to get into George's building. The elevator stank
of roach spray and mothballs.

The radio was turned up so loud he had to bang on the door
over and over before George heard him and let him in.
"George, George," Victor said, "how can you listen to that
junk?" He walked into the room. To work in such squalor. The
reek of acetone, a tipsy brain-crumbling shrillness, almost
knocked him off his feet. Spray paint, fixative, polyurethane.
No molecules resembling oxygen were left anywhere, the air
conditioner was apparently out of order and the windows
sealed shut. The O and CO_2 forced out by the tougher, man-
made particles, which lacerated the lungs as they floated here
and there. George stood sulkily by the door, his long galoot
face surly and elegant, as Victor pulled stuff from the racks.
Scrawled on various half-finished canvases:

USED AFTER A NON-FINITE OR VERBLESS CLAUSE AT THE BEGIN-
NING OF A SENTENCE: TO GET THERE ON TIME, SHE LEFT HALF
AN HOUR EARLY.

USED BEFORE AND AFTER A NON-DEFINING RELATIVE CLAUSE OR
A PHRASE IN APPOSITION, WHICH GIVES MORE INFORMATION
ABOUT THE NOUN IT FOLLOWS: THE PENNINE HILLS WHICH HAVE
BEEN A FAVORITE WITH HIKERS FOR MANY YEARS ARE SITUATED
BETWEEN LANCASHIRE AND YORKSHIRE.

QUEEN ELIZABETH TWO, A VERY POPULAR MONARCH, CELE-
BRATED HER SILVER JUBILEE IN 1977.

George smoked a cigarette while he looked. "Someday
you're going to have an explosion in here," Victor said. The
grim pseudo-African faces, topped with penile projections,
reared from their gloomy canvases. "Now, you should go and
look at the work of Léger, George," he said. "Take a look at
this painting. The composition is all wrong. On the bottom,
over here, should be a thick triangle. And all of these shapes,
they should have a heavy shadow to the right. You have something here, but it's not there yet. How can you work when your
studio looks like a bomb hit it?"

"Victor, did you get my letter?" George's arms were too
long, like a gibbon, shooting from imaginary tree to tree.

"What letter? Why don't you get a chair, someplace I can
sit?" He went and looked out the window. It was bleak here
on Forty-second Street, no sign of vegetable life to prove that
the season was spring. Across the way was a peep show, two
nude women in neon; one, with the tube burnt out in her leg,
flickered on and off. "Give me some paper." George didn't
move. Victor peeled a piece of newsprint paper off the floor
and took a gold pen from his lapel pocket. "I'm excited about
what you're doing, George, but I'd like to see you working from
extensive drawings, it would give me the feeling that you've
spent time working these things out. See, this is what Oldenburg did. He started with small sketches, let's say for his giant
cigarette. He made sketches, these today are worth a hundred

thousand. Then he went out and found cigarettes, hundreds of butts. He studied these. Then he had a craftsman, a master craftsman, make a small cigarette butt from metal. Then he had medium-sized ones made from clay."

"Victor, didn't you read that letter I sent you?"

"Wait, just let me finish. Then you'll talk. This is important, George. This could change your whole way of working. How Oldenburg worked, when he was finally ready, he built his giant cigarette butt in soft sculpture. Whether you like his work or not—"

"I like Oldenburg."

"You have to agree that the man was a genius. So you have the whole gamut, do you see what I'm getting at, here, George? You have the whole gamut, from sketches to paintings to the final soft sculpture; it's not as if he just got an idea and slapped it onto canvas. When you're working, you should do drawings first, then you should make the painting in squares. Each individual square, a segment of the painting, should be as complete and fully realized as the whole work. Go and look at Léger, George. He knew about composition. That's who you could be like, if you spent a little more time on these things." In his excitement the thick, oily feeling rose up in his chest, as if the stomach contents were backing up the esophagus like a kitchen sink. He fumbled for a Tums.

"Victor, can I say something now?"

"What? George, I came all the way up here this afternoon, just to take a look at your work, and I can see you're already on the defensive."

"Victor, I'm trying to tell you: I sent you a letter listing twenty points that would have to change for me to stay with the gallery, and I don't think you even read the letter."

"No, I haven't read any letter! George, I just got back from Chicago, I had to spend all week getting ready for the Madrid art fair, I'm leaving for Madrid tomorrow—what's your problem?"

"I don't know if we should talk about it until you've read my letter. Basically, it's about your attitude. I've seriously been

considering leaving the gallery for a long time now, Victor. I
don't see how I can stay unless you have a change of attitude."

"Attitude! What attitude! George, why don't you come to me
if you have problems? You go around complaining to your
friends, this doesn't make me look good."

"How can I come to you, Victor, when I can't even get into
your office to see you? This is the first time you've come to my
studio in eight months."

He was late for his appointment with his brother; he had a
collector coming to the gallery at three-fifteen. "I'll find your
letter and call you tonight, George," he said. "I haven't been
able to get any sleep in weeks, at three o'clock in the morning
I'm awake, lying in bed, busy making notes about strategies
for handling your work, where we should go next."

"You're not listening, Victor. Don't you see yourself? How
terrible you look?"

"I'm going to call you, George. I would love to stay and talk
this through—"

"I don't want to talk! I want you to read my letter!"

He could hear George flinging objects this way and that as
he waited for the elevator. He would suggest to George the
name of his old psychiatrist. George, whom three years ago he
had found working as a janitor, barely able to make enough to
buy supplies. What did he want from him?

In the taxi he remembered it was Sistina's birthday; he
hadn't gotten her anything. There was something about going
out to dinner that night with Schmuel—Sam—and some of her
model friends. He looked in his appointment book. There was
an opening around the corner he had promised to go and see,
and a dinner afterward for Monica Bell, a painter whom he had
shown two years ago who was still working on new stuff. Sistina wouldn't be home until eight, he would have to tell her
they would have a dinner when he got back from Madrid. Why
was he ever born? Beset upon by roaches—one crawled out of
his briefcase—tormented by his girlfriend; no matter how
much he cleaned up, no matter how many times he told Sistina
to hire a maid to come in on Saturdays while she was at home,

nothing changed. She left crumbs everywhere she went, and the roaches came out as fearlessly as a herd of goats to graze on the congealed morass of cat food which the cat itself disdained to touch. Oh, Sistina, such a beauty, with her halo of reddish-brown hair, her fine features and large, humorless eyes. So he had fallen for a girlish demeanor, sincerity a mere disguise for catlike wiles beneath. On the other hand, maybe he was paranoid. Maybe he had driven her to vixen behavior prematurely. Without him it might have taken Sistina another ten years to acquire it. Why must he be the one to be at war with everyone, not a single soul on his side? Even his army of conscripts whined and complained behind his back, shirked their jobs. No matter how many times he explained a thing, something always went wrong in the execution.

He walked into the gallery rubbing his head; Leo, his brother, was standing stunned in front of one of the paintings at the far end. "Sasha," he said to the blond, bored-looking girl who sat behind the front desk. He could feel her bristle as he got near. Literally begin to bristle. This fury, to be met with it in his own gallery! "I have to have something to eat, Sasha. Would you go around the corner and get me a cup of chili?"

"Madrid called," she said. "They can't get the paintings out of customs."

"Don't speak to me," he said. He started to take off his jacket, limp from the heat.

"What happened to your sleeve?" Sasha said. "There's a big hole in it." He gave her a malevolent look. She had been with him since the gallery opened, the only one to stay this long. She had two girls who worked under her; now she was threatening to leave in August. Sasha had plans: to open her own space in the East Village with some German cowboy-type she had been living with since the summer before. Obviously she despised Victor; she acted as if by working for him she had been sold into white slavery. She used her tininess, her blondness, her lank blond hair, against him. A sour little bud of a face. Women's attractiveness was based on how closely they resembled the fetal stage of life. Sash could have been a

fashion model. In some ways she was more attractive than
bulky Sistina. She was too short, however. Instead, she had
wandered around the world, married and divorced a wealthy
Italian drug addict. A bright girl, like a hornet, with a style for
dress. Black, soigné, chic. No leopard-skin babushkas or hen-
naed hair so popular these days with girls on the street. And
then there was her coldness, her polish: Why didn't she remain
with an uptown crowd? He supposed SoHo held a certain excitement for her; it was strange to think of her as a person with
ambition, however. She knew musicians; French jet-set types
were always stopping by to say hello. She did her work but was
surly; he figured when he was away she probably greeted
clients with hostility. "Can't you call up for some food?" she
said. "I can't leave, I'm the only one here. Everyone else is
out to lunch." She handed him a stack of telephone messages.
He began to paw through them. "Leo, Leo," he said to his
brother, "go sit down, my office is open. Bring us two cups of
coffee, cream and sugar in mine."

Well, he was going to starve to death. The day before he
hadn't gotten home until ten at night. What had he eaten that
day? A Danish, a bowl of lentils, takeout, from some over-
priced vegetarian joint around the corner. "There's some
Chinese food in the refrigerator," Sistina had called from the
bedroom. "You could reheat it." She couldn't have picked up
a steak and asparagus? He paid the rent, he gave her money
—she didn't earn $200 a week, after taxes, had no money of
her own—he always left $50 or $100 around, for food and her
taxis, she never walked and hated the subway. But instead of
getting up to greet him she was sitting on the bed, wearing
filthy sweatpants and a sweatshirt with a pink rabbit, watching
TV. The cat, curled sensuously on the pillow, gave him a superior, baleful stare. "I can't eat that crap," he said. "Old
Chinese food? Sistina, I have enough trouble with my stomach."

He might as well have been living alone. He had gone into
the kitchen and gotten the pile of takeout menus down from on
top of the refrigerator. Meanwhile she yelled out to him from

the bedroom. "So there was this man on TV and he was really amazing. Victor, we've got to try this. He took a watch, and made this woman spin the hands around. He wasn't looking. And then on a piece of paper he drew a watch face, and he wrote down the time on the watch, using psychic perception."

"And did he get the time right?" Victor said. Mexican, Chinese, Indian. He could call the deli on the corner.

"No," Sistina said. "He was about an hour or two wrong. But it was just amazing—" Meanwhile her story, her shrill voice, dragged on and on, lacking point of any kind. How many times had he fallen for this, listening patiently to some elaborate tale that added up to nothing? Also she would tell a story at a party, as if in relation to some subject brought up by someone else. After fifteen minutes of her chatter he would cringe, realizing before the other patient listeners that once again her saga had absolutely nothing to do with anything that had gone before. Nor did it add up to anything else. A story in the *Science Times,* for example. Breeding experiments with cats: the Scotch fold, a short-eared cat. Another, without fur. Mutants.

Yet there was a certain pleasure to be found in watching the faces of the others as they listened intently to her, curiously trying to figure out how she was going to pull off a connection between Manx cats and the previous topic of Joseph Beuys's sculpture. And then the gradual bafflement on the realization that not only wasn't there going to be any connection, there wasn't even going to be a punch line. For Sistina told her stories with animation and enthusiasm; her timing was that of a stand-up comedian. But even Gracie Allen's vignettes added up to a surrealist attitude toward life. While Sistina's were merely outbursts of encyclopedic information, watered down through the television set of her head. Last night she carried out a pad of paper and a wristwatch. "Victor, you draw a circle on this paper, and I'm going to spin the hands of the watch and concentrate."

"Sistina, I'm exhausted. I don't believe in this garbage."

Her full, meaty lips turned down in a pout. Her blue eyes,

smeared with dusky liner, voluptuously fringed, stared at him with childish rage. "Come on, Victor, just try it." She thrust the pad at him. He scribbled hands at the one and three. "Victor! Wait until I'm thinking of the time on the watch! Try and picture the hands in your mind." She ripped the used page from the pad. "Okay, I'm picturing the time on the watch," she said. "Now do you see it in your head?"

"Okay, okay," he said. He drew on the clock, fifteen to seven.

"Let's see," she said. "Look, Victor, look at the watch!" Her wristwatch was set at five thirty-five. "See, it's close," she said. "Only an hour and ten minutes off. Isn't that amazing?"

"It's nowhere near," he said.

"No, it is near," she said. "I mean, you could have written two o'clock, or anything. But you were close." Her tongue, a little blistered flap. Parrots had tongues of the same stumpy variety, pointed, beefy. Her obsession with ESP was perpetual. "What flavor am I thinking of?" "Vanilla." "Close—tomato!" And if he had been able to guess, what would have been the use of ESP of this nature? Often, when she claimed to be cleaning the house, he would come upon her fondling a spoon, attempting—by using psychic energy—to bend it with mind power alone. She insisted this could be done. Yet even if possible, he said, he didn't need or want their spoons bent. "Oh, Victor," she said. "Don't be an old poop." He had ended up with a woman, pretty as a fawn, who used such expressions. "Twat." "On the rag." Words still had the power to offend, coming from a woman. Not by meaning so much as sound.

Years ago, in his artist days, he had written a book. B.B., Before Bomb. The book was called *Mgungu*, it had little text. His wild English friends, decked in sixties' sequins and satins, arrived in Manhattan and posed for a series of pictures: staggering out of a studio-set jungle, indulging in birdlike mating rituals. The book was a spoof. Once he had been an outsider, a marginal figure, capable of making fun. Now he saw things were too serious for that. The world was on the edge of collapse, like a balloon with a pinprick. Yet on this edge it was possible for exciting changes to occur. The artists he had found were like angry babies, furious, spoiled, needing constant attention. Without his nurturing they would hit their heads against the wall, red and squawling, until they beat themselves into exhaustion and died, or gave up. Only through him could they remain in their childlike state of innocence, carefully tended, receiving enough money and attention to enable them to produce.

His brother was sitting on the sofa in his office. Above his head a painting by Stash Stosz: red speckled chickens, pink Bullwinkle moose heads, a man stuck in a gorilla suit, minus the head, arms flailing at the zipper. $5,000. Less discount, $3,800. Fifty percent went to the gallery: not even enough to keep him open for a week. Leo looked uncomfortable. Wearing a cheap pinstriped suit, his face washed-out, as if he had spent too many years under fluorescent lights. Though he was younger than Victor, he looked older—married for twelve years, two children—his wife was a Yemenite Jew, who never came with Leo when Victor insisted he attend the dinners for the artists following various openings. With Leo's sad little twitches—a squint of the eyes, a nervous cough—Victor could not help but feel sorry for him. He had insisted Leo move from New Jersey with his family to Queens, leave his job. Now Leo would manage the gallery business, organize computer records. This would be a change for the better for Leo, though he claimed not to have been unhappy in his dreary life in New Jersey. Somewhere along the line he had died, figuratively speaking. Victor remembered how sparky Leo had been at eleven, playing both teams of an imaginary cricket game in the backyard, a green chiffon scarf around his neck, keeping careful score in a notebook. A tiny, angelic child with pale curls. At some point that imaginative cherub had been swallowed up by a middle-aged English accountant. Now Leo was talking about the house he had finally rented in Bayside. "So I told Orna to call the landlord again. This is the fifth time in a week, Victor. The upstairs toilet is still leaking, and the water is dripping into the ceiling and all the plaster in the living room is bulging, about to burst. Finally the landlord said if we wanted anything done, we'd have to pay for it ourselves."

"What are you renting for? Why don't you just buy the place?"

"I don't have the money to buy a house, Victor. I can't even afford to rent."

"Listen, I wanted you to come in last week. I'm going to Madrid tomorrow night, you're going to have to be here while I'm gone. I've set up an office for you in the basement. The contractor said he'd put in new lighting by the end of the week. All those things we went over, Leo—I'd like you to be able to have files set up on every artist, which paintings of theirs we're holding, where the paintings have been sold to, how much money should be coming in for payments and by whom."

"We went over all this, Victor. I don't know why you wanted me to come in this afternoon. Nothing's unpacked at home, I left Orna with—"

"Because, Leo, this is very important that I feel you understand what's going on here. I want to feel you'll be able to handle any problem that comes up while I'm gone. Don't rush in here like that, acting like I'm imposing on your time or that there's something more important you could be doing. I'm expecting to feel that you're just as conscientious and concerned about everything that takes place here as I am."

"You sound like you need a vacation."

"Yes, I need a vacation. I would love to be able to take a vacation. But when things are happening with the gallery like this, with my artists, it's necessary that I—or someone equally involved—be here every single minute as the problems arise." He could feel himself becoming worked up; why was it that he felt as if he were under water? He had to shout to make himself heard, and even then all he was greeted with were blank expressions.

Meanwhile Sasha was buzzing on the intercom; the collector Larry Nims had arrived and was looking around at the show. Leo stood up to go. "Leo, Leo, don't go. I want you to stay and meet Larry, you're a part of this now."

He led the pudgy Larry Nims down to the storage racks in
the basement. It was late, maybe close to five. The gallery was
empty. He was not unaware of his snobbery. This snobbish-
ness was of an elaborate, complex, obscure order. The rules,
which entailed ratings by family history, personal accomplish-
ments, physical attractiveness, dress and personal hygiene,
also wealth, were so complicated that often even he grew con-
fused, rushing to greet a woman in a pricey mink coat while
ignoring an internationally acclaimed artist who had entered
the gallery at the same time. Larry Nims had no one else vying
for Victor's attention. He came in from Colorado once or twice
a year, to buy in the $3,500 range. He considered himself a big
collector; there were as yet no paintings of Day-Glo colors or
Quick Draw MacGraw up in the ski lodges of Aspen.

"Even in China, on the collective farms," Victor said, "ide-
ology is no longer as important as making money." He was
pulling out a series of lithographs, $1,500 each, that Carl Bal-
low had made the year before. So far mostly unsold. "They
have a saying, 'The rice field is soaked with the sweat of the
peasants, the food on your plate is all hardship, every grain of
it.' That's the quality I'd like my artists' work to have: I want
them to rely on their shoulders, their muscles, the strength of
their bodies."

Larry Nims giggled nervously. There was the feeling that
everyone—Sistina included—was his enemy. They were
laughing at him behind his back. Also they had an intimacy
with each other that he was not privy to. He could not help but
be critical of others, this was something they must have sensed
in him. Especially when he saw so clearly what was wrong with
each of them. Yet underneath this, perhaps they could not tell,
was a feeling of love.

"Victor, I should go," his brother said.

"No, no," Victor said. "Leo, call Orna if you're worried.
You'll both come with me, there's an opening next door I promised I'd look at." He led them back upstairs to his office. From
the minifridge he got out a bottle of champagne and poured it
into three plastic glasses. Meanwhile, his staff—the boy who

helped to hang the paintings and repaint the walls, Sasha, and the two girls—were filing up to the door of his office. "See you tomorrow, Victor," Freddy said.

"You're not going," Victor said. "What time will you be in tomorrow?"

"I—"

"Freddy, try and get here by ten o'clock. What do you have to go now for? Have some champagne." He got out more cups. The other girls were trying to wave good night without coming in. "What are you doing out there? You'll have some champagne."

" 'Bye, Victor," Sasha said. "Your tickets came in for Madrid—first class, Pan Am."

"Wait!" Victor said. They stood staring like hospital nurses, him on the operating table. "Why do I feel so deserted? How can all of you be abandoning me? It's not five o'clock yet—" He wrung his hands; with a tissue he began to polish his black marble slab-top desk.

"It's six-thirty, Victor," Leo said.

"Okay, okay," Victor said. "We'll go now. Freddy, you make sure the downstairs lights are off. Is the burglar system on?" His entourage waited patiently. He saw himself as a mad king, his wretched courtiers fearful and irritated. They could not understand this wrenching he felt nightly in his heart.

He carried his cup of champagne down the street. Larry Nims was waving goodbye, stepping into a cab.

There were specks of lint on his lapel; he asked his brother to brush off the back of his coat.

At the opening he found himself arguing with a Danish woman, someone connected with the Scandinavian-American Association. "And now you people think that England is about packaging old material and selling a new product every week."

The Dane, a leathery attractive blond, in her mid-forties, was nodding, in possible agreement, possible disagreement. A faint smell of Scotch and herrings. Laden with gold: earrings, choker necklace. Somehow she reminded him of one of those preserved bodies found in peat bogs.

"Don't tell me about current English painters," he said. "You don't know about current English painters. Malcolm McClaren has nothing to do with the current English art scene. You can't tell me he's England's genius of the last ten years." He was in a fury now, worn out and filled with bile. He took Leo, standing sipping a glass of wine, by the arm, and led him off into the washroom in back. "I have two lines of coke left, that's all. Come on, you'll wake up a little."

Leo did not seem inclined to protest. He snorted his line of coke and ground his teeth. Victor slapped his brother on the back. "Why don't you go out and get yourself some decent clothes? Did you look at my suit? I had it made for me in Düsseldorf." Here was his brother, mild, admiring. A preponderance of cranial bone, heavy in the brow region, contributed to his look of doggish placidity. "It's going to be good, Leo. I can tell already you're going to be a big help. You don't know the art world, but if you listen to me I think you'll pick up a lot." The tang of the coke filled his mouth. "We'll have a nice dinner in a while, we'll have a chance to talk."

When he came out of the bathroom he found the Danish woman and began again. "There is nothing new! The early Renaissance saw the first introduction of space and used lighting from different sources—unsophisticated space, hardly different than what Vinnie Penza or George Lodge are doing today!"

The Danish woman rubbed his arm. "Ah, Victor, so much enthusiasm, you'll wear yourself out." Some lipstick, bright orange, was smeared across one front tooth.

"Of course nothing's new," Victor said. "What's important is that nothing should be predigested. I've had to start from scratch, that's what's exciting." He wanted to add that collecting young artists required a sense of adventure on his part: he had had to be in the right place at the right time. And that the routines of the old guard were at last beginning to falter. The art scene at present offered infinite possibilities. But she had already turned, twittering, to collect her friends and go off to dinner.

Across the room was his nemesis: Betsy Brown. A small woman, dark, clad in a white linen suit. Even in her red high heels she didn't reach his shoulder. He bludgeoned his way through the crowd to say hello. Cool, infinitely lithe: now his creeping doubts once again emerged, a stricture in his stomach resembling a hand pulling in, tendons like metal veins. She had all the best artists. Those with style, sophistication. He was handling hustling jerks. In ten years, twenty, Betsy Brown would be famous still, while no trace of himself would remain. "Betsy," he said. "How have you been? So what do you think of the show?"

"Hello, Victor," Betsy said. Now she was laughing at him. Such a wily, minxy face. She might have been a movie star from the 1940s, and he the fumbling, sweaty Jimmy Stewart.

"Will you come to the dinner?" he asked.

"I'm afraid I have other plans."

"Yes, yes, me, too. I have to pack for Madrid, I couldn't get away until tomorrow night."

"I'm going on Friday," she said.

"Good, good, then we'll have dinner there. I know a fantastic restaurant—" His nerves were shattered, he felt his bones crumbling to calcium dust inside his arms, his legs.

His brother's car was parked nearby, he told Leo to drop him off before driving to Bayside. Strangely his watch said it was after nine. In the living room Sistina was smoking a joint, sitting next to a packed suitcase. "Hi," she said.

"Oh, my stomach," he said. He went to the liquor cabinet. "Sistina, where are the aspirin?"

She began to cry. "I knew you would forget it was my birthday. You still owe me a Christmas present!"

"I was planning something for you. I just forgot to pick it up. Sistina, don't start with me. I haven't eaten all day, I have a splitting headache. . . ."

"You said we'd all go out to dinner. I knew you'd forget."

"Sistina, why do you think I forgot? I'm busy with the gallery, that's why! I've invested everything I have in it. Not just all my money, but all my love, all my passion. If this gallery doesn't work, I have nothing. I'm doing this for us."

"For us," Sistina said.

"Yes, for us. If things continue to take off, in a few years I'll have the best-known gallery in the world. We can afford a bigger apartment, you can have children. Why don't you stop work and devote yourself to the home? We can't both be putting so much energy into outside endeavors—"

"I don't believe you're doing this for us! You're doing it for you. What am I hanging around you for? We haven't made love in a month and a half, you forget my birthday, you never even wanted to meet my family—"

"Look at this. I have wine spilled on my suit, I don't even have the time to take it to the cleaners. Every night I come home to you and have to deal with another of your temper tantrums. Sistina, why don't you go back to your psychiatrist?" Now he thought she would cry, then he could get some peace. But instead she lugged her suitcase to the front door. "Sistina, don't be like this."

"I told myself, if he comes home tonight late again, and can't even bother to remember my birthday, I'm going to leave."

He was out of Tums. "Wait, wait, Sistina! What am I thinking of?"

"I don't know."

"Guess."

"I don't know what you're thinking! I never know."

"Where are you going? Sistina, don't be like this. Do you want money for a hotel? Maybe we just need a night apart."

"I'm not going to a hotel. I'm moving in with Christopher."

"Christopher? Who's that?"

"Next door." She walked out, dragging her luggage, in a pseudo–Lauren Bacall huff.

He went to the kitchen cabinets and rummaged around, trying to find some aspirin. For a second, before turning, he could see the mangy Snowball, poised on top of the refrigerator. Then with a yowl the cat jumped, landing with four paws of open claws on his back.

who's on first?

I t is August and boring. Stash and I are going to play softball. It starts at ten o'clock at night. The week before, fed up with making jewelry, tired of the city heat and keeping house, I went home to visit my mother. While I was away, Stash attended the impromptu Friday night ball game, up under the Fifty-ninth Street Bridge. He was on a team called the Aliens. The other team was the Sphinxes. None of the teams was really organized—whoever showed up could play. Almost everyone on both teams was in the arts: painters, musicians, writers, filmmakers. Girls were playing, too; in fact, some of the players were so bad Stash felt it would be okay if I joined the next game.

"You sure you want to go?" Stash says from his customary place in front of the TV set. I'm getting dressed, braiding my hair so I can stuff it under a baseball cap with a picture of Pac-Man on the front.

"Yeah, I want to go," I say. "But I'll probably be lousy." I haven't played baseball since I was eight years old. Marie-Angela Montecardo hit me on purpose on the nose with the ball and I beat her up. Mrs. Rourke, the elderly gym teacher, forced me to apologize and made me sit out the rest of the game. Later on, my book bag accidentally fell out of my locker and hit Marie-Angela on the head as she was walking past. I was a fierce, if uncoordinated, child. But in third grade, Mrs. Rourke told me that some of the other children were complaining about me: I was too bossy. Is this what psychiatrists call a peak experience? Since that date, I've never really regained confidence, which strikes me as unfortunate.

Stash seems reluctant to get up and dress. He's watching the "Jerry Lewis Telethon." Sammy Davis, Jr., is singing a song about saving the children. "That is great," Stash says. "Man, I don't even want to go out, this show is so wild." While he watches TV he makes a sketch for one of his paintings. I look over his shoulder. Mighty Mouse is rescuing a bald, baby bird from the hands of a giant Japanese robot in a business suit. I don't know what the drawing means, but Stash is very successful at his work. Though we've only been living together a year, in that time we've traveled twice to Europe, for his shows. Earlier he took me to Haiti, where I was badly sunburned. Stash has a charismatic personality: he's authoritative and permissive, all at the same time. In other words, I can do whatever I want, as long as it's something he approves of. Or perhaps it's true, what he says, I need his approval because I'm willfully insecure, a wimp with a will to be one. Well, I've made up my mind in one way. If I ever get some kind of job security and/or marital security, I'm going to join the feminist movement.

Stash is standing in front of the TV, I have to peer around him to see. A child is giving a wheelchair demonstration. The wheelchair is motorized and crashes into Jerry's legs. "Turn that off, Stash," I say. "We'd better get going." For some reason the telethon—or maybe the impending ball game—is making me nervous. There are at least two more hours before it's over.

We take the E train up to Fifty-third and Third Avenue. Stash molests me on the subway platform—anyway, he grabs me around the waist and breathes heavily down the back of my neck. He knows this makes me squirm. "Take it easy," I say. "There are people leering." Stash is wearing a Crazy Eddie T-shirt and white cotton trousers with zippered pockets. They're stained with mustard from when we went to the Yankees' game two nights ago. Stash resembles a Polish/Italian/

Samurai warrior, with his blond hair and Eastern European complexion. His ponytail hangs in back almost to his waist. He shaves once a week. One reason I was attracted to him in the first place was his dangerous appearance. Before I knew him, I thought he was a member of some motorcycle gang.

I'm not alone in this evaluation. I remember once, Stash hailed a taxi, which stopped; he ran across the street to get it. Just at that moment a woman got out of the cab. When she saw Stash, with his leather motorcycle jacket, his unshaven face, his Confederate Army soldier's cap, she jumped into the air, a look of terror on her face. It took several seconds for her to realize that Stash wasn't going to mug her—he just wanted her taxi. I subliminally enjoyed that: I like associating with such a frightening-looking person.

Underneath, however, Stash is actually quite gentle. He's said at times that it was very immature of me to have been attracted to his underworld qualities. This shows I wasn't looking for a real relationship. But I disagree; I've always felt that people's appearances don't necessarily have anything to do with their personality. Before we lived together, when Stash used to come to my apartment, I'd watch his behavior with Snowball, my cat. Even though it bothered Stash that Snowball didn't like to use the cat box, he was very good with her. He brushed her, bought her catnip. The only thing Stash insisted on was that while he was in my apartment the cat had to stay off the bed. Snowball bit him on the nose once, and he swatted her across the room. I could understand this, but before I moved in with him I had enough sense to give the cat away to my girlfriend.

At our stop we have to climb flight after flight of stairs to get to the street. The escalator is out of order. I'm not one of those girls who like to exercise. At the top of the stairs I'm out of breath. I don't know how I'll be able to play baseball, but I'm determined to try. This is the first time I've lived with a man; I want to be a good sport. Once I bought a book of advice to women about men, and the book told me to read the sports section of the newspaper every day. So far Stash hasn't proposed, although I can quote you the batting averages of the Yankees for the past season.

He takes my arm as we walk up Third Avenue. Cars rush by in the night, furious wasps smoked out of their hive. Though it's dark, the air is hot and dry. In the city at this time of year the people who are left take on a demonic appearance. Their faces are yellow and ghastly. The street toward York Avenue grows gloomier. A large luxury building cuts off the view, but when we cross the street I see the cars are heading up the ramp onto the bridge. The bridge, seen from street level, appears tremendous. I notice turrets and ramparts protrude from the side. Below the bridge is an alcove, hidden from the cars but visible to pedestrians. If things don't work out with Stash, maybe I'll take my stuff and live in that little hole. I'll furnish it with a battery-operated lamp, a worn chair from the street, all the luxuries of home. The idea seems cozy. "There's the field," Stash says, pointing.

We stop at the start of the cyclone fence and look out across the field. Above the field is the underbelly of the Fifty-ninth Street Bridge, ridged with steel girders, shored up in places with planks of wood, like the grille of some immense cage. It's studded in spots with brilliant arc lamps. A hot wind churns up the dust. The ball, covered with a fine brown silt, lies in a pile of empty boxes of Kentucky Fried Chicken, beer cans, and torn newspapers.

Across the field grimy, fierce men—I don't recognize any of them—sock-sock the ball back and forth, faces stony as Aztecs. I feel like some actress who's walked onto the movie set without her script. Obviously I don't belong. Yet I'm not certain I feel any different when I'm at home, pretending that Stash and I are an old married couple. If I had stayed in tonight, by myself, I could have thought some more about the kinds of jewelry I want to design. The best idea I've had so far is to make pins and earrings out of reproductions of food. A plastic company will sell me an assortment of pastries—petits fours, éclairs, strawberry tarts—which I might put onto necklaces and earring wires. Stash has said this idea is not unique enough. He's already seen, in some store, earrings in the shape of sushi and sashimi, with realistic rice, seaweed, and raw fish. He's a harsh critic, but usually he's right.

"Listen, buster," I tell him. "I can't play."

"That's the way I felt last week," he says kindly. "Don't worry, you'll get the hang of it." But he looks skeptical.

"What if I miss?" I say. "All the guys are going to yell at me, huh?"

"Nah," he says. "It's not like that."

Some people are sitting on the cement bleachers. I recognize one person, an artist with a long, pocked face and glittery eyes. His name is Marley Mantello, once he asked me out on a date. This was before I met Stash. I pretend I don't see him—I've figured out that Stash doesn't like me to be friendly with other men—and I follow Stash over to some girl. "Hi, Mame," Stash says. "Have you met Eleanor?"

"Hi," Mame says. She resembles Tweety Bird, yellowish fluff sprouts from her head, her eyes are round and surprised. "Hey, look at this," she says. From a tremendous pocketbook she pulls out an oversized wineglass. Attached to the stem is an assortment of rhinestones—square cubes of emerald, ruby, topaz—arranged around a rubber cupid carrying a bow and arrow. "See this?" she says. "I just got back from Europe. The glasses went over fabulously, I got tons of orders."

I feel a twinge of jealousy. I've been too busy trying to adjust to life with a man to devote all my energy to my work. The world of jewelry and home-furnishing accessories is very competitive. Maybe I should quit doing jewelry and start to do clothing. Stash has been encouraging, but he emphasizes the fact that I don't work hard enough.

"Are you going to play baseball?" I ask Mame.

"Oh, yeah," Mame says. "Listen, I have to do something with myself tonight. I didn't bring any smack with me to Paris, and it was fine. Three weeks and I didn't miss it at all. But as soon as I got back tonight, I went straight to my dealer's. That's New York for you." Mame is very restless. "I hope this game goes on all night," she says. "I don't feel like going home."

I suppose I should be glad that Stash and I are drug-free. I only know two kinds of people, these days: those who used to take drugs and stopped, and those who still do. Stash lived through all that and came out the other side. For myself, I was never physically cut out for the fast lane. No drug I ever tried made me feel good, and even one drink makes me severely hungover almost immediately.

"I'm going out to warm up," Stash says.

"Come on, Stash, you pitch to me," Mame says. I'm waiting to see how good she is and feel relieved when she swings wildly, spinning around in a circle each time the ball is thrown to her. She misses three balls in a row. Her short little arms resemble Tweety Bird's wings; her feet, in pink basketball sneakers, are oversized, cartoonish. Somewhere on this planet, I figure, there is probably a whole tribe of people who look just like her—a neighborhood of Chilly Willy, Sylvester the Cat, Elmer Fudd. At least they probably don't ever have to worry about how to behave.

A long, thin dog wanders around the field, looking morose. The dog approaches a small boy, who is throwing a ball back and forth to the other players. He's about eight, wearing a shirt that says "Oakland A's." A pair of too-large shorts are hiked up to his armpits, his little arms and legs stick out from a larval body. Mame puts the bat down and comes back to me. "Look at him," she says. "Isn't he adorable?"

I look him over again. "I guess," I say.

"I got pregnant," Mame says. "I'm madly in love. It's so depressing."

"Are you going to have a baby?" I say.

"Philippe wants us to have it," Mame says. "We were going to get married, but his mother won't let him."

"This is someone you met in Paris?"

"He lives in Barcelona," Mame says. "I met him last year, then I was with him again this summer. He's addicted to speed, but he's a wonderful musician. I wish I could get enough money to bring him over here and get him straightened out. His mother doesn't want him to, though. You know, strict Catholic and I'm not—his mother doesn't think too much of my background."

Before I can ask her whether she plans to have the baby anyway, a man comes over to us. I must have met him fifteen times, but he's one of those people I instantly forget—he has a bland, innocuous face, sandy hair. It's not until Mame leaps up and throws her arms around him, saying, "Max, Max, my darling, where's the goddamn beer?" that I remember I know him. He's the organizer of the game, and an artist who paints traumatic situations—a rape, a car accident—in a medium he's invented himself, ground bones and blood acquired from garbage pails outside the meat market.

"Are you guys going to play?" he says.

"What the hell do you think I came here for?" Mame says. Her plump white hands are weighted with an assortment of rings, she wears candy-colored plastic baubles up to her elbows.

"How about you?" Max says. "We could use you."

"I don't know," I say. "Let me try and hit a few. If I hit them, I'll play."

I go out onto the field. "Stash, pitch me a few," I say. I swing the bat at shoulder level. To my surprise, a voice comes into my head. "Watch the ball," the voice says. "Keep your eye on the ball. Don't swing until it's over the plate." It's the voice of Mrs. Rourke, my gym teacher, just as spirited as when I was in first grade. Apparently I'm going to have to live with her my entire life; I don't know whether I'm exactly thrilled with this. I swing at the ball and hit it. Even though my hit is low, the ball goes all the way past second base.

Stash looks pleased. "You can play," he says.

Everyone comes in from warming up. I'm assigned to the team that lost last week. They need a catcher, which is fine with me. I remember now how I could never catch a ball out in the field, but if I'm behind the batter's plate, it seems to me, I can easily retrieve the ball and throw it to the pitcher.

My batting position is last. The little kid hangs around looking hopeful. But no one wants him on their team. My team is
up first, we sit around on the bleachers waiting to bat.
"Mickey," Mame says to the little kid, "come over here and
sit on my lap."

Mickey ignores her. "Whose kid is he?" I say.

"You know Eddie, don't you?" Mame says, pointing to third
base.

"Yeah," I say. Eddie has just made a movie—he's written,
directed, and acted in something called *Forget It*. It was about
some people who live on the Lower East Side and sell drugs
that they had invented. The drugs turn the users into members
of the opposite sex. This movie got very good reviews, now
Eddie is something of a celebrity. Soon Eddie is supposed to
leave for California—he's making a big movie out there. But
he still hangs around the club scene and plays ball. I knew he
had a kid who lived half the time with him and half the time
with his ex-wife, but I never actually saw Mickey before. Since
Eddie's divorce, his ex-wife lives with her girlfriend, and Eddie
lives with his boyfriend. More than ever, I realize, everyone I
know is just playing at being a grown-up; I have to include
myself.

I watch Mickey. "Are you going to use my bat this week,
Mame?" he says. "It's a good bat for girls, it's small." He
waves his aluminum bat in the air, almost knocking me in the
head.

A boy with an English accent, wearing an earring made from
a yellow tooth, get up to bat. I should have thought of that, I
think—necklaces made out of animal teeth. I could probably
find teeth in the meat market. This is a slightly repulsive idea,
but I'll see what Stash says. Stash always knows what's going
to be hot; he's got a fatherly, knowledgeable quality to him. I
watch him explain to the English boy how to hold a bat. "Listen, don't you hold a bat in cricket?" he says.

"Yes," the English boy says, swinging the bat as if it were a
tennis racket.

"Here, hold it like this," Stash says. Stash is left-handed.

The boy is right-handed, but he tries to bat left-handed. He swings wildly and misses.

"Strike one!" the little boy screams. Mickey's sitting right next to me, his voice is so loud I involuntarily clutch my ear.

The pitcher throws another ball. The English boy swings again.

"Strike two!" Mickey says. "You're out!"

"What's that, Mickey?" someone says to him.

"Only two strikes to an out in this game!" Mickey says. "That's what we decided last week."

The English boy looks totally puzzled. His face is long and pinched, his nose as skinny as a collie's muzzle. "What?" he says. "What did I do?" It seems as if he's going to cry. This makes me afraid, probably the same thing will happen when it's my turn. Maybe I should just leave. I could easily make my escape and meet Stash later at home. But the thought of stepping out from under the carbon-arc lamps of this imaginary world, a place brighter than day, into the blackness that falls immediately beyond, fills me with terror.

The captain of my team comes over to me. "I'm changing the order," he says. "You're up next."

"I thought maybe I could wait for a while," I say.

"Are you playing, or what?" the captain says. "Everyone's waiting, go ahead. Just take Paul's turn, he went to buy more beer."

I step up to the plate. Stash, the catcher for his team, stands behind me. He puts down his glove and comes over to me. While the rest of the players wait, he grabs me in a stranglehold and kisses me passionately. I disengage. "I have to bat now," I say.

"Take your time," Stash says. "That's my advice to you."

Before the pitcher has a chance to throw the ball, Mickey rushes out from the sidelines. "Wait," he says. "Use my bat! It's good for a girl!"

"That's okay, Mickey," I say. "I like the bat I have, because I practiced with it."

Stash winks at me. I let a ball go by, and then, on the next pitch, I hit one. For several seconds I stand still. I have forgotten what to do next. When I watch the ball game with Stash on TV, things seem to move much more slowly. The time from when the ball is thrown to me and when I hit it seems nonexistent. "Drop the bat," the voice of Mrs. Rourke shouts in my ear. She's more bossy than I could ever hope to be. I drop the bat on my feet and trip over it. Then I start to run. I'm out at first. That's the third out.

"Nice play!" Mickey shouts.

Stash comes over to me. "You hit the ball," he says. "Darling, I'm so proud of you." Once again he locks me in an animalistic embrace. One of his greatest fears—he's often told me—is that he will hug me so hard he'll break my ribs. Once he read something like this in the papers, how a man met his girlfriend at the airport and was so glad to see her he killed her. I don't know what my greatest fear is; maybe just that I'll be caught and discovered, accused of being a child in an adult's body.

Between innings, the little kid comes over to me. "I could be a pitcher, if anyone wanted me to," he says, wiping his nose with the back of his hand. "I could be the catcher if you get tired. Why don't you let me be the catcher, then you can rest."

"Maybe later on," I say. I stand up to take my place as catcher. I don't have a mitt, I'll have to catch bare-handed.

"You mean the next inning I can be catcher instead of you?"

"Maybe," I say. "Maybe later on in the game."

"We'll split innings, that's fair," Mickey says.

"Maybe," I say.

"I'm a great catcher," Mickey says. He squints. "I'm just going to tell my dad that you don't want to be the catcher anymore." He runs off, shouting, "Dad, Dad! She wants me to be the catcher instead of her!"

"Wait a minute," I say. "You said that, I didn't." He doesn't even turn around. "Mickey!" I say. But he is running up and down the bleachers.

All through the inning I get madder and madder. I really want to be the catcher. It's fun, even though I hurt my finger on the ball when it comes at me too fast, bending my finger backward. It takes all my strength to throw the ball back to the pitcher. Most of the time it lands short, and the pitcher has to run forward to pick it up off the ground. I stagger about, trying to avoid being hit when the pitcher throws at the batter. Our team might have gotten a player out at home, but I forget to run to the base when they throw the ball to me. Still, no one yells at me—I'm glad of that. I think to myself: I like being the catcher, now this little kid is trying to take my position from me.

Stash comes up to bat. "You okay?" he says.

"Come on, Frankie baby," someone shouts to Stash from the sidelines. It's Eddie, Mickey's father.

"He always calls me Frankie baby," Stash says. Stash hits the ball and disappears down the field. A cloud of brown dust marks where he ran. I think I'll tell Mickey he can't have my turn as catcher. That's all I need to do, stand up for my rights. I don't want to wait on the sidelines while Mickey catches. Anyway, I know I'm not capable of playing left field. My arms are too weak, and in the glare of the arc lamps I'd have a hard time seeing the ball if it came at me.

After the inning Mickey comes back over to me. He hikes up his pants and rubs his stomach. I wonder what he'll look like when he gets older. His thin lips are cracked, his nose is pug. He resembles a child actor of the 1930s—Jackie Coogan, or Spanky from *Our Gang*. I remember how much I looked forward to being a grown-up: no school, no one telling you what to do. It didn't turn out to be so much fun; I find it traumatic even to make a decision on what to order from a restaurant menu.

"I'm going to ask my father again," Mickey says. "He was too busy before." I guess Mickey seems like a regular kid, it hasn't seemed to affect him that his father lives with a man and his mother with some woman. He runs back out onto the field. Eddie looks embarrassed when his son joins him, he keeps walking.

"Anybody got a joint?" he says.

"She doesn't want to be the catcher, Dad," Mickey says. "She wants me to take over for her."

I run to Stash. "Stash, Stash," I say. "That kid is trying to take my position away from me."

"Well, tell him he can't," Stash says.

"You tell him for me," I say. But Stash pays no attention, he goes to get a can of chocolate soda.

"Hey, Mickey," the captain of my team calls, "are you keeping score? Why don't you be the official scorekeeper?"

"I can't," Mickey says. "I'm going to be the catcher."

"No, you're not," I mumble.

Mickey races over to me, holding a ball in his hands. "My father says it's okay," he shouts from two feet away. He throws the ball into the air, but as he tries to catch it, it slips out of his hands and rolls behind the backstop. "Go get it," he tells me.

"Wait a minute," I say. "You go get it, you go get it. I don't have to put up with this. If you want to be a catcher, you go get the ball. You dropped it."

"Ah, relax," Mickey says, waving his hands broadly. His little face is white and pinched, it must be way past his bedtime. "Don't worry about it," he says. Dirt is smeared in a streak under one eye, I'm ready to send him to Boys' Town. "Where are you from?" he asks.

I don't answer him. All the men seem to take this game very seriously. The women are having a good time, but the men get very angry when they strike out. One guy hits the ball so hard it goes up 150 feet and crashes into the underside of the bridge. The guy looks humbly at the ground, the other team members applaud.

"Foul ball!" Mickey shouts. "Strike one!"

There are murmured complaints from the batter.

"In this game, a foul counts as a strike," Mickey says. "My father says."

The English boy sits down beside me. "What a terrific kid," he says.

"He sure has a loud voice," I say.

"Let me ask you something," the English boy says. "Is getting two strikes the worst thing you could possibly do?"

"No," I say. "I don't think it's the worst thing you could do."

"That's good," he says.

Mame is up next. She hits a ball and runs to first base. Then she collapses.

"It's her legs," someone says. Both her legs have apparently given out from under her. She is carried back to the bleachers, moaning quietly. Then she lies flat on her back on the dusty cement steps. Her eyes are shut. The game stops.

I look up at the bridge. It's like a whole residence up there, mysterious nooks for a human fly. If there was a way of getting a rope ladder up there, a person could arrange a spot to live. This setting is unearthly. It might be two in the morning, it might be the day after the bomb is dropped. After a few minutes a boy drives onto the field on his motorcycle. Mame climbs on behind him, and they race off. "What happened?" I say.

"She pulled some muscles," the English boy says. "It looks bad. Leonard is going to take her to hospital."

I walk over to Stash. "Do you think she's okay?" I say. "She told me she's pregnant."

Stash shakes his head. "That's just the kind of stunt Candy used to pull," he says. "Every time she got pregnant she'd go berserk and do something crazy, then run off and have an abortion."

It bothers me that Stash still talks about his ex-wife. Even though she might have been a little crazy, she sounds to me like she was a very glamorous person; life with her must have been exciting. "Were you trying to have a baby?" I say.

"No," Stash says. "It just happened."

"Did you want to have kids?"

"No," Stash says.

I'm tempted to ask him whether he thinks we'll always go out together. It's a surprise to me, to be twenty-seven with my life still unsettled. I reach out to give Stash a hug, but he's already walking out to the field. I look behind me. Mickey is squatting on the bleachers, shouting, "Strike two! Strike two!" He's jumping up and down, rubbing his crotch. When he catches my glance, a look of shame crosses his face, the same look I've seen on Stash's Dalmatian, Andrew, when he knows Stash is laughing at him for something he's done.

Mickey comes over and points to a can of Diet Coke. "Is this your soda?" he says. "I'm thirsty."

"No," I say. "I don't know who it belongs to." Mickey stands looking at me. "Well, go ahead," I tell him. "I'm sure they won't mind if you have some."

Mickey glances up. "You're safe, Dad!" he screams. I clutch my hand to my ear. The kid is deafening. But Mickey's ecstatic. He leaps up and down on the cement steps, his thin arms waving. "Safe, safe, safe!" He grabs the soda from the steps and drinks eagerly, gurgling sensuously. "Ah," he says. He puts down the can and looks at me. "You sure you don't want to share your batting with me?"

"No," I say. "You can share my catching, but I want my batting."

He shrugs. "Top of the sixth, eight to five," he yells. He turns to me. "I'd make a good umpire, huh?"

Jane, a blond sculptor wearing a black leather miniskirt, her hair tied with ribbons and tiny shoelaces, hits the ball and runs to first base. She's tagged as she gets there. "Safe!" Mickey bawls.

"She's out," the first baseman says.

"Don't argue with the umpire," Mickey says. "She's safe. She had one foot on the base before the ball hit her."

It's Mickey's turn as catcher. Maritsa, a fashion model, is up at bat. The last time I saw her was in a Japanese magazine, wearing something soigné while Godzilla loomed in the background. Mickey races over to her and tries to retrieve the ball, which has rolled between her legs after he threw it in the air. Maritsa nearly brains him with the bat during her practice swing. "Ooops," she says. "Sorry about that."

"That's one way to do it," Stash says from the bleachers.

He gives me a look, grins. Stash is a team player—he shouts to the pitcher, joking around, that Marley (he's out in left field, staggering around in circles) has had one beer too many. The pitcher kids Stash about his baseball cap. I think everyone loves Stash; when we're in public he's really an extrovert, the kind of person everyone comes over to talk to.

Mickey is undaunted by his near bash on the head. He runs around in a circle, carrying the bat and ball, before he goes back to the catcher's position. "Daddy!" he says. "Daddy, it's your turn at bat!" His father jumps up, handing his joint to someone else, and runs over to the plate.

The team captain comes over. "It's my turn," he says.

Eddie turns to Mickey. "It's not my turn," he says slowly. "You said it was my turn, Mickey." I wonder what's going to happen; he seems ready to give Mickey a punch.

But Mickey's like a mouse in the elephant's cage. "You're up next then, Daddy," he says.

By now I'm actually glad that Mickey has finagled my catching position, though I'd never admit it. I'm bushed. This pearlescent, gritty heat, and the smell of the East River—garbagy, exotic—is overwhelming. The game has gone on for hours, it must be getting close to midnight. I wonder if the "Jerry Lewis Telethon" has finally ended. It seems as if everyone is a mile apart from each other. Plus, I have to go to the bathroom.

Stash suggests I go off behind the far bleachers where Max went earlier. Men have an easier time of things. "I can't do that," I tell Stash. "There're probably a half-dozen rapists lurking out there. And probably that little kid would follow me. I can't believe that kid. He has the loudest voice, Stash!"

"Doesn't he?" Stash says.

"I can't believe I let him push me around," I say. "Why doesn't someone discipline him? Why doesn't he take over his father's turn at bat? He stole my position as catcher and now he wants to take over half my batting!"

"But he loves you," Stash says. "That little kid loves you. I can see that."

"Yeah, because he knows I'm a pushover," I say.

The sides change position. Stash gets up to play catcher. Mickey comes back to me. "You know what?" he says. "Last week I was catcher for eleven innings. Eleven innings! There was a girl here who asked me to be catcher for her. She couldn't play at all. Not like you. You're a good player." He scratches fiercely at his thin arms. "Bottom of the fifth!" he shrieks. "Ten to seven, our favor!"

"Yeah?" I say. "You think I'm a good player, Mickey?"

The pitcher stops. "What inning is this?" he says.

"Bottom of the fifth!" Mickey shrieks again.

The pitcher looks puzzled. "I thought this was the top of the sixth?" he mumbles.

"Strike one!" Mickey booms.

"You're the only one who knows what's going on, Mickey," I say. He's not so bad after all, I think. Eight years old, he's not worrying about what's going to happen to him. In a way he's like Stash, grabbing things by the throat, the kind of people who don't worry that something might strangle them first. "You know what's going on," I say again.

"Yup," Mickey says. Jane's dog, the long black-and-tan mutt with a bewildered expression, snuffles around Mickey's ankles. Mickey bends to pat the dog. Then he tosses a stick toward the shortstop. The dog trots out dutifully after it. "Interference on the field!" Mickey shouts. "Time out! Dog on the field!"

turkey talk

So it was that I, Marley Mantello, had a breakfast appointment with plump collector Chuck Dade Dolger for eight in the morning. At a quarter to, I heard a horn honk outside the tenement on Avenue C where I live and paint. I went down the five flights of stairs two at a time. "If he likes you, Marley," my dealer, Ginger, had told me the day before, "then he'll go ahead and buy your work. But remember, he's going to think you're a wimp if you don't eat very much."

It wasn't enough for him to like my work, he had to respect the artist, too. Well, a skinny, unknown artist like me didn't have much choice—but at least I was hungry. It's easy to get that way when you're broke. I figured, not having eaten in several days, that I'd do okay in the eating department. If Dolger took me on as his protégé, so to speak, he would arrange for me to have all the money I needed; then I could complete my greatest work: I'd go to Rome to build my chapel. That was my main lust in life. Sure I was tired of being broke, but what I really wanted was to construct the Chapel of Jesus Christ as a Woman, adjacent to the Vatican. Complete with Her own Stations of the Cross: Washing the Dishes, Changing the Diapers, Self-Flagellation at the Mirror, Fixing the Picnic Lunch, et cetera. Word of my chapel would pass from mouth to mouth, I would charge seventy-five cents admission and have the biggest attraction outside Disney World.

Chuck Dade Dolger was sitting in the front of an old Mercedes, onyx and streamlined, chewing on a cigar. I had only seen him once before. I had forgotten how much that guy weighed; he was like a human sofa, jammed behind the steering wheel.

"You're late, buster," he said by way of hello. "I get up at the crack every day. That's what you should do if you ever expect to get anywhere."

"I've been up since six," I said. "Got two hours of sleep last night."

"Didn't sleep a wink, myself," he said. Sitting next to him on the front seat was a white pit bull terrier with a crooked mouth and a sexy leer; to my surprise my dealer, Ginger Booth, was in the back, wearing a pair of sunglasses and looking glamorous, if a little fatigued. "Ginger!" I said. " What are you doing here?"

"I thought I'd have breakfast with you two before going to work," she said.

This just went to show that Ginger was working for me as hard as she could; I don't know why I had my doubts about her. I told her often that I was the best artist she handled; she was lucky to have me, even though my paintings weren't her biggest sellers. That was because they were original; the original is always disliked until it is imitated. "Glad you could make it," I said.

"Get in the back," Chuck said. "The dog rides in front. She gets a a little carsick. Let me tell you something, Marley: I love girls, especially Ginger Booth, but oh that dog!" He pulled out from where he had double-parked, without looking at the road.

"God, Chuck, watch where you're going," Ginger said shortly.

"I could use a cup of coffee, that's for sure," I said, cracking my knuckles.

"Coffee!" Chuck said. "No wonder you're so skinny. Coffee will poison your system quicker than anything. I gave up coffee a year ago; haven't touched a drop of liquor in three years.

Pretty soon I'm going to give up all refined sugar. My ambition is never to die, and so far there hasn't been a goal of mine I haven't fulfilled. How about placing a little bet on it, Marley? If I live forever, you pay me; if I keel over, you try and collect!"

"I have a better idea," I said. "Something that will make you immortal without giving up sugar. I have this idea, a genius idea, that's not to say my head isn't crammed with them—"

"Chuck, take a left here at the lights," Ginger said. "Chuck has owned the same house in Manhattan for the past five years, but he's so used to being driven by his chauffeur he can't find his way home without help." Her voice was brittle; I turned around to look at her. Dressed in a carbuncle-colored sweater, she lit a cigarette and flicked the match into the ashtray as if she were killing a fly. Well, she had hurt my feelings by interrupting me, but this was one of the things an art dealer always did, to try to keep the artist in his place. Still, she put up with Chuck's driving in grand style; she sat in the back seat as if the front of the car was unconnected to her in any way.

Every time Chuck had something to say, he took his eyes off the street and turned to the back, so he could look at me. "Happens I drove an ambulance for Medical Division during WW2," he said. "Which is where I got my driver's education. I was in Paris at the time with my first wife. A boy of twenty-two years of age I was, and I sent Lady home by boat and joined Volunteer Services over there until the Occupation. Tried to enlist in the regular army but my feet were as flat as a dog. Ended up with thirteen medals, though."

"Anyway, this idea for my chapel—" I began.

Ginger gave me a punch on the shoulder. Meanwhile even the taxis were steering clear of his tank as we charged up Park Avenue. It didn't sound too great—it had a sort of groan in the transmission, but that didn't stop him from hitting the gas. "My daughter's car," he said. "She left it with me while she's in Ireland—she went over to buy some art for me. I gave the driver the day off, so the other car's in the garage."

"Turn around, Chuck, you've driven too far uptown," Ginger said.

"Goddammit, Ginger, if you're so great at driving, why don't you just take over this thing," he said, letting go of the wheel and holding both hands in the air.

"Do you have breakfast with Chuck a lot?" I said to Ginger.

She gave me a funny look and picked up one of her feet, clad in a little pony-skin boot. "Chuck and I are old friends, Marley," she said.

"So then you must have told Chuck about this idea I have," I said.

"Tell Chuck what new artists you like, Marley. We've been wondering who's showing now that Chuck should buy, outside of the artists that I handle."

"Well, there's a guy I know—Stash Stosz. He's doing paintings based on the difference between good and evil. He uses cartoon characters a lot: Babalooey, Chilly Whilly, Bullwinkle, Mickey Mouse, and various Byzantine figures. He's good; not as good as me, of course, but he's good. Why don't you look at his work?"

"Well, of course," Ginger said. "He's your friend, of course you'd like his work."

"*Credat Judaeus Apella*," I said. "That means 'tell it to the Marines' in Latin."

But meanwhile Chuck wasn't even listening. He muttered to himself, "Ginger never drove a day in her life, except once into a parking meter. Now she thinks if she tells me where I'm going it's going to help me get there." And he turned east, narrowly missing a pedestrian, and started back downtown.

When we got to his house, Ginger mumbled something and tried to pull me off to one side, but Chuck took me by the arm. "Come on, come on," he said. "Got to get going with the fixings."

"I'm going upstairs to lie down for a while," Ginger said. "I'm getting a headache. When you get a chance, Marley, come upstairs. There's a Roy Lichtenstein in the bedroom I think you'll like."

The place was a fine brownstone, built like a coffin, with mahogany walls of Van Dyck brown, and a big painting by Eric

Fischl above the fireplace, of a naked boy masturbating in a wading pool. I went over to see. "Bought that to shock my mother," Chuck said, laughing. "Died last year, age ninety-seven. I can laugh about it now, I'm a changed man, but I broke that poor woman's heart. Come on, I'll show you around later."

I followed him into the kitchen, where he made me sit down at the table while he put on a big white chef's hat. The whole table was covered with food—a bottle of taco sauce and a huge pitcher of honey, another marked sorghum, and an old-fashioned bottle of cream. On the grill he put a dozen or two vehement pink sausages which began to spit angrily away like so many frying cats; he broke open eight or ten eggs into what he said was "hot monkey grease"—each egg with a double yolk. From the oven he took a bowl stocked with biscuits resembling overgrown turnips and dripping with butter. "I'm an expert master at the rolls," he said. "Boy, what do you want from life?"

"I should have been born in ancient Rome," I said. "I would have liked to be an early Christian martyr."

"Why, son, I'm a Christian myself," Chuck said. "After a life of being your ordinary American capitalist, something just snapped in me."

"Oh, then you'll appreciate my idea," I said.

"You have a point about ancient Rome," he said. "See, I would have been a senator back in those times. It's like this—" And he kept talking while he cooked. The table was covered with a blue-and-white-checked cloth, but you could hardly see it for the food. It was like eating on the farm— where all that stuff came from I couldn't figure out. I wouldn't have been surprised to learn he kept a couple of cows and pigs out back. I was so punchy from hunger that it was all I could do to concentrate on the visuals. Chuck had a huge, ripe face, and a booming manner. His tiny eyes twinkled away, jovial as Farmer Brown; meanwhile, talking to himself—at least, I wasn't listening—he took a basket of mushrooms out of the refrigerator and flipped a couple up into the air. One left a little spot where it hit the ceiling. "The help'll clean this up later," Chuck said. "I like to have a good time when I cook."

He sat down next to me at the table. The dog was sleeping right next to my feet and let out a big snore that made me jump. "The old dog is asleep," he bellowed, tossing six hot biscuits on my plate. "We better keep our voices down. She's a fighting dog. Oatmeal to start with?"

"No, just the grapefruit," I said. Chuck let out a little snort. "I'll have the oatmeal after I finish this," I added, trying to size up what that snort meant. I poured a little honey onto the grapefruit; he must have imported it from Texas, it was about the size of a basketball, and the meat was pink and juicy. There was nothing I hated more than oatmeal first thing in the morning; grapefruit followed a close second.

"Well now, I have to tell you," he said, getting up and bringing a saucepan of baked beans to the table, and then returning to divide up the eggs and sausage he had placed on a platter. "And, by the way, get started on all this before it gets cold, I have it in mind to make us some fine blueberry pancakes— wild Maine blueberries—when we've finished this. I have to tell you—I'm thinking of buying one of your goddamn paintings."

"Mm," I said, though my mouth was full of food.

"Eat, Marley, don't talk. I don't know what the hell is wrong with you. If you can't eat, how the hell do you expect to paint? I don't have much faith in a man unless he's one of your true Renaissance men. Now take me for example—" And so on and so forth. Greedily I devoured a biscuit, lathered with benign butter.

Chuck watched me cunningly. "Now, I think your work is a pretty thing—that picture in your show at Ginger's, not that big ugly thing, what do you call that big one, by the way?"

"It's called 'The Party of Beauty,' " I said. "It's a big get-together of all the beautiful people, the Venus of Milo, Aphrodite, Hebe, the Graces, Peri, Houri, Cupid, Apollo, Hyperion, Antinous, Narcissus—"

"Didn't think much of it. But that small one she's got in her

office, the one representing 'Geoffrey Chaucer's First Date.'
Now what did you paint that with?"

"Gouache," I muttered, and skewered a sausage. The big
painting was the finest thing I had done to date. I had to put
three of the little stuffed mushrooms—bread crumbs, Parme-
san cheese—down my gullet in rapid succession in order to
keep from arguing with him, as if it meant nothing to me. In
fact I was already feeling quite full. Maybe my stomach had
shriveled from living for months on nothing but canned Chef
Boy-ar-dee once a day.

"Gouache, you say. Well, that painting is as fine a represen-
tation of a pair of lady's breasts as I have ever seen. Use a live
model?"

"Dirty magazines," I said.

"Keep your voice down, Mr. Marley, we don't want Princess
to take offense at our talk." He tossed a sausage to the sleeping
dog below, who roused herself long enough to wolf down the
meat before instantly plunging back into what seemed like
permanent narcolepsy. "Whoops, don't tell Ginger I'm feeding
the dog under the table. She don't approve, she says it leads
to bad habits whenever she tries to throw a dinner party. See
that little camera up there in the corner of the room?"

I glanced over my shoulder and kept my hands busy by
letting a biscuit accidentally drop to the floor.

"Got electronic surveillance all over the place," Chuck said.
"Art collection here is worth close to three million, if you count
the stuff in the basement. Ran out of wall space. Ginger insisted I put in the electronic system. She does boss me to
death. With my wife, Lady, before she died, things were different. Of course, times were different then. I managed to
make my wife's life a misery for twenty-odd years. In Paris,
back in the late thirties, I sent her home to look after the
turkey farm while I had an affair with a White Russian countess. Never cared much for the countess, don't know why I did
it. Tall women always went for me. I'm only five-seven, you
know. Don't look it, but I am."

"I like Paris," I said. "But my true love is Italy, Rome in particular."

"I did love my wife, Lady, dearly, she was a tiny little thing, the runt of the litter, came from one of those fine old New England families that never took to me. Anyway, the only way I could get rid of that countess woman was to take up driving an ambulance. I never did intend to break Lady's heart, but that's what I did, I guess. Can't say she wasn't made of strong stuff, though. She left me in Paris with that White Russian and came back and supplied the U.S. Army with turkeys weighing up to fifty pounds, the whole time I was gone."

I broke open the runny egg yolks with the tine of my fork and studied the goo as it ran out over the plate. Egg yolks. I couldn't help but think of those frescoes in the basement of the San Marco monastery in Florence. I would definitely do some frescoes in wet plaster in my chapel. . . . "I guess I didn't really realize you were Ginger's boyfriend," I said. "I mean, she told me about you, but you know how it is. I'm the kind of person who's wrapped up in my work."

"Oh, well, Ginger," Chuck said. "Now she's sitting there upstairs someplace worrying that I'm convincing you to make me a new painting, for less money."

"Oh, is that what's bugging her?" I said. "Listen, my paintings are cheap at the price Ginger's charging for them. Believe me, any work of mine you buy now is a great investment."

"I'm not going to argue with you, Marley," Chuck said. "But there's a lot of young artists out there, I don't take risks unless they're guaranteed."

"With the project I've got in mind, you'd make a fortune. It's going to be bigger than Disney World. Even Ginger says—"

"Oh, Ginger. What she's got is a tough facade, but underneath that, what I have is a little girl who calls me up at three in the morning on those nights when we're apart, crying to me that she's never going to get to whatever place it is she thinks she's going. She gave up painting to become an art dealer—

her and fifty other gals all have the same idea in mind. It's a tough world out there, Marley, you need more than a facade."

"I have more than a facade," I said. "Listen, I have the blueprints all drawn up. I could have been a great architect if I wanted—the inside is going to be made from marble, rubber, and glass. In the center I've got plans for a giant bathtub, a kind of fountain filled with sulfuric acid—"

"I told Ginger, in a couple of years, maybe, if we're still together and I've built up her ego sufficient, I'll let her have a kid. For the time being, I've taught her to knit. See, I like to knit, I have some creative talents myself. Don't ever let them tell you that things like cooking or knitting aren't artistic in their own way. Take a look at this sweater I have on."

I looked him up and down. He had on something Argyle, of bishop's purple and garter blue, which would have been normal if not for the neckline, wrinkled like the wattles of some big bird. It disturbed me to hear so much about Ginger that I wasn't entirely sure I wanted to know; after all, I had come to depend on her to take care of me. I mean, an artistic genius can't be expected to do more than create his works. "I guess old Ginger would like to get married," Chuck said. "I'm sixty-seven years old, I'm leaving my money to my daughter."

"Ginger doesn't need any kids," I said. "She's got me, you know."

But Chuck looked nervous; he changed the subject. "Let me bring out something I think you'll like to try," he said, noting that my eating had slowed somewhat. From a drawer in the pantry he took out several tiny green cans labeled PINEAPPLE JAM, C-RATIONS, U.S. ARMY.

He opened up a can with the electric opener. Inside was a small amount of crusty, yellowish salve, smelling powerfully of some kind of detergent. "The cook tried to throw this stuff out the other day, and I near to had a fit. I got a whole truckload of them for thirty-five dollars. You know what this would cost on today's market? I thought I could sell it—genuine collector's items, these are. Not that I need the money, but I've got to keep myself occupied. Collecting art don't take every minute." He put some on a biscuit and watched as I tried to eat it. "Not bad, huh?"

As soon as he looked away, I let the biscuit slip under the table to the dog. I had to make a fast clack with the fork and knife to cover up that powerful sound, the crunching of jaws.

Meanwhile Chuck had put away four or five of the eggs liberally doused with taco sauce. " Goddammit, you're slowing down. When I operated the Ballroom in Newport, we used to attract the sporting trade. You know, Marley, I never saw a professional golf or tennis player who would buy his own god-damn drink. Those fellows could eat; let me tell you, I could judge at breakfast who was going to win that afternoon."

"What was the Ballroom?" I said.

"Try some of the taco sauce on the mushrooms, brings out the flavor. Imported the stuff myself from a restaurant in Tex-arkana. Don't tell me you never heard of Dolger's Starlight Ballroom. There wasn't a day in the papers there wasn't some mention of the goings-on at the place. Lady and my mother were horrified; so was the community. It was their belief that a person's name should never appear in the paper but for three times—birth, marriage, and death. Hell, my mother and Lady never got used to some things; both of them society ladies. Place didn't last too long though—nightclubs are generally short-lived. Ripped out the whole main floor of the mansion, put in a stage and a wet bar out by the swimming pool. At one point I turned the whole back lot into a miniature golf course. Newport never saw the like. Had an orchestra—a different one every two weeks—up from New York. I was just a kid then. Have a couple more eggs, there's room on your plate. Or are you ready for some dessert?"

The dog got up under the table, emitting a slow, painful groan, and shuffled over to her water bowl. I tossed a few baked beans off my plate. Well, so it is that history is passed from mouth to mouth, *virum volitare per ora*. I guess the old guy just wanted me to know how it had been for him. Still, I was frantic to get on with my own life; I was willing to listen, though, if the end result would be my getting some money.

"All set," I said. The dog came back from her water bowl, pushed the beans around with her snout, and sunk back again. "Whoops, looks like I just dropped my napkin," I said, bending over to try to retrieve the baked beans.

"I guess you might say I was a rebellious kind of guy, Marley. But I was a self-made man and generally people who have been brought up the way I was don't like to make money. Not me, though." He stopped talking to give the red-eyed dog a halfhearted kick. "Love that dog—she looks just like me. *Tch tch tch.* How about a drink to go with the eats?" He went over to the cabinet and came back with a dusty bottle of brandy covered with a parchmentlike paper he held up to the light.

I couldn't help but be fascinated with his face, so sad and elephantine. Big rheumy eyes folded in delicate tissue. Maybe I could use him as my male Madonna.

"Had to give up the booze," Chuck said wistfully, pouring out a snifter of stuff the color of rotten apricots. "But I sure miss those elevenses. Now I just cook. Believe me, cooking is creative. Why, I could write a cookbook of my own recipes. Reminds me of when I used to make my own ice cream during Prohibition days. Tutti-frutti. I had bonded rum in storage just for flavoring. I never considered it a waste of booze. Like paint, you can't stint on your art supplies if you want to succeed. Neighbors used to send their cooks over to my kitchen just to buy a quart—I had direct contact with the finest rum-runners from Cuba. Finish up this last sausage, sonny."

"*Esto perpetua* to you!" I said, holding up the sausage on my fork, while with the other hand I reached down and tried to loosen my belt. Meanwhile trying to record the man. A handsome face, combining the most gracious aspects of a moose and a doorknob. I could see the old genetic lines at work, a certain nobility and foghorn dignity. Yet it was an irritation to me that he had enough money to finance my genius idea, and I couldn't bring him to see the point. Oh, hope told a flattering tale: I still thought I might persuade him to fork over the dough.

Chuck leapt up from the table on his big feet, the chef's hat flopping over to one side, and brought on the coffee and some fat jelly doughnuts that were greasy and soft to the touch, but brown and gritty with sugar on the outside. "Have one of these," he said. "Made them myself. Special treat."

I blinked politely and bit into one. It was filled with loads of gooey, blackish grape jelly that blurted out over the sides of my mouth. "Good, good," I mumbled. "By the way, you haven't told me yet what you think of my project."

Meanwhile he had forgotten about the smoked trout. "Too late. Well, just try a little taste, Marley. I only took a couple out of the deep freeze, but I'll get out more if you think you want a snack after breakfast."

"Yeah."

"Where was I? The Starlight Ballroom. Well, when the neighbors took up in arms about the place, I turned it into a turkey ranch. Dolger's White Mountain Turkeys. Hah! The neighbors were even less happy about that, but they couldn't do a thing—they had made sure the neighborhood was zoned for livestock. They were thinking about their horses, I guess. Ever see a turkey make love?"

"No," I said.

"Or a hen straining to lay an egg that won't come out?"

"No."

"Ever cook up a bird, and when you open it there are hundreds of little turkey embryos, some in an egg and others getting smaller and smaller until the last one is tinier than a pearl?"

"No."

"All of this is leading up, I guess, to how I'm thinking about becoming a Catholic. I lived my life by biting into it like you would a person's arm. The neighbors should have complained less about the Starlight Ballroom; you should have heard them squeal about the farm. It was one of the finest turkey operations around. None of this chemical stuff; my birds were happy. I didn't make much money, though. Take your average Thanksgiving bird, for example—ten, twelve pounds. What family needs or wants a fifty-pound bird?"

"Maybe a large family," I said.

"Nope," Chuck said. "Don't have a large enough oven. But my problem was, I had a lot of other projects going—I started a magazine publishing dynasty, and got out at the right time, and made a real killing—and I lost interest in the whole bird endeavor. I could have been Frank Perdue today. Maybe not, though. The reason those birds got so big was that I hated to kill them off. The only kind act in my life as a young man. I let the birds live until they turned mean and sour and had to be ground up into turkey roll for the U.S. Army."

I was thinking about my stomach, a tender instrument. I could feel it down there at the bottom of my esophagus, like a woman's glove stuffed with snails and lye. "That's terrible," I said.

"I've always been a farmer at heart, though you wouldn't think of it to look at me. Got kicked out of prep school for raising ducks in the dorm room."

"Don't pay Chuck too much attention," Ginger said, wandering into the kitchen and pouring herself a cup of coffee. "We should all be so lucky as to be the kind of self-made man that Chuck is."

"These are men talking, Ginger," Chuck said.

"I'm going, I'm going," Ginger said. "Marley, you haven't been telling Chuck about your project, have you? Why don't you let him buy a couple of your paintings before you start in on him." She left the room, but not before shooting me an expression—I could see what Chuck meant, she was a nervous little thing, with those concentration-camp eyes popping out of a rich American face.

Chuck gave me a wink. "Raised a couple of pigs, too, before the neighbors got on my case. Those pork chops, Marley, were not to be believed. Each two inches thick, I stuffed them with bread crumbs. Swimming in cream. Mmm mmm mmm. I've had to give up eating pork, though, you'll notice I only had a taste of my homemade sausage. Trouble with the digestion, it's a shame how the body starts to conk out on a person. How were the sausages, by the way?"

"Delicious."

"You think so? Let me wrap up a couple for you, a little snack later on. Anyway, what was I telling you? I have an attention span that is shorter than a goddamn dog's. Let me tell you, since I got on this art collecting kick, I've come to realize that in my youth in Paris I could have picked up quite a few paintings for a song that would have gotten me more than a million today. Well, I saw how you put away that food—you did all right, boy, though let me tell you that in my heyday I could have eaten you under the table. Take the dog out for a walk, son, and then I'll drive you back home and speak to Ginger about that painting of yours. It's a pretty enough picture, 'Geoffrey Chaucer's First Date,' though I think Ginger could do a little better on the price."

I should have been content with what I already had; but I was like the fisherman with his magic fish, I couldn't help but ask for more. "What about funding for my project?" I said. "You'd be like the Medicis with their own chapel—"

"Marley, at this minute I have a man who calls himself an environmental artist moving heaps of mud from one part of Montana to another. I have a man attempting to get permission to cover the Golden Gate Bridge in Band-Aids. I have a gal handcuffed to a Korean and a Dalmation making a videotape of every moment of their year chained together. All this is costing me, but that's the price I'm willing to pay for my interest in the art world. I tell you what, though: I'm going to buy your painting."

"Well, would you consider my project? Just consider it before making up your mind? I'll send you the complete prospectus, and slides of the altarpiece that's already finished."

"I tell you what: I'll do that."

So I was pleased. For I knew that even though Ginger would let Chuck talk her down some on the price, I would still see enough on the deal to pay my rent for the next couple of months—and still have something left over to eat with besides, if I ever felt like eating again. And in the meantime I would figure out a way to make Chuck come around to my point of view, even if it meant holding Ginger hostage or doing away with the woman making the videotape while handcuffed to the Korean and the dog.

Just as I was about to snap the leash onto the dog's collar to take her out, Chuck called, "Maybe you'll walk off a bit of that food. Come back and have another cup of coffee and we'll start on lunch. Or you'll have a piece of goddamn apple pie. Baked it myself from the finest apple trees in New England. Let me tell you, some people call me an artist, an artist who works in food."

"Where do you want me to take the dog?" I said.

"Let me show you something, Marley," Chuck said, coming over to the door. He lowered his voice from a bellow to a whisper. "Sit, Princess," he said. The dog looked at him but didn't move. "She's a fighting dog, Marley, so be careful out there with her. See, a dog has got better hearing than a human being."

"So will she attack or something?"

"Could happen. When you get out there with her, don't raise your voice or you'll be in trouble. There's no need to shout at her. Just take her around the block."

I was prepared for the worst; but on the street I realized that the dog was so fat all she wanted to do was snuffle up a few droplets on the pavement and go back home to sleep.

Maybe the old guy really had gotten the best of me. All I knew was that if I went back into that kitchen to eat some more, I was going to die.

I crept into the living room to find Ginger, sitting knitting on the pigskin sofa. The place was done up like a hunting lodge, circa 1910: all that dark wood, everything manly and antique, except for the big pictures studding the wall, work by Sol LeWitt, Alfred Jensen, Neil Jenney, a curious jumble of stuff, some junk, some not so bad. I wouldn't have minded looking around; it was the sitting down to eat I couldn't take.

"Ginger, I have to get out of here," I said.

Ginger nodded. "I'll tell him you had to meet some friends for lunch," she said. "See that moose head?" She pointed to a big animal above the fireplace, with one antler askew. "I keep that up there as a reminder to Chuck of what he was like before he gave up drinking—he got mad at me one night and threw a pewter mug at me, but he missed and hit the moose. Since he stopped drinking he took up collecting art. Marley, you didn't try and tell him about your chapel, did you?"

"I tried to," I said. "I don't know if he was listening."

"Because he's been seriously thinking of converting to Catholicism. His daughter's Catholic, he's very close to her."

"Well then, he'd like my chapel."

"I don't think so—many people may be offended. I'm just telling you this so that your hopes aren't dashed."

"I don't buy that," I said. "I didn't realize that Chuck was the guy you were going out with, by the way." It occurred to me I had never bothered asking Ginger anything much about her life before; I was more concerned with the job she was doing in looking after me. Well, this just went to prove I was getting to be a better human being.

"I really do love Chuck," Ginger said. "For years I've stayed with him several nights a week. He always brings me breakfast in bed, but he can't make any kind of commitment to me . . . I think partly because of his daughter. She doesn't approve. Besides that, he's been having an affair with the woman next door for years now, so on the nights he's not with me, he's with her. And she's trying to convince him that I'm not a good adviser to him. She says I'm just using him to buy work from the artists I handle . . ."

"Marley!" Chuck bellowed from the kitchen. "You back with that dog yet? How about having a drink and coming on in here for some of that pie I was telling you about?"

"Quick, you better go," Ginger said. "I'll try and explain to him why you had to leave."

"But maybe he won't buy my painting then," I said.

"Marley, go!"

So I snuck off fast, to walk downtown. This would give my skinniness a chance to rest, and thus I could cultivate my thoughts at their ease. For I was certain that Chuck had indeed

taken a liking to me, and soon I would have his financial en-
dorsement to buy a site in Rome, where I would live happily,
building my chapel. I don't know why, but I have always
counted on my intuitive knowledge. I was so certain of all of
this it occurred to me I should have asked Ginger for a little
advance money; it probably would have been possible to have
gotten a substantial check from Chuck that very morning, had
I pressed the point.

A great sense of joy rose up in me. To my surprise I was
getting hungry: to me this was what joy had always been. With
the last buck in my pocket I darted across the street to a pizza
joint; stuffing the cold slab in my mouth, I began to tell the guy
flipping the dough about all of my plans.

physics

After I got my hair cut at High Style 2000 on Lexington Avenue, I was hit by a car. It wasn't even a very nice vehicle, just a blue-and-white Chrysler. I was trying to cross the street in the middle of the block, and the car backed up and hit me in the legs at knee level. I didn't realize that I'd been struck by a car; it felt more as if someone came along and punched me in the legs. Then it pulled forward. I was stunned. I kept staring at the license plate: it said 867-UHH. I tried to memorize it. The car wasn't going anywhere—I guess the driver was waiting to see if I was seriously damaged. I was angry, even if it *was* my fault. I glared at the car and tried to give the driver the evil eye. He leaned out the window and yelled at me, "You stupid, or what? Did you see how many feet from you I was?"

Now, I am a word person and have never been good with mathematical problems—how many miles a train can travel in five hours if its speed is forty miles per hour, and so forth. I always think, What if a cow gets in the way? Probably because of this, I almost flunked high school physics. Every night my mother made me memorize phrases from the textbook, but it didn't do any good. The teacher tried to help me after school, but I still got a D. Faced with the driver's hard question on Lexington Avenue, I wanted to do something—to scream at him, for instance—but I was afraid.

I remembered my mother telling me how, at age two, she

was taken on a trip from Atlanta to Manhattan and when her mother took her outside to play in the courtyard of the building they were staying in, someone opened a window and poured a pail of water onto my mother's head. Whoever it was didn't like the fact that my mother was singing under the window at nine o'clock on a Sunday morning. Of course my grandmother dried her off (or the water evaporated quickly or slowly, depending on the coefficient of diffusion), and called the police and the newspapers. My mother still has the clipping with the photo from the *Herald Tribune*, captioned A MINUTE MYSTERY. It showed my mother in Shirley Temple ringlets, with chubby legs, and the article described how little Sonia Silverman, up from Georgia on a visit, had been the victim of a nasty prank.

I stood in the gutter. I was trembling. Either I was extremely happy, or I had just received a jolt of adrenaline from being hit. It was hard to tell the difference. I wasn't dead. It was like finding $20 in the gutter. What a thing I was! Finally I went across the street and into a pizzeria, and I ordered a piece of pizza—pepperoni, mushrooms, onions, and peppers. I had to wait on line while it was heating in the oven.

There was another girl waiting ahead of me, and when the chef finally took out her slice, I tried to reach for it. But she reached first and the chef handed it to her. "Is this the type that you ordered?" I said. I rarely speak to strangers, but I had to say something. I didn't believe that the girl had gotten the same type of pizza as mine because (a) it was an unusual choice to make and (b) almost everyone else seemed to be ordering the plain slices.

The girl gave me a dirty look. "Yes, it is," she said snippily.

The cook said to me, "Don't get impatient, honey, just relax." This only made me feel more foolish. The slice that he gave me, however, was really sparse. Most of the ingredients had slid off into the oven. I was embarrassed and would have said something along the lines of "I can assure you I'm not impatient," but nothing came out of my mouth. The cook, I was certain, had gone out of his way to make me look pushy, when obviously it was unintentional on my part.

The pizza was like a metaphor for my entropic life. The girl whose piece of pizza I tried to steal was carrying one of these trashy novels about Hollywood. I was incensed. This was her reading material, yet she still felt superior to me. At first I thought she was about to sit down at the only table left and I would be forced to sit with her. My hot pizza was leaking through the paper plate. But finally I found another seat. I felt so grateful I almost threw myself into my seat. At the next table was a woman with a crewcut, a kid about six years old, and a guy with pale-blue hair who looked like the woman's brother. He kept taking food from the little kid's plate and the kid said, in a fury, practically heartbroken, "Leave my food alone." He was eating spaghetti; I wondered if it tasted as good as my pizza, which was absolutely delicious—chunks of chewy mushrooms, dense and meaty, cheese like stringy bubblegum, and salty, sparky bits of pepperoni.

On the ceiling, over the steam trays, giant papier-mâché haunches of meat were hanging from ropes. I kept thinking, "I was just hit by a car."

On the bus home, I reminded myself not to tell Stash about what had happened or he would kill me. How would it be if he picked up the *Post* and saw JEWELRY DESIGNER, 28, KILLED BY HIT AND RUN? First of all everyone would know that I got my hair cut in a cheap joint on Lexington Avenue and not at some SoHo or East Village spot. Plus, who would come to my funeral? I had no friends. All the other jewelry designers I knew had plenty of friends. They threw big parties for themselves at various clubs and their pictures were published in the most fashionable magazines. Maybe they were receiving outside financial assistance. I had no money to throw parties, although I had a hunger for things I knew realistically I didn't actually care for.

When I got in the door, Stash was lying on the bed next to Andrew, our Dalmatian. Stash's thick blond hair, loose from its ponytail, was practically covering his face. He had an ominous, unshaved look. He wasn't wearing a shirt; his hairy chest had an animal ferocity. Andrew's legs were sticking up in the air and his neck was resting on Stash's arm. Andrew had a snoring problem; he snored so loudly that he used to wake Stash and me several times a night, until Stash devised a solution. He attached a rope to Andrew's bed, and during the night whenever Andrew began to snore Stash would yank the rope and the abrupt movement would wake Andrew and he would stop snoring for a while. I used to tease Stash, telling him this was cruelty to animals—after all, would he have liked it if someone tied a rope to our bed and gave it a jerk every time we drifted off to sleep? But Andrew was so good-natured —or dumb—he didn't seem to mind.

Stash and Andrew didn't even look at me. I felt left out. "Hi," I said. "I got my hair cut." I had red, corkscrew curls, almost to my waist: my hair didn't have a real style, it was just a mess. Stash had begged me never to change it. "It doesn't look one iota different, does it? I spent ten dollars and told them to snip the ends. What do you think? Will I look nice tonight?"

Stash didn't answer.

"Is something wrong?" I said.

"No."

"Are you sick? You have an earache?"

"No."

"Did you eat today?"

"Yes."

"What did I do?" I said. "I forgot to defrost the refrigerator? Is that it? *You* defrost the goddamn refrigerator."

"Eleanor, I would have defrosted the refrigerator, but you've got too much stuff in there. You made me help you pick eight quarts of cherries last summer and you never made pies. Why don't you throw them out?"

"I didn't make pies because you said we were on a diet. I come home and you're mad at me about the refrigerator?"

"I wasn't even thinking about it until you reminded me. I'm mad about that article on the table. Go look at it." Sometimes I felt as if I were the sole member of the Bomb Squad: I had to defuse Stash. I picked up the magazine lying on the table. It was a nice table, like something that might be found in a camper's dining hall. Stash had bought it for me a few months back, saying that since I complained so much about not being able to have anyone over to dinner he would get me a table. So far, though, every time I suggested we invite someone over, he said the house was too messy and gave examples. Number One, I had stuck black and white adhesive tiles in the space between the kitchen counter and the cabinets, and when they peeled off, a short time later, all the paint on the wall peeled off with them, leaving brown spots.

In the magazine was a reproduction of one of Stash's paintings, "The Wisdom of Solomon," in which Quick Draw MacGraw and Babalooey are sawing an Eskimo baby in half. Underneath the picture was a long article. In the first paragraph the man said that while he couldn't dismiss Stash's work entirely, it was nevertheless the mindless scrawling of a Neanderthal.

"Well, that doesn't sound so bad," I said when I put it down.

"Doesn't sound so bad?" Stash said. He shook his head disbelievingly. "Sometimes you amaze me."

"Well, things could always be worse," I said. "This could be Russia, where they come and knock on your door and take you away and shoot you if they don't like what you do."

"Russian Constructivist art is my favorite," Stash said.

"At least you're getting attention!" I said. "I'd be thrilled if anyone wrote an article about me, even a negative one."

"I don't know if I feel like going to the dinner tonight," Stash said.

A fancy dinner for forty of the world's most famous artists was going to be held at a swank Italian restaurant, to honor the fact that they had agreed to decorate a nightclub. Stash was one of them; they would all be there this evening. My girlfriend had told me that dinner for two, with champagne (one bottle) could cost more than $200 at the restaurant. Luckily, we wouldn't be paying.

"You do, too, feel like going out tonight," I said. All the other artists will envy your appearance in that magazine."

"Do you think?" Stash said. "I don't know."

"First of all, everyone wants publicity," I said. "Secondly, as long as you're an underdog, you can have respect—like Vincent van Gogh. If you get too popular it makes you seem phony and commercial." I probably would have said anything —I really wanted to go to the dinner. It was going to be an event: never had so many diverse and famous artists been collected under one roof. They ranged from people famous for sports illustration to the latest East Village star.

"I was in a good mood until I saw this article," Stash said. "Then when I got home I found you still hadn't defrosted the refrigerator. Not only will I never be able to get the money to buy a loft now, I don't see the point anyway. If we did have a decent place to live, it would always be a complete mess."

"Didn't you ever hear of a self-defrosting refrigerator?" I said. "You were just looking for an excuse. Don't you try and punish me, Stash."

"How am I punishing you?"

"Because you promised me we'd start looking for a bigger space to live in, and now you're going to try and weasel out." One half of me had known all along we would never move— we were too uncomfortable here. Low rent (subsidized housing for artists), and a nice river view—we were used to it. On the other hand, a friend of Stash's was trying to buy a building nearby, and Stash liked the way the deal sounded. He could buy a whole floor and rent out half, thus making his mortgage payments.

I started to get the things out of the refrigerator and put them into the sink. I'd defrost overnight. I felt like clobbering Stash over the head. I was practically thirty years old, unmarried, and my marketability was going downhill fast. My career hadn't taken off the way I had hoped. I had had to quit working on my jewelry full-time in order to take on a job two days a week as copy editor for an East Village newspaper. I also had to be burdened with my lousy personality. If I had been more outgoing maybe I could have been more successful with my jewelry. That was the way things worked in Manhattan.

Where I grew up, in South Carolina, social graces didn't count. Max, my father, had a mail-order gardening business. We raised peonies, daffodils, daylilies, hyacinths, iris, all kinds of bulbs and perennials. For my fourteenth birthday Max named a new variety of pink camellia after me. I wasn't thrilled —I really wanted a subscription to *Seventeen*—but I kept my mouth shut. Max also taught horticulture at the local university, part-time. When we children came home from school, everyone had a job to do. The stove was full of baked potatoes, and that's what we'd have—baked potatoes with yogurt and goat cheese. My mother raised angora goats, she sold the wool to weavers across the country. My parents had made a choice: they would remain poor but live off the land, in a lifestyle unaffected by the progressively commercial and false world around them. It was taken for granted that we would all work hard. In other words, we didn't have a TV set.

Well, I had also made a choice: I would rebel against my parents and join the rat race. I wanted things, and the things I wanted weren't inexpensive. Unfortunately, somewhere along the line I got sidetracked. For one thing, I had never, in my wackiest dream, imagined that I would grow up to be a poor person. My mother had warned me about New York, but I was prepared to work hard, and I figured eventually I'd make it. I wasn't the only one in my situation. Most of the people I knew were doing one thing but considered themselves to be something else: all the waitresses I knew were really actresses, all the Xeroxers in the Xerox place were really novelists, all the receptionists were artists. There were enough examples of people who had been receptionists who went on to become famous artists that the receptionists felt it was okay to call themselves artists. But if I was going to have to do something like copy edit two or three days a week, I didn't want to lie to myself and say I was a jewelry designer. I figured I should just accept reality and say I was a copy editor.

I was embittered. It was hard not to live in New York and

be full of rage. I was thinking of all this while I fixed some instant flan—using up all the rest of the milk so it wouldn't go bad being outside the refrigerator overnight. On the side of the box the only ingredient listed was sugar. I felt I should have made Stash flan from scratch.

At that moment he came into the kitchen. "What are you doing?" he said. "You can't even focus on one activity! You're trying to defrost the refrigerator and cook at the same time!"

It was strange how most of the time we got along so well, but then there were these periods when it was a good thing the knives were in the drawer and not out on display. "You're picking on me!" I said. "I do things as I please! Look around you—the junk that's here is yours, not mine. I had to clear off four of my bookshelves and mail my books back to my mother so you could have space to put all that junk from the table— and now the table has new junk on it."

While I yelled, Stash hacked at some of the loose ice in the refrigerator. When he had filled a bowl, he carried it over to the sink. "Where should I put it?" he said. "The sink is full of food—plus the dirty spaghetti pot."

"In the tub."

"I can't throw it in the tub," he said. "I'm going to take a shower."

"Well, run some hot water on it," I said. "The melting point of ice is zero degrees centigrade or 32 degrees Fahrenheit."

He had to restrain himself from throwing the ice at me. "How can I buy a loft when you put too much food in the refrigerator? Why should I go into debt when you're going to turn a new place into the same kind of disaster as here?" he said.

"You lash out at me because you're angry about the article!" I said as he went into the bathroom.

I imagined grabbing my clothing, throwing it in a suitcase, and storming out. This seemed so real to me that when Stash came out of the shower, wrapped in a towel, arms extended toward me, I was surprised.

He clutched me like an orangutan. "Let's be friends," he said.

"Don't pick on me every second of my existence," I said into his ear. "It makes me feel like I'm a fly and you're pulling off my wings."

"Yeah?" Stash said. "Don't give me that wings-being-picked-off business."

I knew he was afraid of letting me get too sure of myself: this was as much of an apology as I was going to get. He said we could go to the party. Quickly I slurped down a yogurt before we went out. It tasted exactly like cold cream. I was only interested in helping the stomach not to complain, with its little lump of cold cream balanced neatly in the center. At these dinners, food wasn't served until eleven o'clock, or even eleven-thirty.

Even though the dinner was scheduled for ten, we didn't get there until ten-thirty, and most of the other people were just arriving. At the door, we had to sign a release, stating that if our pictures were taken they could be used in publicity.

The restaurant was quite a pretty place. Every table had a mammoth floral display, like complete trees, in the center, and there were little nameplates and gifts at each place. My nameplate said GUEST OF MR. STOSZ—I was seated next to the nameplate of STASH STOSZ—and my gift was apparently selected by someone who must have known my situation as well as my vocation: it was a large fake diamond engagement and wedding ring set. Stash got a set of tattoos, water soluble, and a toy motorcycle—Stash had a motorcycle himself—which, when he wound it up, zipped across the table and fell over. Other artists received Etch-a-Sketch kits, voodoo dolls, exploding cigars, wind-up jack-in-the-boxes in the shape of clam shells which contained Botticelli's Venus leaping out to music, and their signatures made into rubber stamps.

The food was really delicious: slices of raw meat, thin as paper; angel-hair pasta speckled with shreds of crab meat and roasted peppers; little fried fish hot and curling on platters, with their teensy eyes still intact. In one corner of the room a man played the accordion—various haunting tunes—possibly as a special treat in honor of the occasion. Or maybe he was there all the time. For an appetizer I had a plate of slightly sandy mussels in a sauce of vermouth and garlic. Stash had smoked mozzarella with basil and tomatoes. We had agreed to share. But frankly, I couldn't enjoy it as much as I would have liked. For one thing, by eleven-thirty at night my appetite was gone and I was ready to go to sleep, and for another, I only liked to eat alone with Stash. I wanted to relish my food without having to worry about why I wasn't being included in the conversation or whether I was getting food on my chin. This was my sad but minor handicap, not something that revealed a character trait: sometimes food or grease would get on my chin and I couldn't feel it. I had had a minor operation when I was fifteen and the sensation never returned. It wasn't the most glamorous of handicaps to have, but it was mine. The one handicap that really appealed to me as tragic and romantic was the one that Laura had, Laura of *The Glass Menagerie*— she was lame. There aren't too many lame people around these days, nowadays they just limp.

I was seated next to a girl wearing a rubber dress; it looked like a coat of latex paint. The sign in front of her plate said SAMANTHA BINGHAMTON, and every two seconds one of the photographers would come and snap her picture. She had wild black hair (maybe a wig) and a long skinny neck, which was either very elegant or goosey—I couldn't decide. So much for my one fancy evening outfit of sequined top and black velvet skirt—it was nothing compared to what Rubbermaid had on. I could have strangled her. The people across from me pretended I didn't exist. While twirling pasta with my fork, I quizzed Samantha on her life story. She had known her husband—he was seated on her other side—since second grade. He came from a fabulously wealthy family and now had one of the hottest galleries in the world. She used to be a top-notch agent—she was best friends with Dustin Hoffman and John Huston, and one of her clients was in the movie that swept the Academy Awards last year. But even though she was only twenty-eight years old and close to the height of her profession, she decided she wasn't happy. Since her husband could support her, and she didn't really need to work, she quit two weeks ago to become a rock star. This was what she really wanted to do. So far she hadn't landed a manager, but it seemed likely that this would happen soon.

Maybe I had had a little too much champagne: it certainly was delicious, with large, real, lumps of raspberries stuck in the bottom of every glass. "Isn't it strange," I said, "to be trying to land an agent and a record contract when this is what you used to do for other people?"

"No."

Her best friend, in a feathered tutu, was seated across from us, and when the tutu girl got up to go to the restroom I asked Samantha what her friend did. "She goes out with Fritz," Samantha said. Fritz was a sculptor, famous for his work in lemons and mirrors. "She's only eighteen and a real witch." So much for best friends, I thought.

In the restroom we applied various kinds of makeup from Samantha's handbag. "That guy next to you," she said as she powdered her nose, "you're with him, right?"

"We live together," I said. "That's Stash."

"That's what I was going to ask you," she said. "He's Stash Stosz, right? Who just got a terrible review?"

"Yeah," I said.

She took a joint out of her bag.

"Is he rich?" she said, lighting the joint and handing it to me.

"No," I said.

"Are you?"

"No."

"Well, why would you go out with him?" she said.

"I—" I said. I was stunned.

"Come out with us after the dinner," she said. "My husband has a brother who'd love to meet you—we'll go with Fritz to the club."

I smoked some of the joint with her. Maybe she had had too much to drink, too.

Back at the table Stash was having an active argument with a racehorse painter, a man with a goatee and rabbit teeth. "What you're doing, that's not art," the horse painter was saying. He was wearing a cowboy hat of soft and furry felt.

"I've seen your work," I said to him. "My mother bought some paper plates one time, for a cookout, and your paintings were on them."

Everyone had changed places. The photographer was walking around taking candid pictures. One artist, with his long white arms curled around the back of the chair next to him, and his round, bloblike head, resembled an octopus. Another made strange movements with his mouth like a kissing gourami. One artist was so famous he refused to sit with the rest of us: he had his own private table on the balcony, where he was seated with a famous French movie actress. The one sitting across from me was quite drunk; he had a red face and a superior attitude. While he was talking to someone he picked up a full ashtray in front of him and emptied it under the table.

When the dinner was over, one of the artists picked up a plate of cake (a special kind of Venetian cake known as a "pick-me-up") and dumped it on the head of a less-famous artist. The less-famous artist didn't even blink, just called for the photographer to come over.

Stash got stuck talking to someone at the coat-check room and I went outside. Samantha rolled down the window of a limousine and leaned out. "Eleanor, come here," she said. "I want you to meet my brother-in-law, Mitch."

I squinted in the window: some guy with red hair and a beard was sitting next to Samantha; he had the wild eyes of a trotter at a fifth-rate racetrack, hopped up on who knew what. "Nice to meet you, Mitch," I said. He handed me a glass of champagne.

"Where are you going now, Eleanor?" Samantha said.

"Downtown."

"Come on, get in with us," she said. "We'll take you."

I thought for a second: I should wait for Stash, go home with him, walk the dog, and watch TV. I'd try to tell him about why all these people drove me crazy. How I was tired of everyone being wrapped up in themselves. But I knew all he would say was that I had had too much to drink. Or I could open the car door, jump in, and whizz off someplace. Even if I changed my mind, Stash would probably forgive me, eventually.

"Stash is still inside," I said. "I'm waiting for him. I don't want to keep you, I'll call you next week. 'Bye, Mitch." Samantha shrugged and the window rolled back up. I was left standing on the curb with a glass of champagne in my hand.

By the time we got home I was pretty depressed. While I brushed my teeth and cleaned my contact lenses, I thought about Samantha, in her rubber dress. Let's face it, she wasn't prettier than me, or more intelligent, and what did she do? Just one out of the millions who want to be rock stars. So how come she kept getting her picture taken and all the men were making a fuss over her and asking if they could snap her latex wear? Because (a) she had an important husband who ran a big gallery and (b) she probably hung out with these people every night, taking drugs—cocaine or whatever—whereas it was a rare thing for me just to smoke a joint. On the other hand, maybe she really had a better personality than me, and really was more attractive physically and psychically, and I was just deluding myself.

I realized that I really did want to be where I was—with Stash, in this hovel. I ran through all the parts of my life, trying to figure out which thing in particular wasn't working for me. I supposed I could get a nose job and take one of those courses that teaches chutzpa. (I had read the leaflet on it in the supermarket.) But would this make me a more spiritual person? I doubted it. It was hard for me to keep up with all the various aspects of reality. Finally I figured it out: I wanted a baby.

Obviously, based on this evening and others like it, I wasn't meant for any glamorous night life or fast lane, but I would be a good mother.

I pictured myself with a giant Buddha baby with a fat belly, a shock of blond hair, and a surprised expression. I would give it baths in a basin and wheel it around the block in a little go-cart, speaking to the other mothers. Stash could take it to openings strapped on his back. I had often seen men doing this in art galleries and nightclubs. Finally, when it grew up, it could tell me how wonderful I was. Stash and I would finally be bonded and we could have a joint checking account and I wouldn't have to be so worried about finances. These weren't such great reasons, but what counted was the unconscious level—the feeling that something was missing from my life, and I had finally guessed what it was.

I went out into the bedroom—anyway, the end of our apartment where the bed was. "Listen, Stash," I said. "I've been thinking. You're middle-aged, and I'm not so young, either. It would be a good time to have a baby. We've been kidding about it for a while, but let's be serious." Looking at him, I knew our baby would be cute, though if it inherited Stash's chest hairs and my head hairs it would practically be a gorilla. There wouldn't be one hairless inch.

"What are you, drunk?" Stash said. He was lying on the bed, watching a Frankenstein movie on TV, Andrew alongside him. "You can't bring a baby into this world. At least not in the city. Didn't you hear the news before?"

"I was brushing my teeth."

"This forty-nine-year-old widow was walking down the street and all of a sudden a forty-ton crane toppled over and hit her. She was pinned under it for more than six hours, partially crushed, just like that. That's why you can't have children in New York." Stash looked as if he was ready to kill me. It was hard for him to believe that a person could be so stupid. I knew I irritated Stash in the same way that my brother used to irritate me when I was kid. Roland's foot tapping used to send me into a rage, I would start to scream at him when he wasn't even aware of what he was doing. Now I knew what it was like to be the source of irritation, without being irritated in return: I looked at Stash with the same puzzled, hurt expression that my brother had when I lashed out at him for no good reason.

"I'm taking the dog out," I said. "Come on, Andrew." Andrew shot up and plunged up and down at my feet. Every time he went out he acted as if he had been locked up in a kennel for a year. His whip tail slashed my legs. Unfortunately, this was the only time he ever paid any attention to me, even though I had been with him since he was only a year and a half old. He was Stash's dog. I had worked hard to make him love me. He was wearing a collar I had designed just for him—plastic dinosaurs, turtles, and square, varicolored rhinestones which I had attached to the leather with little grommets. I had done all kinds of things for Andrew. I decorated him, sometimes with baseball caps, sometimes with slogan sweatshirts I cut down from Woolworth's boys' department, and once I painted additional spots on him with food coloring. Well, Andrew wasn't the brightest of dogs, but he did have a sense of humor and a certain dappled elegance.

It was late at night, and I didn't bother to put him on the leash. He sniffed the stunted trees and the metal signposts with the utmost of delicacy, as if he were rooting for truffles. A fishy wind blew off the Hudson. Stash was probably feeling guilty and would be nice to me. Probably I had made the right choice. If I had gone off with Samantha and taken drugs I would have shifted into higher gear, but how long could I keep that up?

"Get over here, Andrew," I said. I wanted to go upstairs. "Hurry up." Of course he wouldn't move. He was deaf when he wanted to be. I gritted my teeth, annoyed. He went on calmly rooting as if I wasn't even there. The rotten animal obeyed Stash, but not me.

Finally he followed. The elevator was broken and we had to walk up seven flights. I'm not in such great shape. Believe me, I'd like to be one of those women with all the muscles, but frankly I don't like the idea of doing all that work. Once I took an aerobics class—I thought it would give me more energy—but every day I had to come home after class and sleep for a couple of hours.

When we made it back to the apartment Stash was standing near the window with a funny look on his face. "You wouldn't believe what just happened," he said.

"What?" I said.

"A transvestite and a john came over to the bushes under the window. Well, I don't want transvestites and tricks in our courtyard. So I went to the sink and took the spaghetti pot and dumped the water in it onto them. A direct hit!"

I started to laugh, involuntarily, but I stopped. "Stash," I said.

"Well, I didn't know that there were things in the pot," Stash said. "I really was mad and I just dumped the whole soapy contents out and I didn't realize there were some spoons and a bowl in it."

"My Russel Wright dish!" I said. "Stash, how could you do such a thing?"

"What do you mean?" he said. "You were out there with Andrew. Something could have happened to you. I wanted them to get the idea they can't come around here."

"What happened when the water hit them?" I said.

"They just walked away, shaking their heads."

"You could have killed someone," I said. I felt very badly for the transvestite: she was just trying to get along in the world and had ended up covered with soapy, greasy water, spaghetti water, and would probably be freezing cold for the rest of the night.

"The bowl hit the trees, it didn't hit her," Stash said.

"It's not your job to throw water on people," I said. "You should either have yelled something to get them away, or called the guard."

"I did feel sort of demonically possessed when I did it," Stash admitted. "What do you want? I'm only a mindless Neanderthal." I could tell he would have liked to have undone it as soon as the water was halfway down, but it was too late, as had been demonstrated in another age by Galileo, who threw some stuff off the Leaning Tower of Pisa.

I suddenly wished I could go back to school and take physics again; I knew this time I would understand it. The notion of random particles, random events, didn't seem at all difficult to comprehend. The whole business was like understanding traffic patterns, with unplanned crackups and hit-and-run accidents. Somewhere I read that increasing the rate of collisions between positrons and electrons will result in interesting "events" that physicists can study. Quarks, quirks, leptons, protrons, valance electrons, tracers, kryptons, isotropes—who knew what powerful forces were at work? I saw how emotions caused objects to go whizzing about. If I had gotten into the limousine earlier that evening I'd be in the same mess, only in a different neighborhood; at least in this place I had love, a feeling that came at a person like a Dodgem car in an amusement park, where the sign says PROCEED AT OWN RISK.

lunch
involuntary

For many years I have eaten the same thing on certain days of the week: Monday, Salisbury steak, mashed potato, roll, apple cup; Tuesday, sausage in tomato sauce, buttered corn, mixed fruit cup; Wednesday, island sandwich (ham, cheese with pineapple), salad with French dressing, crackers, Wonder bar; Thursday, sloppy joe bunwich, vegetable sticks, onion rings, apricots; Friday, cheese pizza, buttered mixed vegetables, chocolate pudding with topping.

This completed the weekday menu.

For many years I had eaten the same thing on certain days of the week: Monday, Salisbury steak, mashed potato, roll, apple cup; Tuesday, sausage in tomato sauce, buttered corn, mixed fruit cup; Wednesday, island sandwich (bun, mixed fruit cup, meatballs), zucchini squash, nuts and bolts; Thursday, collard greens, Tater Tots, peas and carrots; Friday, corn niblets, fishwich and cheese on a seeded roll, chocolate pudding with topping.

This completed the weekday menu.

The food was dished out by the dietitian on a green plastic tray, and at the end of the line there were forks, knives, spoons of two different sizes, and napkins in a black-and-silver metal container. There were three tall canisters like sump pumps, and each day the solutions in these dispensers varied: ketchup, French dressing, mustard, and syrup were only a few of the different things available to put on the food.

I did not like to interrupt my enjoyment of the meal by speaking to anyone, so I sat alone in one corner of the dining hall. In any event, it was obvious to me that I was superior to the others—I do not mean this in any derogatory sense, only that I was better than they—and would not have had much to say to them, grim and noisy in their grease-covered coats.

Still, I could not help but be filled with happiness as I ate my meal. How tactful I felt toward everyone! How kind! And they to me, for they left me quite alone as I dined. The mashed potatoes so creamy, bland, and gently refreshing. How pale and thin was the metal fork, and how fine the roll, with a tender brown crust and white interior, as if a bird had died in my hand. The carrots like young girls smiled on my plate, the macaroni and cheese, pure, nearly inedible, swam down my throat like living goldfish, and the chocolate pudding, dense, sooty, tasting of powdery grit. Around me the forks and knives of the others clattered like the most glorious of harpsichords.

No seconds were allowed, but generally, if I waited until the very end of the lunch hour, I could go back and get another roll with a pat of margarine, or even, on occasion, another portion of dessert. This was only because the dietitian and the cashier knew me and did not mistrust me in any way. The cashier did not take money but different colored tickets: I myself always had the green tickets, daily I gave her two. The meals lasted two hours: from eleven forty-five to quarter of one every day.

After two and a half years I began to notice that my portions were dissimilar to the portions received by the others. At first, I assumed this was simply due to sleight of hand on the part of the dietitian: after all, I remembered how on several occasions I had gotten more than one and a half times the normal amount of batter-fried fish and cheese on a bun, because after all fish was by its very nature not a mathematically exact form. I had not complained on those occasions when I received too much, but now, getting less, I began to feel offended.

After all, everything was weighed and cut into equal portions beforehand—the meat always weighed two and a half ounces, the mashed potatoes were dished out by ice-cream scoop, the pineapple tidbits were measured into tiny paper cups. Therefore, though the first few times I received smaller portions it might have been an accident, the deviation from the norm could not have been so frequent *without being done on purpose*.

At first it was just by a little bit that my portions were cut, and while others on line in front of me got a whole cup of Jell-O with fruit cocktail, I noticed that I received only half a cup. After several weeks, my rationing grew even shorter: one ounce of meat, two or three carrot sticks instead of five, two peas, and then at last only one pea and nothing else, one pea alone on my cafeteria tray.

Why? What had I done to deserve this? It was unjust, unjust, and in the cafeteria dining hall I saw the faces of the others sneering half-wittedly at me, as if to say, now you have gotten your comeuppance.

As if this wasn't enough, my tray was very dirty. The dietitian had organized the trays so that when I came in, the tray on the top was very dirty, and to pause on line for even a second, even for the second that it took to get a different tray, would mean being trampled by those behind me on line. I had seen it happen, I had seen elderly and infirm hurt and kicked for their slowness on line.

My nails were bitten to the quick. There was no peace of mind to be found in eating one pea for lunch.

The dietitian and the cashier acted as if they did not know me. They looked through me as if I did not exist. I had always felt such a closeness to them, especially the dietitian, who more than anyone had grace and an animal surety.

At the end, when I tried to give the cashier my tickets, she would not accept them. I hestitated to speak out loud, knowing how the others would turn to leer at me, they who had once been so tactful though crude, but I could not control myself. "But why?" I said. "Why?" She did not answer, and I realized I was the only one using the green tickets. The green tickets were no longer being accepted. But this at least was an explanation, something I could live with.

Slowly I took my tray to the disposing area, I put it on the rack, the spoon I placed in the silverware container, I did not know what else to do. . . .

in and out of the cat bag

The next day was Saturday. Or maybe Sunday. I set out for a walk, thinking this would clear my head enough to decide what to say to the judge when I went to court to protest my eviction notice. I had less than a week left before I was officially supposed to be out of my place.

While I was worrying about this, and thinking how unfair it was that I, Marley Mantello, sensitive artist, should get kicked out of such a crummy place, I almost tripped over Sherman.

Old Sherman was my best friend; or at least one of them. He was a sculptor, working in colored resins that resembled flatulent balloons. I was startled to find him so far uptown, knowing how he usually refused to travel above Fourteenth Street, claiming it led to mental decay. Also he was on crutches, with a plaster cast up to his left hip. "Sherman!" I said. "What are you doing here? And what the hell did you do to yourself?"

I was pleased to see him: I thought maybe he could help me figure out what to say in court. But he looked most terrible. He had the face of a woodland tuber, something unexpected and white springing up from the dense humus of the street. Well, this had always been true of Sherman to a degree. In demeanor he was funguslike, agreeable and yielding, and always had an innocuous comment at hand. To run into him was exactly like finding a mushroom, cause for mirth, though there was a darker side to this. Often I longed to give him a bruising poke, not out of malevolence, but from curiosity, the desire to kick at something helpless and spongy. But then, I had been the sort of child who did like to kick mushrooms. After a rain I would walk in the woods and collect mushrooms of every hue —creamy purple, frilly and voluptuous yellow ones, stout gray toadstools. And then, my mound before me—grim amanita, red porphyry, quivering polyps—I would smash and injure the palpable flesh.

"I'm afraid I don't feel like speaking to you, Marley," Sherman said, and kept walking.

"Don't feel like speaking to me?" I said, perplexed. "To me, or just in general?" For the latter was something I would have been able to understand, but not the former.

"To you," Sherman said. "For one thing, if you want to know, I've been thinking."

"Yes?" I said. "That must be nice for you." I was annoyed with his tone and lack of interest in my predicament, even though he didn't know anything about my upcoming eviction. Some friend he was! But I kept walking alongside him, as he bumbled along on crutches.

"I suppose I owe it to you to tell you why I don't consider us friends anymore. I'll tell you, just to help you from repeating this with someone else in the future."

"Fine, fine," I said. "Go ahead. Care for a cigarillo?" And I got one of my special little Tuscano cigars out of my pocket. But Sherman shook his head. "So," I said, "before you tell me, let's make small talk. How's Lacey?" Lacey was old Sherman's girlfriend; they lived together, and were scheduled to get married.

"We split up," Sherman said.

"Split up!" I said. "Say not so! But you two were all lovey-dovey, when last we spoke."

"Yes, well, we don't live together anymore. And if you want to know, I think you're pretty much responsible for what happened between Lacey and myself. When I didn't sell anything from my show, she moved out."

"I don't understand what I have to do with it," I said. It was

true I had always found Lacey attractive, with her blond cer-
tainty, and Lady of the Lake pallor. All I could think was that
perhaps she had a crush on me, and had left Sherman thinking
that I might date her.

"Frankly, Marley," Sherman said, "your way of thinking
isn't much to my taste. And it's cost me."

"Cost you?" I struggled to slow down to his pace; already I
was half a block in front of him and had to stop just to hear
what he was saying.

"Yeah, cost me," he said. "Your way of thinking is always
to talk about success as if there's nothing else, as if success in
the outside world is the one thing to aim for, and nothing else
matters except making big bucks."

"I don't think that's the case, Sherman," I said, but he
refused to listen.

"Well, when I was living with Lacey maybe it wouldn't have
mattered if you just talked to me. But no. You always went on
when Lacey was there, and you always had to mention how the
Cooper Hewitt Museum was thinking of putting three of your
religious paintings in their new show, and how you spent the
weekend with a rich collector. While meanwhile my career
wasn't going anywhere at all. So your words had their effect;
hell, I can see that now. After a while, Lacey got fed up with
living with me. She compared me to you, and said that I would
never make anything much of myself and that she had no
interest in supporting a starving artist for her entire life!"

My first thought was to ask him if he was drunk, and to tell
him he was nuts, but something stopped me. It was so painful
to see Sherman wandering the streets like this, reeking of
alcohol and plastered into a cast. An outcast. By comparison
things were going remarkably well for me; my career was at
last beginning to take off, and I had a few interested collectors
who faithfully bought my work. "Well, Sherman," I said, "I
just can't agree with you. I can't see that I had much to do
with your breakup with Lacey. Hundreds of couples break up
every day, and not all of them hold me responsible."

Yet I did have to stop and think about what Sherman had said. Well, obviously I couldn't have been the cause of the breakup of their relationship, but was it possible I had had something to do with it? I did know that on some evenings, while Sherman was at home painting, I used to drop by the delicatessen where Lacey worked, and maybe I had said a couple of things to her alone that I wouldn't have said in front of Sherman—things that weren't too nice, not in actual words, maybe, but in attitude. Maybe I made it clear that I didn't think Sherman's work was so great.

Okay, I was the kind of guy who had to be superior to everyone all the time, whenever I could. In some ways I was very vain, but everyone knew this about me, and it was an endearing part of me that my true friends were able to accept. Did this mean I wasn't really a saint?

My mother would have said that a real saint is not a perfect person, that he would be a god if he was. A real saint was just an ordinary person, irritable, hard to live with, and then almost accidentally doing a saintly deed now and then. But I, Marley Mantello, had always thought of myself as coming pretty damn close to saintliness. And now, seeing Sherman like this, miserable and blaming me, I had to stop and reevaluate: maybe I wasn't so noble as I thought.

I shrugged. "So what happened to your leg?" I said. "It must have been a terrible blow to your ego."

"I walked into a bus while drunk," he said. "The bus hit me sideways, my leg is broken in three places. See you around, Marley." And he walked off, slowly, on crutches.

I thought that this was the end of the matter and walked off morosely in thought: for some reason I hated to end a friendship. Only a few minutes later, while standing waiting for a red light to change so I could cross the street, I felt a tug on my shoulder. "Ah, listen, Marley," Sherman said, with a forced grin, "I know you think I'm a jerk. Anyway, I've got a terrible hangover. I'm being an asshole, I know."

"Yes," I said.

"Listen, come by later tonight for a few drinks."

What was all this about? "I don't know," I said. "I don't know if I'll feel like coming over to your place."

"I'd meet you somewhere, but with these crutches it takes me too long. I've lost all the hair under my arms because of them."

"Well, come over to my place," I said. "It's the last week I'll be there, I'm being evicted."

"Oh, I didn't know," Sherman said. "Well, sure, that'll be great. There was something I wanted to ask you. See, I've been in touch with Lacey since we split up, and I sort of told her that I might be able to come up with a job for her. She lost her job at the deli, and I mentioned that you were probably going to hire someone as an assistant to help you get ready for your next show."

"I don't know," I said, taken aback. "What happened? How did she lose her job?"

"Ah, this guy came into the deli and asked if they sold half a grapefruit. Lacey told the guy they didn't sell grapefruit halves, only whole ones. But this guy was very persistent and didn't believe her, and insisted she go and ask the manager. So she went into the back room, not realizing the customer was following her. And she yelled 'Hey, Eddie, some asshole out there wants to buy half a grapefruit.' And then suddenly she realized that the customer was standing right next to her, and she said, 'And this gentleman here would like the other half.' Anyway, I think they were planning to fire her long before that: she used to carry home half the food in the store with her every night."

"Mmm," I said. "Tell her I'll let her know; yeah, I'd love to have an assistant, but I don't know if I'm going to have enough money."

And we parted, this time on good terms. I felt a bit better—my feelings had been hurt, but I wasn't so bad as all that. I thought, All right, Sherman, so you're not a genius (for this is what I felt was the true source of his rage against me, that I was a genius and he was not). So you're not a genius, but what do you care? Life can still be good to you. Break down and get a teaching job, you'll paint a little when you get the chance, on weekends and so forth, and life will be pleasant enough. There are a million painters in this world, how many of them are really going to be any good?

But I was sorry for thinking Sherman was not any good—I remembered all the fun we had had together, such as how we would go to a restaurant, when we had some money, and play this little game we had invented. We would decide in advance that any time the waitress said a certain word, such as "get" we would fall off our chairs. So that when she said, "What can I get you?" off our chairs we would flop. And when she came back, asking "Can I get you anything else?" we would collapse again.

It was a long time since we had played such games; thinking about this made my eyebrows twitch. They felt so brittle I thought they were possibly going to drop off. It was a peculiar sensation, and I wondered if I didn't have some disease of the skin or hair follicles. If I went bald and lost my eyebrows it would be terrible.

I arrived home some hours later. I was exhausted, but like Dickens I have always loved to walk and some afternoons would walk a good ten miles. My apartment, the sublet from which I was being evicted, looked just as terrible as when I had gone out earlier—worse, even, for there was a foul reek of something fecund and feline, like the stench of old lion spore upon the veldt.

Turning on the lights I noticed a curled black pile on top of the messy bedclothes, and on closer inspection I realized some animal had performed its ablutions right in the middle of the bed: animal, human, or supernatural.

A kind of omen, perhaps—but who would be so deranged as to inform me in such blatant fashion that they thought I was full of shit? The being had climbed on top of my desk and scattered papers everywhere. A pool of bright yellow piss was not even dried. Was I to take this as coming from some being from another world? There was no sign of a real entity.

"Jesus Christ," I said. I couldn't even deal with it; without looking around any further to examine the desecration that had taken place in my absence, I went into the bathroom. But before I even flicked on the light, I noticed two toffee-colored eyes glaring near the toilet. Rather than look further, I clasped my hands over my eyes, and strangely they were freezing and clammy cold.

Then the creature let out a yowl. It must have been some kind of a cat—well, if it was a cat sent from Satan, then probably it would disappear under fluorescent lights. So I turned on the switch, with my eyes still covered.

Then I looked. It was a cat, a malevolent animal weighing at least twenty-five pounds, with a tough, stumpy muzzle and ears built low and small like a fighter. It was standing on the edge of the toilet seat. What it was doing there was hard to fathom: perhaps drinking from the joyous pot, perhaps ready to take a dive into the sewers. I took a step forward and the damn thing hissed at me—a cat that was part-snake, with a set of fangs inside its mouth that were quite unnecessary. "I have no desire to tangle with you," I said.

Meanwhile, I was growing very nervous unto myself. I had never seen such a malicious animal. Maybe it had rabies. It examined me as if I were some kind of intruder. It balanced on three legs, while it raised the fourth, clawed and vicious, in my direction. "Indeed, I suspect you are from the Other World," I told it. "But whether that Other World is sacred or profane I wish you would clue me in." For the cat has always been a sign of the devil, at the same time an animal worshiped by the ancient Egyptians.

But the cat did not respond. While talking to it, I backed out of the bathroom and sat down on the broken chair in the kitchen, before I remembered it was broken. I got tangled up in the cane seating and sprang to my feet, thinking maybe there were two cats now and I had sat on the second.

And then had to defibrillate my sweater threads from the chair caning.

How had the damned animal gotten into my place? Possibly through the broken window in the bathroom, above the fire escape. This was *my* territory it had invaded, bringing with it no doubt fleas and disease, perhaps even bubonic plague. Was I to be put out of my place even before my eviction notice was up by this vituperative alley cat?

I decided to ignore the problem. It occurred to me I might read for a little while, huddled under the blankets. The place was freezing cold: murder was in my thoughts, for I had murderous intentions toward the landlord, Vardig, who never bothered to heat the building and did such a poor job at repairing broken windows that a stinking cat could slink in. This was the reason I hadn't paid my rent in so many months, but because of this the old goat Vardig had managed to present me with an eviction notification.

Well, I have always had that skill of being able to escape my immediate surroundings by diving into a book; but tonight the book I was reading didn't hold my full interest. Which was odd, because I was normally totally absorbed by any book about insects. I was in the middle of a chapter about how wood ants feed their grubs. In return for food the grubs exude a glandular fluid. This stuff is pleasurable beyond belief to the workers who feed them. It was all part of a mutual exchange system. Why couldn't I accomplish the same thing with Ginger, the art dealer who handled my painting sales? Wherein Ginger, the grub, would get food, and I, the worker, would get pleasure. But all that seemed to be happening in our relationship was that I was working and she was getting the pleasure of handling my paintings.

While I was thinking about this Sherman came knocking at the door, carrying a bottle of Stolichnaya. "Listen," I said. "I've been reading this book."

Sherman leaned his crutches against the wall and cleared a space on the couch to sit down. "Oh, my underarms," he said, rubbing his pits.

"These grubs exude a fluid so important to the workers that the grubs are beyond measure in value to them."

"What grubs?"

"Ants," I said. "If there's a battle, or if the colony is attacked, the baby grubs are the first thing to be saved. This ensures the future of the colony."

"I can't walk anymore, my arms are so sore. How about getting us a couple of glasses for the vodka?"

I went over to the sink and tried to find a couple of coffee cups that weren't broken. "At first I was thinking how the worker ants are like the artists, and the art dealers are like the grubs. But on second thought, artists are the highest symbols of man's civilization, right?"

"Oh, sure," Sherman said bitterly.

"So they should be the first to be saved, for example, in the case of a nuclear disaster. But that's not how it would happen. In this country the first ones to be saved would be the politicians and the corporate executives, and lastly the lunatics who have been building shelters."

"I don't know what you're talking about," Sherman said, opening the bottle and pouring the vodka into the two cups.

"Well, what I'm saying is, this would be the equivalent of the worker ants struggling to save their own hides, without remorse or thought for the future."

"Do ants have hides?" Sherman said. "Jesus, Marley, what smells in here? Do you have a cat or something?" He took a swallow of his vodka, and limped over to his crutches. "Where's the light in your bathroom?" he said.

"Wait, don't go in there!" I said. But it was already too late: I heard the proud war chortle of the cat, and a yowl out of Sherman; I rushed into the bathroom to find the cat had leapt off the back of the toilet and had thrown itself at Sherman's neck.

"What the hell hit me?" Sherman said. I grabbed him from behind and pulled him out of the bathroom; his crutches fell to the floor. The cat had managed to sink its claws into the side of Sherman's neck, pointillistic dots of blood were now appearing. "There's some kind of demon in there!" he said.

"I tried to tell you," I said. We stood at the doorway of the bathroom, I switched on the hall light. The cat was now standing on the edge of the bathtub. That animal was a fighter, heavy in the testicles, torn up in the ears and a big scab across its nose, which made me wary. He gave Sherman and me a superior gangster glance, proud and condescending. Resembling as he did Baby Face Nelson, full of gism and loathing.

"Let's go finish our drinks," I said.

"Wait a minute," Sherman said. "My crutches are in there, I can't go anywhere without them."

"Well, I'm not going in there to get them," I said. I slung Sherman's arm around my neck and helped him back to the couch. Meanwhile we guzzled two cups of vodka in rapid succession, attempting to recover from the shock.

"Is that your cat, Marley?" Sherman said. "It's insane."

"No, it isn't my cat," I said. "I don't know how the fuck it got in here." Then a thought occurred to me: I went and opened the door to the hallway. Then I went back to the bathroom. "Here, kitty," I said. "The door's open now." I avoided its eyes while I bent over, trying to reach Sherman's crutches without going into the room. The animal turned around and sprayed some distasteful fluid right at me. It had good aim, and got me all over my arm and chest. Then it let out another war cry. "Keep the crutches," I said. I went into the living room.

"God, Marley, this place is freezing," Sherman said, pulling an old shawl over himself that was covering a hole in the couch.

"Have some more vodka," I said. "This place has been freezing cold for months, that's why I stopped paying the rent. And now that son of a bitch is evicting me."

"Well, did you try talking to him?" Sherman said.

"I tried," I said. "But when I call him he has this goddamn answering machine and never returns my calls."

"Where does he live?" Sherman said.

"Downstairs."

"Go see him!" Sherman said. "Go see him and tell him you're dying in here, and there's a monster in the bathroom, and you're going to sue the pants off him!"

This was something that had not previously occurred to me. Swallowing another glass of vodka, I stood up and went out to tell that rotten bastard just what I thought of him.

Old Vardig lived down in the basement. I knocked on his door and had to wait five minutes or so. I could hear his crabbed shuffle as he grumbled to the door. "Who is it?" he said.

"Emergency!" I said. "Emergency! I'm from the ASPCA, open the door at once!"

This trick seemed to work; old Vardig opened the door and I slipped in. Jesus, his apartment was even worse, if such a thing was possible, than my own. It was furnished with a variety of old cast-out furniture, broken chairs, and a sort of rotten desk with one leg held up by books. No windows, and old scabbed walls, cracked from the water pipes, which were covered in a fine, furry mildew.

"What do you want, Mr. Mantello?" old Vardig said. He had the accent and persona of many nationalities—a big handlebar mustache encrusted with food, but whether this was an Armenian, Greek, Spanish, or Jewish mustache I couldn't say. The room had a rank smell; I saw he was in the middle of heating up some kind of food on a gas burner. And there, lying on the chair, was a big, sleeping cat—it might have been the brother or son to the monster that had taken over my bathroom upstairs. Old Vardig looked at me with soulful eyes. "I was just heating up a little soup for dinner," he said. "Care to join me?"

I thought to myself, Don't let the fact that he is pretending to be a kindly old geezer, all alone in the world, fool you. This guy is a rat, collecting rent and not bothering to heat the place at all.

He was a wheeler-dealer and conniver who owned half the

buildings for miles, though he acted as if he were poverty-stricken, obliged to live in the basement and feed himself off cans of ravioli and peanut butter. But his arms were in good shape, burly, and sticking out from his gray slobbery undershirt.

Oh, I was in a rage: his basement hovel was toasty warm. He had a couple of kerosene heaters going, no wonder he was so deranged, he probably suffered from some kind of carbon monoxide poisoning. Still, I knew he was very timid in his soul, I was going to force him to listen to me. He bustled at the stove, pretending I had come down for nothing more than a chat. "So, how goes it with you?" he said.

"Listen, Vardig," I said, "I have a sick friend upstairs. I'm trying to paint. Damm it, I need the heat. You haven't heated this fucking dump all winter."

Vardig shook his head; his brown eyes appeared luminous and filled with sensitivity. "Marley, I'm glad you told me this. You know, this is the first complaint I've had, it's a good thing that someone told me. It's a shame you didn't tell me earlier, but just stopped paying your rent—you know I had to evict you, and I already have a new tenant lined up. You'll be out of here by Monday, I believe that's right. Well, there's only one thing to be done, so the new tenant doesn't suffer. I'll get some more oil, have my son take a look at the burner when he returns . . ." And he showed me to the door, still jabbering.

I was speechless, I couldn't understand how I had just been bullied in such fashion. The man was a veritable magician, he had hypnotized me for the length of time it took to show me to the door. I banged on the door once or twice, but he didn't answer. Finally I went back upstairs.

"The man is insane," I said. "Is that cat still in the bathroom?"

"Yeah," Sherman said. "I didn't see it come out, anyway. How am I going to get my goddamn crutches?"

"Listen, you'll stay here until the cat leaves," I said. "I'll fix us some supper."

For dinner I made up a large bowl of pancake batter, omit-

ting any kind of baking powder or soda because I liked my
pancakes to be very thin, though for some reason they always
came out soggy—like large, flat, lumpy maggots. But this
didn't stop me from trying again. I cooked up the cakie-wakes
on the burner in a bunch of margarine. There wasn't enough
margarine to keep them from burning, so I added some Crisco.

While they were cooking I suggested to Sherman that I help
him around the loft so I could show him the paintings I was
working on. I took his arm and slung it around my shoulders
and dragged him to the back of the place. "I want you to get a
good look at the big canvas," I said.

"What is it?" Sherman said.

"It's going to be a painting of Ulysses getting home after his
twenty years of wandering," I said. "This part is where he's
being greeted by his filthy old dog. Right now it's just a rough
outline, but I plan to make the dog one of those beagles that
should have been put to sleep long ago, overweight, with not
much hair left anymore: not even able to get up on all four
legs, only the front, and with a soft, pleading look in his
rheumy eyes."

Sherman shrugged. I could tell he wasn't too impressed.
"Don't you think that Ulysses shit has been painted enough
times already?" he said.

"You don't understand," I said. "Ulysses is going to be this
kind of wild-eyed guy with a beard, wearing a denim jacket
and blue jeans—like Larry Rivers or Larry Poons. Late forties,
the kind of artist you see hanging around a bar, hasn't made it
and never will. Not exactly talentless, just gets enough attention from time to time to make him feel justified in leeching off
a wife who has to support him and the kids—a minor member
of a school."

"Which is how you think I'm going to turn out," Sherman
said.

I ignored this. "Anyway, Ulysses gets home and his wife is
living in a sort of Cape Cod beach house. Stuck between a
hamburger joint and an ice-cream stand: he's back after

twenty years to see if his wife has got a couple of dollars she could maybe loan him . . ."

Well, I was all excited just talking about it. But something in my words depressed Sherman. "You're not exactly in sync with the times, Marley," he said. "Maybe you know something I don't, but your work seems like a lot of stuff that was done in the late seventies."

I pushed his arm off my shoulders and let him try to balance on one leg. "Oh, look, I don't mean to turn on you," Sherman said. "It's just that whenever you start talking, I think about Lacey. I know I wasn't easy to get along with, I have this tendency to sulk and stuff, but I mean if it wasn't for all those ideas you put into her head I know we'd still be together. Can't you give her a job and tell her good things about me this time?"

All of a sudden I could smell something peculiar emanating from the stove. It had taken me awhile to notice it; that cat shit was an effective block to all other odors. "Aw, fuck, the pancakes!" I said, running to the stove and leaving Sherm in the middle of the room.

While I was juggling with the burning pancakes on the stove, the telephone rang. "Could you get that!" I yelled to Sherman.

"I can't!" Sherman said. "The doctor said I'm not allowed to put any pressure on this leg, it was a serious break." He bent over on his hands and knees and started to crawl to the couch.

I turned off the burner, but the pancakes were still sizzling away. I tried to pick up the frying pan, but the handle was burning hot to the touch. "Yeah, who is it?" I snarled into the receiver.

"Hello, Marley," a girl's voice said. "What are you doing? I'm right on the corner. I'm coming over. I thought I'd try to seduce you."

Before I could figure out who it was, she had hung up. But to me there was only one person it could have been: and that was Lacey.

spells

t's Daria's thirtieth birthday party. There are fifteen or twenty people in the room; I don't know most of them. Stash and I sit on the couch and watch her open her presents: the gift from us of a Godzilla lighter (flames shoot out of Godzilla's mouth); a record of Maria Callas singing *Norma*; a silk survival map of the Arctic Circle; a glue gun; a cassette tape of Teenage Jesus and the Jerks; a large black plastic object with a pink pyramid-shaped cover (possibly made by the Memphis Design Collective) which might be a breadbox or an ice bucket; a ten-pound bag of Eukanuba health food for dogs; a book about wrestling; and a Statue of Liberty hat—a spiky helmet of flexible foam. Daria puts it on.

I know that this assortment of gifts means something specific and symbolic about people my age who live in New York and are involved in the arts. A list of gifts received by a flapper in the Jazz Age could tell you things about the period, and this stuff has significance as well. But what the gifts actually represent, I have no idea.

Daria's dog, Textron, half-collie and half-greyhound, is in bad shape: he's very elderly, and ten years ago he was injured in some sort of accident. Now his back legs are partially paralyzed, and frequently give out from under him, some of the fur is missing from his tail, and he has a drooling problem. On the other hand, he's a happy animal; at the party, he lies on the rug wagging his tail and grinning. He has a long snout and tartar-stained teeth. Daria must have some positive character traits, since she's kept Textron alive and happy in the city; it can't be easy to walk him.

After Daria opens the presents, I make a point of finding a seat on the opposite side of the room from Stash: at parties, he likes me to be independent. As soon as I get up, Daria comes over and sits down next to Stash. He looks very animated; I watch him lean forward, almost touching Daria's legs with his own.

I start to plan his funeral. This is something I do rarely, when the mistral—or some kind of violent wind—blows in from Long Island. At times like this everyone in New York behaves bizarrely, as if a bunch of sparrows have pecked up a spill of rye bread infected with ergot fungus.

Of course, I'll be devastated when the phone call comes, informing me of his abrupt demise—taxi accident—yet eventually I'll make the adjustment. I think how upsetting it must have been for Lee Krasner to have been told of Jackson Pollack's death in a car crash (especially since he was with two women at the time). It will probably take me at least a year to get over the trauma, though of course during that time everyone will be extremely kind to me, inviting me out to dinner parties, et cetera, and I'll be very busy managing his estate.

Stash and Daria would make a cute couple. They are both so blond and beefy. Daria is attractive, in her tight-fitting dress with the holes cut out in the back and stomach. But her art is nothing to look at. I get up and walk around the room to examine its contents: a sort of candelabra thing made from bent, pink metal and ornamented with cherubs; a piece of wire twisted into a Picasso-head silhouette; a rococo door studded with plaster figures of satyrs made from molds, like some summer-camp crafts project. I'm mildly horrified. The stuff reminds me of the decoration to be found in some Italian restaurants in Brooklyn. Yet Daria obviously intends no irony. I can hear Stash—he's a painter, much more well-known than Daria—telling her how much he likes her work.

I go over to the table: there's a display of various cakes,

each with a little sign to indicate the type: Grand Marnier; a mocha butter cream; an apple tart; and a homemade coconut cake, shaped like a hat and fringed with white shreds and flecked with brown dots. It's wonderful to see so many cakes all lined up like that. Sometimes, for recreational purposes, I sit and read an old cookbook: it belonged to my grandmother, and is falling apart, but it's filled with fascinating recipes for cakes that require twelve eggs and a pound of butter and cups of nuts ground to a fine paste, and which have names like Miirb Teig, Lady Baltimore Cake, Lalla Rookh, and Lebkuchen.

Daria's mother, Georgette, comes up alongside. "This is the one I made," she says, pointing to the coconut cake.

"Then I must try it," I say. I eat a forkful. What a disappointment! The cake is illusory, I mean, it looks like a gooey, fluffy coconut cake, but some basic ingredient such as sugar or coconut has been left out. "Delicious," I say.

I go back over to Stash. "Stash, I think we should go pretty soon," I say. I notice his legs are now pressed up against Daria's.

He looks annoyed. "In a while, Eleanor," he says.

I'm worrying about whether I should sit down next to him and join in the conversation, when Georgette leads me off by the arm.

"I lent her my car for six months," she says, sitting me in an uncomfortable butterfly chair, "and when I came into the city to pick it up, I found that the whole right side was smashed in. Now what can you do with a girl like that?"

The record on the stereo is so loud I can barely hear what she's saying. "I don't know," I say.

"How do you like her dress?" Georgette says. "Stephen Sprouse. Believe it or not, it's made out of cotton, but the label says to dry clean only. I said, 'Daria, forget the dry cleaning, you'll throw it in the sink.' A three hundred dollar cotton dress."

"She looks good in it," I say. The chorus of the song on the record is a girl singing, "It's all my fault." Daria's mother's hips wiggle from side to side to the music. Her date, Mr. Arnazian, watches with admiration. He's a short man, seventyish, with thick glasses and suntanned skin. He hands me a glass of champagne and I sip it quickly. It's like drinking freeze-dried headache. Georgette starts dancing with Mr. Arnazian.

I see a girl I know; she has a heavy Iron Curtain accent and owns a hair salon, a trendy place with barbershop chairs and paintings that incorporate hair clippings of famous customers.

"I always meant to ask you—where are you from?" I say. "Originally."

"Where am I from?" she says. "Where am I from? What kind of question is that?"

Is my question in terrible taste, or is she crazy? It's hard for me to figure out how to be a social being: I'm alone all day with Andrew, our Dalmatian, either working on my jewelry designs, or at the East Village newspaper where I have a part-time job doing copy editing in a closet.

I do get to have one real conversation: Daria's boyfriend, Simon, talks to me about the tickets he has to a private screening of a remake of a zombie movie. Simon's cousin played a zombie in the original film. I tell Simon how, generally speaking, I'm not a moviegoer. It makes me uneasy to sit in a chair in the dark. I can't say this to Stash, because it would have made him mad to think of how many movies he has taken me to.

As Stash and I leave, Daria says, "Good night, Stash. I'll call you tomorrow about going to meet Victor."

"What was that about?" I say in the elevator.

"I'm going to try and help Daria get a gallery," Stash says. "Her stuff is good, don't you think?" I don't answer.

When we get down to the lobby I feel a little queasy. "Hold on a second," I say. I totter over to a vinyl loveseat. "Let me sit down." I figure I'm probably the first person in forty years to make use of the lobby. I see the source of Daria's influences: the lobby has Plexiglas chandeliers, and a grimy fountain without water.

"What's wrong?" Stash says.

"For a second there, I felt a little dizzy," I say. "Fine now. Let's go." I stand up. On the street I only manage about a block before the smell gets to me. There's an awful lot of garbage on the street; some bags have broken open, and chicken bones clutter the sidewalk. Around the edges of my vision things are starting to go dusty and curl up. "I'm not too good," I say. "Let's just lean against the car over there."

"How much champagne did you drink?"

"One glass," I say. I'm in a cold sweat. "I just can't continue," I tell him, ripping off my raincoat.

"Well, if you don't feel good, let's at least go home," he says.

"I can't move," I say, and sit down on the sidewalk. "If I stand up, I'm going to faint." I know Stash must be getting miffed: I stand up and stumble a few feet farther down the block. "I believe I'll just sit on these steps for a few minutes," I say. To my surprise I lie down across the bottom step. There are times when the body just takes control. Certainly its actions have nothing to do with me.

"What are you doing?" Stash says. "You can't stay there."

"I can't move," I say. "I can't walk. You're going to have to get a taxi."

Stash flags one down. He has to help me up and into the cab. "We'd like to go two blocks away," he tells the driver.

I lie straight across the back seat, utterly blitzed; the symptoms are faintness, weakness, perspiration, and general malaise. I once knew a girl who married three times and fainted at every single wedding. But I can tell my problem isn't psychological: although my body has intrigued against me, my mind is as clear as Waterford crystal.

Stash pays the driver and half carries me into the building. I have to lie on the floor while we wait for the elevator. "You better go see my doctor," Stash says. "If I hadn't been there with you, and you were alone, lying across the sidewalk, you could have been in big trouble. Are you going to go to my doctor tomorrow?"

I stretch out on the bed. It's as if I've been hypnotized, or fallen into a trance. "Uh," I say. "Something's wrong with me. I don't think I'm the same person anymore."

"Why don't you listen to me? That does it. We're going to go to the emergency room right now."

"No, no," I say. "I'll go to a doctor tomorrow. I will. I promise. I'm feeling much better now. But will you please walk the dog tonight? I don't think I can make it."

"How many pieces of cake did you eat anyway?"

"Three or four. But I'm telling you, they weren't big pieces."

Although I feel fine the next morning, I make an appointment at the clinic I belong to. Stash is displeased when I tell him I won't be able to see a doctor until next Tuesday. It's a real effort for him to keep his mouth shut, but I'm proud of him. The minor strains of living with another person are almost unbearable. That much I understand.

It's fun standing on line for the special screening of the zombie movie, up near Forty-second Street: I recognize lots of people from nightclubs. Daria and Simon are already waiting. Daria seems so perfect, in her Nehru jacket, unwrinkled, a dab of gold gloss on her lips, her large Op Art earrings dangling from clean ears. By comparison—though it's true I'm much skinnier—I feel sooty, a Dickensian waif with hunched shoulders and a greasy sweatshirt. Maybe I'm exaggerating. Of course, probably if we could have switched brains for a minute, I probably would find that she feels like a big galoot next to delicate me. Well, once again I am silently rambling on. I have to reel myself back in like a fish.

"You look very handsome," I tell Simon. He's wearing a tremendous suit jacket—it must be ten or fifteen sizes too large for him—made of some shiny blue material like wallpaper, with a raised velvet paisley design.

"Thanks," he says. "I'm in shock. I was arrested for littering this afternoon."

"Really?" I say. "What happened?"

"I was walking on Wall Street and I dropped my apple core in a flower bed. I swear, I don't know what's going on in this city—it's like some kind of voodoo. The next thing I knew, a person dressed like a meter maid was giving me a ticket. I tried to explain that an apple core was biodegradable, and would provide fertilizer for the flowers, but she wouldn't have any part of it."

As we go into the theater there's a mass scramble for seats, but we finally find four in a row. While we wait for the movie to begin, I nudge Stash. "Don't you think I'm different now?" I say.

Stash rolls his eyes.

"What?" Simon says, leaning forward in his seat next to Stash.

"Have you noticed my personality has changed?" I say. "I think I'm more outgoing."

"Yes, yes, I have noticed," Simon says. "I thought you seemed more outgoing and I really felt glad, because I like to talk to you, but there usually seems to be a wall separating you from . . ." His voice trails off.

"A wall separating me," I say, pleased with this image. I realize, however, that Simon is simply supplying me with what he thinks I want to hear: certainly I've never found it terribly difficult to talk to him.

I remember how once Simon came up to me on the street, at a traffic light, and said, "Hello, you old rattlesnake." I jumped about a foot in the air. Then he said, "What's wrong? Why do you look that way?"

I told him I wasn't used to being called an old rattlesnake. "I thought for a second you were the East Village rapist." He was terribly embarrassed: I guess I had made him feel stupid.

During the credits, while the audience is cheering, I have a real craving for mocha-chip ice cream, and whisper to Stash, "Could we go out for ice cream afterward? To Big Top's?"

"Maybe," Stash says.

But during the movie, while the zombies are devouring living human flesh, I start to feel guilty about our dietary habits. Since Stash only wanted cake for dinner, I just heated an old slice of mushroom pizza for myself. This type of meal probably should not be rewarded with dessert, but after the movie Stash suggests to Simon and Daria that we all go somewhere for ice cream. I would have liked some acknowledgment for coming up with the idea; I don't say anything, though.

"Big Top's is really one of my favorite places," I tell everyone when we are seated in a booth. There's something so reassuring about being in here. The boxes of stale chocolate-covered caramels arranged at the cash register behind us, the Muzak—nothing bad, aside from poor service and lousy food, could ever happen here.

Stash can't figure out what to order. "I don't know whether to get dinner or dessert," he says. "I took a nap before we went out, and when I woke up I had angel food cake."

"Mmm," Daria says. "I haven't had angel food cake in years. Who made it?"

"I did," I say.

"You make angel food cake?" Simon says. "Boy, that's really something. She's really something, Stash."

I keep my mouth shut and merely look modest: I don't admit that I made the cake from a mix. Honestly, it tastes better than the same thing made from scratch. A girlfriend of mine works in a restaurant where spectacular angel cake is served. I begged her to steal the recipe, and she confided that the cake came from a packaged mix. The one time I tried to make the cake from scratch, I used up twelve eggs and ended up with a new plastic product. Stash thought it was delicious: he likes rubbery foods in a big way.

"How can you not be able to figure out what to order when the selection here is so marvelous?" I say. "For example, the Wizard's Fried Clams have always been a favorite of mine."

"Really?" Stash says. "That's funny. That's what I was thinking of getting. But do you think it's safe?"

"What you're getting is something frozen and reconstituted," I say.

"Daria, would *you* order the Wizard's Fried Clams?" Stash says.

I'm irritated that he's asking her. Why would she know more about the safety of the clams than me?

At the last minute Stash decides to have BLT on white toast, and Simon says, "That sounds good. I think that's what I'll get, too."

"Very good," the waiter says. He's about our age, and resembles a stand-up comedian in a Catskills resort: reedy mustache, red bow tie, a tic in one eye.

"What kind of bread do you have?" Simon says.

"We have rye, wheat, and white."

"I'll have whole wheat," Simon says.

"Good choice, excellent choice!" the waiter says. He notices we're all looking at him—he's like some sorcerer's apprentice. "Well," he says nervously, "there were only three possibilities available to you, for a BLT sand.—rye, wheat, or white. Of course, some people don't get bread at all. Do you want bread?"

"A BLT without bread?" Simon says.

"Sure," the waiter says. "Didn't you ever hear of a tuna sand., hold the sand.?" I love how he calls a sandwich a sand. He goes on, half mumbling, "That means the person just wants tuna on a bed of lettuce."

"I'll have my BLT on rye toast," Simon says.

"Here we call rye 'Robert.' "

"Not 'Roger'?" Simon says.

" 'Robert.' "

"Okay, then a BLT on Robert and a Heineken."

"Something to drink with that?"

"To drink with the Heineken?" Simon says, peeved.

"Oh. I didn't hear that," the waiter says. Daria and Stash give each other a look.

"And I'd like a soda," I say, since no one asks. "I'd like to have mocha-chip ice cream and chocolate syrup." I figure part of my new personality is to make my wants known.

"Wait," the waiter says. "We only have milkshakes, and they're premade—there's only a choice of three flavors. It's a bottled mix."

"I'm very disappointed," I say. "But in that case, I'll have a tuna sand." This isn't what I want at all, but it's good when it comes: it fact, that tuna salad is like a shot of heroin and goes right to my bloodstream. I look at Daria and think, Go ahead, make my life easier. "Your dog," I say. "How did it happen?"

"Oh, he was hit by a car," Daria says. "He was only two years old then. Of course, it was my fault; I should never have let him off the leash. Anyway, I was hysterical, and my husband at the time wrapped him up and we took him off to the veterinarian college. At first they said it was hopeless, but Textron didn't try to bite anyone, which is unusual for a dog in that much pain. The veterinarian college was extremely impressed with his disposition; they decided to try and treat him, and though the work they did on him should have cost three thousand dollars, they said they wouldn't charge us. In fact, they wanted to keep Textron to conduct experiments on— because of his disposition."

Daria wants to know if we are going to Sakhalin Island afterward: there's going to be a party at the club for the director of the zombie film. Before Stash can say anything, I speak. "I don't think so," I say. "If I go out tonight, tomorrow's a lost cause."

"I was going to go, but I guess now I won't, either," Daria says. "I put on high heels and everything. But maybe I'm too tired."

I cross my legs and feel what I think is Daria's knee pressed against Stash's—but maybe it's only a table protrusion.

Stash drinks a chocolate milkshake while he smokes a little cigar. He asks Daria if she remembers his old girlfriend, Andy.

"Oh, sure—Andy Dime, I see her name a lot these days," Daria says.

Stash says that Andy got to be very successful because she worked hard all the time.

"I like to rest, myself," I say.

"In fact, Andy worked harder at costume design than anyone else I ever knew," Stash says. "From six A.M. until five P.M. she worked, then she would go to dance class. Then she would have dinner—vegetarian—and then we would go out dancing until three in the morning."

"Amazing," I say.

"Maybe I won't go to the club, either," Simon says.

"You can share a cab with me," Daria says. "You'll drop me off at home first."

There's a silence. I can hear Stash guzzling. "Great special effects, huh?" I say. No one answers. "Like where that head got chopped? With the eyes?"

"Yeah," Simon finally answers.

While we're looking for a taxi, near a video arcade, a policeman waving a gun comes running toward us and knocks into Simon. Then he dashes into the arcade.

Simon is white. "A gun!" he says. "He crashed into me with a gun!"

I tug Stash's arm. "This isn't a good place to stand," I say.

There are no cabs in sight. A couple of Buddhists (maybe they're Zen monks) walk by in front of us, dressed in very plain and beautiful robes. I wonder what they're doing in this part of town so late at night. I'm tempted to go over to the chief monk and ask him to give me a koan, but probably he doesn't speak English.

When we finally grab a taxi, Stash says he thinks maybe we'll go to the film party; in fact, he's definitely going. He starts to tell the driver, "But we'll be making a stop first, at—" when Daria interrupts.

"If you guys are going to Sakhalin Island, then maybe I'll come with you," she says.

I don't say anything. I take out my little mirror from my pocketbook and check to make sure I'm still here, then I put on more eyeliner and lipstick.

It's not so bad at the club after all. Actors, dressed like zombies, stagger around with trays of zombies: fancy drinks with four or five types of alcohol, in drinking bowls that resemble coconuts and skulls. Daria and Simon go off to the room where there's dancing, and Stash and I go to the room with the piranhas in the fish tank and say hello to people that we know. As usual when I go to a club I can't hear a word anyone says; all I can do is grin and try and nod at the right places. Since Stash gets involved talking to an old friend about the Velvet Underground, and I don't know too much about the topic, I lean against the wall and sip a zombie. As the room gets hotter and more crowded, I start to get weak. Once again my vision is gathering detritus.

I pull Stash by the arm. "Hey, listen," I say, "I feel weird. I think I'm going to faint again. I'm going to go sit down."

Stash is in the middle of a sentence. He looks distracted. "Okay, okay," he says.

"I'll be over there," I say, pointing to some chairs. Unfortunately, all the chairs are taken. Once again I'm in a cold sweat. I kick a man gently in the ankles. "Excuse me," I say. "I'm in trouble. I'm going to faint." I'm embarrassed but feel I have no choice.

The man, dressed in what appears to be silk pajamas, stands up immediately. "Sit down, honey," he says. "Are you pregnant?"

"No," I say. "I just feel faint. I know I'll be okay in a chair."

"I was going anyway," the man says.

I put my head between my legs and feel the blood rush around like a herd of buffaloes trapped at the edge of a cliff. I'm better almost at once, but I'm afraid to get up again, especially if it means losing my seat. Anyway, I enjoy just watching the scene: a boy with long hair, wearing leopard-skin leotards and white lipstick, is busy taking pictures of another man dressed as Captain Hook. Then I study a girl who's wearing a Victorian dress, complete with bustle—she's got on Day-Glo red mascara. On her shoulder is a parrot, but whether it's stuffed or alive I can't tell. I watch the crowd for hours; in fact, I float into a sort of trance, and when I look at my watch it's after 2:00 A.M.

I spot Stash on the other side of the room: he and Daria are leaning against a railing near the piranha tank. The room is too crowded to push my way through to them. I try to catch Stash's eye, but he's busy talking. Finally he sees me. I wave at him, trying to make him understand I want him to come over to me, but he doesn't move.

Around three, Stash is ready to leave. In the taxi he wants to know what's wrong with me. "You don't talk to people, you sit in a chair all night," he says. "Daria said to me, 'What's wrong with Eleanor, she looks terrible.' "

I don't even know most of his friends' addresses to notify them about the funeral. Maybe I should request, "In lieu of flowers, contributions to the Museum of Modern Art." "My behavior is my business," I say. "I'm not a performing dolphin; I act as I please." My words sound feeble even to myself. I try not to be so sensitive; at least I don't burst into tears the way I did in the early years of our relationship.

In our apartment Stash is silent, and it makes me sad to go to sleep without getting a chance to analyze every person we've bumped into that night. I picture the room getting blacker, beginning at the edges and gradually disappearing into a hole resembling a bathtub drain.

I'm shocked at how cute the clinic doctor is. He has brooding, vampire eyes and a strong smell of foreign aftershave. I'm glad I didn't go to the person Stash suggested. Even so, I'm nervous—I'm used to my family doctor, Dr. Henness, who is at least eighty years old. When I was eighteen and went for my college examination, he begged me not to get undressed. He never really seemed to remember my name, but at least he represented stability and some sort of security. With him, I knew there would never be anything wrong with me. But with this guy—Dr. Bartholdi—things are ominous right from the start. He sulks at his desk, jabbing something that lurks in the top drawer.

I assure him right off the bat that I'm not pregnant. I describe what's been happening to me. I want to prove to him that I'm not flaky; because of this, perhaps, my hands are rummaging wildly through my hair, I'm talking a mile a minute. I explain that I never take drugs, due to the fact that they don't make me feel good. Nor was I drunk on the recent occasions when I practically fainted.

But Dr. Bartholdi pays me no mind. In fact, he examines his fingernails while I talk. Then he makes me pull up my shirt. He presses his cold stethoscope against me. It's difficult, with such a handsome doctor, not to feel violated. I imagine marrying him, dutifully undergoing such examination nightly. Then I tell myself he's a medical person, not a human being.

I'm lying flat on my back on scratchy paper, waiting for the verdict, when Dr. Bartholdi tells me I can sit up and tuck in my shirt. He writes furiously on a pad: probably dialogue for some autobiographical best-seller he's working on. "Chapter 23: The Case of Eleanor T."

"Your blood pressure is low," he says. "Probably if you get up too quickly after you have a few drinks, you'll feel dizzy."

"I didn't have a few drinks," I say. "I didn't feel dizzy. I almost passed out on the street. If I hadn't lain down, I would have blacked out completely."

"You wouldn't believe how many people I treat in nightclubs. People faint all the time. Vasovagal syncope."

"Yeah?" I say. I wonder why Dr. Bartholdi would even bother to go to nightclubs, if he has to spend his whole evening treating hysterical fainters.

He sends me for a blood test, saying, "You can call me on Thursday for the results, but I don't think they'll tell us anything we don't know."

It gives me a certain satisfaction to get jabbed in the finger. I watch as one large, ruby dot of blood appears on my skin, miraculous as jewelry. I think of the dot of blood as full of life and motion and drama like the lives of the people around me. Microbes, corpuscles—who knows what deathly battles are fought all the time between white blood cells and alien invaders?

On the other hand, on the subway ride home, I do wish I had something more critical to tell Stash: that I have anemia, pleurisy, an electrolyte imbalance. I'd like to inform him that shortly I'll be reduced to life in a wheelchair, that I'm counting on him to push me across the street. I'm disappointed that Dr. Bartholdi dismissed me so abruptly, without even trying to get my phone number. I could have given him Daria's; that might have taken care of her for a while.

Stash isn't home, and after hours of waiting, at eight o'clock I fix myself some hamburger and blue cheese on an English muffin. I like ketchup. It's a good thing Stash isn't home, because I gleefully finish off a bottle. This would certainly drive him crazy. I take my plate to the bed, at the far end of the room, so that during my meal I can watch TV; there's a program on about how rich people make more money. This pastime takes up an entire life.

I'm annoyed at Stash, but by the eleven o'clock news, with the water shortage and the story about the sculptor who was murdered by junkies, I start to get worried. Andrew, our dog, waits patiently for him by the door: he's not even interested when I offer him a bit of hamburger.

I don't really want anything to happen to Stash, although I enjoy planning his funeral from time to time. A lot of things can occur in the city: muggings, shootings, women accosting him from the windows of limousines.

At twelve-thirty Stash walks in. "Where were you?" I say. "What's happened? Why didn't you call?" These are the very words I've resolved not to say.

"Daria," Stash says. "Her dog died."

"She has her own boyfriend!" I say.

"I had to go with her in the dog ambulance to the hospital," Stash says. "She was hysterical."

"The dog was twelve years old!" I shout, jumping up to empty ashtrays. "What was she hysterical about? Why didn't you call me?"

"She let the dog off the leash," Stash says. "It was her fault. Textron got attacked by an Akita. Straight to the jugular."

"We have a dog *here*," I say. "Tell me you're having an affair."

"There's nothing between Daria and me," Stash says.

"We've been friends for years and years. We used to hang out together."

"I paid for half of that Godzilla lighter for her birthday," I say. "She never even thanked me. What about me? I had to spend the day at the doctor's."

"What happened?" Stash says wearily. He opens the refrigerator and moves a jar of Mexican hot sauce to one side.

I imagine the hands on my wristwatch stopping, then turning backward. I see myself dressed in black, my face very white, a red rose clutched in one frozen hand. I change the red rose to a lavender one. "It was weird," I say. "He spent hours examining my breasts."

"What?" Stash says. "Report him! What do your breasts have to do with fainting?" I've gotten to him. He's indignant and furiously snatches a hunk of cheese from some hidden recess inside the fridge. I watch him sink his teeth into it; I want to tell him to use a knife, but I don't say it.

"He had to listen to my heart," I answer at last.

Stash poises over the cheese like a puma made nervous at a fresh kill. "So what did he say was wrong?" he says.

"Vasal-vascular syncope."

"Which means?"

"I faint in nightclubs," I say. "Or if I stand up too quickly. It's a common problem. Maybe he said something about a vagal-vasal system."

Stash shakes his head. "Why do you go to that crummy clinic? They don't know anything there."

"I'm a member," I say. "He was a doctor, with a medical degree from an accredited university."

"He said there was nothing wrong with you? But I saw you! Why didn't you go to my doctor, like I told you?"

"She should have put that dog to sleep long ago," I say. "It's cruel to keep a suffering animal alive."

Stash comes over to the bed where I'm sitting. "There's nothing between us, Eleanor, really," he says. He puts his arm around my shoulder. "Don't be jealous. She loved that dog. Now she's all alone. But we have each other." He strokes my hair, and with his free hand he takes a Tuscano cigar from the packet in his pocket. "Who was on Johnny Carson tonight?" he says. "Anybody good?"

I move to the edge of the bed, bend over, my head between my knees. My hair touches the floor. In my veins—some thin and twisty, others fat, ropy—I can feel my blood, thrown for a loop, struggling to flow uphill where only a second before it was flowing down.

the new
acquaintances

For several weeks Clarence Mullens had been sharing his apartment with a girl he met on the street. It was his sixth year in college. Because he was so inconspicuous in appearance he had developed the habit of dressing outrageously. All of his clothing was made for him by an elderly tailor familiar with the styles of 1928.

Clarence was an exceptionally tiny person, nearly featureless. Yet over the years he had become accustomed to his looks. He was the youngest child in a family of three boys: in some way he had been cheated, for his brothers, though not especially striking, had succeeded in snatching more distinguishing features than he. His oldest brother had a chin; the middle one a nose. Yet even they, as well as his father, the third in a multigenerational family of publishers, were quite nondescript.

"What do you think?" he said to the girl, as he put on a striped bow tie.

The girl, Inez, lay on the bed staring at the ceiling. "You always look the same," she said, without glancing in his direction.

"If you intend to stay in my apartment," Clarence said, "I suggest you compliment me from time to time." Instantly he was filled with remorse. He picked up a stack of records from the couch and put them on the floor. Then he sat down. "We'll go out now and get a drink," he said in a flat voice. "Unless you'd care to look at my collection of photographs?"

"You've shown them to me eight times," Inez said. "You go for a drink. I'll rest." She sat up abruptly and began to hum in a low voice. Her hair was quite short; her face, more masculine than Clarence's, consisted of a pair of gray, slanted eyes, a bumpy nose, and thin mouth.

"We're expected at my parents' house for dinner," Clarence said.

"I have no interest in meeting your parents," said Inez, lighting an unfiltered cigarette.

After a short discussion, it was agreed that Clarence would pay Inez five dollars to attend the dinner at his parents' house.

"I've told my parents we intend to be married," he said. "They want to meet you."

At this remark Inez slid her legs over the side of the bed and scowled. "Where are those bridal magazines we bought?" she said in a sullen tone. Clarence picked up the magazines and sat next to her on the bed. As she turned the pages, Clarence slid one arm around her shoulders. Inez appeared not to notice, but shrugged his arm away.

Clarence's apartment was at the edge of the ghetto near the university. It was in an old brownstone which had formerly been a one-family residence. The wallpaper in the hallways was peeling, a curious cucumber pattern. The kitchen, which had formerly been a closet, was not large and contained a tiny Frigidaire and a gas stove with two burners. Numerous insects roamed at will.

They walked down the street to the bus stop. In an alleyway, two boys were hitting a small animal with a stick. Inez ran over and punched the weaker-looking boy in the head. He spat in Inez's face and ran off. Before the second boy could escape, Inez grabbed him by the arm. With her free hand, Inez picked up the yowling animal, a blond kitten, from the ground. It clawed her fiercely across the arm, but Inez held onto it.

"Inez," said Clarence, "what do you think you're doing?"

The boy, although smaller than Clarence, appeared very

dangerous. Clarence did not trust even the ten-year-olds in this particular neighborhood. Once a gang of boys had tormented him in the park, succeeding in embarrassing him no end. His valuable watch and antique eyeglasses were stolen.

Inez turned and walked back to him, dragging the boy by his ear. His hands waved violently in the air. She flung the scratching kitten into Clarence's arms. "Ask him where he lives," she told Clarence.

"Inez, please, let's go," said Clarence, holding the kitten before him. "We're going to be late for dinner. I thought you might like to take in a show at a club afterward, so I've reserved seats. A well-known, rather elderly transvestite, who used to star on the French stage, is doing a cabaret act on the other side of town. Unfortunately, as you may have noticed, there is not much in the way of night life in this city."

"I said, ask him where he lives," said Inez.

Clarence looked at the boy. He was no more than eight or nine years old, and was dressed in a prep school uniform. No doubt, thought Clarence, he attended the parochial day school on the block. "I don't want to get involved, Inez," said Clarence.

"Then screw the dinner at your parents," said Inez.

Clarence thought for a moment. "Where do you live?" he asked the boy.

"Six Hundred West 109th," the boy said.

Clarence looked at Inez.

"Not anymore," she said.

After a short conversation the boy agreed that he would stay with Clarence and Inez, provided that his mother did not mind.

They left the small boy watching television, having first removed his clothing so that he would not attempt to escape. He had made friends with the kitten, and was amusing himself by tying its back legs up with a bit of string; unfortunately the animal was covered with fleas.

After locking the boy and the kitten in his apartment, Clarence announced he would get his car out of the garage. They were now so late for dinner that Clarence felt he had little choice, though he hated to drive. It was only with the greatest of difficulty he could see out over the dashboard; the car was very old and the dashboard unusually high. He felt it would appear undignified to sit on pillows.

"Do you think the boy will be all right left alone in our apartment?" he said nervously when the garage attendant had brought the car around to the front of the building.

"Clarence, do you want me to drive?" Inez said.

Clarence assured her that he would prefer to drive his own vehicle. His life had become so interesting since his accidental introduction to Inez, he could now scarcely imagine how he had filled his days before. His primary activities were listening to opera and cutting out pictures of food from magazines, which he then glued onto paper plates. However, he had so many incompletes in his classes, some dating back three years, that he went through each day under a crashing anxiety; even the two aforementioned activities he could not really enjoy. Now, in the space of only a few weeks, Inez had finished all of his work for him, and while the papers were rather odd —Inez had read none of the books or attempted even the slightest bit of research on the various subjects—they were nicely typed and of the correct length.

Inez was indeed a remarkable person. She lived life on a daily basis; some mornings she woke up in Clarence's bed and had no idea of where she was, or even Clarence's name. Clarence had learned to greet her directly each day. "Hello, Inez," he would say upon waking. "My name is Clarence Mullens, and we're engaged to be married."

She came from a wealthy family; her father and grandfather had been politicians, but her family would have nothing to do with her. They found her behavior disruptive; twice she had attempted to burn down the ancestral home. At present she survived on the streets, though as she was not a terribly attractive person, prostitution was out of the question. Her manner was far too abrasive and abusive, without necessarily appealing to the sort of man who hoped to be dominated. "My true dream is to run a business where I go into people's homes and help them decide which items of clothing to throw out and which to wear," Inez said on several occasions.

Clarence's parents were quite old and feeble. They lived in a luxury apartment building, in four small rooms decorated entirely in the color scheme of light green and avocado.

Clarence rang the doorbell. His father appeared at the door, clad in a bathrobe. He appeared perplexed to see Clarence. Clarence wondered if he even remembered who he was. Certainly he had never been the favorite in this family. It was sad but true that his parents had not been young even at his birth; they had hoped their third child would be a girl, and had never gotten over the shock of Clarence's entrance into this world.

"Hello, Father," Clarence said. "How are you feeling?"

"What's that?" his father said.

"Dad, this is my fiancée," Clarence said. His father held out his hand to Clarence. "This is Inez O'Brien, Dad," Clarence said, pointing to Inez. "I believe you're familiar with her father, Senator O'Brien."

Mr. Mullens looked upset. "I must be getting senile," he said. "Shall I take your coats?" He took Clarence's and Inez's coats and handed them to Clarence.

Inez followed Mr. Mullens into the apartment. "Care for a drink before dinner?" Mr. Mullens said.

"I'd like a Perrier and water, if you've got it," Inez said.

"No Perrier," said Mr. Mullens. "I can offer you club soda and water."

Clarence found he was blushing with embarrassment over his fiancée's remark. Was it really possible that Inez was the daughter of Senator O'Brien? Her manners, her accent, her mode of dishabille were not what one would expect. Still, the sons and daughters of the rich and famous were often highly unusual. Clarence considered himself to be out of the ordinary, though few people connected him immediately with the distinguished publishing house of Winston Mullens and Sons.

He threw their coats on the floor of the closet and led Inez firmly by one arm into what had been his childhood bedroom. "I thought you might be interested in examining my childhood photograph album," he said. "You would probably be amused to see what I looked like in prep school. My hair at that time was down to my shoulders. Throughout high school, I was heavily into drugs; following my graduation, my parents arranged for a series of treatment at an upstate sanatorium. Luckily they were of the sort where they put you out before the electroconvulsive shock. But during high school I played in a band; even then I was interested in electricity."

Inez seated herself on the bed and removed her rather worn pumps. She lay back and lifted her stubby legs in the air. Her stockings had numerous runs; her thighs, white and juicy, were visible.

If I don't prevent her, Clarence thought to himself, she'll pull that skirt all the way up and God knows I don't wish my parents to discover her without underpants.

"Let's go have a drink," Clarence said, walking quickly from the room.

Over dinner, Inez brought up an unfortunate experience. As a sixteen-year-old she had been overpowered by a sex-crazed creep, brutally assaulted at a rowdy rock concert.

Clarence's father, still dressed in his robe, sat at one end of the table toying with his soup. He perked up momentarily as Inez stubbed out her cigarette at the side of her plate. *"Tch tch tch,"* he said.

"What are you publishing these days, Dad?" Clarence said.

"It turns my stomach to hear you were raped," Clarence's father said. "Would you like another drink?"

Inez shook her head. "I believe I was in the middle of a story," she said to Clarence in a reprimanding tone of voice.

Clarence's mother was extremely pale. As always, she was dressed in peach. This evening she had on a peach-colored cashmere sweater and a wool peach skirt that was several sizes too large. Lately she had lost weight; heavy bags under her eyes had not been obliterated by recent plastic surgery.

"Do you find this sort of story distasteful, Mother?" Clarence said, finishing the watery pea soup and reaching to the center of the table for a handful of oyster crackers.

"Don't be an old fuddy-dud, Clarence," his mother said. Her weak blue eyes glittered as she reached across the table and cracked Clarence across the hand with the back of her spoon.

Clarence dropped the handful of crackers. "May I please have the crackers?" he mumbled.

"Would you excuse me for just a minute," Inez said, rising from the table.

During her absence Clarence's father drooped once more. His head sunk weakly into his concave chest, which was visible through his partially opened robe.

"An unusual girl, Clarence," Mrs. Mullens said. "I'd like another Scotch."

Clarence stood up and went to the sideboard. He poured some Scotch into his mother's glass and drank it quickly, throwing back his head. Then he poured out another shot and brought it to his mother.

"Senator O'Brien is on the House Ways and Means Committee," Mrs. Mullens said.

Clarence's father did not look at all well. It occurred to Clarence that he should be checked for Alzheimer's disease. His eyes fluttered shut. Then they opened and fixed themselves on Clarence with a steely gray stare. "Grammy's doing just fine, Clarence," he said. "That nursing home is one of the most beautiful places I have ever seen. You and Inez will have to come out with us next weekend to visit her. I'm sure," he said more loudly now as Inez came back into the room, "that Inez would be fascinated with Grammy's reminiscences about Ernest Hemingway. She doesn't have much longer to live; someone should listen to her."

"What do you do, dear?" Mrs. Mullens said to Inez.

Inez was standing at the head of the table, near Clarence's father. "Look at this," she said, pointing to her leg. "Would you believe it? My stockings have a run." She kissed Mr. Mullens on top of his head with a wet, smacking sound and sat down at her place abruptly. "I hope you don't mind that I kissed you like that," she said. "I'm a rather spontaneous person. It's not often I tell people how I was raped by a burly, nineteen-year-old marine. I wouldn't want you to learn about it secondhand. Because of the enormous crowds, women were permitted to use the men's restrooms during the concerts, but guards kept the men out of the women's bathrooms. A man offered to stand guard as I used the men's room; unfortunately, after escorting me inside, he pushed me into a stall and ripped off my clothing. Several men in the bathroom yelled 'Right on, right on!' during the procedure."

"Clarence's father and I always tried to discourage Clarence's interest in music," Clarence's mother said.

"Oh, yes," Inez said. "Clarence and I hoped for a rather informal wedding, perhaps in a garden somewhere in the city, in a few months. It will have to wait, however, until I'm settled into my new job."

"Oh, not an informal affair," said Clarence's mother. "When Blake was married—last year, to a lovely girl—we had the wedding out at our summer home in New Paltz. It was really lovely. Nearly a thousand people came, and though the weather was not what might have been hoped for, the enormous tents kept everyone dry."

"It really was splendid, Inez," Clarence said.

The maid brought out herb omelets and French fries. She was not a good cook; however, she had been with the family for years. The omelets were rather dry, and filled with a dense padding of dried herbs. The French fries were greasy and already cold.

After dinner Clarence's father offered to show Inez slides of their trip to Peru; but Inez, smiling gently, took Mr. Mullens's hand in her own and explained that a young boy, who was lost on the street, was waiting for them back in Clarence's apartment.

"We must go off and join the young people, you know!" Clarence said, standing suddenly. "We're a very desirable couple—can't spend the whole evening with you!"

Clarence's mother escorted Clarence to the door, while Inez had a brief word with Mr. Mullens.

"I am so glad you're getting married and settling down at last," Mrs. Mullens whispered in Clarence's ear. "God knows we've had our difficulties with you, Clary, perhaps in part it was my fault. I always did want a girl, though I suppose it's not unusual that you kept your hair long until college. It was the times, you know. She seems like a nice girl."

As Inez walked to the door with his father, Clarence could hear her saying, "Major multinational insurance company. I'll be instructing foreign companies in insurance against revolutions, political risk, that sort of thing. Exporters selling to private buyers abroad want to make sure they'll pay their debts. For example, an American company sold twenty million dollars' worth of software to Brazil. Now they have twenty million dollars in Brazilian currency in a Brazilian bank, which can't be converted."

"Sadly, I'm not interested in that sort of thing," Clarence's father said, patting Inez gently on her behind. "Literature's my game. You might be interested in stopping by the office one of these days, Inez. I'm bringing out an extraordinary first novel about World War Two."

"Don't you mean the Vietnam war, Dad?" Clarence said.

Mr. Mullens ignored him.

"It's lucky that a man came in while I was being raped and scattered the sickening mob that had gathered to watch," Inez said, taking Clarence's mother's raincoat from the closet and putting it on. She smiled sweetly at Clarence's mother. "You'll never miss this old thing," she said.

Clarence felt the dinner had been a big success. "My parents rarely take to anyone as they have taken to you," he said when they had gotten into his car.

The young boy was sitting in front of the television set just where they had left him. When Clarence stepped into the bathroom to wash his hands, he noticed a grimy ring around the top of the tub. "Did you have a nice bath?" he said, going into the kitchen to look for the Ajax.

"I have to go home now," the boy said. "Unless you have something to eat."

"But of course," Inez said, going to the refrigerator. "Clarence, what can we make with one egg and some oil?"

"Mayonnaise," said Clarence. "Unless you want to order something in. I really don't feel like going out again this evening. I'm not a strong person emotionally. That dinner with my parents was probably about as much excitement as I can take for at least a week."

"All that will change after our marriage," Inez said. "You just have to get into the swing of life, Clarence. Why don't we make some mayonnaise? There's some old bread here—the boy could have a mayonnaise sandwich."

"My name's Andrew," the boy said. "I don't have a father. The guy my mother is married to appeared only recently. Both he and my mother drink heavily. According to my mother, I am the victim of immaculate conception. Could we order a pizza? A friend of mine works nearby—he would be glad to deliver."

Clarence told the boy to go ahead and order the pizza. Inez was at work making mayonnaise, using a hand egg beater. The procedure was fascinating. With only two simple ingredients, Inez explained, plus a little vinegar, lemon juice, and dry mustard, she could create real mayonnaise. "Watch," she said. She broke the egg into the bowl, added vinegar, and instructed Clarence to slowly pour the oil in while she beat. Within a half-hour, the whole bowl was filled with yellowish, soupy mayonnaise. Inez took the bowl to the television set, where Andrew was sitting. "Andrew, would you like to try some?" she said in the gentlest voice imaginable.

"My mother is attempting to bring me up as the second Messiah," Andrew said. He leaned forward and changed the television channel to an interesting program about sexual surrogate therapy. A large accountant was describing his experiences with premature ejaculation. "I realize my mother has

problems, stemming primarily from her drinking problem,"
Andrew went on. "However, the idea of thinking of myself as
the new Christ does not displease me. I don't mind doing good
deeds; I'm doing my best to maintain a childish innocence,
though in these times it's not easy. Did anyone call in for that
pizza?"

"I thought you were going to do it, Andrew," Clarence said,
picking up the phone.

After a half-hour the buzzer rang. As Andrew was involved
in grooming Inez's hair, Clarence was instructed to go down
and open the door. "My friend's name is Ferenc," Andrew
said. "Why don't you bring him upstairs? I think you'll find
him enthralling, Inez."

Clarence raced down the four flights of stairs. In the entry-
way was a dark man, in his early twenties, dressed in parami-
litary garb and holding a large box printed with a design of a
man in a chef's hat holding a slab of dough.

"Ferenc?" Clarence said through the glass. The man nodded. Clarence opened the glass door. "Andrew is upstairs,"
Clarence said. "Do you have a moment to come and join
us?"

"That will be eleven dollars and ninety-five cents," Ferenc
said.

Clarence reached into his pocket. "I believe I've seen you
around the campus before," Clarence said. "Do you go to
school here?"

"That's right," Ferenc said, following Clarence up the
stairs. "I'm working my way through school." He had a slight
accent; Clarence determined that he was from Hungary, or
some other Iron Curtain country. Yet he hesitated to pry.

On the landing he turned around to address Ferenc. "Only
another three flights," he said with a slight smile.

Ferenc was dark and clumsily built. His thin, dark mustache
seemed out of place on his potato face.

When they arrived at Clarence's room, Ferenc studied Inez
hungrily. Then he turned to Andrew, seated next to Inez on

the bed. "Not you again," Ferenc said. "The little Messiah. Has he been telling you his delusions of grandeur?"

"Aw, Ferenc," Andrew said in a whiny voice. "They're not my delusions—they're my mother's. I thought you'd be glad to see me."

Ferenc smiled and put the pizza down on the coffee table.

"Hey," said Clarence. "Don't put the pizza down there— that's where I keep my cutout pictures for my artwork." He raced over and lifted the box, but it was too late; most of the pictures of food he had meticulously cut out from magazines were stuck to the grease oozing through the bottom of the box.

"Do you know, apart from Inez, you two are the first new people I've befriended in a long time," Clarence said. Neither Ferenc nor Andrew responded. "Apart from Inez," Clarence said again. Andrew picked at a scab on his elbow. "It's true," Clarence said, more loudly than he had intended. "Believe me or not, but it's the truth."

Ferenc had seated himself upon the bed and was intently examining a painting of a cow which hung above the fireplace. At last he spoke. "I perpetually build these cages and then put myself into them," he said. "I might have been a proctologist, had I not met a girl who introduced me to heroin. Now I've had to change my major from pre-med to finance."

"I know exactly what you mean," said Clarence. "Because I was afraid of writing a bad paper, I procrastinated, each summer I had more and more incompletes to write, until the work load became overwhelming. It has taken me more than six years to get through college; I still have a semester left. As for the statement that you two are the first new people I've befriended—I almost never speak to anyone, lacking social grace. It was only because Inez inflicted herself upon me that I became engaged to her, and through her, have now met you, Ferenc and Andrew."

Andrew glared angrily at Clarence. "This sort of dribble doesn't interest me in the least," he said. "If this is what you locked me up here for, you can bet I'm not sticking around any longer. Give me five dollars. I want to go play some video games."

"That sounds like fun," Inez said. "I'm coming with you."

"Should I come?" Clarence wondered aloud.

"Clarence," Inez said, "one of the first signs of a bad relationship is the inability of one partner to allow the other his or her independence. You have a nice chat with Ferenc, listen to your opera or whatever, and give me the extra set of keys. I'll be back later."

As Andrew and Inez walked to the door, Andrew said, "Although I'm only nine years old, I'm very highly sexed. People don't realize how much of a sex life even small children have. After we play the video games, why don't you come home with me, Inez, and I'll introduce you to my mother? Then we can go to my room and listen to records."

"You little devil," Inez said, reaching under Andrew's arms and tickling him ferociously. She turned and grinned wildly at Clarence. "Don't get maudlin, Clarence," she said. "Easy come, easy go!"

Clarence suspected this was Inez's idea of a joke. Yet the thought she might not return did not bother him nearly as much as it had on other days. He turned to Ferenc. "How did you escape?" he said.

"What?" said Ferenc.

"How did you ever escape from Hungary?"

"I'm not Hungarian," Ferenc said. "Nor do I have an accent. My father is Lithuanian. I come from Chicago."

Clarence puzzled over this remark for some time. "To me," he said, "you resemble a dark, mysterious James Dean."

Ferenc stood up and walked restlessly about the apartment. "Some folks might say I'm too self-absorbed," he said at last. "I brood a lot, trying to figure out the mysteries of life. You'd do well to remain friends with Andrew, though he's only nine years old. For all that he is irritating, I wouldn't be surprised if he turned out to be the modern Messiah. He has a long way to go, however."

Clarence felt something jolt in his chest. Tomorrow, he thought to himself, I will go to the health center for tests. "But you're the one who's unusual, Ferenc," he said. "It's you!"

Ferenc picked up a stack of photographs lying on the mantelpiece. His hands were trembling. "What's this?" he said.

Clarence hurried over to Ferenc's side and took the pictures from his hand. "Those are my Polaroid photos," he said. "Would you like to look at them? Here's one of me in my bath."

"Not right now," Ferenc said. "I have to get back to my job. I have a lot of deliveries to make. Why don't you come with me? We'll make the rounds, and stop off for a drink later. We could talk some more." He turned and knocked into Clarence, who clumsily dropped the stack of photographs.

Clarence knelt to pick them up from the floor. "I would love that," he said, looking at Ferenc's grotesque army boots. "I would love it. But I have to wait for Inez to return. Perhaps some other time."

"I understand," Ferenc said. He turned to leave.

"Wait!" Clarence said. "Before you go, let me give you a tip." He handed Ferenc a five dollar bill. Then he picked up his Polaroid camera from the radiator. As Ferenc turned to shake his hand he snapped three pictures of him, one right after the next.

"I have these pictures of you," Clarence said. "You know my address, I hope you will come back to look at them sometime."

"Goodbye," said Ferenc.

Clarence sat down on the couch and looked at the photographs as they began to develop. I wonder when my fiancée will return? he thought. I do hope she'll bring Andrew back with her.

In the closet something scratched at the door and began to yowl in a high, thin voice. Clarence picked up a dripping slice of pizza and carried it slowly to the closet door.

fondue

For dinner that night I made cheese fondue. I had a terrible craving for the stuff, had for two days. It came in one of those packages, Swiss Knight, $3.50 at the supermarket. I opened the box. Inside was a little metal packet, all I had to do was warm it in a double boiler. I toasted some French bread in the oven. Stash wasn't coming home until late. I ate without him, carefully putting half to one side.

I turned on the TV. While I was dipping the bread into the cheese, I started to cry. The fondue was already salty enough, big tears slid off into my face and into the bubbling cheese.

The last time I had fondue, I was eighteen and studying in England for the year. The fondue was chocolate. My mother gave me the names and addresses of various acquaintances of hers who lived in London: one was a lord, a professor at one of the branches of London University.

I wrote to all her friends, with a letter of introduction I composed with difficulty:

I am a young American girl studying abroad in London for the year. Never before have I left the environs of the United States. My mother told me to write to you. I feel it is your duty, as a brilliant English personage, to assist a youthful, ignorant girl in acquiring culture.

On the envelope of each letter I drew a tiny face, hairy, with various animal attributes: giant furry ears, a dog collar and leash, a man's head with a long, toothy snout. My mother had always encouraged my artistic tendency; she didn't know whether any of these people would actually remember her, since she had only spent a week in London once, ten years ago, but she thought I should pursue all avenues.

Every day I checked the mailbox in the student lounge. Some of my mother's friends wrote asking what it was that I wanted from them, informing me that they were very busy. Others didn't even bother to respond. Then, after three weeks, an invitation to lunch from Lord Simeon.

The other American girls in the dorm were excited by my invitation. In the cafeteria, over dessert—a bowl of pale green, slippery gooseberries topped with hot custard—my best friend suggested I become Lord Simeon's mistress, if he would have me looking the way I did. "Why don't you go instead of me?" I said. I knew my mother wouldn't approve, but I didn't see how I could face this man with green hair.

What happened was, in one of my excursions down the back streets of London, I passed the Vidal Sassoon hair salon. I had long black hair down to my waist. Some of the stylists, smoking cigarettes on the sidewalk, stopped me and asked if I wouldn't do some modeling for them. "Okay," I said. "Can I get some pictures to mail home?" They took me into the salon. A whole crowd of stylists stood behind my chair, playing with my hair and remarking in shrill English accents. I could hardly understand what they were saying. I felt as if I were the first white person ever seen by some isolated African tribe.

I was told the coloring wasn't permanent, but would wash out. It took three days of work, from nine in the morning until early evening. First my hair was bleached, then dyed, then given a permanent wave. In recent years my mother had gone once a week to a beauty parlor, I didn't see how she could have stood it. This business was painful, I felt like a prize pig.

The hair show was on the evening of the third day, at the Royal Albert Hall. The audience was a group of two thousand Japanese hair designers, who had traveled to London to learn the new techniques. I was placed under a sheet, with only an opening for the head, along with five other girls. Then we were pushed out onto the stage.

We were to represent a bowl of fruit—I was the green grapes. Another girl had hair cut in a bowl. She was an apple, with red and green hair. In front her hair was longer than her eyes, so she clutched me for support. The top of her hair was completely smooth except for a narrow strip twisted with pipe cleaner to serve as the stem. The others were banana, strawberry, and an orange, with hair colored and fashioned appropriately.

From the stage the two thousand Japanese hairdressers all looked exactly alike, with shiny black hair and blank faces, giggling politely. I tried to pretend I was somewhere else. Several photographers shouted up to me: "Hold up your head! Give us a smile!" They must have been in communication with my mother. I scowled, blinded by the flashbulbs. The apple, unable to see from beneath her hair, stumbled off to one side. No one seemed to know in which direction we were supposed to move. We were like a Siamese quintuplet, staggering under the white sheet. But the fruit got a big round of applause.

I went home to wash my hair. There were no showers in the dormitory, just bathtubs. The tub was filled with green water, but after my bath my hair still looked the same. Only a little of the dye had washed out.

It was two days after this that my luncheon with Lord Simeon was scheduled to take place. At the college where I was meeting him, in the long, dark halls, I passed a glass case with a sign that read: HERE REST THE MORTAL REMAINS OF JEREMY BENTHAM, FOUNDER OF THE COLLEGE. But the case was empty. Hordes of students walked to and from classes. My green hair got me a lot of attention; I was sure that none of them even suspected that I, the same age as they, was about to have lunch with one of their professors.

I took the stairs up to the fourth floor. Lord Simeon's office was like a private library, lined with books, an Oriental rug on the floor. The secretary, very proper, asked if she could help me. "I'm Eleanor," I said. "I'm here for lunch."

"Oh, yes," the secretary said, rising from her desk. "Lord Simeon is in a meeting, but he'll be with you shortly. Would you care for a glass of sherry while you wait?"

"Okay," I said. I felt nervous. I grew up in the woods, in South Carolina. The only thing I knew about situations such as this was what I had read in books. What I had grown up reading was limited to what my mother had given me. Though my mother had always told me I could be anyone I chose, I couldn't make up my mind among Marjorie Morningstar, Tess of the d'Urbervilles, Isabelle Archer, and Miss Gamelon. It was hard to fit these characters to the present.

Well, according to my mother, life was supposed to be an adventure. If adventure didn't come to you, you had to go out there and force it, just as forsythia can be made to blossom prematurely in winter. I had only met one person to whom adventure constantly happened: my roommate from freshman year. When my mother helped me to move into my dorm room, she took one look at Sage—six feet tall, blond, wearing blue platform shoes—and told me I was in luck, that here was a person who could show me around. But Sage would have little to do with me, I had to live her experiences vicariously. She would return to our dorm room early each morning and relay the events of the previous evening: picked up by a well-known rock star in a limousine, taken to a fancy nightclub, given quantities of cocaine. Later this girl flunked out and married a med student she had known since high school. But at the time, it was a big disappointment that she rejected me socially. This girl was rich, she wore tiny hats with veils that cost $60. I was trying to get by on work-study. I served dinner in the cafeteria, soggy Brussels sprouts, flabby chicken thighs, smothered liver and onions.

But in London, as my mother had predicted, things did seem to happen to me. A girl with my looks was quite exotic: everyone in England was pale and blond. Once a man followed me around the Tate and invited me to a party. He resembled a youthful Andy Warhol. He came from Neptune, New Jersey, and had something to do with the fashion department of the

Victoria and Albert Museum. I thought he was kind of creepy, but then he introduced me to his English wife, Fiona, who was a stripper at lunchtime in various pubs. After this introduction I felt a little more comfortable with him—after all, he was married, it wasn't your usual pickup.

Anyway, this particular adventure didn't work out too well; I went to dinner at their house, where I was shown a display of various sexual devices. I acted friendly and interested. After dinner I helped with the dishes. Fiona showed me the gowns she wore for her strip act, and suggested that if I was short of cash she could get me a job.

"But, Fiona, I'm quite flat-chested," I said.

"That doesn't matter," she said. "What they want is variety. You could easily make thirteen pounds a day."

I said I'd think about it. Then we went to the party. It was near the Tower of London, at the home of a well-known shoe designer. The shoe designer was dressed like the Mad Hatter. He wore a bright blue top hat and a row of light bulbs around his waist which flashed on and off. The party was in honor of Pancake Day, an annual English celebration. At one in the morning the guests gathered outside and raced across the lawn flipping pancakes in the air. I wasn't impressed. Mitch and Fiona came around to collect me. It was time to leave, and they seemed very insistent that I go home with them.

I said thanks but no thanks. They lived in the wrong direction. The subways had stopped running and there were no taxis in sight. Finally I begged a ride with a group of French people; none of them spoke to me on the drive home.

It was something to write to my mother about. In my letter, I described the pancake toss in great detail: the drunken guests, clad in polka-dot taffeta ball gowns and jumpsuits made entirely of rubber and fake gorilla fur, staggering across the grounds with huge frypans, lumpy pancakes landing everywhere. I left out the part that no one had spoken to me all evening.

In the office of Lord Simeon, the secretary poured me a tiny, paper-thin glass of sherry. I drank it in one gulp. Then I real-

ized my faux pas. I pretended I hadn't finished drinking it, and
continued to sip from the empty glass. I was sorry now about
the green hair. The secretary was wearing a tweed suit, her
blond hair neatly coiffed. I sat gingerly on the edge of a leather
armchair, hoping she'd offer me another glass of the stuff. My
palms were hot and sweaty. I couldn't understand now why I
had ever obeyed my mother's command and written such a
strange letter to Lord Simeon. I should have at least been
smart enough to go to the library and find out what it was that
Lord Simeon had written. Perhaps he was an expert on dis-
eases of tropical birds, or Renaissance furniture (I was taking
a course in this, so I knew something about the subject), or
Sheridan's plays.

Finally a group of men entered the room. I half rose, half
sat, half rose again. There were all kinds of rules of etiquette
that I only faintly remembered my mother mentioning. Well,
my lack of manners had always been due not to rudeness but
to nervousness and stupidity. Sometimes I was far too formal,
at other instances I slammed doors in people's faces.

So far, however, people had always pointed out my tasteless
behavior to me. One afternoon, in my meanderings across London, I stopped in the lobby of a hotel to use the restroom. As I
was drying my hands, a woman burst into the women's room
and began to shout at me: "Look at this place, it's an absolute
mess! Why haven't you changed the towels in here!" She was
dressed in white, she looked totally demented. I shrugged my
shoulders and walked out. I was too afraid to point out to her
that I didn't work there.

Another time, following my modeling fiasco, I made an appointment with a modeling agency. It was my dream to become
a top fashion model. From abroad I would send my mother
money to buy a sports car, a fur coat, our lives would be
changed. In the office of the head of the agency, I took out a
red lollipop—my mother had sent me a box, following a particularly homesick letter from me—and began to lick it while
waiting for her opinion. She gave it to me: I was extremely
rude to lick a lollipop in her presence, how and where had I

been brought up? I was humiliated, of course the woman was correct. Still, wasn't it just as rude of her to embarrass me? She went on to tell me that I had potential: if I would pay her one hundred pounds for photographs, she would consider taking me on. But I was too ashamed to tell her I had no money for such things.

Lord Simeon, very jovial, introduced himself to me. He was plump and quite bald, with a pair of half-sized spectacles that hung precariously on the end of his nose. The other men looked at me with curiosity and kept staring at my hair. Introductions were made; Lord Simeon commented that he was an old friend of my mother's. I wondered whether we were all to lunch together, around a long medieval table in some great hall, toasting each other with pewter mugs. Then I remembered what my mother had told me: "You will be Zuleika Dobson, Zuleika, the belle of Oxford." Everyone was in love with Zuleika; out of unrequited love the jolly dons and Oxford lads threw themselves en masse into the local river. My mother had said that all of London was waiting for one such as me, I had to get over this business of low self-esteem. I shook everyone's hand and smiled, tossing back my green hair.

With great reluctance all the gentlemen except Lord Simeon said how nice it was to meet me and left the room.

Lord Simeon asked if I had had a glass of sherry.

"Oh, yeah, thanks," I said.

"We're to lunch in the tower," he said. "I hope that's all right, generally I take lunch here, rather than go out and fight the mob."

On the way up the stairs, I questioned him about the empty case in the entrance of the building which stated it contained the body of Jeremy Bentham.

"Oh, there's a rivalry with King's College," he said. "Their rugby team annually steals the body and returns it for a ransom."

"Yeah?" I said, stumbling up the worn stone steps. It was too bad we weren't going to dine out, I would have liked to have had interested, prying eyes upon us, no such luck. His study was four flights up a set of very narrow steps. The room was octagonal, with tiny slots for windows. The table was set: china patterned with the college's seal, a bouquet of flowers on the center of the table.

A tall Indian man, dressed in a white Nehru coat resembling a strait jacket, entered the room. I stood up. "How do you do?" I said.

"This is my valet, Virez," Lord Simeon said.

The valet glared at me. Lord Simeon pronounced the word valet with a hard "t." The whole business really struck me. I had never met a valet before. The valet poured us wine from a bottle breathing on the table. "Well, cheers," Lord Simeon said, holding up his glass. "I'm so terribly pleased to meet you at last, I enjoyed your letter a great deal."

"Oh, that," I said, drinking my glass of wine in one gulp.

"Just a light luncheon, I hope that's all right with you," Lord Simeon said.

"Fine," I mumbled.

"I never eat too much at lunch, it puts me to sleep." He poured me a second glass of wine.

The valet brought a silver platter to my side. It contained an arrangement of very dry-looking pieces of salami and some cubes of cheese. I helped myself with the fork and spoon, sullen, thick instruments. At home, we had dined on plastic plates. "Now tell me," Lord Simeon said as I struggled with a cube of cheese, "how is Clarice?"

"Oh, you mean my mother?" I said.

"Do have some bread with that," Lord Simeon said, passing me a basket containing large, hard rolls.

I glanced over at the valet. He was leaning against the wall with his eyes shut. His face was long and Dickensian, a sallow brown. He let out a sigh. His eyes opened momentarily, glared at me, then shut again. I drank my second glass of wine. "She's fine," I said. "She got divorced. Then she remarried."

"What a remarkable woman, your mother," Lord Simeon said. "How marvelous of her to put you in touch with me."

"Yeah, really," I said.

"It must be ten years now since I saw her last," Lord Simeon said. "Your mother was absolutely stunning. Of course, she didn't have your green hair."

"It's red."

"You know, when I was eight years old I was sent to stay with my Aunt Helen," Lord Simeon said. "Ever since then I've had a weakness for women with tiny mustaches. I shouldn't ought to admit something like that, I suppose."

"Why not?" I said. "It's very interesting. Like my brother —in second grade a little blond knocked him down on the playground. To this day he won't even look at a brunette."

"What fun," Lord Simeon said, refilling my glass. "Will you have some salad?" The valet brought around a plate of lettuce. I sneezed. The dressing was made of mustard. I quickly drank more wine. "Oh, this is so delicious," I said. "I love the dressing."

"Do you?" Lord Simeon said. "Do you really? Oh, I'm so pleased. It's my own special formula. You know, I made it myself." The valet returned to his leaning position against the wall.

"It's really good," I said. The wine tasted like bitter mold. I was afraid to ask the surly valet for a glass of water. "I'd love to know how you make it," I said.

"You know, it's my very own special secret recipe," Lord Simeon said, leaning forward. "But I'm going to tell you how I make it; I'm afraid I'm just not appreciated by my family. I use a teensy bit of dry mustard, walnut vinegar, and olive oil. Then I crush the peppercorns—"

I chewed on a bit of salami and removed a strip of paper from my mouth. The valet let out a sigh.

"Now, I want to hear everything about your experiences in London thus far," Lord Simeon said.

I told him about my experiences as a hair model. Lord Simeon muttered, "Extraordinary. Extraordinary." I wondered again about his age. He appeared so terribly ancient, with his bald head, his ruddy complexion. The room in the tower felt as if it were spinning around. Probably he was about forty-five years old. What a shame, he really was so nice. But I couldn't see myself becoming the mistress of a man who was such an antique. I drank some more wine. Lord Simeon asked me how I liked curry.

"I've never had it," I said.

"Never had curry!" Lord Simeon said. "But you have to have curry! I make a delicious curry!"

"That," I said, putting down my empty glass, "that would be wonderful."

"Or, I know a terrific Indonesian restaurant, you'll have to promise to join me for dinner one evening."

"Oh, yes," I said. I took a dark purple lipstick out of my pocketbook and smeared it carefully across my mouth.

"Now, will you have tea or coffee with the sweet?" Lord Simeon said.

"Coffee," I said.

"Just as I thought!" Lord Simeon said. "I know how you Americans love coffee."

With the coffee the valet brought out a fondue pot of wonderful, bitter chocolate, into which we dipped huge English strawberries. By now, however, I was too drunk to enjoy this. The combination: the wine, the dry salami, the salty cubes of cheese, the lettuce with mustard dressing, the coffee, and now the chocolate—didn't seem terribly auspicious. The strawberries, almost as large as tomatoes, certainly looked beautiful, each dark red and flecked with green seeds.

Lord Simeon and the valet appeared very pleased with this dessert; the valet emerged from his position against the wall by about two steps, and though he tried to maintain his bored expression, he kept glancing over at me. "But you must have another," Lord Simeon said. "I'm terribly afraid this lunch wasn't to your liking."

"No, everything was very good," I said.

"I'm so glad," Lord Simeon said. "Did I tell you I've been called in as consultant on a movie? It's rather fun, actually.

They're filming at Elstree—I'm coaching Al Pacino on his accent."

"Yeah?" I said. "Neat."

"Well, I must be going," Lord Simeon said. "I wish I could stay here all afternoon, but I have all kinds of dreadful appointments."

I stood up. "You know what?" I said. "I can't wait for that curry dinner, I'm really looking forward to it." I looked into Lord Simeon's face, I figured I'd ask him then if I could go with him to visit the set of the movie.

"Oh, I'll ring you soon," he said, shaking my hand. His eyes did not look into mine.

As I passed the students in the hall, I wished there was some way I could announce to them that I had just had lunch with their professor. Really, it wouldn't be all that terrible to have an affair with him. It would open endless doors for me, I would have the most interesting time. My mother would be pleased.

During the bus ride back to my dormitory, the bus rounded a curve and I slid off my seat onto the floor. The bus was empty except for the conductor, who came to my side and helped me up. "Had a tot too much?" he said. "That's a nice color hair you have, love."

As soon as I got back to my dorm room, I lay on the bed and shut my eyes. I was thinking about my mother. She had tried to teach me to be a femme fatale, I don't know why her lessons hadn't taken before. I guess she had started too late. Now I could see my life was going to be different. Then I passed out.

Anyway, that was eight years ago. Lord Simeon never called me for dinner. I made jewelry that didn't sell too well, and had a boyfriend who didn't want to be seen with me in public. It was hard to be almost thirty years old and so unlovable. My mother's second marriage had worked out quite well: she had two sets of antique dishes, and liked to give parties.

Weeping into my fondue, with Stash's dog Andrew looking up at me with a worried expression, I decided to call my mother for reassurance. Our relationship had always been good. I still took my directions from her, even though it did seem a lot of the time her ideas backfired. I let her phone ring once, a signal for her to call me back. That way the money I owed Stash for phone bills was kept to a minimum. "My apartment's all ready," I said. "A moving man from the *Village Voice* is coming to help me move my things tomorrow. He said he weighs two hundred and seventy-five pounds." I started to bawl. "Stash is right," I said. "My self-esteem is too low, I'm too messy, no one can live with me."

"That's not true," my mother said. "No one can live in one room with a man who sulks; what are you, crazy? As for being too messy: I remember when you first moved into his apartment, the bathroom carpet was so mildewed, something resembling Rice Krispies was growing around the toilet. This you told me yourself. Stash was so lazy that when Roland came to New York he had to change the toilet seat cover for you. Do you want me to go on? I will: Stash wants to be a bachelor type, and what you're looking for is something more."

I had to think. It was true that what she was saying was true. Intellectually I knew our relationship had its problems. But I had been prepared to find solutions. My little nerve endings were frazzled. "Maybe you're right," I said. "I'm in pain, however."

"I remember when your father and I divorced," she said. "I never thought I'd get over it. But after a few months, I thought to myself: Did I really want to go on making goat cheese for the rest of my life? Obviously I had just been playing a role. As soon as I saw the possibilities in life, I threw out all my natural cotton garments and got myself some fancy underwear. Then I met Stanley, who bought me a microwave and took me to Club Med."

"That's how you are," I said. "That's not how I am. I'm going to be lonesome, I'm going to sit alone in that apartment and make fondue and cry into it."

"Give me a break," my mother said. "What was so great about this guy anyway?"

"I don't know," I said. "He was nice. When he wasn't sulking, sometimes he used to dance around the apartment and sing me a little song."

"That doesn't sound so different from any other man."

"You're kidding," I said. "The thing is, for two years I was never really certain if I actually wanted to be with him. As soon as I decided I was genuinely in love, he told me he would never marry me because I went out for coffee with a man last summer."

"Get a tape recording that tells you you're wonderful," my mother said. "Stash had a way of treating you like a leper. Go back to London, men appreciated you there, didn't they?"

"I was thinking about my lunch with Lord Simeon," I said. "Even though when I met him he hadn't seen you for ten years, he remembered you at once. You must have something that I don't. Did I tell you how a few months ago I went to hear him give a lecture at Cooper Union, on ethics and morality?"

"So what happened?" my mother said.

I started to cry again, my mother was a good audience. "I'm eating dinner now," I said. "I had this terrible craving for fondue. For two days I had this craving, finally I went out and bought a package of it for dinner."

"You got that idea from me, didn't you?" my mother said.

"No, I didn't," I said. "What do you mean?"

"I must have told you," my mother said. "Two nights ago I had some people over for wine and cheese. At the last minute one woman called and said she couldn't make it to the dinner. So I panicked, thinking that all these people expected dinner, and I went out and got a package of that Swiss Knight fondue. There was only enough for two people, but I thought it was delicious."

"You didn't tell me," I said.

"What kind did you get?"

"Swiss Knight," I said. "It cost three-fifty."

"I paid five dollars," my mother said. "Maybe the next time you come to visit us you could buy a few packages and bring them. I thought it was delicious. Are you sure I didn't mention it?"

"No," I said.

"So what happened when you went to hear Lord Simeon?"

"I went up to him afterward," I said.

"Wait a minute," my mother said. "This is a very bad connection. Can you hear two people talking?"

"No," I said.

"I have to hear this," my mother said. "This girl is saying she's going to burn her briefcase. Interesting." I waited while my mother listened to the other voices. "Okay, okay," she said at last. "So what happened?"

"After Lord Simeon's lecture I went up to him and asked him whatever happened to the body of Jeremy Bentham. He was pleasant enough, but he obviously didn't have the slightest idea of who I was. He looked frightened. As soon as he got a chance he moved away."

"He has such nice eyes, though, doesn't he?" my mother said.

"I guess," I said. I wondered what that body actually looked like: wigged, befuddled, decked in a bowler hat and frilly bows, imprisoned behind fingerprinted glass. I could almost picture his face: amused, slightly superior, maybe a touch of wistfulness. There he was in the hallway, the students passing endlessly before him, in a kind of life after death. Or perhaps he was still tucked away in some closet at King's College, still unransomed.

on and off the
african veldt

Ginger Booth, my dealer, handled only male artists
and I was the most important. She had said this
to me often, when I called her at three or four in
the morning just to check. I had to bring some paintings over
to her—she had to take a look at them to decide whether or
not we should include them in my upcoming show. Before now
she had always worked out of her SoHo apartment, but she
was finally about to open her own gallery. This made her frantic; she had workmen redoing her apartment, and she was also
running a couple of blocks away to supervise putting up the
walls and floor of her new gallery.

So she was in a bit of a snit when she let me into her apartment. The first thing she said was, "Marley, why couldn't you
have gotten this stuff to me sooner? You know I've got a buyer
coming over in fifteen minutes to look at some things—how
can I sell your paintings to her if I haven't even seen them?"

"Because I didn't even finish putting the details on them
until late last night!" I said. She was going to have a group
show of some of her artists as her first show in the new place,
but as I put the largest painting on the ground, the one I
wanted her to use in the opening show, a big chunk of clay fell
off the upper left-hand corner and crashed onto the floor.

"But what do you call this?" she said, picking up the pieces
and crumbling them further in her hand, so that there was no
likelihood of my sticking them back on. "Marley, what could

you be thinking of? I can't sell this. The painting's falling apart."

"That's all that's going to happen. The rest will stay on. I guarantee."

"I can't sell paintings of yours if they're going to fall apart, Marley. What am I going to do if ten years from now a client comes to me with one of your works he's bought from me and it's all fallen down to the bottom of the frame in a lot of pieces?" And she got all huffy and frittered around her apartment like a potato in hot oil, leaving me to feel embarrassed at the empty table. She was a good sort, with a little manikin face and a brittle New York fashion, fine for keeping me in my place. I didn't pay her any mind: I had a hot date for that night, believe me I had more important things to worry about.

Meanwhile, she went into the bedroom to see what the workmen were up to. "You can leave the ladder here, for the time being. Do you think you can put the rest of the putty in around the window tomorrow? Because I'd like you all to start work on the gallery as soon as possible, and the rest of the work on my apartment can wait." She lectured some big wall painter like a terrier going after a bull; the big lummox never even knew what hit him. Then she came back out, without bothering to look at me.

"These are the last works I'm going to paint on clay, Ginger. So it won't happen again." This seemed to placate her a bit. She took the other two paintings out of the carrier and stood them up against the wall.

"This is gorgeous, Marley. What do you call it?"

" 'Ode to Hero of the Future #5,' " I said. It was just an old thing I had given to my mother, then later retrieved. In the center was a gray gunsel sitting with a piece of metal in his hand, inside a metal box. In the background were some gray buildings, ominous and filled with gasoline, and some grasses —like the oil refineries outside Newark, New Jersey, voluptuous with sorrow and evil. "It's not finished," I said. "I have to add in a few details. But I thought you would like to see it. You

see, in times of antiquity there were real heroes, known for
their great achievements. But in today's world, all we have are
celebrities, people known for their well-knownness. Creations
only of the media. Well, a century ago men were more heroic
than people of today; and some guys in antiquity were even
more heroic, while people in the times of prehistory were real
gods. That's because they didn't have *People* magazine to create men, but the men created themselves, through their great
works. But my feeling is, in the future we will have real heroes
once more. Like me."

"How much do you think I should ask for it?" Ginger said.
She seemed a little nervous. What a distinguished bottom my
dealer had, sizable and with a nice triangular shape. Then she
looked at the third painting. "This is the weakest of the three,"
she said. "Actually, it's no good at all. The center part is all
right: but there's too much blue outside it."

I shrugged. I didn't mind that she said something like this,
because I had a simple way of dealing with it—I didn't listen.
"You're wrong," I said. "This painting is among my best. By
the way, are you going to Sherman's opening tonight? You
should see the girl who's meeting me there—"

"If I can make it," she said. "I'm going to try." She looked
harried. Really, she might have shown a little more interest in
my existence. It was not easy being an art dealer, that much I
could understand. Oh, well. A fondness for this person washed
over me, she seemed about ready to crack into little pieces.
Well, she was only a few years older than me, and had for the
past five years been operating privately out of her SoHo apartment. It was just now that she was going to open a place at
ground level, where street traffic could come in; it had taken
her this long to work up the strength. "Ginger, when am I going
to get paid for that last piece of mine you sold?" I said. I turned
a chair around and sat in it.

Unfortunately I heard a crack. It was only one of those little
spindly chairs like those in an ice-cream parlor, nothing I
would have allowed into my home. Ginger had a sort of moth-

ering way about her, on the whole—still she sighed and gri-
maced and didn't handle it all that well, at least not as I would
have done.

"Goddammit, Marley," she said. "And I just bought these
chairs, too. Listen, I'm really very busy right now. This woman
is coming over in a little while to look at your paintings, and
the men are fixing up the bedroom; my mother is visiting me,
and she's eighty, so things are a little hectic."

Well, I got up to leave. But she was ashamed of her abrupt-
ness with me, she smiled with an abstract, crispy little smile,
and walked me to the door. "Marley, I would advance you the
money that you should get from the last sale, but right now I'm
totally broke, what with opening a gallery. It's turned out to be
terribly expensive. But as soon as I get the check from the
buyer, I'll call you up and you can come and pick up your half
of the check. All right, honey? I'll speak to you soon." She
kissed me on the cheek.

"There's just one thing I want to say," I said.

"What's that?"

"I have a great idea for when I get rich. I'll hire John Lennon, Shakespeare, Puccini, and Jimi Hendrix to write an
opera. I've been thinking about this for a while. Isn't that a
fabulous idea? Just think about it."

"They're dead, Marley."

"I just want to tell you one more thing," I said.

"I've really got to go, Marley," Ginger said. "Maybe I'll see
you at Sherman's opening."

But she had made me morose, and I insisted on speaking.
"If I don't get this goddamn grant to build my chapel in Rome,
I'm going to give up painting."

"You're not going to give up painting, Marley," Ginger said.
"You're a genius. Besides, there's nothing else you can do."

"Do you think so?" I said.

I was pleased. And as there were some hours to kill, but not
really enough to accomplish any work in, I decided to cheer
myself up. I was nervous about meeting this girl later at Sherman's show. I had to kill hours: I would go to the Museum of

Natural History. Nor was it to cheer myself up entirely. I had to examine the stuffed lion group behind their glass wall to see what their fur looked like at close detail. Such details were essential in my work; there was going to be a lion in the "Feast of the Gods" painting.

It was violently cold out, and at the same time raining. It was no better or worse than being in Siberia—the World Trade Center was covered in grim, yellowish fog, and the tops of the buildings disappeared into the gloom. The stuff was pouring down from the yellow sky. I wouldn't have been surprised if it was the end of the world by flood.

Which made me think about old Noah. He was an Armenian, this explained his great love for animals. For some years some guy in New England had been building his own ark; it occurred to me I would be well advised to send him a check when I got rich. In that way I would be assured of a position on the boat if indeed the flood came.

I tried to leap over a puddle: a small lake was more like it, for though I estimated where the lake finished, I was wrong in my misapprehensions—the lake kept going, and I landed in water up to my ankles.

My cowboy boots would be ruined, no doubt, but I trudged onward. The water was a very tricky obstacle, for under it was a sheet of ice. The few other souls who had dared to come out were slipping this way and that; like one big comedy routine from a silent film. What a miasma!

But I made it to the subway. I got on an uptown express train that would stop at Seventy-second Street. Then I planned to get out and walk the ten blocks uptown. But it didn't stop: the conductor announced the next stop would be 125th Street. "Goddammit," I said. And a man sitting across from me said, "You can change trains here." As if I didn't know! So I had to say, "Yes, mister, I know. I'm from the city. But these trains are fucked." After that he didn't speak to me again. But there was no denying I was right.

At 125th Street I saw the downtown train come in: I dashed up the stairs and down the other side and flung myself onto the train, which said it was a local. *But it was no local.* At Eighty-first Street it didn't stop, nor at Seventy-second—I let out a scream. The other passengers looked up from their news-papers at me. "Goddammit!" I said. "If I was in Rome the goddamn fucking subways wouldn't do this to me. The fucking train says it's a local and it doesn't stop. What kind of shit is this?" I glared at them all. But nobody else even seemed per-turbed. They were so resigned about their lot they didn't even utter a fuss.

There was a terrible stink in the car. I couldn't figure out where it was coming from. I looked down to the other end of the car. There was a bum-girl sitting there. This person smelled so bad the entire car stank, and yet they allowed her to ride the subway. She couldn't have been very old, shrouded in wet newspapers and a blanket, which she constantly plucked at to rearrange upon herself. A tremendous smell, not easily cultivated. Did she not notice it on herself? And she was without shoes; God, I was sorry in my heart and yet filled with fury—in Rome there were no bums on the trains. With all this money in the United States, they couldn't find this bum a better place to sit out the winter?

With a groan she rolled over onto her side, filling up the whole seat. There under the seat was a pair of jogging sneak-ers, missing the sides and backs, mostly rotted away. Which had a lot to say about how I felt about joggers; and this was the only thing this creature had to slog along in.

It was devastating. Why I could not feel more compassion for this person I did not know. Is there no harnessing human emotions into something useful? But meanwhile half my brain was blabbing on about the disgustingness of the subways, doing nothing but burbling to myself. By now there was hardly even any use in going to the museum: I had spent the whole day resting up, my watch said it was well past four. If the museum closed at five there was little sense.

But I sloshed back up anyway; I had to change cars while the train was in motion, and for a second, poised between cars, I considered stepping off and throwing myself onto the track.

Though, knowing me, I would not be killed but maimed for life. Still, if I had genuinely set my mind to it, I could have bumped myself off: I saw before me, in my damp misery, the next ten or twenty years of my life, broke and unknown, to end up no doubt like the bum riding the train endlessly. Then the second of contemplation passed: I had my date with Lacey to look forward to, after all, and if I continued to live I would sooner or later be able to teach them all a good lesson. Hah!

When I got off the train at Eighty-first Street, I went down the wrong exit, not the one that led directly into the museum. There on the stairway was still another bum, poised halfway up the stairs, able neither to walk up nor to come down. Wearing flipflops on his feet instead of shoes—and emitting that same stale, hideous reek, neither urine nor sweat but something much worse: the formaldehyde of decay.

An old Toulouse-Lautrec of a bum, unable to go up or down the stairs, with ponderous hunch and hunch along. He clasped the railing: I had to brush by him, thinking, Ah, what is the use if I help him up or down, when what he will arrive at will be the same at either end, probably worse than where he is now?

The measliness of myself and humanity struck me to the core.

But luckily the museum was open that evening until six, which made matters a little better. For I believed that museums should be open twenty-four hours a day, and should not cost anything, as was the case in England, so that I might roam about the African Plains Hallway at four in the morning with thoughts of the African veldt deep in my head.

Meanwhile, I was scrounging in my pocket for some money to buy my way in. There was a sign that said, "Pay what you wish, but you must pay something. Adults, $2.50."

I did not wish to pay $2.50. No, I would pay what I wished. And I was standing there, searching for some coinage, when the girl who was working the register looked at me with a smile and said, as if reading my mind, "You can pay whatever you wish, you know."

"I know," I said. I handed her fifty cents, but abruptly I saw myself as she must have seen me: soaking wet, wearing gray pants covered with paint, my long hair chopped and ragged. And umbrellaless; for this article I had lost a multitude of times. With some green paint on my face, which I later noticed when I went to take a piss; and shaven badly, for as it is said, the greatest artists don't give a damn about the physical amenities of society.

But I went in. I was at the entrance where the great Indian canoe full of wooden Indians was built. Which had been there for as long as I could remember—how many times had I seen it as a child and longed to climb in.

Oh, there were many exhibits that moved me greatly: the African peoples and their baskets, and the costumes made of shells and straw, like a large house to wear upon one's person.

I spent the most time in front of the king cobra. This animal filled me with glee. The skin, for one thing, a rippling cheese-cloth of the other world. And its immense, incredible power, for it could kill in a matter of minutes.

There was a new exhibit: artificial and not real, of a group of army ants. These in the middle of completely devouring a large horse tethered in their path which could not escape.

These ants never settle down but march constantly, devouring everything in their path; never deviating they go onward, cutting a swathe many feet thick through the ranks of the living creatures on their trail. Vultures fly above to eat the small animals which their coming start from cover, the rank smell of carrion surrounds them. Ah, how human and more than human! Because they must search everywhere for food for the eighty thousand adults and the squirming brood of young.

I wandered down to the African veldt and jungle. How cleverly the small exhibits were put together. The perspective had to be painted on the background so keenly that it blended in with the foreground. It was all painted like in the old Hudson River School. If only I was rich enough to purchase a stuffed warthog. I would have built a room just like one of these for it.

Only I would not stick to re-creating perfectly the animal's natural environment, but would add laser guns and flying horses and all the rest of the modern world to the background.

I couldn't help but be impressed with what had been done here. Like two gazelles and a heron down at a pool of water. Using a piece of glass and some old leaves, the designer had made it look like real water. And the pride of lions—with withering hair, aged, fusty lions, with partially bald backs. It was very well done. But the air had deteriorated the grouping a little. Still, these things had all been there for eternity.

And in the background the hooting of children sounded. Oh, there was loads to see, and I was in a very cheery mood. I witnessed dinosaurs, evil and forlorn, some without skin and just bones, others with skin added. The allosaurus, with his large head designed as a weapon of destruction. A meat eater who did not need to stalk his game—the other dinosaurs were too stupid to run—but simply needed to pit his teeth and claws against weight and tail.

There were only two forms of defense against this ferocious dinosaur: one was to get out into the water and stay there, the other was to grow armor. Not easily done in a hurry.

Everywhere I went I saw how similar other forms of life were to mankind. Only mankind was the worst. And the art world—the business part—was worse than that. I would have numbered myself in with the rest of humanity, only I was one step above it: by that I mean I was an artist, which redeemed me.

After this I went off to Sherman's opening. But Ginger wasn't anywhere to be found, which was sad, because I wanted to hear once again from her lips that I was a genius.

I wandered around the Borali Gallery. The whole room was like a steam bath; there were so many people crowded into the place I couldn't even see Sherman's work. There was Lacey, my date, crushed next to a wizened poet/art critic named Rene LaRoue—they already knew each other and were talking, but I ignored him, for once when I had admired one of his poems

that was framed on the wall of the Gulag Archipelago (my
favorite bar) word got back to him and he tried to ask me out
on a date, the thought of which made me sick.

I went over and kissed Lacey; I wasn't unhappy to see her.
On this, our first real date, she looked even more delightful
than I had remembered—clad in something black and smol-
dering, and belted with the skins of leopard and various orang-
utans. "These were made from old coats that belonged to my
grandmother in the twenties," she said. "So I cut them down
and accidentally I kept cutting and cutting and all that I ended
up with were some belts."

"You look great," I said. "I had no idea that you were so
adorable." And I became certain that we would go out with
each other. Whispering in her ear I invited her to come to
dinner with Sherman and Willow and myself and Sherman's
dealer, Borali. This was to take place after the opening. It was
supposed to be a secret that we were all going out. Sherman
didn't want to offend any of his friends who weren't invited.

Lacey breathed heavily into my ear in one corner of the
room, while I was talking to different friends about Ginger:
how at last a decent dealer had agreed to take me on. My life
was going to be uphill from now on, I could see that. And the
general consensus was that I was very lucky, for Ginger was
going to be a hot new dealer in a matter of time, and we would
make a great team.

When the room cleared out I found Sherman: he was barely
able to stand on his feet. In his hand he was holding a glass of
white wine that I guessed was not his first or his fifth. "How
are you doing, Sherman?" I said. "Fantastic show. Are you
pleased?"

He scowled at me, but I did not take it personally.

"I invited Lacey to come with us to dinner," I said. "Which
I'm sure is all right."

"Why not?" he said. "Nice to see you. What's that around
your waist, dead rats?" But Lacey did not answer, merely
smiled mysteriously. "Go across the street for a drink," Sher-

man said. "Willow and I will come by in a few more minutes, and then we'll go to dinner."

I wandered around the room for a bit more, so I could get a look at Sherman's work. Well, the room was too small for such massive pieces. They possessed a great deal of energy. Sadly, they were nothing that anyone would want to hang on the wall. It wasn't that they weren't pleasant to look at: they weren't. But it was more a question of how many people would have a fifteen-foot wall that they would want to inflict such large girders of pink and blue upon?

While I was thinking about this I bumped into Jeff Smyll, another one of my roommates from art school whom I couldn't stand. He was small and ridiculous, filling me with loathing. I was sorry to run into him; here I had fantasies of being nominated for sainthood, I considered myself a saintly kind of guy, and yet more and more I was realizing there were thousands of people I couldn't stand.

I tried to think of what it must be like for him. He had always had a thing about his height, and now for him to bump into me like this at an opening, when I was doing so well and he was still just short, must have been painful for him. He was basically a smart guy, basically talented. But the basically that I'm speaking of is basically mediocre. I had to live with him in room 132, back when I still lived in the dorm my first year. He looked like John Denver, and that made it worse. I tried to smile. "Jeff," I said. "Jeff, how are you?"

"Marley," he said. "Marley Mantello, right?" As if he didn't know. He grinned and smiled at Lacey. But sadly Lacey's name slipped momentarily from my mind, and so I didn't introduce them. Because all at once I was remembering why I couldn't stand him. This made my lack of saintliness a little easier for me to accept.

"Eaten any ham lately, Jeff?" I said.

When this guy was my roommate, he never did any work. He always seemed to get by miraculously. For his art project he spent a whole semester copying three fruit carton labels

onto little graphs. This was years after Andy Warhol had already thought of the idea. Jeff spent four months on this project—he was the biggest pothead in the world, with a terrible
taste in music. But I was still thinking of the ham. I asked him
what he was doing.

"You know, I'm home for vacation," he said, grimacing. "I
sell pizzas in L.A."

Had I no sympathy? Was I reduced to gloating over a mari-
juana freak who had spent art school replicating labels? But
still, I remembered what he had done, and taking Lacey to one
side I told her the story, before she could warm up to him too
much.

This guy had bought a ham, a canned ham. He put it on the
shelf in our dorm room. I said to him, "Jeff, you have a canned
ham—" I was a pretty hungry guy in college. The canned ham
gave me ideas.

"Yeah," he said, "I'll make it tomorrow or something."

So I went back to work, but I thought to myself, When you
cook that canned ham, buddy, I'll be right here. Because I had
to live with him, I might as well get to share in the good things,
too.

A week later that canned ham was still there on the shelf,
on the side of the room that was his. I said, "Jeff, when are
you going to get to that canned ham, it's going to spoil if you
leave it up there."

"Yeah, yeah," he said. "I'll get to it."

Another week went by.

"Refrigerate that ham," I said. "It's going to explode otherwise and I don't want to be here when it happens." Every day
I said, "Jeff, will you do something about that ham?"

But weeks passed. One night we were both in the room—I
was painting and he was duplicating fruit labels. Listening to
music and working. All of a sudden there was an explosion.
Splattering all over the room—on his side—was the ham. The
stench was so bad it was unimaginable. Rotting ham that went
off like a bomb. The ironic and funny thing was that nothing
on my side of the room was touched. His ham was situated at

such an angle that only his side of the room was covered with rotten particles of ham. But the air was so full of fumes I literally had to run out of there so as to save myself from vomiting.

Inside of ten minutes the entire dorm was empty. No one could stay in the building. Jeff went back into the room, his face covered with a wet towel, and threw the remains he could collect into a garbage can. They had to burn the contents of the pail. The entire dorm smelled for a week.

Lacey and I each had a quick drink in the Korean joint across the street. The specialty of the house, a ginseng cocktail, was made with shaved ginseng, so it had an extrapowerful kick. "Maybe I shouldn't drink this stuff," I told Lacey. "My stomach—very sensitive." But I left her there and went back across the street to the gallery to find out what was keeping Sherman and Willow.

Willow was a sorry elf. How she made her living I don't know. She wasn't poor, she lived in a big, whitewashed loft, with built-in couches covered with dirty white cushions vaguely reminding me of straitjackets. I used to like to go over to her place, with Sherman or alone, because she had a huge color television, the largest kind made before movie-screen size. It was the same kind I planned to buy as soon as I got rich. She was another of Borali's artists—but she couldn't possibly have survived on what she made through Borali's gallery, because Borali didn't make money for anyone except himself.

Willow's sculptures were made from Plexiglas, some kind of polyurethane substance, ethereal and resembling large turds made of spun sugar.

Well, I was very fond of Willow: I liked her. She reminded me, as I say, of a sort of fatigued-looking elf, a Peter Pan who had aged perceptibly but refused to accept it. Her pale red hair was wispy and stuck out from her head like duckling down. It may be that she resembled my sister; there was some connection there, the very vagueness of them.

Anyway, Sherman and Willow came back out to the Korean

place for a drink before we went to meet Borali and his assistant in a Japanese restaurant, Willow already a little unsteady on her feet. From what I had seen she lived on a diet of champagne cocktails and diet cigarettes. She, like Sherman, could be found in the farthest recess of any seedy bar; the Three Roses on Canal Street, Stanley's down near the World Trade Center, the Gulag Archipelago . . . crammed into the back of a bar, drinking alone or with friends, her ghostly white face with childish circles under the eyes and a perky snout of a nose that turned up just a trifle too much at the tip. The nose seemed to say, "I'm a jaunty, easygoing sort of person." When in reality she was superior in her attitude and at the most innocuous of comments from anyone would jump to a fight. Which amused me greatly, for when we sat down at the bar next to Lacey I started to complain about deodorant commercials. "What the hell does anybody need deodorant for?" I said. "You know, I never wear the stuff—I never smell, and I think it's all a hoax thought up by big corporations to get the American public to shell out money."

"Yeah, you're right," said Sherman. "I don't smell, either. What a rip-off the whole idea of deodorant is."

But Willow was very indignant. "Well, I do smell," she said. "Deodorant prevents me from smelling. Just because you guys don't use the stuff there's no reason that the rest of us shouldn't be allowed to use it."

Just speaking absently I had put her on the defensive.

"What do you think, Lacey?" I said.

"It's not a question of what anyone thinks," Willow said. "You guys think of yourselves as so superior that the world should be changed according to your beliefs."

"I smell," Lacey said, trying to placate Willow.

"You can say that again," Sherman said.

"Then you should use deodorant," I said. "Your show was great, Sherman. You should feel great. I bet you get reviewed this time."

But Sherman was morose and slurped up his ginseng cocktail rapidly. I helped myself from a dish of maraschino cherries

that were behind the bar. Being a tall guy, my arms were long
enough to reach. Before I knew it, the Korean bartender came
back and moved the whole bowl away. Willow was drinking
her champagne cocktail. She had that poise to her; an attitude
of being above and beyond those around her, though she was
dressed in a shabby deranged raincoat of pink psychedelic
plastic, and old platform-heeled boots. I asked her what she
was doing these days—I hadn't seen her in some time.

"A bunch of us are collaborating to make an animated film
of my work—with the music from my old rock-and-roll group."
For she had been the lead singer in a defunct band, not a bad
band, but lacking in talent.

"You know," I said. "I have a great idea for a collaboration.
I'd get John Lennon together with Shakespeare, Puccini, and
Jimi Hendrix to write an opera."

"A good idea," Lacey said, her face all shiny from the ginseng whoop-de-do. "Weird, but a good idea."

"You couldn't do it," Willow said. What a little piccolo voice
she had, like a living character from a Walt Disney cartoon. "I
mean, it's possible you could get Shakespeare to collaborate
with Puccini, and Hendrix with Lennon, but I don't see what
Shakespeare and Lennon would have to say to each other."

She put a damper on my evening, she really did. "I think
you're wrong," I said.

But she was already talking to Sherman about the fact that
Borali had said he would take Sherman out to eat at a Japanese
diner after his opening. "That guy is really getting off easy,
Sherman. He knows how to save himself money. I tell you, he
really is cheap. You've only invited a few people. At least he
could take us someplace expensive."

"I thought it would be nicer with just a few people," Sherman said. "I can't face very many people right now." He
glared at Lacey. "And I like Jap food." It was curious to think
that Willow was so interested in money, when she pretended
otherwise; wearing a sort of shabby shirt beneath her raincoat
she had made herself, of some dingy metallic substance, which
looked out of date and was not elegant. While Lacey was mut-

tering, "Oh, I love Japanese food. And I hope you don't mind my coming along, Sherman; I know we're adult enough to be friends, Marley did ask me to come along."

"Well, I mind," Sherman said, and this was his attempt to be funny, a humor that I understood but one which left Lacey with a jarred expression. "But Marley doesn't go out with girls too often, and you're pleasant enough to look at."

We went over to the restaurant. Borali was sitting there with his assistant. His head was a bit too large for his body, and his hair was most peculiar, a sort of little bowl-shaped haircut that made him resemble a monkey. I examined his legs protruding from the end of the table; oddly spindled legs, as if he never used them. Even the knees were visible behind the gray flannel of his suit. His assistant was an older woman who at first glance appeared normal. But then I noticed that everything on her face was askew. Her eyes were set at different heights and one was slightly closed while the other was open. Even her mouth turned up on one side and down on the other. And while she was older than Stephen Borali, she was much the meeker, and barely acknowledged my existence while being intro-duced. I felt bereft with sadness. Still, I didn't know what to say to her; she was jammed in the corner, morose, with that half-shut eye. So I ignored her.

But Borali was like a bowl of Jell-O; he popped up in his slim, elegant suit, begging us to sit down, have a drink. "There you are, there you are," he said. How cheerful he was, he and Willow were like two pixies, and Sherman, too, was small and ratlike, physically he was another hairless type. I felt a little embarrassed to be there with Lacey—the two of us with so much hair and much taller than those around us.

It made sense for Borali to have artists so alike in type; their work was quite similar as well—immensely tropical, ephem-eral balloons of pink and topaz taffy, or like flamingos with bashed-open heads and twisted legs.

While I was thinking all this, I didn't know what to order; I got a plate of sushi, the same as the others. A tiny geisha of a waitress brought out a pile of labial raw fish on huge ashtrays. I took one look at it and ordered a vodka.

"You're not going to eat anything, Marley?" Borali said in a little chipmunk voice.

"Don't worry about it," I said, jabbing at a lump of tuna with my chopstick. "I have to be careful of my stomach. It never occurred to me a restaurant would serve their fish raw. If it doesn't agree with me I'll be in big trouble. But I can always get a bite to eat later on at McDonald's."

"God, you're suave, Marley," Sherman said violently. But the others all laughed, though I was quite serious.

Nobody had much to say. Borali looked at us with his bright eyes. Sherman appeared to have fallen into some lower depths; well, he had been drinking for weeks before his opening, now he had to sink even further. Willow, the fairy elf with two front teeth that protruded far beyond the realm of human probability, was wolfing down the fish. Lacey had ordered tempura. She was crunching away at it; she wasn't a talkative type.

"Have you thought about having some work done on yourself, Willow?" Borali said.

"How much does it cost?" Willow said.

"My surgeon is willing to trade work for paintings."

"In that case," Willow said, "I'd like to have my whole self redone. But not my hair."

"It was very interesting how he did my hair transplant," Borali said. "First a number of artificial hair plugs were implanted in my head, as well as the remaining hair on the side of my head, which was spread thinner. The whole thing was covered with a thin layer of skin grafted from my thighs. When the true hair grew out, the artificial plugs were removed. My father said, 'Stephen, I don't know why you're doing this, you look perfectly all right bald.' But you know, I'm only going to be alive this once, and I wanted to look good during that time."

"You're a lot more outgoing since you got your hair," Willow said. Sherman let out a sharp snort.

"Maybe you'll want to have the lines under your eyes done, Willow," Borali said.

I wasn't really listening to the conversation but watched Lacey—an angelic mouth; she caught my eye and smiled. Sherman let out another of his curious noises.

"By the way," I said to the assembled, "what's the most disgusting meal you've ever eaten?"

"Ah, that's a very good question," Borali said. Eagerly he picked at his pickerel. Anyway, it was some sort of greenish fish, perhaps a porgy or plum fish. This gave me thought for the food I was going to paint in my "Feast of the Gods." I'd do a sort of bacchanalia, with all different food crouched around the bottom of the painting: small green and white cakes, large colorful fish of pearly-white and gold lamé, mysterious fruits, some resembling the human head, others like chestnuts and bits of amber. Even the insects from the insect world would be there, huge flies with gaily striped wings . . . in the background I'd have a swamp, with creeping things hanging from the vines and stunted trees resembling artichokes. Also a kind of sickly flower plant, with murky leaves.

And I'd do the women up in all different sorts of hairdos, some with tangled manes, bluish-silver, decorated with weeds and flowers; and there in the middle would be Poseidon, a kind of flabby guy in a fish suit, mucking about at the edge of the water and looking something like Borali, only more substantive. Maybe even an old geezer in the corner: Zeus in his old age with bits of corn and other foodstuff in his coppery beard —kind of Howard Hughes-ish. I looked at Sherman, scowling away on the other side of the table. These people I was with now—they were nothing more than furious elves and fairies, in twentieth-century disguise. But this is what has happened to gods and pixies in the twentieth century. They have forgotten their true selves and are out trying to make a buck and win influential friends. Still, in my picture most of the people would be having a good time, drinking out of goblets of red glass, yawning and carousing. The whole thing maybe twenty feet long.

Meanwhile, Borali had taken my question about meals and was flying along with it. "That's a good question, Marley," he said. "There's one meal I've eaten that was so disgusting I don't know if I can tell it at dinner."

"You can't," his assistant said bluntly. This was the first thing she'd said since our arrival; I was surprised she could speak at all.

"But there's another meal," he said, "which is also pretty disgusting." He leaned forward across the table; I noticed his tie was about to fall into the mustard sauce. "You know, when I was in Singapore I was in a restaurant with a number of businessmen, all Asian except myself. I was eating something called rice birds. Actually, I was feeling quite proud of myself for being able to eat them. Rice birds are tiny birds caught in the wild and deep fried. They come on a plate beneath a silver cover, and you eat each bird whole."

"Beak?" I said.

"Yes."

"Feet?" I said.

"Yes. The birds are very tiny, you just pop each one in your mouth. Curiously without flavor, but a lot of crunch, Marley." He looked at me and smiled, as if there was more to his words than met the eye. "There was a big cage of monkeys in the corner of the room, which wouldn't have been allowed in this country, but in many Indonesian and Asian countries they don't have any regulations about animals in restaurants, you know, so I didn't think anything of it. But I did notice that in the center of each table was a large round hole. After the businessmen had eaten their soup, the waiter took one of the monkeys out of the cage and brought it over to the table. All the men nodded and said that it was fine, as if the waiter had brought over a bottle of wine. I began to feel uneasy. The waiter placed the monkey in a sort of stool and strapped it in. The monkey began to scream in a way that was extraordinarily human. Then the waiter brought the monkey underneath the table and placed the chair holding the monkey beneath the hole so that the monkey's head was sticking up through the hole."

"I don't want to hear this," Sherman said. He put his hands

over his ears. Willow looked most fascinated; she picked up a tiny brush made from scallions at the edge of her plate and crushed it into her mouth. Then she lit a cigarette.

"The monkey stopped screaming and began to moan. As if in sympathy, the other monkeys in the cage hooted and rattled the bars. I felt very much as if I was witnessing an execution in the gas chamber, though I didn't know what they were going to do to the monkey; but the businessmen were so detached, they seemed like newspaper reporters, watching but not commenting. The waiter came back to the table carrying a large chef's knife. With one stroke he sliced off the top of the monkey's head. The monkey was still alive. Its eyes were moving. At least, I thought it was still alive. Each businessman picked up a spoon, leaned forward, and began to scoop out the brains of the monkey and eat it."

"Alive?" I said.

"Oh, yes, the monkey was still alive, at least briefly. Well. It was all I could do to keep eating my rice birds. I don't like to watch my food die in front of me; I like my meat to be killed and cooked offstage before I eat it." For a moment Borali looked embarrassed, as if he had revealed something he shouldn't have. Yet why had he told this story? He turned to me triumphantly. Was he trying to tell me I was no better than the monkey eaters, that I should put aside any hopes I had of achieving sainthood?

Naw.

"Ugh," Lacey said. Her face was even paler than usual, her nose could have used a little powder, it glowed like a tender bulb. Sherman took his hands away from his ears.

"Finished?" he said.

"What's the meal that's even worse?" I said.

"Get out, Marley!" Sherman said. I ignored this.

"I have a strange fear of opening cans," Willow said. "Though when I bother to eat I live mostly out of cans: some tuna fish, canned asparagus, mandarin oranges. It's the simplest way to eat. And yet, I have this silly fear of opening cans

—that I might find the wrong thing inside. A tip of a finger, perhaps, or something chewy and not quite identifiable . . ."

"Ah, don't let me get started on my cannibalism stories," Borali said.

"What are they?" I said. I was quite eager to find out.

"Well, I don't really think I should bring them up over dinner," Borali said, looking at me slyly across the table. "Maybe you'll come over after dinner for a drink." And then he looked around the table. "I don't think the rest of you could take it."

Then for some reason Sherman just fell apart. "I thought I could keep my mouth shut but I can't. You've totally wrecked my fucking dinner, Marley. Whenever you're around everything totally deteriorates. This was supposed to be *my* dinner! You show up with my ex-girlfriend, egging people on to tell disgusting stories—I don't know how I got to be friends with you in the first place, but I sure as hell made a big mistake. You have absolutely no feelings. You, too, Lacey, but as far as I'm concerned, at this point you don't even exist."

Well, I could tell he was mad. His face was bright red; as the waitress went by with a platter of drinks he snatched one away and gulped it down, without bothering to look. Even Willow was nodding her head in agreement, though Borali just looked amused. These were the politics of the art world.

"I think I'll turn down that offer to stop by for a drink," I told Borali. "Lacey and I have got to go home so that I can do some work. Thanks for the dinner, though." And I helped Lacey into her coat and went out, snatching up another handful of maraschino cherries on my way past the bar.

So we left. I was starving, and told Lacey we were stopping off at McDonald's for a quick bite.

Inside there were a few dried mice of customer-service attendants: no makeup, just extruded faces topped with pie-shaped platters for hats, and wearing the most adorable of costumes! I was sincere when I thought this—the clothes they wore reminded me of superhero costumes, and I would have liked to do a piece about superhero waitresses. A sort of nylon sheath in brown, ringed at the neck and sleeves with bright orange.

The tables were covered with effluvia, but I wasn't going to complain; as I explained to Lacey, "At least I can afford some food here. By the way, do you have any cash on you?"

"Some," she said.

"Fine," I said. "Hand it over."

I purchased a chocolate milkshake, fries, and four hamburgers, tender slices of meat wedged between two soggy buns. Screw the raw fish! I was meat happy. "I could live on hunks of bloody red steak every day of my life," I said.

"When I was in Paris my checks didn't arrive at American Express and I was broke for a while," Lacey said. "So I had to live mostly on oranges. Small, sweet-smelling oranges—two for a franc—that were very sour, tasting almost like lemons, and brilliant crimson inside. To me, when I think of Paris, I think of these oranges. But then, I really don't like meat."

I could have figured that much out just from looking at her. She had the pale hair and bright eyes of a llama or other herbivore. So much for getting myself all worked up over our date—really, I couldn't figure out what it was she wanted from me. "Well," I said, "I'm a carnivore. I don't even like to use a knife and fork. If I have a steak or roast beef I'd rather tear it off, bite by bite, with my teeth. There's nothing like the texture of meat, dense and red, the smell, the bloody taste. Of course, I'll admit, I don't want anything to do with killing. I don't want to see any cows bawling, I just want to eat them. Someday I might open a restaurant, 'Where the Elite Meet to Eat Meat.' Someday I'll cook you a roast beef."

"That would be nice," Lacey said.

"I cook roast beef brilliantly."

Next to us was a family I couldn't help but study, not having had much contact with the nuclear American grouping before. A puggy father, who looked like he was about to go out of his mind—he lit one cigarette after the next—and across from him was the mother, the female of the pair. Stuffed between them

at the table were the children, a girl and two boys. The older
ones kept up a sort of battle cry, "Mommy, Mommy,
Mommy," while she tried to talk to her mate. "At work today,"
she said, "Jim put his finger through the window. There was a
lot of blood, he had to go to the hospital for stitches."

The kid sitting across from her, the littlest, about six, had a
pinched face and a bird-snout of a nose. There was red all over
his chin from some sort of frozen pop he was eating, something
pink and dripping. At last he put down the pop and stuck a
finger up his nose, pulling out a long string of snot. I put my
hamburger down on my plate. Why must I, Marley Mantello,
be the one to bear witness to such events?

Yet I knew these tribulations were given me for a reason. To
see that family was like getting one of those little things that
float sometimes in the corner of your field of vision and look
like molecules. Edvard Munch got a permanent one of those
things in his eye in the shape of a bird with a long beak—he
was sixty-seven at that time and all of a sudden he started
painting pictures with these birds with long beaks in them.

Not that the point about vision defects matters when it
comes to painters; nor is it of any use in explaining why El
Greco painted such elongated figures, even though some people say it was because of myopia or something else wrong with
his eyes. But the guy had to be crazy to paint in the first place,
and whatever else was wrong with him was only secondary.

"Come on," I said. "Let's get out of here." I jumped up,
pushing the stuff on the table away. "Let's walk downtown," I
said. "I'm in the mood to walk." For I had to be careful and
make sure I didn't indulge too freely in the pleasures of life,
such as taxicabs. Like Raphael, who was crazy about women
and wasted a lot of time over them, and then died when he was
thirty-seven, which was probably what would happen to me. It
was something I thought about occasionally, every five or ten
minutes.

So I would walk off the evening as penance.

"But do we have to go to your place right this minute, Marley?" Lacey said. "I feel sort of bad about what happened at

dinner. I know Sherman is kind of mad. We could go find him at the Three Roses."

"Listen, I have to work," I said. "That's the way I am. But I'd love to have you there while I paint."

So Lacey smiled at me, and we continued down the gray, windy avenue. It was freezing cold; I put my hands in my pockets and took long strides, preoccupied with my thoughts.

case history #15: melinda

Melinda was tiny and blond with the luminous dark eyes of a loris or some nocturnal animal. At night she worked in a bar; she had come to New York to be a dancer with an experimental company but had broken her leg in a taxi accident and now hoped to get into choreography or set design.

With the money she collected from the insurance company she was able to buy a small apartment with a backyard near Tompkins Square Park. When she had some extra cash she would go to the ASPCA and buy animals that only had one day to live and take them home with her and try to find them new homes. Almost always she grew attached to the animals and couldn't bring herself to give them away. The animals were a substitute, she thought, for a man and a real relationship, but there were no men interested in her and the animals loved and accepted her in a way that no man ever could.

She lived with eight cats and five dogs: an elderly Schnauzer with no teeth who reminded her of her grandfather; a German shepherd-collie mix that supposedly had been trained as an attack dog but was afraid of everything, including the cats; a pair of schipperkes that liked to howl in unison to the stereo; and a dachshund that had to be strapped into a little pair of wheels as he was partially paralyzed from the midsection down. The animals took up all her time and were spoiled and demanding, but this didn't bother her; in fact, Melinda rather liked playing mother.

Once late at night she saw a tiny baby rat crossing the street very slowly. It was missing a leg and Melinda scared the rat into a paper bag and took it home, where she kept it in an aquarium. A short time after she took the rat home her dogs and cats all came down with a bad case of fleas but Melinda loved the little rat and also sometimes found pigeons that were hurt and other wounded and delicate animals. In the yard was a stack of cages in which she kept rabbits and ferrets she had bought from a run-down pet store on Houston Street.

The bar where she worked was a regular neighborhood kind of bar where a lot of male artists hung out watching the ball games on TV or shooting pool and most of them had tried to date Melinda at one time or another. Quite often Melinda would invite them back to her place for a cup of coffee, but when they saw her tiny crowded apartment (which was full of angry barking dogs that were all busy defending Melinda or trying to rape her guest's leg, and yowling cats and the rat in the cage) they never returned to visit her again.

Most of the men she knew didn't mind their own mess but it was quite a different story in a woman. Melinda didn't care, however; in a way she looked upon the chaos and terrible odor of her apartment as a kind of test. When the right man came along he would be willing to overcome the circumstances in much the same way as the princes in fairy tales were willing to slay the dragon or go off in search of the magic potion in order to win the princess.

One night, in her bar, a pretty, exotic-looking boy came in. He had dyed black hair and was missing one of his front teeth. He looked like a crazed angel. None of the regulars had ever seen him around before.

After he had drunk four beers Melinda suggested he pay his tab as the bar was about to close. The boy broke down and began to cry. He said he was only twenty-three (though he looked younger) and had no money and was out on the street. His name was Chicho, and he hoped to get a job, either working with the elephants at the zoo or studying dolphins in Florida.

Melinda felt sorry for Chicho. She said he could come home with her, and in fact he could stay with her on a temporary basis provided that he help clean and care for the animals. Chicho said that would be fine.

After a few days Melinda realized she was falling in love with Chicho. He was so naive, so gentle and innocent, he reminded her of a little injured puppy. Behind his facade of street toughness was a true child who worshiped Melinda and thought everything about her was wonderful.

He was very good with the dogs and took each one out in turn for its exercise so that Melinda would have more time to work on her dance project ideas. He even cleaned up the yard, which was filled with cat droppings and mud. "It's true I'm educated and you're not," Melinda told him. "And also you're ten years younger than me. I always thought these things would be a problem in a relationship. But now I see the ideal relationship is based on trust and kindness, and the rest is unimportant."

One day they discovered that the stunted rat in the aquarium was missing. Melinda accused Chicho of letting it go or somehow getting rid of it—of all the animals, the rat was the only one he didn't care for—but he assured her the rat must have escaped on its own. No doubt it was running around somewhere in the walls, or had made its way back to the streets.

She didn't really believe him, but she didn't want to pick a fight. She was thirty-three years old and Chicho was the first man who had shown any interest in hanging around. It was true he was good with the dogs, but aside from that he was a lot of work; he still could not find a job and Melinda had to give him spending money, and he expected dinner to be cooked for him whether she had to work that evening or not. But any stray, Melinda knew, was a lot of work at first and it was possible, through years of gentle persuasion, to train even the most abused and wild animal.

A short time later she came down with a mysterious disease. She grew quite ill and no doctor had any idea what was wrong with her. Finally, after extensive tests, she was diagnosed as having Weil's disease. This was an extremely rare ailment which most doctors had not seen or heard of. It was acquired from drinking liquid that a rat had urinated into. It was possible that the deformed rat had been wandering around late one night and urinated into the glass of water that Melinda always kept near her side of the bed.

She was taken to the hospital and was there for many weeks, but during that time Chicho only came to visit her once. She forgave him, however; he was like a wild animal who did not understand even the most ordinary laws of etiquette. She knew Chicho was probably thinking about her all the time.

It was not expected that she would recover; she could feel herself growing weaker and weaker and she thought how sad it would be after her death when all her stray animals and Chicho had no one to look after them.

To everyone's surprise, however, she got better. She went home in a taxi and when she walked through the door of her apartment she found Chicho in bed with her closest girlfriend. All of the animals were gone—he had apparently given them all away or let them loose—and the apartment had been neatly repainted and cleaned up. "Man," Chicho said, not even bothering to wrap a sheet around himself, "what are you doing here?"

She had to get the police to have Chicho evicted; it was expensive to get the locks changed, and difficult to accept the fact that she had been betrayed by one of God's creatures, but eventually she got a new bunch of crippled and stray dogs, forgot Chicho, and settled into her old ways, neither joyful nor despairing.

patterns

In the morning I'd go across the street to the delicatessen
to get a cup of coffee and I'd see the butchers in their
bloody coats, with hooks and knives slung around their
belts. It was after I had broken up with Stash. I'd moved into
an apartment in the meat market district; I liked it. The streets
were filled with puddles and bones, and a particular variety of
meat-eating pigeons, like carrion birds, that hung around the
neighborhood, pecking up bits of gristle and fat.

It was hard living alone, though: I kept waiting for someone
to come home and yell at me. At first I missed Stash terribly,
but then one day he stopped me on the street and said that he
had seen an episode of "The Mating Game" or some such
program, and one of the questions asked of a woman in her
late thirties was, "On what basis do you know if someone's
right for you?" And she answered, "There are four categories:
Spiritual, Physical, Intellectual, and Emotional."

Stash said that he had thought about this for a while, and
realized that we had only been compatible in three-and-a-half
categories. "Listen, Eleanor," he said. "Last week I had three
dates with a beautiful Swedish model, and she wanted me to
go to Czechoslovakia with her, but I realized I was only compatible with her in two of the four categories—Intellectual and
Physical."

After Stash told me this I stopped missing him. I just didn't
care to spend my life with a man who based the merits of his

relationships on something some woman in California had said on "The Mating Game."

I knew then it was up to me to negotiate a new life for myself. I remembered a guy I had met and I wrote him a letter. His name was Wilfredo and he was a very well-known fashion designer. Recently he had gone bankrupt, but everyone admired his work, he was talked about all the time, and I knew for a fact he would soon be on his feet again.

Wilfredo based his designs on all kinds of things: clothing he found in thrift stores, costumes borrowed from a theatrical clothing warehouse—pirate outfits and gorilla costumes and old Victorian numbers. Then he combined the various elements, had them remade in beautiful fabrics such as silk and cashmere, and faille and when the entire ensemble was together (such as a sequined vest with a cotton T-shirt and a brocade jacket and tiny wrinkled pants) the whole thing looked gorgeous and sold for thousands of dollars. He had light, brilliant brown eyes, almost yellow, and turned heads when he came into a room (I had seen him in nightclubs). When I met him I was struck by his extreme shyness: he could barely bring himself to speak to me in a voice above a whisper. About a year before I broke up with Stash, I was walking Andrew, our Dalmatian, in the courtyard one night, and this very cute guy came over to me with *his* Dalmatian, a bitch, and said he had seen me around before, walking the dog. After he started mumbling, I identified him as Wilfredo, the famous designer. I was very flattered when he said he admired my ambiance. It was late, and drizzling a little bit, and I certainly didn't look my best: I was wearing an old, dirty dress and a padded Mao jacket of Stash's (he had had Velcro sewn into the front but it still didn't close) and my hair was frizzy. I thought I looked like Elsa Lanchester in *The Bride of Frankenstein*, but maybe I was only flattering myself.

But I said to Wilfredo, "Listen, Stash and I would be delighted to breed Andrew." I gave him our phone number. Stash and I had often talked about having puppies, not that we needed another dog, but it would have been fun.

Stash was observing me out the window, and when I got back upstairs I was very excited: I told him that we were going to breed Andrew to a famous fashion designer, and that I had given the guy our phone number.

Stash got up and put Little Richard on the compact disc player. The music—"Tutti Frutti"—was so loud it hurt my ears. Then he turned and yelled across the room. "How could you have given out my number like that to some guy?" he said. "That guy could be a killer; now I'm going to have to get my telephone number changed to an unlisted one, and that will cost me forty-five dollars a month."

"What do you mean, *your* phone number?" I said. I tried to explain that all Wilfredo wanted was to breed our dog to his, and that I did have at least a modicum of sense and was able to recognize the difference between a killer and an internationally acclaimed fashion designer when I saw one. I figured that Stash was probably jealous.

As it turned out, Stash didn't speak to me for five days. I ended up apologizing, even though it was against my judgment to apologize when I didn't feel I had done anything wrong.

After the breakup, when I was settled in my new apartment, I decided to write to Wilfredo. I realized that I didn't know if he was interested in me or not. So when I wrote to him I simply explained that I had met him with my dog on the street (I included my physical description of the time, long red hair, tiny blue eyes, and an orange minidress with a peace symbol cut out over the stomach) and I said that I was a jewelry designer (in case he had forgotten) and if he was ready to breed his dog I could arrange it. Then I added, in a postscript, that I admired his work very much, and perhaps he could meet me for a drink.

I figured this way he could assume that I was interested in some kind of collaboration with him, perhaps in getting him to see my jewelry which he might possibly use to accompany his clothing. Or he could guess that I was trying to ask him out on a date.

Tons of men these days were getting married, and one of the most interesting things Wilfredo had said to me on that rainy night when we discussed breeding dogs was how much he would have loved to have kids. He had a brother who was married and raised bison in the Midwest, and sometimes Wilfredo would go there and baby-sit for him; his brother had three children, who were really great. So I thought, in retrospect, that there was a possibility of Wilfredo being interested in me, at least if he wanted to start reproducing quickly.

Anyway, a few days later Wilfredo called to tell me he had had his dog spayed. "That's a shame," I said. It was probably for the best, because Andrew was Stash's dog and Stash wasn't speaking to me at present. "But maybe you wouldn't mind looking at my jewelry—either my slides or actual pieces which I could bring by at your convenience?"

Wilfredo said that would be fine, he was looking for a new jewelry designer—he had some ideas for things himself, and maybe we could work together. Even though he was temporarily bankrupt, he was getting a new collection together to show backers in the fall.

I packed up a lot of stuff in my suitcase to take to him. I had gone to this place upstairs on Fourteenth Street, where bones and skulls were sold, and I had constructed various necklaces of small animal skulls, bracelets made of bones and forks, belts made from teeth and rhinestones and silver chunks.

I also, on a whim, brought along some hats I had made (in a fit of pique, fed up with doing jewelry, I had thought momentarily of going into the millinary line) and the hats were really neat. Some looked like pancakes, others looked like pizzas, some like cheese soufflés—made of the kind of brocade used on chairs. And they were decorated with small skulls in the front. A clothing critic might have called them African-influenced. I was a little uneasy, because the hats really smelled like mothballs: they were mothproofed. I had found most of the fabric for the hats in a garbage dumpster in SoHo. When I wore one of the hats—a turban style in the shape of a cobra,

head ready to strike—to a party someone pointed out that
there seemed to be a couple of moths flying around my head.
The man I was talking to pulled apart two of the cobra's coils
and several more moths flew out—the hat was infested. The
hostess of the party said that because of me she would have to
have the place exterminated. Maybe she was just a little high;
usually she was a very friendly, sweet person.

I agreed to meet Wilfredo for a drink the next day. It was
great to be in love again, particularly so soon after being in
despair. I didn't even care whether Wilfredo liked me or not.
He had nothing to do with the way I felt in the thirty-six hours
before I was to meet him. There I was, there was Wilfredo,
and then there was my great love for him. The night before I
was to meet him I sat in my apartment, drinking wine (Château
Bonnet, $4.99) and thinking about how I had finally achieved a
feeling of contentment. I put on my silver leather coat to go
across the street to the delicatessen (roast beef sandwich, rye
bread, Russian dressing, and tomato) and I felt pretty zippy.
Manhattan was just waiting for me to conquer it. On my way
back from the store the woman who lived two buildings down
(she was always sitting on the stoop) started to point at me and
laugh. "Look at that silver coat!" she said. I knew this was
just part of living in New York, but it did bring me down.

I had to celebrate with more wine when I got back to my
apartment, and the next day I puttered around, working out
some new designs and generally pampering myself. My mother
always told me, when there's nothing else to do and the phone
isn't ringing, you can use the opportunity to pamper yourself.
Finally it was time for me to leave and meet Wilfredo. I walked
down the street (it was around seven in the evening) and everything seemed just great, except for my hangover. But even my
hangover seemed necessary, it was a part of nature and gave
me a sense of affinity with the inanimate objects such as the
buildings and garbage cans around me. I passed the fat woman
who had pointed at me and laughed the night before. She was
sitting on the steps with some guy. "Listen, honey," she said.

"You know what? That was a beautiful silver coat you were wearing the other day." She was around fifty years old, with long gray hair and a tiny red potato face.

"Yeah?" I said. "Thanks."

"This is my friend Rico, by the way. He wants to meet you." She pointed to the stallion sitting next to her. He had a Fu Manchu mustache and limpid eyes. Well, it seemed that when I was in love everybody wanted to be my friend.

"No, I don't," Rico said.

"And it's a wonderful evening," the woman said. "And it's so nice to see you with all your energy. You look like a person who would never hurt another person."

"It's nice to hear you say that," I said. "Except if you knew the way my head feels, you would think twice about my energy level. Also, this suitcase is rather heavy." I was just saying this to be modest.

"Oh, listen, I'm tired, too," she said. "What's your name?"

"Eleanor."

"I'm Agnes. Listen, Eleanor, I stay up all night, watching TV, and I have to listen to my cocaine addict friends tell me they want seven hundred dollars to go to Seattle. And I say: Do I need this? But that silver coat you've got—when I saw you wearing it yesterday, I thought, Wow, now there's a person who doesn't mind standing out."

"That coat is special," I said. I didn't want to remind her that she had humiliated me the night before by pointing and laughing.

"I'm going to give you my card," Agnes said. "I'm a psychic, I can give you a discount. You can call me any time, day or night. When did you move into the neighborhood?"

"August," I said.

"Oh, you're just a baby," she said. "I've been here thirty-three years, four months, two days, and seven hours."

Anyway, I took her card and grabbed a taxi to the restaurant where I was meeting Wilfredo. He was already there, lurking at a back table and wearing a straight black wig and a ban-

danna around his forehead. He had supreme style. I watched
him give the waitress elaborate instructions for how he wanted
his coffee prepared. He liked his coffee with hot, steamed milk
on the side; in other words, a cappuccino in two parts. The
restaurant was very romantic, with Art Nouveau paintings on
the walls, and other gaily dressed young people. I noticed they
were all eyeing us. It was pleasant to sit with a man who was
recognizable—even if this was a shallow thought on my part.

I ordered some white wine. Over our drinks, Wilfredo and I
discussed how talented he was. He was a deeply sensitive
person who had only had one lover in his life, and this person
he had broken up with recently. "The way I see it," Wilfredo
said, "I have trouble connecting with people because of my
upbringing. My father was an architect—and though he was
kind to others he was very strict and distant with his own
family. He designed a sort of double-envelope house that was
solar heated on the roof. The solar heat warmed rocks that
were under the foundation. Then at night the heat would be
thrown from the rocks back to the house. It was a real ecolog-
ical breakthrough. Anyway, after the divorce my brother and I
lived with our father, in the prototype house. Because it was
the first model, it had some design problems—water retention.
Between my father's aloofness and the mildew, obviously this
affected me. I have trouble getting close to people."

"Well," I said. "That's good. It just shows you're not a
casual person." He took my hand across the table, which I
thought was a very spontaneous, affectionate gesture. "I'm
just getting over a breakup myself." I asked him not to stroke
my hand, as it was making me forget what I was saying. "You
don't know what it feels like," I said. "It's like hypnotizing an
alligator."

Wilfredo dropped my hand. "What do you mean?" he said.

"You know, sometimes at the zoo, they have these demon-
strations—they hypnotize a small alligator by turning it over
and stroking its stomach and it goes into a trance."

Wilfredo looked alarmed. "That's not what I had in mind,"
he said. "I just thought you had nice hands."

"Do you get along with your father?" I said. I had to speak loudly; two men at a nearby table were arguing.

"Oh, we're great, great pals," Wilfredo said. "We used to fight a lot; in fact, for many years he disowned me. Now the only thing we argue over is who cooks the best linguine with clam sauce."

"But wasn't he upset when you went bankrupt?"

"No," Wilfredo said. "In fact, he was very supportive. After all, when he was starting his architectural firm, there were two times in the early years when the whole thing fell apart. But he had faith in himself. The only problem now is that he wants me to find independent backing."

Then something happened: the two men who had been arguing at the nearby table stood up and began to flail at each other. A waitress came over and tried to hold one of the men back; apparently she had studied judo or wrestling, because she knew the right holds. One of the men was calling the other a Communist. In the scuffle, our table got knocked to the side. Wilfredo's coffee sloshed across the cloth. I stood up quickly. "Maybe we should leave," I said. I went to the restroom while Wilfredo paid the bill. When I came out, the men had gone.

"That was something, wasn't it?" I said.

Wilfredo asked if he could see my jewelry. The waitress had put a clean cloth on the table and I took everything out, including some slides and two hats. "Do you smell mothballs?" Wilfredo said. I shook my head. "This stuff is fantastic," he said. "I really wasn't expecting anything like this at all. I know in your letter you said you designed jewelry, but I just thought you'd have the usual old stuff."

I could tell he was genuinely excited. I wasn't really surprised that Wilfredo hadn't heard of me or seen my work before, but I did explain that ever since I broke up with Stash my jewelry design business had really taken off: I was getting invitations to work with all kinds of fashion designers, a fashion magazine had called me up asking me to do an article on tips for wearing jewelry, and I was planning a trip to Europe in the spring. "I wouldn't be telling you all this except for the fact that I think you're the most exciting designer around," I said. "And you're the one I'd like to work with. But I'm normally very humble. Believe me, I'm humble: I've been humiliated too much of my life not to be."

Wilfredo said he understood. Then he asked if I'd like to go out to dinner with him, not tonight, because he already had other plans, but maybe sometime the following week. I said that would be fine.

I really felt I was getting to know him. Even though he was busy, he managed to find the time to talk to me on the phone: we had long conversations, discussing his latest designs, the difficulty he was having with patterns, and the kind of effect he hoped to achieve in his spring line. He also had a lot of ideas for the kinds of things I should be making to accompany them. He was thinking along the lines of historical monuments, and fourteenth-century Japanese warrior. This sounded good to me.

On our first date we had a romantic time—we sat by the water holding hands, while Wilfredo complained about his ex-lover and I said things about Stash. "He was a crazy artist type," I told him. "I couldn't take the sulking, and one day after a six-week sulk I said I was fed up and was walking out. Naturally I assumed he'd call me at my girlfriend's immediately, begging my forgiveness. Unfortunately, that's not what happened. Now I feel fragile; it seems hard for me to believe that a person could live with someone for many years—two, anyway—and then one day, quite without warning, it's over."

Wilfredo said that in the case of his lover, the person fought all the time and the temper tantrums became unbearable. Both of us agreed we loathed and despised fighting. It was unnecessary. You could either tell your partner what was wrong and both of you would make the needed negotiations, or the relationship was better off forgotten. There was definitely an instant rapport between Wilfredo and myself. Both of us liked to put on strange accents while making an important point.

Maybe I said too much. I knew it was a mistake to tell a new man about a past relationship. But I said exactly what came into my head, and then I was sorry. Because most of the time I didn't even agree with what I was saying. But once I had said it the words hung in the air like stalactites, or whatever those things are that hang off the ceiling.

Wilfredo had a car, and he drove me home, but not before we had spent some time kissing passionately. Anyway, at my door Wilfredo said he had had a great time, that he was really becoming attached to me, and that he would call me soon, if not immediately.

A few days later he invited me out on another date: he said he had asked a bunch of people over to dinner, and I could come early and pretend to be the hostess. I found the idea appealing: I pictured myself in a gingham hostess outfit, serving canapés and chattering amusingly, while my husband—or some kind of fiancé—looked on admiringly.

Wilfredo was glad to see me, but his dog, Dora Mar, at first decided I must be a burglar. She was small and liver-spotted, and stood barking at the entrance. But after Wilfredo spoke to her gruffly she gave up and allowed me to come in. Wilfredo had a small, cluttered apartment, and while he was busy cooking in the kitchenette I looked around at some of his stuff: a large octopus in a jar of formaldehyde, a stuffed swordfish, a pair of snowshoes, a Japanese silk kimono hanging on the wall, and a large fish tank with several ugly pink fish. Wilfredo was puréeing tomatoes by hand, squeezing them through a colander, and when he was finished he gave me a glass of fresh tomato juice to drink, but I said I'd stick with the wine.

While we were kissing in the kitchen, the guests began to arrive. The first couple were named Mike and Hank, two men in their fifties. Hank was skinny and blond, and had a number of interesting quirks. The major one was his habit of switching the subject, so that one minute he was talking about Ezra Pound and the editorial slaughter job that Pound did on Eliot, and then a minute later he was arguing with Mike about who had been at fault ten years ago when a man broke into their apartment and left them tied up with paper bags over their heads only minutes before a hundred guests were due to arrive for cocktails.

I started laughing, maybe a little nervously. "Why, you have wonderful friends," I told Wilfredo. "Just wonderful."

Then an artist and his boyfriend, who was an art critic, showed up. Everyone congratulated the artist on his recent show. "I didn't think it was as good as his last," the art critic said. "I told Roger to start painting on bigger canvases, but he wouldn't listen."

Mike took me to the couch to show me one of Roger's paintings hanging on the wall: it showed several tiny figures squatting on an idyllic lawn, eating what appeared to be a massive quantity of peas. "I think Wilfredo really likes you," he whispered in my ear.

"Really?" I said. "Why?"

"He's never gone out with anybody with such long hair before," Mike said.

I had to keep drinking wine, out of anxiety, and Wilfredo's food wasn't ready until after eleven, but it was a jolly evening. Dora Mar had a chair to herself at the table. All the men fed her treats. She had a big pink nose, which I thought was rather unattractive, and a goofy, pleasant expression. It was true I didn't know much of what the conversation pertained to, but I was used to that. At one point, when it seemed they were discussing a couple they knew who were in the middle of splitting up, I decided to insert a contribution. "Women these days are supposed to be tough and independent," I said. "But I don't see what's wrong with wanting to be bonded to another person."

"Oh, come off it," Mike said. "If women were really tough then they'd know their career is the most important thing; if some guy comes along that's fine. But all the women I know are just as obsessed with Lane hope chests and *Bride* magazine as if it was the 1950s."

They all looked at me, but I didn't have anything else to say. Dora Mar waved one clawed paw at me. My old dog, Andrew, was a lot more attractive and less spoiled. But maybe in time

I'd get used to Dora Mar. Or maybe I was just remembering Andrew in a whitewashed light.

While Wilfredo was in the kitchen he called for me to join him. He was preparing some type of pasta with sun-dried tomatoes and fresh tomatoes and tuna fish. When I got to his side he said he missed me.

"That's great," I said. "I like to be near you, too."

Finally, around one in the morning, the guests left, but not before Hank and Mike had a little fistfight—well, Hank slapped Mike across the face to make a dramatic point about why he had the right to see other people if he wanted, and then Mike stormed out, so Hank had to follow him in a hurry. When they had all gone, I mentioned that it must be nice to be part of a couple that had been together for a long time. "Don't you think?" I said. "When people are together for ages, there must be almost a psychic connection between them."

Wilfredo gave me an inscrutable look, his eyes were amazingly yellow.

"Of course," I said, "it's awful that Hank and Mike got into a fight. This is the second time that people near us have started squabbling."

"I don't like to fight," Wilfredo said. "Makes me totally claustrophobic. Any kind of game playing—I'll just walk away first."

"I've never been able to figure out the rules," I said. "Even as a kid—with Parcheesi or Milles Borne—I never did learn what I was supposed to do. At this point it's probably too late to even try."

Wilfredo said he could appreciate this quality in me.

In the morning, over reheated pasta, Wilfredo said that everything was great: he liked my personality, my physicality, and my jewelry. "I feel as if I already know you," he said. "But the best thing is that even though I feel so comfortable with you, we have all the time in the world to get acquainted."

He went out of his way to see me home in a taxi, and left me at my door after kissing me fervently and saying he would call me either later that day (he wasn't certain if he would, because a friend of his was just getting back from Chicago and he really wanted to see the guy) or else the next morning.

"Don't lose my number," I told him.

For the first couple of days I just floated around, in a kind of trance: I felt ephemeral. But then when he didn't call by the third day I started to wonder if I was crazy and had imagined the whole thing. I tried to call him at his studio and also at his house—but in both places a machine answered. I did leave a few messages, but he never returned any of them.

I tried not to leave my apartment in case the phone might ring. While I waited, I studied a book I had bought about how to make men fall in love with you. The book seemed to suggest I had done something wrong. First of all, I should never have left messages on Wilfredo's machine—this showed I was too interested—and second, I hadn't made an attempt to communicate with Wilfredo in his own language. According to the book, Wilfredo fell into the "visual" category of men. To make him fall in love with me, I should have done two things: spoken in "visual" language, using terms such as "It *looks* like we're going to have a lot of fun tonight" and also by "mirroring" him. Mirroring meant that, for example, while we were sitting at a table if he touched his chin with his hand, I should do the same.

I wasn't sure if I necessarily believed all of this, but thinking about it did pass the time. After a while I started to feel angry at Wilfredo for not calling. I remembered making a vow to myself, years ago, that I would never sit around waiting for some man to call the way my girlfriends did; it was bad enough to be at the mercy of this person, but even worse to have broken a promise to myself.

It was almost like having a physical illness. I walked around my apartment as if I had been punched in the stomach, and three times I called the telephone company to see if my line was out of order. After a few more days I didn't feel any better, and I called my mother. She said I should call up her friend who lives in Oklahoma for advice. Her friend was an expert at

getting men to fall in love with her, and really understood
them. I phoned her and told her the whole story. And my
mother's friend said, "Well, it sounds like things speeded up
too fast. You should never talk about your own needs—at least
not in the short run. This may sound devious, but that's the
way it is. You should be affectionate, but not intense. Now,
here's my plan. If you haven't heard from him within three
more days, you can try calling him again. Be light—say you're
calling to say hello. But don't be too available. Seem aloof."

"It's hard for me to pretend to be aloof when he's not paying
any attention in the first place," I said. The whole business
was so painful. I had seen those *National Geographic* wildlife
specials on TV, and it didn't seem right that animals met each
other, performed some little courting dance, and mated for
life. They knew exactly what to do; they relied on instinctive
behavior that had not given their parents and grandparents any
problems either. Maybe my mother had taken something during my prenatal months that interfered with my evolutionary,
collective knowledge.

"Are you sure this guy isn't gay?" my mother's friend said.

"It's strange you mentioned that," I said. "What do I
know?" Then I thanked her for her time, and said I had to go
because it was long distance.

After I hung up I went to the closet and put on my studded
leather wrist band and black leather motorcycle belt with the
spikes protruding that Stash had given me for my birthday a
couple of years back. Thus prepared, I sat down on the couch
with my Tao Fire Healer. This was a piece of plastic I had
received in the mail (my girlfriend had ordered it for me) which
I had to hold twice a day for fifteen minutes—it was supposed
to burn off my bad karma, leaving me with just the positive
aspects of my psyche. The bad part, from what I could figure
out, was my poor taste in men. I had to face it, this wasn't the
first time I had fallen for a man who wasn't interested in me.
But even people with ugly living room furniture could, through
years of interior decoration therapy, learn to move up a notch

on the esthetic scale. I had always thought of myself as superior to such people. Now I knew I was—on some level—no
different from them. I had all the regular human qualities—an
unlimited capacity for suffering, and spending money.

The instructions that came with my Tao Fire Healer said my
life would be straightened out in no time, as long as I used my
device. The piece of plastic was green and pink, and there
were small white dots attached to it. After I held it for fifteen
minutes, the white dots got black—probably from absorbing
my bad energy. I sneered at myself for being so vulnerable: I
felt as if I had been conned, just like elderly women I had read
about who fell for a con routine in front of their banks. Someone would approach them with an envelope of money, which
they claimed to have found and wanted to share with the
woman, provided that she put up her own money in trust, so
to speak. The con artist would take her envelope of money and
hand over the "found" money, which invariably would turn out
to be a bunch of blank paper.

But in my case, I couldn't figure out what the con was;
maybe I had really been conning myself. Why would someone
bother to pretend to care for me? It was difficult to sit still for
fifteen minutes when I kept thinking thoughts such as these,
and all I really wanted was for the phone to ring and for it to
be Wilfredo.

By Friday evening I was so nervous from sitting around waiting that I didn't know what to do with myself. I had no map,
no guidelines, no role models for how I was supposed to behave
in the modern world. I didn't know why I couldn't achieve
some kind of peace just from being alone. Then I found the
little card in my pocket that Agnes, the psychic up the block,
had given me, and I decided to call her. I was sort of embarrassed to speak to her, but I wrote down a few questions that
I had about Wilfredo, such as "Will he call me?" and "What
did I do wrong?" and a few others I had about my career, and
I dialed her number.

A tough-sounding woman answered and wanted to know who I was. When I explained, she put down the receiver and yelled, "Agnes!"

Then Agnes got on the phone. She didn't seem surprised to hear from me, but she said that she had a cold and that though she did give readings for some people over the phone she would probably have to keep interrupting the reading to blow her nose, and so it would be better if I came over in a day or so with $30. I told her okay, except that right now I was obsessed with whether or not this guy would call me, and that was what was making me nervous. I said, "Can't you tell me anything right off the bat?"

Agnes said that Wilfredo probably wasn't very important in my life, and that sometimes people—meaning me—went through a period where they just didn't want to be alone and wanted someone to care for. But that due to something that had happened to me in one of my past lives, I was bent on repeating the same pattern over and over; in other words, I was interested in a particular type of guy who made me feel rejected. In a little while, however, I would meet a man called Lenny, and he would be the right person for me.

I was reassured, except I would have liked to hear that Wilfredo was going to call me. I felt so adamant that Wilfredo and I were meant to be together. Agnes didn't seem to understand that what I was experiencing was like a metal hand squeezing my torso. It was like I was stuck on a soap opera inside a tiny TV, and the plot wasn't going the way I thought it should. "Would it matter if I tried calling him again?" I said.

"Just keep it light and merry if you do," she said, hanging up.

I decided to go uptown and skulk around near where Wilfredo worked and lived. There was always a chance I'd catch him leaving his apartment on his way to his studio: I knew he kept odd hours.

On the subway I read an article in the paper about a whale in San Francisco named Humphrey who kept trying to swim upstream away from his whale school and the ocean. Scientists

studying him believed there was a reason for his aberrant behavior. Maybe he was a pregnant female. In that case he was
acting in an understandable way—looking for a quiet place to
have a baby. Obviously these scientists believed in an orderly
universe, where there was an explanation for everything if they
didn't know what it was.

Just at that minute a man got on the car and hit me in the
legs with his briefcase. I didn't really pay him any mind. He
was respectable looking, some sort of brown briefcase and a
brown suit, quite innocuous. I went back to reading my article,
but then a few stops later an altercation broke out, right in
front of me. The man was getting off the train and smashed his
briefcase into someone else who was getting on. I looked up
just as a very tough-looking street girl—about fifteen, wearing
sneakers with fancy laces and a leather jacket—was screaming at the man, "Don't you say 'Excuse me?' "

The man started to curse at the girl. "Get off the train and
fight me," he said from the other side of the doors.

The girl shouted a few swear words back. She was standing
with a couple of urchin girlfriends. "I'm going to get you!" she
said.

The man managed to throw a side kick, karate style, at the
girl. The girl backed into me just in time, as the doors were
closing, and I saw the man's grinning face as the train pulled
out. The girl was really upset, obviously she wasn't as tough
as what she hoped she was projecting. I wanted to tell her the
man had hit me, too, but she looked too angry.

The man must have been one of those pathological people I
had previously only read about, like the man who enjoyed
stomping on women's insteps. I pictured him trudging through
a crowd at Grand Central Terminal, casually hitting one
woman after the next with the pointy edge of his briefcase.
Such random rage made no sense to me yet maybe this man
was following some natural law. Who was I to have less faith
than people who had studied such things for many years?

When I got to the stop where Wilfredo lived I hung out on
the street for a while, standing in the slight drizzle and watch-

ing the faces as they came along, one after the next. Everyone had the same features—two eyes, a nose, and a mouth—yet every face was slightly different from the next. I didn't see any two alike, though each appeared to be set in recognizable expressions: despair, fatigue, joy, ennui. I think I could have stood for hours, watching the people go by. Some urgency was diminished. The faces seemed a partial answer to a question I couldn't even articulate. But after a while it started to rain harder, and I went into a bookstore. I bought four books: Dale Carnegie's *How to Stop Worrying and Start Living;* a book on transactional analysis to write your own life script; *How to Make a Man Marry You in Thirty Days;* and something on reincarnation. The four books cost me almost $30, and I was going to wait until I got home to take them out, but as soon as I hit the street I ripped open the bag and pulled one out, starting to read as I walked to the subway in the rain.

ode to heroine
of the future

My sister in the end jumped naked from the window of the top floor of a seven-story building. This was after a long string of events. She couldn't get her license back. The state had made her take a drunken-driving evaluatory test and, because of this, she fell in with some dangerous characters—a kind of guru who made her think that what she did made no difference at all. Such were the fates of the heroes in ancient Greece: some perished under seven-gated Thebes, which was one battle; others died in Troy, fighting for Helen. These were the sons of gods and mortal women.

But it is not written how the others died: some by being constantly harassed, some by being picked at, some because the world around them was too great a place and they were not meant for it. Anyway, the sons and daughters of gods and humans were never destined to be around for very long; my sister was a throwback to these earlier times. In ancient Greece the first race of man was made of gold, and they lived like gods without labor or pain, and did not suffer from old age, but they fell asleep in death. But I'm referring now to my sister. The race of the men of gold were hollow inside and easily bent and melted. I only saw her once more before she died: I had arranged to meet her in one of the bars she spent all her time in—all she did besides take drugs and drink and pick up men. I met her one evening in the Gulag Archipelago with her current amigo. He played in a rock-and-roll group—an ex-junkie in his thirties. He had made it big in the early seventies in a rock group that wore women's clothing and makeup: a heavy drag quartet. But the band was good; I remember at the time I had listened to their music quite frequently. Now for years he had been out on his own, and he had finally managed to put out a solo LP, and made decent bucks in the clubs in Europe and New York, though the life was grueling.

Or so he said. I met them on an evening when he was playing at a nearby club later that night. I didn't trust him—he had the face of a con man, sly and foreign. Besides, he was a Frenchman, and my preference has always been for the Northern Italian type. I didn't like the way he flicked ashes from his cigarette in my sister's direction, nor the way he shook her off when she tried to put her arm around his shoulders—there was a puppyish quality of despair to my sister I hadn't remembered seeing before. I got a kind of nasty feeling about him, as if whatever it was he did with her in bed gave Sis a gratification that was primarily secondary, if you undertake my meaning. He had long curly black hair and high cheekbones; he was dressed in an old sweater with little puffed shoulders. I guess it had once been a girl's sweater, it appeared too small for him. Though in it he looked awfully cute, a cunning little queen. When I looked down at the floor to pick up a dollar I had dropped, I saw he was wearing long winter underwear, flannel, with four or five pairs of socks on over it; each sock with holes in various places, exposing the pair beneath, and a pair of tattered cowboy boots. When he rose to shake my hand I couldn't help but be amused at how the flannel underwear, with nothing on over it except the girl's sweater, gave him a kind of Robin Hood appearance; he should have been wearing a codpiece, egads.

He didn't appear to have evolved much from the sixties. Which was all right with me: I had just gone back to wearing a ponytail myself. "You do look like John Paul Jones with your ponytail," my sister said, rising to kiss me.

"Yes," said Jonny Jalouse, "or like—what was his name? Paul Revere and the Raiders." He spoke with a little lisp, and a lilting French accent. There were many of these lizardy guys crawling around all the time at the Gulag—this one was prettier than most, and if my sister had picked him up he must have had something going for him. He wasn't a bad musician. It was his mouth that interested me: as if a kiss had been planted on his face in the womb, and this later grew into a mouth.

He chain-smoked Gauloises; really, I shouldn't have been disturbed by him. In a different place I might have been reminded of my pal Sherman, a gentle soul. But my sister did have a black eye, and I didn't want to ask about it. When this character smiled he revealed two black stubs of teeth.

I felt so upset I had to go over to the jukebox and put some Frank Sinatra on; when I came back to the table the guy got up all over again, exaggeratedly polite. "I can't tell you how glad I am to meet you," he said. "You will come to hear me play later?"

I shook my head. "Can't make it," I said. "I've got a deadline: I have to finish this painting before I go to Europe."

"And when will you be going?" Jonny said.

I wanted to take out a cord of dental floss and whip it between his teeth; God knows he would have appreciated that. Or some kind of mitering device, with which I could round off the corners of his canines: what a spiked Dracula he was. His stage makeup—or maybe he wore it all the time, I don't know—was far too heavy: black eyes, red guppy mouth. "I'm going to Italy," I said. "Roma. I'm going to get a studio there and paint."

"Amaretta tells me you are a painter?" the guy said.

"Yes," I said. "Let me have a double vodka on the rocks, will you." Jonny Jalouse took out a hand-rolled cigarette and lit it. "With hashish," he said. "Would you like some?" I shook my head.

My sister was in bad shape. Sitting next to this guy, her hair was dirty and there were pimples on her face. What she was wearing was something like an old silk shirt, very tattered, and a leather jacket. She had the look of a person who needs a shower, much abused; by this I figured she had been taking too much cocaine. "What happened to your eye?" I said.

"I'm anemic," she said. "I walked into a cabinet door and because I'm anemic it gave me a black eye."

"That certainly seems to run in the family," I said.

"I practically put my eye out. At first I thought, Well, it's all over with me now, I'll be a blind person, and then I don't even need to worry about where I'm going to find a drunken-driving course."

"Yeah," I said. "What happened with that?"

"I had to go to this place in Trenton to take an evaluation test. I thought that these people were really going to help me. There were about forty of us, all in one big room, and they gave us a test to do. On it were questions such as, 'How often do you get drunk?' I thought I was supposed to be honest in answering. I didn't know that all around me people were putting down 'Once or twice a year.' I put down 'Four or five nights a week.' Well, really I wouldn't get drunk if I didn't take the coke. But I need something to bring me down after I get wired, and so I have a couple quarts of beer just to relax me."

"You really must stop doing this so much," Jonny said.

With that I suddenly felt a great joy in my heart for Jonny, and I nodded. "This guy knows what he's talking about, Amaretta," I said.

"Shut up. There were a lot of other questions on this test: 'Do you drive after you've been drinking?' I was completely honest. So when we all handed in our tests, it looked like I was a lunatic. Everyone else had lied. And they seemed sane, while for being honest I was now in real trouble. So they called me into this little room. They told me they couldn't help me at all, that my problem was too big for them to handle. I was supposed to seek therapy or find a program that lasted for more than four hours of classroom time: more like thirty. I wasn't going to get my license back. So I went back to the New York

State license bureau, and they said there was nothing they could do. But one guy there felt sorry for me; he agreed to let me into his class. 'You are trying to change, I think,' he said. 'Maybe I can help you. The mess you're in is your own fault, but still . . . we'll see.' Anyway, he turned out really to be my savior, a real guru. A little shrunken guy, who always dressed in black. 'Because if you can project energy wearing black, you can do anything,' he used to say."

"I'm getting bored, Amaretta," her pal said. "I'm going to play some pinball."

"Nice guy," I said, after he had left.

"Yes," she said. "He's really been great . . . a real stabilizing influence on me, Marley."

"Well, did this guru help you?"

"Oh, yes," she said. "He made me go to a class called 'How to Make Money Doing Anything.' I thought this was sort of a neat idea. The other people who were enrolled in the course thought so, too; that it would be about how you could turn your hobbies into money-makers. Like knitting, for example. But as it turned out, the first class the guy spent talking about how everything that happens to you is because you want it to. 'You can live forever,' he said. 'You only die because you want to.' 'You mean to say I wanted to be mugged?' a girl said.

"He said that yes, she had wanted to be mugged. Well, don't look like that: I didn't go back after the first time. I went back to my guru. He sent me to a class in how to be a whirling dervish. It's part of the Sufi religion, you know. We had to chant for hours, and a man showed us how to weave our necks into circles. We were told not to think of anything at all. This is very difficult, you know: too difficult for me, and I didn't go back to that class, either. But I'm fine now, since I've met Jonny. He's very stable and a good influence on me. . . ."

As if to prove what she was saying, Jonny came back to our table with a couple of German drug dealers I had met before. They were all jabbering in French. My sister sat humming to herself at one end of the table, weaving back and forth gently, as if she were still in the whirling dervish class.

Even as a mess, my sister was beautiful: I was bereaved at
how badly I had treated her most of my life. Those clear eyes,
which nothing could muck up—like the color of the Caribbean
in a *National Geographic* magazine photo. And that smell of
raspberries she had always about her, raspberries in a field on
a hot summer day. With some bees flying about: these represented her thoughts, random to others, but making sense to
herself. Even in a scruffy leather jacket she looked fine—like
a great lioness after a feed, basking with a bloodstained mouth.

One of the Germans brought another drink for my sister.
She drank it in one gulp: something of a gold-cream color,
maybe it was sherry, but I doubted it. They were all giggling
in shrill French that lapsed into German, and they were all
highly decorated, in a primitive way: gold clankers and leopard-
skin boots and 'gator belts. And fur coats, so I guess they were
doing all right. "By the way," Amaretta said, "did I tell you of
my lesbian experience?"

"No," said Jonny. "That sounds amusing . . . do tell us."
He had to explain something in German to one of the drug
dealers: the guy didn't speak English, though he seemed to
vaguely understand. So they were all quiet. I could tell they
were interested.

"After my divorce papers came through I kept the summer
house Rafe and I had. I was out there alone last week . . .
bored out of my mind. In desperation I went to the lesbian bar
in town. I had no place to go, and the evening hours to kill as
usual. I had walked to the end of the pier and looked at the
fishing boats tied up and tossing in the stiff winter sea . . .
stout little ships, laden with ropes and nets and all the other
equipment they use to catch fish, and it was suddenly like
being in a different time . . . some snow was falling and the
waves were very white at the crests. I was carrying my little
dog . . . he was shivering under my jacket. It was very cold
and wild, without the little dog I would have felt quite sad, but
there he was, shivering under my jacket. . . .

"I wandered back into town and saw a sign that said The
Cellar, and below it a narrow flight of stone steps that led to

the place. When I opened the door it was very warm. It had
been blowing outside. It was warm in there and lit with rose-
colored light. Girls were talking and laughing, shouting with
laughter, how happy they all seemed. But when they saw me
come in, suddenly they all stopped talking at once . . . they
stared at me. Only the television blared on in the background.
I thought, How nice, to see a whole bar of women like this, all
talking and laughing and carrying on, what a friendly place!
But then they all stopped talking, and I realized, Oh, this is a
lesbian bar, of course, these are all gay women! I was embarrassed . . . one of the girls let out a long, low whistle . . . but
then I thought, Let's not be ridiculous, what do you care what
the sexual persuasion of these women is? And why should they
care about mine? It was a warm place, and I liked the look of
it. . . . My little dog needed a place to get warmed up. . . .
Still, I had to force myself to go in, sit at the table, put the dog
down, and get a drink from the bar. I was all aquiver . . . I
was very nervous. You know, I enjoy those moments of nervousness; just as I think I will never feel nervous again something occurs to make me blink. As if a skin had formed over
my eyes and I am able to be blasé, then something happens to
. . . shock me and I feel very alive again. Perhaps that is why
I went to that place by myself. Well, why am I so cynical? Why
do I think of myself as such a tough cookie, and the rest of the
world even worse? Too much television, perhaps . . . child of
a broken home, or some other reason easily written up as a sad
bit of information about our times in the daily paper—why
children take drugs, or a letter to Dear Abby. There's an answer both intelligent and wise, yet solving nothing for the person with the problem."

The Germans were getting restless and my sister seemed to
sense this and got back to her story.

"Nobody would speak to me at first. The girls, for the most
part, didn't appear any older than eighteen . . . chopped-off
hair, leather jackets, sulky expressions. At first none of the
women spoke to me: I must admit I was relieved. For a long
time I sat and listened to their talk, memorizing all their names

. . . Betty, a woman who had waited on my table earlier that evening when I went out to dinner, came in shivering from the sea breeze, her hair flecked with snow that quickly melted. When she came in she didn't acknowledge me, but went to watch a television show. . . . When she wasn't laughing at the TV she was petting Amy, her little friend who sat mouselike at the bar while Betty stroked her and kissed her neck, but only during the commercials. I thought, How funny that I like to sit in this place . . . there was a moment, the first second I came in, that it seemed so inviting. But now it seemed rather sad, as if to make friends with anyone there I had to have the same sexual orientation. Though to be honest, it seems as if to make friends there must be something rather symbiotic between the two partners in a friendship. I have a rather sarcastic view of friendship: I believe friendship is based on human beings using one another. To look at it my way, two girls get to be friends because they need someone to confide in . . . or they have the same job and need someone to eat lunch with. Or, quite often, they each would like to meet men, but don't want to venture out alone. Well, a genuine friendship is a rare thing . . . people are quite disposable; if one friend moves away an attempt to correspond is made at first . . . then a few long-distance phone calls, a postcard from a vacation retreat . . . then broken promises to visit. . . .

"Billy, the bartender, was dressed like a man. . . . She would have been attractive if perhaps she let her hair grow a little longer, in a way that was more flattering to her plump face . . . and did not find it so necessary to pose like a man. Perhaps when she first learned she was gay she needed to announce this fact. But by now her butch act had become something else. She was hardened, there was no longer anything in her that could be touched by another human being, so she had given up. . . .

"And I thought, What is the worst that can happen to me? I'll wake up to find a woman's face in my cunt instead of a man's. Big deal. But still that didn't get rid of the ominous feeling for me. I was familiar with the hungry looks of men, but in a crowd of women the feeling was something quite different. They all seemed to be in disguise, hard little mugs . . . most of them looked alike. Out here in the sticks they were not the choicest group of lesbians. They were sort of working class. Maybe they had summer jobs as waitresses and stayed out over the winter, I don't know.

"Damn! I felt like a young chicken in a group of foxes. About ten, twelve of them. . . . They all had short hair of a neutral color, and most of them were wearing black vests, men's vests. Funny, because if I were going to be attracted to another woman, I would want one who was very pretty, with a big mouth and long curly hair . . . wearing something like an old Victorian nightgown. I guess I'm saying I'd be more attracted to a woman who looked like me: narcissistic, I guess. I myself am envied by many of my friends, though I freely admit I am unhappy . . . but I like my littleness, I am little, my bones are light, I once had a boyfriend who clasped my wrist in amazement and said, 'But, Amaretta, your wrist is so little I could snap it with my fingers!' My hair is peach-colored, peach and amber (my little dog is the same shade; I chose him because he matched), and my skin used to be clear, very clear . . . when I walk out in the cold my cheeks get very red . . . with tiny teeth, I have tiny square teeth that I floss each night and brush until they absolutely gleam . . . my hands are very long and thin . . . once, in a jewelry store, where I was trying on rings just to kill some time, the jeweler said, 'Ah, what fine hands you have, you should be a pianist!' But I do not have that sort of creativity. Though I might have been a dancer . . . my little dog dances when I fling my clothes about and parade naked before the mirror! He enjoys that, he likes to prance, too. . . .

"But even the women who didn't have short hair and a man's vest had something hard about them: plucked eyebrows. Strange, because why pluck out your eyebrows if at the same time you are trying somehow to look masculine, or at least androgynous? I can't stand plucked eyebrows . . . they take all the expression off a person's face, and made the girls look very hard.

"I still can't place what was so ominous about them . . . except they looked at me and at each other in a way that lacked feeling . . . well, it was purely sexual. Like they had come out looking for one thing. Well, even in a straight singles' bar most of the guys look pretty scared and are happier just getting to talk—usually about the plots of different movies that they've seen—aren't really interested in ripping your clothes off. I mean, even the ones on the make are usually just showing off for their friends and have a braggardly attitude to them that is pretty much a joke, an act.

"But anyway, I'm getting off the track. The evening was drawing to a close and Betty was tenderly wrapping little Amy up in a fake fur jacket, and Jacy was complaining about the reception on the TV set, and Karen was dancing by herself and crying . . . because Jacy was not speaking to her, Karen did not want to see Jacy ever again, but in this town there was nowhere else for the girls to go. I sat at the bar for a last drink, and I was thinking of getting home, my little dog was trying to sleep. . . .

"And a woman came in who interested me, oddly enough. At first I thought, Well, if I have to pick up a woman—for all the time, I have forgotten to say, there was a nasty voice in my head telling me to do this and that, things I really didn't want to do—if I had to pick up a woman that evening, I would make it a pretty one. And there were a couple in the place, one of them had glossy black hair and was wearing a long sweater-tunic, and another was like a little girl I had gone to grammar school with, very pale and freckled . . . but they were so second-rate I discarded them. A girl with long blond hair, but what a fat ass! What would I do in bed with so much rear end?

"As I say, a woman did come in . . . it was getting to be after eleven . . . she was a lot older than the others and a real old-school dyke. This one not only had short hair, all gray, but was a real bull: dressed up in a man's suit, man's shoes, gray

Shetland sweater . . . really did look like a man at first glance
. . . had a very teeny braid in the back, like a question mark,
an afterthought. It was all part of the same thing—you know
I've had a thing lately about men with little ponytails or braids
in their hair: not like antiquated hippies but as part of a style,
more Italian let's say, or European. Well, am I boring you?"

"No, no," said Jonny Jalouse. "Finally you are getting to the
good part, go on. I find this very funny."

He was getting all stirred up, wiggling in his seat . . . I felt
quite sick. "Yeah, Sis, tell me the rest of it later," I said.

"No, I want to hear this," Jonny said.

"Well," Amaretta said, "Jonny, give me the coke." They
kept the cocaine in a little bottle of nasal decongestant so they
could sniff it in public. In between times they were rubbing
their noses in a tube of eucalyptus menthol, something for
colds that cleared their sinuses.

"If you don't want to hear this you should leave," said one
of the Germans. It was quite vicious and without warning; well,
I have noticed that cocaine sometimes does this to people,
makes them criminally vicious and there is no hard feeling
behind it.

"I have to go soon anyway to work on my painting," I said,
ignoring him. Meanwhile I sipped my drink.

"This big bull dyke, six feet tall. The young ones didn't seem
to have to play butch or femme; but this one was into playing
what I guess she assumed was the man's role. . . . I was sitting at the bar, and one of the girls was kneeling on the floor
petting my dog and another woman said to her, 'As long as
you're down there, Marie, why don't you . . .' But the rest of
the sentence was lost as all the women giggled. I felt as if this
was in some way addressed to me . . . like I was supposed to
be shocked or something. A sexual joke, but of a crudeness as
to bely the fact that they were women, that they might have
had any idea of the sense or sensitivity of real women. . . .

"Meanwhile, the voice was even louder in my head—Amaretta, you're a coward, why, you'll never do it, come on, go
ahead, make your move *unless you're too afraid!*

• 255 •

"So I said to the old gray-haired dyke—who at least had some intelligence in her face, with a heavy jaw, a square terrier face, rooted in grief; I had the feeling if given half the chance she would have attached herself to my leg and hung on tenaciously—I said, 'Excuse me, do you have a light?' A pitiful line, I know, but the only line that would do in such a situation, the only thing this old-school lesbian would have understood.

"We didn't really talk. 'Buy you a drink, hon?" she said. I nodded. The other women faded away . . . it was so tacky, I can't begin to tell you, at least if I were going to do this I might have chosen a place in Manhattan, some place jazzy and fun where the women were artists and dancers . . . my kind of people.

"The other women were mostly dancing . . . a slow song came on, my dyke and me were sitting at the bar. 'You wanna dance?' the woman said. So I nodded again . . . there I was on the dance floor. If she had breasts it was no worse than the pair to be found on many a guy . . . she was nuzzling my neck, I kept my eyes quite shut, I was very drunk and let her push me around, I didn't want to make a fool of myself by falling down . . . anyway, it's all very stupid."

"Don't say that!" Jonny snapped. "I want to hear what happened. You're a tease, Amaretta."

"Well, all of a sudden I was yanked away . . . her girlfriend came out and pulled us apart, slapped me in the face. . . . 'Tough shit, Angela!' the woman I was dancing with said. 'I'm fed up with you!' Her girlfriend wasn't very nice-looking. An older woman, no makeup, with a wretchedly thin nose, trying to beat at my face. Very sad. How trivial human beings are, worse than the dogs we used to have at home, always snapping at each other over a bone. . . . Dykey—I shouldn't call her that, she told me her name was Denny—took me to a washroom, she got a bunch of paper towels and wet them and put them on my face . . . I was crying, too drunk to know what I was doing. The other woman had scratched me. 'You from around here?' the woman said. I told her my

car had broken down, I was staying in town at the local hotel
until my car was fixed.

"She took me back to her apartment. It turned out she was
a certified public accountant. How incredibly dull! And her
friend was an assistant professor of philosophy at the state
university . . . this was the only place in town they felt comfortable at. I asked her for another drink, she didn't want to
give me one. But I leaned forward and touched the back of her
neck. It was as if all the air went out of her. This tough old
dyke became very helpless, like a cat hypnotized by a snake.
She didn't want me to touch her . . . how gently I ran my
fingers along the nape of her neck. And then I took my cigarette and puffed on it and put it back in the ashtray. . . . She
didn't want to be undressed by me, one part of her was fighting
it, but she forced herself to relax . . . her body was like a piece
of china, very old and cracked. White, flabby skin with blue
veins along her groin. . . . She became almost doll-like in her
resignation. She knew for once she wasn't going to be allowed
to be the aggressive one. . . . I removed her brassiere. It had
left a pink line under her breasts. 'Why do you wear your
brassiere so tightly,' I said. 'Look how it is damaging your
flesh.' Her breasts were very small against her thick rib cage.
I held each one in my hand, weighing them. The nipples were
brown, tinged with pink. I took one in my mouth and bit the
nipple tip. . . . It was funny, doing this to a woman. And then
I took my cigarette out of the ashtray and stuck it into her side,
very quickly, before she had a chance to jump up.

"I don't know what came over me. I got out of there fast,
though. Luckily I was completely dressed, and I knew how to
run through the woods to get back to my house."

The Germans and Jonny Jalouse all started to laugh. I felt
sick and got up and went to the toilet to take a piss. When I
came back my sister and Jonny J. were laughing about a movie
they had seen about snakes: a trained king cobra is set free to
murder people that the deranged hero doesn't like.

"*Oui, oui,* and the poison sets in, that is the best moment,"

Jonny said. "When she turns green and is in convulsions and the rest of the people are standing there saying, 'Oh, la la, what to do?' "

"The king cobra is among the most poisonous of snakes," I said. "But the reason it is so interesting is that it can be trained. How did you guys get to see that film? It hasn't even opened yet."

"Anyway, Marley, you missed the end of the story," Jonny said. "Amaretta, tell him what happened."

"Oh, the next day I was downtown getting some groceries, and I saw the old dyke in the store. She came over to me, really friendly, and I was so nervous when she asked me for my phone number I gave her my real number in the city, and she's been calling me up ever since. She says she forgives me and wants to see me again, she wants to take me to Florida— Florida, for God's sake! She'll rent an apartment for me . . . after what I did to her!" My sister started to giggle.

I wanted to smack her. Here I had always thought she had feelings and now she seemed worse than all the other sleazes and crummy people New York was elemented with.

"And I forgot to tell you!" my sister said with a shriek. "She wore Jockey undershorts!"

"No!" said Jonny.

"Yes!" my sister said. "I just remembered! The old dyke actually wore men's Jockey shorts! Oh, God, how awful! I said to her, 'For never did I behold one mortal like to thee, neither man nor woman: I am awed as I look upon thee. In Delos, once, hard by the altar of Apollo, I saw a young palm tree shooting up with even such a grace.' I was laughing my head off. You know, that's from *The Odyssey*, where Odysseus speaks to Narcissus. You know, Marley had practically the whole thing memorized when he was a kid. We used to recite different parts out loud to each other. It was like a joke to me, undressing this big quivering horse, while she moaned with pleasure. I was like a goddess mucking about with a mortal. I knew what it was like to have power, but it left a nasty taste in my mouth, coming too easily."

One of the Germans, bored, took Amaretta by the arm and they all got up to go. My sister seemed half out of her mind and didn't even say goodbye to me. I should never have let her go. But she had always looked after herself, and she would have belted me in the face if I had even tried to tell her what to do.

So there I was, alone in the Gulag. And after I had another vodka I went home to paint. But the next day, about eight in the morning, I got a call from the cops of the Fifth Precinct. They hadn't been able to track me down until then. My sister had jumped out the seventh-floor window of Jonny J.'s building. When I spoke to Jonny he said he had tried to stop her; but they were heavily coked up, and he thought she was just playing around. When he refused to give her any more coke she climbed out onto a windowsill and he screamed at her to get inside; she was standing on the window ledge and then she slipped.

Well, there aren't many more thoughts in my head. Only a few, like something quite defunct and forgotten in the closet: an old cheese sandwich, perhaps, or a half-empty bottle of root beer. Or worse still, old socks green with lichen and mold. It might have hurt me less if they hadn't published those pictures in the paper, the kind of picture that should be outlawed: my sister like a broken cup, flecked with dust and pencil shavings on the pavement.

matches

A voice came into my head and told me I should give a party. I had always wanted to give a party while I was living with Stash; now that I was alone there was nothing preventing me except that I didn't want to do it. I was afraid.

I thought about it for a while—giving a party—and then I thanked my lucky stars: I didn't have a table or chairs. So that ruled that little whim out. No one could have a party without a place to sit. But the voice kept nagging, "You must give a party, Eleanor. It will be good for you," and finally I broke down. I found myself in a store, purchasing two chairs and a table and arranging to have them delivered.

I could see what my actions were leading to. I understood that I was at a period in my life when everything was falling apart. If I could pull off a successful party then it meant that eventually I'd be able to pull my whole life together.

I knew my room would only comfortably hold four or five people; since I hated to use the telephone, I sent out twenty invitations. The invitations read "Please Come to My Tiny Hovel for Cocktails."

I invited around fifteen men and five women. What I planned to do was introduce all the men I wasn't interested in to my three single girlfriends (the other two women were married and coming with their husbands).

Unfortunately I was certain I had probably called each girlfriend, following my various dates with the men, and given them the dish on each man's peculiar habits. My only hope was that they wouldn't remember.

The day of the party everything went wrong at once. My table arrived in a box, about fifty pieces of it; it came with instructions in inscrutable English (apparently translated from the Chinese). If I had known it wasn't going to be sent to me whole, I never would have bought it. I tried to screw the various aspects together, but after two hours I had to give up. In appearance the table resembled a table, but the top was merely balanced on the legs, and the whole thing wiggled uncontrollably.

Then I tried to cook some kind of dip (I had a recipe from *Women's Day* for something using cheese and jalapeño peppers) but I couldn't get the stove to work. It was an electric stove, and my electrical field had been shot to hell for a while now. After I broke up with Stash, I went to visit my mother and every time I tried to make a piece of toast the toaster caught on fire. Either that, or it shot flaming pieces of toast halfway across the room.

Nothing was working right around me. I had to replace my answering machine four times in two weeks as soon as I moved into my new apartment: it kept breaking down. Anyway, after I couldn't get the stove on I went down for a minute to retrieve the mail—a Con Ed bill for $90. I couldn't even believe it, I was certain it was a mistake, a $90 bill for one month. I was living in a studio apartment that was so small I had to buy a folding sofabed—otherwise the whole room would have been filled up with just a bed—and a folding table and folding chairs. In other words, if it didn't fold, there was no room for it. And it was early September, hot, I wasn't exactly using the stove for a lot of cooking. I had used the air conditioner for one or two nights, but not $90 worth. I could see I was going to be reduced to lighting candles at night, just to keep my bills down.

I called up the tenant who had lived here before me, and he said when he lived in my apartment if he used the air conditioner every night for a month his bill came to maybe $40. No wonder I was so jittery! I was being utilized as some kind of outlet or channel for excess electrical energy. It was pouring straight from the walls into me. My bill said that if I had any questions, I should call up a man named Albert Menendez, so I did. "Ninety dollars, Albert," I told him. "This is crazy."

"Not to Con Edison," Albert said.

But it *did* seem crazy. This made me think about objective reality. What a shame it was that nobody had it besides me. I realized I was working myself up into a state, and the party wasn't until eight that evening. So I went out for a walk.

I was sitting on the pier and this man came over to me. "Are you playing hooky?" he said. I thought; I am almost thirty years old. But in a way I wouldn't have been surprised to find myself arrested and shoved back into first grade. I looked at the guy. He was attractive, maybe even too handsome, in a rugged, cigarette advertisement kind of way. He had blue eyes, curly brown hair, and was wearing a plaid shirt.

"Playing hooky from *what?*" I said. The man seemed chagrined. But we started talking. He was a furniture designer, he liked the furniture of Frank Lloyd Wright, though not his buildings, and the work of somebody whose name I didn't know but pretended to anyway. The man—his name was Jan —said he was playing hooky from work to ride his bike around. He had a red motorcycle—BMW 800—parked in the lot at the end of the pier.

I said I was depressed; I had gone out the night before with a girlfriend and drunk too much and now I was suffering the consequences: (1) physical symptoms such as headache, fatigue, and vitamin C and B complex depletion, and (2) anxiety. "I don't mind the physical business as much as I do the anxiety," I said. "I just keep worrying about this party I'm giving later on."

Jan sat down next to me. It was a hot, grayish day, the air smelled of turpentine. Jan said that he was Hungarian—anyway, his parents came from there, and he was an excellent cook of such dishes as goulash and paprikash—and he had grown up in a small Hungarian community in New Jersey. He spoke a few words in Hungarian: I guess he was trying to prove his honesty to me. He wanted to know how old I was, and when I told him "twenty-eight," he peered anxiously into my eyes. It was a weird thing but these days everywhere I went people seemed to be asking each other their age. It was like an epidemic, everyone trying to pin each other down by their age as if they were insect collectors. "How old are you?" I said.

"Thirty-four."

"That's *old*, honey," I said.

"Should I leave?" Jan said.

"No, no," I said, "I'm just kidding you." Then I told him a story: An elderly man (seventy-two) who was a friend of the family's, called up to take me out to lunch. After the meal (arroz con pollo) he said that he would like to come back to my apartment and make love to me. Even though I said it was better that we remain friends, and reminded him that he was happily married, he still made a grab for me at the door. As I fled, his parting words were a compliment about a portion of my body. "Isn't that awful?" I said.

"Why do you seem so shocked?" Jan said. "You must be used to stuff like that."

"Seventy-two years old?" I said. "The animal." I tried to explain that the men I knew who were my age never laid a finger on me. "When you take someone out," I said, "if you decide to go to bed, it's pretty much mutual, isn't it? I mean, you don't attack her at the door or anything."

Jan said that this was true and he agreed. Someone was playing the trumpet, very badly, one pier over, and the sound carried across the water. The musical background gave the general atmosphere of a scene from a movie; anyway, I felt as if I were in one. I explained to Jan that I was sick of men placing value judgments on me. "Most of the men I go out with come up with these adjectives," I said. "But you can tell any man or woman that he or she is deeply upset and it will be true at least fifty percent of the time." Jan didn't seem to understand.

"You don't seem upset to me," he said.

"I'm not," I said. "Well, maybe just a little, but that's because I'm nervous about giving a party. And I'm not strange or weird, either. Everybody's strange or weird around here, but I'm not. I know the difference."

"Um," Jan said. He offered me a ride on his motorcycle. I decided to accept, even though the last time I had ridden on a motorcycle Max, my father, bumped into me on some back road—he recognized Ricky, the juvenile delinquent I was riding shotgun with, and then he recognized me. He made Ricky stop, made me get off, and forbade me to ride on a motorcycle ever again.

I figured that by now Max's statute of limitations had run out, but I did feel a little nervous. Max hadn't been entirely wrong; I knew I was doing something dangerous, possibly even pathological, but I figured on the city streets how fast could Jan drive his machine? He gave me an extra helmet, which he apparently kept locked to a front wheel, and I tried to shove my hair—it was long and red—up into the helmet. It felt like a vise clamping down. "Don't touch this," Jan said, pointing to some lump on the side of the motorcycle. "You could get burned."

Then he kicked up some kind of kick stand, started up the engine, and we took off. Driving in heavy traffic, careening between taxis and onto the sidewalk, I felt as if my knees might be shorn off at any moment. I shouted in Jan's ear to make a right down my old boyfriend's block. For a moment I pictured myself, glamorous, waving to Stash as Jan and I screamed through a green light on his bike; I could see Stash, first bewildered, then running madly through the streets after us. Of course Stash wasn't there, but it was pleasant to indulge in momentary fantasies.

Jan took me on a whirlwind tour of lower Manhattan and finally dropped me off near my apartment. I started to say goodbye, but then I had a thought. He was handsome and affable, and I figured even if I had no use for him maybe one of my girlfriends would. I considered myself to be a reasonable judge of character, and Jan had gone to West Point and dropped out to attend Bard College. So I gave him my address and invited him to my party that night. He said he would be delighted.

Even though I had burned up quite a bit of adrenaline on the motorcycle, I still couldn't face my apartment and the impending party. I thought I'd go and get some lunch, and I walked up my street. Agnes, the psychic on my block, was sitting on the stoop and she stopped me as I went by; she pointed out her husband. He was standing in the gutter with a weary dog who resembled some old stuffed Steiff toy. "We've been married thirty years," Agnes said. "We're very compatible: he hates people, I love them and talk to everyone. He can't see very well, but he has good legs. My legs are bad, but my vision is fine. Also, we have separate apartments."

I nodded. "See you later," I said. "I'm going to get something to eat; then I have to buy wine. I'm having a party." As I turned the corner along Bleecker Street I caught a whiff of beef. Garlic, packaged onion soup mix—not bad. I had the sensation of having experienced this before. It was nearly three in the afternoon.

Then I saw two men I knew; each of them was wheeling a stroller with a baby. "Hi, Eleanor," Mark said to me. I crossed the street to walk alongside them. "Our wives went to a baby shower," Mark said. "We're taking care of the babies. You know Beauregard, don't you?"

"Yeah," I said. I looked down at the baby Beauregard was wheeling. It was exceptionally homely.

"It's not mine," Beauregard said. "It's my niece."

"How are you, Eleanor?" Mark said. He gave me a pitying look. I hadn't seen him since before I broke up with Stash.

"Great, excellent," I said. "My career's going well, got a cute apartment—"

Mark looked nervous. "That's nice," he said. "We went to see 'Goldilocks and the Three Bears.' "

"Did you enjoy it?" Beauregard asked his niece. The infant

had a fat face and a sour expression; I thought she might be around one and a half.

"It was fine, thank you," she said.

The two men seemed very glum. "And how did you guys like 'Goldilocks'?" I said. Nobody answered. "There was a street fair yesterday on the next block," I said. "Maybe it's still there today. You could look." I pointed to my studded leather wrist band. "I purchased this there for a mere two dollars. I wish I had bought more. Some had spikes. Frankly, I'd like to have wrist bands up to my neck. Nobody would mess with me, then."

Beauregard suddenly perked up. "Where did you move to, Eleanor?" he said. "You look wonderful."

"Yeah, Eleanor," Mark said.

So I ended up inviting them to my party.

Then I went into a diner and selected a hamburger and French fries. I needed something to restore myself. The food seemed almost deliberately bad; this fascinated me. Ice-cold French fries, nearly uncooked; watery ketchup; a thin piece of meat between two cold slices of bread. Spiteful. I was giving off nervous vibrations—I kept looking at my watch as the hour drew late—and at this time of the day the only people in the place were precarious. I knew my atmosphere was having an influence. A bearded hippie type was harassing the waiter. "What's the matter?" he kept saying. The waiter didn't seem to speak any English, he was dark and surly. "Why are you in a bad mood?" the bearded man said. "Come here and I'll straighten you out. Where are you from?" The waiter didn't answer. "I think you're great," the hippie said. "You're sweet, but you're great."

Behind me were two women who were talking; apparently they had just visited someone in the hospital. "I think that her doctor's gone nuts," one said to the other. "Did you look at her chart? Under 'Patient's Diet' he wrote 'Bedrest.' "

Finally I got myself out of there and bought the wine and went home.

There were a lot of messages from my guests on the answering machine; I had forgotten that I had left a message that said, "Hello, for breakfast today I had a doughnut, black coffee, and cranberry-apple juice. I'm having a party; please feel free to attend. Leave a message after the beep."

When I played my tape back, I had a lot of people saying, "Hi, for breakfast I had two eggs, scrambled, toast, and hot chocolate. See you later on tonight." I couldn't figure out for quite a while why all these people kept telling me what they had eaten for breakfast.

There was only one piece of bad news: all the women I had invited suddenly couldn't make it. One was sick, one had to leave town, another made up some lame excuse. They had spent so much time complaining to me about being single, I couldn't believe they would cancel on such an exciting event. But at least there would be me and my girlfriend Amy; she was in the middle of a divorce, and surely would be happy to accommodate as many men as she could, in order to prove she was on the rebound.

Before the guests came I was so jittery I felt like putting a sign on the door: DIED EARLY LAST NIGHT, GO AWAY. But as it turned out, my downstairs front door buzzer was broken, and many of the guests didn't get in anyway. Everything was a bit skewed. I had to cover my table with a crepe-paper tablecloth (even though it wasn't Halloween the cloth was decorated with various pumpkins, it was the only thing I had been able to find) and I made a display of some hunks of cheese and some tiny triangular spinach and phyllo pastries that I had found in the freezer at the supermarket.

It wasn't the most elegant extravaganza I could have imagined.

But I myself looked splendid: I had purchased green satin Chinese pajamas and I wore these and a pair of gold sandals. I prepared my camera, with fresh film and batteries: I was definitely going to record the event.

Then the guests started to arrive: Mike, Fritz, Barry, Marley, John, and Ted. And Bill, Stan, Larry, and Russell. I

seated them on the couch, on the chairs, and on the floor.
Everyone seemed genuinely affectionate toward me, even
though I could hardly remember who they were. The men all
brought bottles of wine and flowers. Amy arrived dressed in a
leopard-print see-through blouse, tights, and spike-heeled
shoes. She stood at the sink, defrosting a hunk of pâté she had
stolen from the caterer's where she worked. "Come in and
meet Marley," I said. "He's gorgeous, humble, and heterosex-
ual."

"I can't," Amy said. "I'm frightened. I'm the kind of guest
who likes to lurk in the kitchen."

"I don't have a kitchen," I said. "Just an alcove. Why didn't
you tell me this before? You're the only other woman here
besides me!"

The room was crowded with cigarette smoke, men were
rummaging through my refrigerator looking for more bottles of
wine. I thought of myself as Audrey Hepburn in that *Breakfast
at Tiffany's* movie: Truman Capote was hunched over in the
corner (actually he wasn't Truman, just some male friend who
liked to make fun of me) and the rest of the room was filled up
with men and my one girlfriend. That wasn't exactly how I had
planned things, but that was how they turned out.

Of course, during the party itself there was plenty of food
for thought. Was Mike getting along with Fritz (they were talking about tuna fishing and then moved on to what Eastern
European tennis players wore on the courts); was Amy talking
about her divorce for too long to Marley? Ashtrays, refills of
wine, changing the tape from Nino Roti's movie scores for
Fellini films to some modern African bongo-bongo music—I
was looking for any activity that prevented me from associating
with my guests. How the hell had Holly Golightly ever been
able to have a good time? The buzzer kept ringing and ringing,
but no one else ever arrived at the door (I didn't know then
that fifty percent of the time it wasn't working). It seemed like
hundreds of people would arrive at any minute, but when this
didn't happen I climbed out on the fire escape to see who was
downstairs; maybe they had rung and left.

"Wait, Eleanor!" I heard one of my guests shouting. "Don't do it! Don't jump!"

Then for a moment I did feel truly glamorous; in my green satin Chinese pajamas, crawling out the window to the fire escape, I was certain I looked like a genuine hostess.

Now, if only the door would ring with some man I was interested in, my evening would be complete. But I was expecting no guests that I was intrigued with, or even much liked.

Finally the front door of my apartment did ring, and I scurried off the fire escape to answer it. It was Jan, complete with suitcase. I quickly finished my glass of wine. "Hi," he said. "How are you?"

"Okay," I said. "Do come in. But I hope you weren't planning to move in with me—it's rather crowded in here all ready." I was a little put off by the suitcase.

"Don't worry," Jan said. "My girlfriend threw me out this afternoon. I just thought I'd stop by your party before I checked into a hotel."

"Have some wine," I said. I led him across the room to where Amy had arranged herself like a Spanish maja reclining on a bed of soapboxes. Actually she was sprawled on my futon, which was a bed as well as a spare chair. I took out my camera for incriminating photographs. Then I looked at my watch. I wasn't having a bad time, I just couldn't wait until the event was over and I could genuinely enjoy myself. I was sick of having fun. I found fun very traumatizing, difficult even. In some ways it was more fun not to have fun. To me, having fun was almost identical to feeling anxious. I thought I preferred to sit at home by myself, depressed.

Meanwhile, Mark and Beauregard arrived, apparently having come together. "Hi, guys," I said. "Where's Tina and Betsy?" I had assumed they would bring their wives.

"Uh," Mark said. He took out a cigarette and wandered off to look for a light.

"We didn't know we should bring them," Beauregard said. He looked embarrassed, and went to the table to get some food. His foot must have touched one of the table legs; he leaned forward and the whole table collapsed abruptly, spilling half-finished wine in plastic cups and cheese on to the floor. Three men knelt to clean up. "Oh, God, I'm so sorry," Beauregard said.

Jan propped up the table, crawled under it, and quickly screwed it into normalcy. I looked at him with new interest. "Don't worry about it," I said. "I don't think that table was meant for actual use. It was just a Platonic ideal."

Everyone was smoking cigarettes but the strange thing was nobody had any matches. It seemed that every surface was littered with empty matchbooks. As long as one person had a lit cigarette, though, somebody else could light up from them. Ted trapped me near the refrigerator. "Tell me, Eleanor," he said, "do you think children are just born the way they are, or do the parents have any effect on their personality?" Ted had an eight-year-old son who was already making it big: the kid had a rock band with a hit record.

"I don't know," I said, trying to escape. "I was in SoHo the other day and a woman was carrying a large chimpanzee—the chimp was dressed in a suit and little boots. Strange, huh?"

"I saw some of your jewelry featured in *Vogue*," Ted said.

"Excuse me," I said. I locked myself in the bathroom. When I came out it appeared most of the wine was gone; I was finally able to get rid of my guests. It was a peculiar thing: each of the men seemed to think I had invited him because I was in love with him, when in fact just the opposite was true. Each one kissed me at the door and said not to worry, that he would call me soon. "Did you get to meet my friend Amy?" I said.

Apparently they had all taken her number.

I thought everyone was gone, but Mark and Beauregard and Jan had seated themselves on the couch and were polishing off a two-liter bottle of wine they must have hidden away. Since I could see they weren't going to leave, I lay down on the futon and held out my glass for another refill. "Oh, God," I said, clutching my head. "Remind me never to do this again."

They sat there like the Three Stooges, waiting to see what I would do next.

"This might have been easier on me if I had a boyfriend," I said. "Someone to share the responsibility with. I'm starting to think I'll never meet anyone."

"Let me tell you something," Beauregard said in a slurred voice. "You shouldn't act so desperate."

"Let me tell *you* something," I said. "I was just as desperate when I had a boyfriend. I consider life itself to be an act of desperation." Beauregard looked puzzled.

"She doesn't like to have value judgments placed on her," Jan said.

"Thank you," I said. Nobody said anything for a few minutes. The tape had come to the end and the room was quiet for the first time. "Well," I said again. "Thank God that's over."

"What is it that you had hoped to accomplish, Eleanor?" Mark said.

"It was a party," I said. "Where was Tina tonight?"

"I told her I didn't want her to come," Mark said. He was pretty looped. "I said I needed to go out without her sometimes." I wondered why in that case he was spending so much time with Beauregard. Obviously it wasn't that he wanted to be independent; he just didn't want to be with *her*.

"I think I miss Stash," I said. "So did I do anything terrible tonight?"

"You didn't do anything wrong," Beauregard said.

"No worse than anybody else," Mark said.

I was drunk, and exhausted. "I know it," I said. "One part of me knows that—but the other part of me berates myself constantly."

"You don't get what you think out of a relationship anyway," Jan said.

"So it's impossible then," I said.

Beauregard fumbled for a cigarette. "Damn, I keep forgetting," he said. "There's no matches. Wait a minute, why don't I just go light the cigarette from the stove?"

"It doesn't work," I said. I remembered how when I was a child my parents gave me instructions in how to use electricity —always hold a plug from the back, never turn on an appliance with wet hands. Surely they left out some essential directions.

"The stove doesn't work?" Beauregard said.

"I have to call Con Ed tomorrow," I said. Mark leaned forward and poured us some more wine.

kurt and natasha, a relationship

Kurt, a handsome blond German artist, could be found almost every night in a different club. Though he always wore the latest fashions—oversized brocade jackets with gold satin lapels, silk bathrobes in tiger prints—he always seemed as if he should be dressed in lederhosen, marching with the Hitler Youth. He was in his late thirties, but with his pale blue eyes, his boyish, Luftwaffe face, many people thought of him as in his early twenties.

He was a fairly successful artist. He exhibited at a small gallery in SoHo—paintings and conceptual pieces about various instruments of torture. One such piece (never actually constructed) showed a copper-lined pool, to be filled with sulfuric acid. The idea was, as people came into the gallery to view the work, they would be forced to walk across narrow planks over the pool.

It was clear Kurt was well on his way to becoming a major art-world figure.

Natasha met Kurt at one of his openings. She was tall—almost as tall as Kurt—with masses of black hair, milky white skin, and green eyes. Though she was dressed conservatively, in a skirt and baggy top, she had a distinct aura about her: that of a Forty-second Street stripper.

Natasha was trying to start a small hair salon in the East Village. However, she was having a bit of trouble getting money. That night, at the art show, she decided she was going to pick up Kurt.

Following the art opening there was a dinner in Kurt's honor, and Natasha managed to get herself invited along. She got to the restaurant early, and stole the nameplate opposite Kurt's seat, where she arranged herself like a cheetah in an Avedon photo, about to dine on some particularly choice chipmunk.

By the time Kurt arrived, she had already consumed two vodka martinis and was at her most charming. Though Kurt, who had grown up in Berlin, was accustomed to dating blond women, he found himself quite infatuated with Natasha; as the guests were leaving, he told his date that he was tired and was going home alone. Then he whispered in Natasha's ear, "Why don't you come back with me to my place? We'll watch TV."

Kurt lived in a drafty loft, filled with plans, drawings, and models of his art. He had several large cages, built of steel and aluminum, in the center of the room. Cans of paint, oily rags, broken plates, newspapers were piled everywhere. The only place to sit was a mattress on the floor. "Sit down," he told Natasha, pushing her to the bed. He poured her a shot of vodka and told her to drink it quickly. As soon as she had put down the glass, Kurt took out a roll of adhesive tape, strapped Natasha's mouth closed, and wrapped her wrists together behind her back. He felt her struggling on the bed; he ripped off her clothes and began to make love to her.

When he had finished, he lay back on the mattress and looked over at Natasha. Then he picked up a cigarette and lit it. Her green Russian eyes, he saw, were wide with fear. Slowly he peeled off the bandage from her mouth.

"When you were a kid," she said, "which program on TV was your favorite? 'The Munsters' or 'The Addams Family'?"

Kurt thought Natasha must really be very drunk; there was every reason for her to have been terrified. He decided to make love to her again, this time without the bandages, but it was not as satisfying to him as the first time had been. "I have to get some sleep," he said, "I'm just exhausted."

He lay back on the bed, but found it was almost impossible to keep his eyes shut; Natasha was wide awake, talking, and cleaning his apartment. She swept the floor, and piled all the junk and garbage neatly into one of the cages.

Around six in the morning he got up and made them both some coffee.

"Don't you ever sleep?" he said.

"No," Natasha said. "It must be something genetic. No one in my family has ever needed to sleep. I remember back in high school—my dates used to drive me home at two in the morning, and the whole block would be dark, except for my house. My date would say, 'Do you think something's wrong?' 'No,' I'd say, 'it's just my family.' My sisters, my mother, my father—all of us were awake all night."

Within a short time Natasha and Kurt were living together. Kurt would make Natasha clean the house while dressed in Frederick's of Hollywood brassieres and thigh-high boots; sometimes he would chain her to the radiator and go out for half the day.

It was Kurt's idea to put on performance pieces in Natasha's hair salon, at night—she performed, and if any members of the audience wanted their hair cut, her two assistants took care of business. Kurt knew everyone in town, and not only got Natasha a lot of clients, but convinced the right crowd to come to her place and hang out.

"Kurt, this is more than I can handle," Natasha said a short time after her salon started to take off.

"You will do as I tell you," he said, and that evening when Natasha was getting ready to go out, he insisted that she wear a tight leather corset and an obscenely short miniskirt.

While Natasha felt awkward at first, she was pleased with all the attention she received that night.

Soon she was being written up in trendy magazines; an art collector gave her financial backing to open up a bigger space that became even more successful.

After six months, some of Kurt's friends began to wonder

if he was sick; he was losing quite a bit of weight. "Well,
I'm not getting much sleep," Kurt said. "Natasha's up all
night."

Yet Natasha, who was forced to cook elaborate Russian dinners night after night, dressed in only a G-string (this made
frying uncomfortable, as often grease would spatter from the
stove), was more voluptuous than ever. Kurt found he couldn't
concentrate on his work the way he once had. It took up so
much of his time to think of humiliating things for Natasha to
be commanded to do; and so often, just when he thought he
had broken her spirit, he would find her chuckling to herself
as she scrubbed the floor with a toothbrush.

In the fall Kurt had another show, but though he expected
that sales would start out slowly and pick up during the latter
days of the exhibition, this year not a single painting sold.

One day Natasha's sister came to town. She was almost an
exact replica of Natasha—the same full breasts, slanted Tatar
eyes, white skin—but she was much smaller than her sister.
As they looked so much alike, it was hard to tell that Natasha
was so much larger unless they stood side by side. Kurt
wouldn't have thought anything about it, had he not been walking down the street with Natasha's sister, when he realized he
was barely as tall as she.

Yet only the year before, he had been taller than Natasha.

While Natasha was onstage, during a performance, he took
her sister into one of the back rooms at the hair salon, and,
after bandaging her mouth with tape, made violent love to her.
When he peeled off the tape, Natasha's sister began to giggle.
"That was fun," she said.

As he was lying in bed that night, Kurt thought about how
great sex with Natasha's sister had been. He thought he would
leave Natasha and go off with her. Then something occurred
to him. At home, Natasha had two, three, or perhaps even
more sisters. He imagined them, each one a replica of Natasha, each one progressively smaller in size, like those
wooden Russian dolls that fit one into the next. And he

saw himself, over the years, growing smaller and smaller, as each sister matured and it was time for him to accommodate her.

In the morning, while Natasha was in the shower, her sister, who was staying with them, tried to get into bed with Kurt, but he pushed her away. "What skinny little arms you have," Natasha's sister said.

A short time later, Kurt threw Natasha out of the house. At first she wept, saying that she had thought they'd always be together, growing more famous. Also, she had spent a year fixing up his apartment trying to make it inhabitable, and what kind of payment was this in return?

But after a week or so, Natasha met an artist who told her it was a well-known fact that Kurt was a has-been, and she ended up going off to live with the new man.

Kurt discovered he missed Natasha more than he had expected. He found other girls to tie up and practice bondage on, but somehow it wasn't the same.

He tried seeing a psychiatrist on Sixty-second Street. In the waiting room a parrot kept screaming, "*Ach du*, Herr Freud?" and other German phrases. The doctor explained that the acorn for Kurt's neurosis landed in fertile soil during his first postnatal feeding months. Therefore, Kurt both adored and feared women. There was no use coming back, the doctor said —the problem was incurable.

By now Kurt was quite tiny and had no inspiration for new constructions or paintings, though his apartment had deteriorated back to the way it was.

Once, while standing on line to use the bathroom at a party at Natasha's hair salon, he tried to squeeze into the bathroom with Natasha, who was in front of him. She was now so huge she almost filled the doorway, but Kurt was able to push his way inside.

"Natasha, Natasha, Natasha," he whispered in a tiny voice. "I need you, therefore I am!"

In the bathroom he took out his roll of adhesive tape. Yet

before he could break off a piece of tape and place it over Natasha's mouth, she thrust his head to her bosom and snatched the tape from his hand. He found himself smothered in her tremendous breasts, and he could hear her muffled laughter as she ripped the tape and started to wrap it around his wrists.